"DO YOU HAVE A WOMAN IN YOUR LIFE RIGHT NOW?" LEXIE ASKED.

"No one special." Almost against his will, Tremaine's hand moved upward, cupping her chin.

"Jenny McBride?"

Tremaine swept in a breath. "Who have you been talking to? Jenny and I are just friends."

"And there's no other woman in Portland?"

"No." His thumb slid down her throat to the hollow of her neck. Slowly he bent his head.

"What are you doing?" she asked, drawing back.

"What does it feel like?" he whispered.

Lexie made a sound of disbelief. "You're not going to . . ."

"Kiss you?" His mouth twisted. "I believe I am."

Lexie reared back as far as her body would allow, but he pulled her inexorably forward, his dark head descending toward her trembling lips . . .

Lady Sundown

Nancy Bush

POCKET BOOKS

New York   London   Toronto   Sydney   Tokyo

For my grandmother,
Sarah Emma Kate Dickey:
Happy 96th

An *Original* Publication of POCKET BOOKS

POCKET BOOKS, a division of Simon & Schuster Inc.
1230 Avenue of the Americas, New York, NY 10020

ISBN: 0-671-66821-8

First Pocket Books printing August 1989

10 9 8 7 6 5 4 3 2 1

POCKET and colophon are trademarks of
Simon & Schuster Inc.

Printed in the U.S.A.

Prologue

*New Orleans, Louisiana
June, 1864*

The drunken man weaved and stumbled and finally fell across Joseph Danner's table, managing an idiotic smile before losing consciousness altogether. Joseph, who had been holding his beer about a foot off the table, calmly took a long draft and absently wondered why no one, himself included, even cared.

The smoky bar was lit by quivering oil lamps and the brightly colored beads strung across the back door led to dim, red rooms and innumerable sinful pleasures. Not that Joseph much cared about that, either. Since Sarah's death he'd found precious little in this life to interest him.

"Could I interest you in anothah draft, sir?"

The mountainous barmaid showed him a smile missing several important teeth. Joseph considered. "No, but you could do me a favor. My son's asleep upstairs. Room four. I'd like someone to check in on him."

"I'll be happy to check on him. You from up north, then?"

Joseph hesitated, just for a fraction. "Boston," he said, lifting the mug to his lips once more.

"Jes passin' through?"

Normally, he wouldn't consider giving out his destination; he didn't want anyone he knew to find him and try to talk him into returning to Boston and starting his practice again. What kind of doctor could he be, when he hadn't been able to save his own wife's life?

But Joseph didn't see how conversing with the friendly barmaid could hurt. "I'm going to St. Louis and then on to Oregon."

"Well, then, you should talk to Brett." She inclined her stiff blond head toward the barman. "His brothah went on the wagon train jes last summah."

Joseph looked around, surprised by this bit of luck. "Thanks. I will."

The barmaid smiled again, dropped one fat hand on the scruffy collar of the drunken man, hauled him from Joseph's table, dragged him a few feet, then let him fall facedown on the grimy wood floor. "I need hep with this un," she hollered, heading toward the back stairs, which led to the upper rooms.

Feeling eyes on him, Joseph glanced up. A woman was seated at a corner table on the other side of a marred oak pillar. Her face was obscured by a black veil, but the rigid and still way she sat revealed an upbringing not in keeping with the regulars at this backstreet bar.

To his intense surprise she suddenly rose, rustling in layers of taffeta petticoats, picked up a bulky valise, and walked straight to his table. "May I sit down?" she asked, a soft southern drawl rippling through an already dulcet voice.

"My pleasure, ma'am." Joseph stood up and pulled back a chair. His courteous manners brought snorts of laughter from the other customers, and the woman herself seemed surprised.

She tugged nervously on the fingers of her black kid gloves. "I heard you say you were going to Oregon. I wondered, how are you traveling?"

"Overland, ma'am." Joseph studied her thoughtfully. Blond hair was swept up into a pillbox hat and slanted blue eyes met his gaze directly. But her lips quivered almost imperceptibly and any loud noise had her starting from her chair. "Is there something I can do for you?"

He was dying to ask her what she was doing in this part of

town, in this smelly, run-down hotel, which was little more than a brothel. But he kept his thoughts to himself and waited.

She drew a deep breath. "I want to go with you to Oregon."

Joseph rubbed a hand across a two-day growth of beard. "In what capacity, ma'am? A lady traveling with a man might—"

"I'm aware of what people may think," she cut him off harshly. "I want to avoid—notoriety." Her fingers climbed to the cameo brooch at her neckline, betraying her anxiety. "It's imperative, in fact, that I make this trip without creating a lot of attention."

"Are you in trouble?" Joseph asked quietly.

"Of a sort." She smiled faintly and extended her hand, a small cinched satin handbag swinging from her arm. "My name's Eliza Smythe. I've been watching you and your son for the past few days."

Joseph was astounded. Had he been in such a fog that he hadn't noticed this beautiful woman before? "You've been here?" he asked incredulously.

"Here and there. I heard you mention that the boy's mother is dead."

Joseph drew a breath. That must have been when Tremaine asked him if he would ever have another mother. Joseph had explained that he didn't count on the future bringing any such good fortune. "She died about a year ago. I've been—traveling ever since."

Drifting was a more accurate term, he supposed. Or maybe running away. The image of his wife teetering on the upstairs windowsill, reaching her fingers toward Tremaine who'd climbed out onto the moss-covered roof and was too afraid to come back inside, was indelibly etched on his brain. He could still see the way her foot had slipped, could hear her echoing screams. He'd screamed, too, running to catch her, but she'd fallen at his feet. Then for weeks she'd lain unconscious, barely alive, while Joseph had done everything possible to save her life.

The day she died he sold the house, turned his infirmary over to an associate, and took off with Tremaine. He would never again practice medicine. A man who couldn't even save his own wife wasn't fit to be a doctor—or so he told himself. He wasn't certain what he wanted to do but he knew he could never go back to the life he'd led before.

He felt the woman's eyes on him and surfaced as if from a dream. "What's your name?" she asked.

"Joseph Danner," he said gruffly. "And if you've been watching me, you probably know that already."

She looked down at her hands, as if embarrassed, and gave a curt nod.

"I don't see how I can help you," Joseph told her, finishing his beer and wiping his mouth with the back of his hand. "I'm not in a position to take on another responsibility."

"Mr. Danner, I have money."

"Money?" he asked blankly.

"You can have all of it." Her gaze was steady. "Come with me and I'll show you."

"Wait a minute . . ."

But she wasn't listening. Hauling up the heavy valise, she headed for the narrow back stairway.

"Miss Smythe," Joseph protested, blinking, but when she showed no signs of slowing he muttered a curse, dropped some change on the table, and followed after her. The odor of cooked fish and rotting vegetables rose suffocatingly from the kitchen below as Joseph mounted the stairs, but he barely noticed. His gaze was trained on Eliza's straight back.

At the top of the stairs he met the barmaid, who was hurrying from the other direction. The barmaid flicked Eliza a glance before turning to Joseph. "He's doin' fine, your son is," she said. "A regular heartbreaker, that kid. He's gonna be a looker."

"Thank you."

Joseph sought to squeeze past her, but the barmaid stopped in the center of the narrow hall, her corset seemingly stretched to breaking beneath her faded red velvet dress. She touched Joseph's arm companionably, and glanced wistfully after the elegant woman who'd just passed. "A woman like her in a place like this means a pack of trouble, mistah. Ah've seen 'em come in before. You'd best watch more'n your wallet."

With that piece of advice she stood aside, and Joseph,

though forewarned, followed thoughtfully after the mysterious Eliza Smythe.

She was waiting for him at the door to room four. His room. Joseph twisted the key in the lock and stepped back. She moved past him in a cloud of French lavender perfume. "Close the door and lock it," she said softly.

Joseph glanced at his son. Tremaine slept fitfully on the narrow bed, his eyelids quivering, his small hand clenching the threadbare bedspread. Was this some kind of strange seduction? he wondered. Was this woman merely a bored housewife, seeking a way to liven up her evenings? Did she have a husband somewhere? Just what did she plan on doing with Tremaine sleeping on the only bed?

With surprising strength Eliza tossed the valise on the creaky mattress, drew a silver key from a ribbon around her neck, unlocked the case, and threw open the lid. Inside were neat stacks of money. More money than he'd ever seen in his life.

"It's all mine. I didn't steal it," she said with a trace of humor. "You can have it if you take me with you to Oregon."

"You're running away from someone," Joseph said.

She inhaled through her teeth, hesitating. The seconds ticked by. Finally, she admitted, "I'm running away from a past I'd rather forget. That's all I want to say. Oh, but there is one condition."

Of course. He'd known there would be.

"I want you to marry me before we leave."

"Pa?"

Joseph looked dazedly at Tremaine. The boy sat up, rubbing sleep from his eyes. Eliza shut the case and locked it, waiting.

"Go back to sleep, son," Joseph said.

"Who's she?"

Eliza sat down on the edge of the bed, smiling at him. "I'm someone who needs a family."

Tremaine's blue eyes regarded her with the steady, stripping appraisal that most people found unnerving. "We need a mother," he said.

Joseph cleared his throat. Both Eliza and Tremaine looked at him expectantly. He was about to negate this foolishness once and for all, when a tiny voice inside his head asked "Why?" Marrying a woman he knew nothing about seemed about as sane as drifting aimlessly from town to town. And Tremaine was right when he'd said he needed a mother.

Still, what did he know about her?

"Mr. Danner, I will make you a good wife," she said quietly. "You won't be sorry."

His palms were sweating. He'd taken chances in the past. Being a risk taker had served him well on more than one occasion. Clearing his throat, he said in a strange voice, "We don't need to go overland. There's a steamer heading out around the Horn the day after tomorrow. It'll be a long trip but I don't think we're in any hurry. It might make less—er—commotion than hooking up with a wagon train. . . ." Joseph trailed off.

Eliza's eyes shone with unshed tears. "I would like to be married before we leave," she said, so softly he could barely hear.

"Yes, ma'am." His mouth was as dry as shoe leather.

"Will you make the arrangements?"

"Yes, ma'am."

"You can call me Eliza, . . . Joseph," she said haltingly, gathering her skirts as she headed for the door. "I'll see you tomorrow."

"Yes, ma'—Eliza," Joseph said as he held the door for her. "Tomorrow."

Two days later Joseph Danner stood at the railing of the *Bonnie Lynne* with his son and new bride. A hot, moist breeze trembled against Eliza's veil and tossed Tremaine's too-long black hair into his eyes. Eliza's hand gripped Joseph's so tightly he wondered if she were having second thoughts.

Three blasts from the ship's horn signaled their departure. Eliza shifted closer to him, tense and tight. He put his arm around her, and she melted into his shoulder. The pitch of the steam engines altered and the sailors pulled in the lines. Beyond, the sun rose from a shifting sea of pink and scarlet.

"I'm pregnant," Eliza said as the shore slipped away. "I thought you should know."

Joseph absorbed this in silence. Since he and his young bride hadn't had a chance to discuss the physical side to their marriage, let alone do anything about it, Joseph had to add this uneasy bit of news to the already disturbing picture he had of his new wife.

"She'll be born in February."

"She?" For a moment he thought she somehow knew the sex of her child. It wouldn't have surprised him.

"I think it's a she," Eliza admitted, blushing. "I hope so. I want to name her Lexington."

"Is that where you're from? Kentucky?"

"Yes," she said in the clipped way he was beginning to recognize. The subject wasn't open for future discussion.

"Eliza, I need to at least know about the child's father."

"He's dead." She pulled away from him, as if the memory alarmed her. "Someday I'll tell you everything," she said. "I promise."

Joseph wondered if he really wanted to know.

She glanced at Tremaine. The boy, as if feeling her eyes on him, dragged his gaze from the diminishing shoreline and looked her way. She smiled. "The barmaid was right," she said softly. "He will be a heartbreaker. Those eyes . . ."

Joseph Danner gave his son a long disturbed look. Those eyes had seen far too much, he thought. They had seen his mother die. They had watched the decay of his father's life.

What, Joseph wondered, would those eyes see in the uncertain future ahead of them?

Chapter One

Rock Springs, Oregon
Spring, 1882

Tremaine Danner slid from the sweating bay horse, his blue eyes narrowed on the tumbling crystal stream that cut between the Danner and Garrett properties. But it wasn't the stream that held his attention. It was the sight of a young man holding out his hand, helping a lithe blond woman across a series of waterswept stones. Tremaine drew in a sharp breath. Dusk had fallen, turning the cloudy day into a shrouded gray evening. He could barely make out the two figures, but the woman's laughter—Lexie's laughter—fell like chimes on the clear mountain air.

It made him want to rip out Jace Garrett's throat.

Soft rain poured downward, staining the shoulders of Tremaine's leather jacket, running off his black hair in steady droplets to slide down a hawkish nose and onto a pair of stern, sensual lips.

His horse blew through his nose and Tremaine automatically rubbed its forehead. "In a minute, boy," he said, cursing himself for the whim that had made him leave the buggy at the end of the lane and ride Fortune bareback. He'd been impatient to be home, impatient to see Lexie.

8

And that impatience had forced him to see the one thing he feared most—Lexie with another man.

Tremaine's hands balled into fists. He couldn't stay and watch, yet he couldn't seem to look away, either. His heart beat deep and painful, thundering in his chest, as he witnessed Lexie lift her face to Jace's, her lips parting expectantly for his kiss. Frozen, Tremaine saw Jace's fingers wind through her hair as he took what was so eagerly offered.

Turning blindly to his horse, Tremaine was astride Fortune before his mind was fully in gear. He rode back down the lane, the damp leaves scraping his shoulders, wetting his face.

There was a saloon in Rock Springs. A damn good place to get drunk. He would spend the night there and arrive home by buggy tomorrow—the way he should have done today. No one was expecting him anyway. Certainly not Lexie . . .

Lexie reached a toe down to the next rung of the hayloft ladder. Below her and around the corner was a cluster of men: her father, two of her brothers, and Doc Meechum, the horse doctor. She could see the way Meechum was examining the listless Jersey cow, his craggy face lined with concern.

"Looks like she's got hollow horn," he said.

Hollow horn. They always had hollow horn. Why not just say you don't know what's wrong with the poor animal? Lexie thought in disgust.

Harrison, Lexie's younger brother by less than a year, ran his hand down the drooping neck of the ruddy cow. "So what do you propose we do?"

"Only one thing you can do. Split the tail and rub it with salt."

Pieces of straw, disturbed by Lexie's movements, slid from the edge of the loft to wisp softly to the ground. None of the men noticed but Harrison, who glanced up, spied her, then gave an imperceptible shake of his wheat-gold head, his gaze shifting anxiously toward Pa.

Luckily, Joseph Danner was looking solemnly at the Jersey, his silver hair glowing in the light from the lantern.

Lexie knew exactly what Harrison was trying to tell her; Pa wouldn't like her butting in where she didn't belong.

But the poor Jersey needed someone to care for it, and Calvin Meechum, whose reputation as a drunk far outstripped his renown as an animal doctor, wasn't doing his job.

Climbing down, Lexie jumped to the barn floor, scattering dust motes up in a whirling cloud. Outside rain poured torrentially beyond the open barn door, sending up the tangy scent of wet earth and pine, but inside the dusty smells of hay and grain and dried mud from the swallows' nests prevailed.

All four men glanced her way. Lexie's next younger brother, Jesse, raised his brows, a smile on his lips. Unlike Harrison, who was worried about Pa's reaction, Jesse looked forward to any kind of confrontation.

"Matilda's problem isn't hollow horn," she said distinctly. "I think she's got some kind of infection. Look at the way she hangs her head. And just this morning she started favoring her left hind foot."

"She's not favoring it now," Joseph pointed out, his mouth tight. Aware of his disapproval, Lexie forged on nevertheless.

"Is her leg hot?" she asked, knowing that Meechum hadn't even checked.

The horse doctor flushed. "Now, little lady, your Matilda has all the symptoms of hollow horn. See the way she holds her head? It's tilted."

To Lexie, Matilda just looked weak and depressed. She turned to Harrison, who shared her wish for better animal care and, like Lexie, hoped one day to be a horse doctor. "Please feel her leg," Lexie implored. "If it's swollen it may need to be lanced."

"That's enough, Lexie," Pa said in a voice that brooked no argument. "We'll let Doc Meechum give the diagnosis."

A crimson tide washed up Lexie's cheeks. Setting her jaw, she murmured, "Yes, Pa," knowing it was useless to argue. Her father couldn't abide disrespect for anyone, and her feelings about Calvin Meechum's ability were painfully clear.

"Why don't you finish feeding the Herefords," he said in a kinder voice. "We'll be done here soon."

She turned on her heel. She would check Matilda later herself. Whether her father believed her or not, Lexie knew how to help the suffering Jersey.

On the other side of the barn the Herefords waited expectantly, trampling on one another's hooves when they saw Lexie approach. Grasping the pitchfork, Lexie shoved it into a shock of hay, then scattered the dried straw into the manger above the cattle's eager heads. "Slow down," Lexie said, managing a smile at their antics. "You'll all get a turn."

The rain battering against the weathered barn roof drowned out the sounds of the men's voices on the other side of the barn. But Matilda's bawl of pain echoed upward, making Lexie's teeth clench and the swallows leave their nests to swoop agitatedly around her head.

"Meechum, you ignorant fool," she muttered. Splitting Matilda's tail and rubbing salt into it wasn't going to do anything but make the poor cow suffer more.

With a vengeance born of frustration, Lexie forked more hay over the side of the manger. She could smell the scent of scorched hide as Meechum burned the open wound. At least he wasn't going to let the cow bleed to death.

Lexie never asked herself why she was so certain his methods were wrong; she just knew they were. More learned people than she trusted in the horse doctor's wisdom, but Lexie, who'd grown up communing with the animals on the farm, possessed an insight she trusted unthinkingly.

If only she could become a horse doctor someday . . .

The men's voices drifted away and through the open barn door Lexie saw them walking toward the house, their heads bent against the rain. She dropped the pitchfork and ran to Matilda's pen.

"You poor thing," she whispered, wrapping her Turkish split skirt up in one hand and tossing a leg over the rail. She dropped lightly toward the floor and approached the Jersey whose eyes were white-rimmed with fright. "Relax. It's okay. Everything's all right."

Lexie touched the cow's hide, which shivered under her hand. Matilda shifted sideways, let out another plaintive bawl, then nearly gouged Lexie with a horn when she bent to touch her back leg. "Whoa, girl. I'm not going to hurt you."

There was just the faintest bit of swelling around the site of expected injury, but Matilda's hide was hot to Lexie's touch. The Jersey switched her tail and swung her head around and Lexie jumped backward, out of harm's way from the lashing horns.

Moving to the side rail, Lexie bit her lip. She was right. Infection was developing right below the surface. If something wasn't done for the animal soon her father would send for Meechum again and who knew what horrors that man would perform next.

What Matilda really needed was to have that hot spot lanced. The infection was painful and potentially lethal.

Lexie thoughtfully returned to the pile of hay and the hungry Herefords. She would have to help Matilda in secret; her father would never approve of her treating the cow on her own. Tonight, before she met Jace, she could come back to the barn, drain the wound, and stitch it up with the catgut she had stored in the tack room. The whole thing would be over before her handiwork was discovered, and by that time Matilda would be on her way back to good health.

Lexie slowly let out her breath, uneasy. She was directly defying her father's wishes, something she almost never did. But Pa just didn't understand. The first time she'd told him she wanted to become a horse doctor, he'd looked at her as if she were not quite right in the head. He'd explained, kindly but determinedly, that women didn't treat animals—especially livestock, on whose heads might lay a farm's entire welfare. It simply wasn't a job for a lady.

"The farmers around here want a man to help them," her father had pointed out, reasonably. "Women just aren't strong enough, Lexie."

Of course she'd argued, long and hard. But in the end she'd only grown frustrated and infuriated. Nobody wanted to listen to her, not her father, her mother, or any of her brothers. Harrison was the most sympathetic, but that was only because he was hankering to be a horse doctor, too. Even Jace Garrett didn't seem all that keen on the idea, Lexie had to admit. And that was even a bigger problem.

She leaned on the pitchfork, listening to the drumming

beat of the rain. Jace Garrett. Just thinking about him made her mouth curve in a secret smile.

"I'm in love," she whispered to the feeding cattle. "But don't go telling anyone just yet."

The wind tossed a peppering of rain through the open barn door, dampening her white cotton waist and the faded blue split-skirt which her mother didn't approve of. Icy cold, the rain took her breath away, yet it was sharply sensual, reminding her of last night's meeting with Jace and the feel of his lips pressed against hers. She smiled a little at the memory of Jace's kiss. She'd kissed him back, too, maybe a bit too eagerly. But what did it matter? She and Jace were going to be married. Jace had asked her and she'd accepted.

Lexie sighed. Pa wasn't going to be thrilled at the idea of having a Garrett as a son-in-law, but Lexie was confident she could overcome that obstacle. After all, it wasn't as if the Danners were feuding with the Garretts. The two families just had a difference of opinion about property lines that flared up every time the stream veered onto a new course.

She scooped up the rest of the hay and tossed it into the manger. Tonight, at dusk, she was going to meet Jace again. Her conscience twinged her a little. It wasn't proper to be having these clandestine meetings; her mother would be shocked. Even the sight of the Garrett buggy on their property was enough to send Pa for his rifle. Not that he would use it, of course, Lexie assured herself hastily; her father was the kindest man she knew. But it certainly wouldn't help her relationship with Jace any to be looking down the barrel of her father's Winchester the first time he came calling, so Lexie had taken matters into her own hands.

Indulging herself, Lexie closed her eyes, imagining Jace's kiss. She felt a twisting in her stomach at the memory, an anxious aching. Had she been too eager? He'd seemed to draw back, as if she were too—

"So here you are. I should have guessed," a familiar voice drawled, breaking into her thoughts.

Startled, Lexie gasped, her eyes flying open. "Tremaine," she exhaled in a rush of breath. "What are you doing here? You scared me."

Her elder brother regarded her through narrowed blue eyes. "You looked like you were dreaming."

"I was resting," she said primly, resenting his lean form in a way she'd never completely understood. Her relationship with him had always been strained. She'd never felt the same closeness with him as she did her younger brothers. Now, as he lounged against the open barn door, rain spattering the shoulders of his worn leather jacket and darkening his breeches, Lexie felt impatient. "We haven't seen you in a while. Pa said you've been busy."

"I've been pretty tied to the hospital," he admitted. "It would be better if I had my own practice."

"Well, can't you?"

"I suppose," he mused, straightening. "But I don't know if I want to stay in Portland. I think I'd rather be in a smaller town."

Lexie's shoulders stiffened involuntarily. "You're not thinking of setting up practice in Rock Springs, are you?"

"No. Don't worry. I'll find somewhere else to go."

His bitterness was unwarranted, Lexie thought. Ever since she'd caught him with Mary-Anne Laytham near the stand of cedars by the hot springs, rolling on the ground, Mary-Anne's drawers a conspicuous ten feet from where they lay, Tremaine had treated Lexie as if she were afflicted with the pox. Was it her fault they'd been so indiscreet? Tremaine was just lucky it hadn't been Pa who caught them!

"I'm not worried," she told him, tossing back her blond hair. "I just wondered, that's all."

"Well, I'm not going to settle here." Tremaine straightened, shoving his hands in the pockets of his breeches, the soft buckskin stretching around his thighs. "Maybe I will just stay in Portland. It's better than Rock Springs."

Resentment grew from a seed to an all-out blossom inside Lexie's chest. "What's wrong with Rock Springs?" she demanded. "Or do you think you're better than we are? Is that what being a doctor in a big city's done to you?"

Tremaine's brows shot up. "Well, maybe you do want me here after all."

"I don't care what you do."

Silence fell around them and Lexie realized resignedly

that nothing had changed between herself and her older brother. He had a way of getting under her skin like no one else.

"Have you had a change of heart about Rock Springs?" he asked. "The last I heard, you wanted to apprentice to become a horse doctor."

"I still do," Lexie said testily. "But I'm not leaving Rock Springs. This place could use a decent animal doctor."

"You don't fancy Doc Meechum's skills?" Tremaine asked, amused.

"You know as well as I do that he barely knows one end of an animal from the other."

"Careful." Tremaine's smile was a gleam of white. "Pa still has some faith in the man."

"I don't know why. Pa was a medical doctor once. Like you," Lexie offered, a bit self-consciously. "He ought to be able to see what an impostor Meechum is."

"And you could do better, I suppose."

His needling bothered her. "Yes, I could," she said boldly, her green eyes defiant. "And that's why I'm going to stay right here and become the best damn horse doctor in the county!"

She expected him to revile her for swearing; her mother and Pa sure would. But Tremaine just centered his gaze somewhere past her left ear and said, "You sure your decision to stay doesn't have something to do with Jace Garrett?"

Lexie could only stare at him. He knew! How could he know? No one knew, not even Harrison, to whom she told everything but her very dearest of secrets. "I . . ."

"Yes?"

Amusement lifted the corner of Tremaine's mouth and to Lexie, that was unforgivable. Defensive, she gripped the pitchfork tighter and asked, "Did you come to the barn looking for me?"

"Your mother wants to see you." Her stranglehold on the three-pronged fork hadn't escaped him and his smile deepened. "Oh, come on, Lexie. Let's not fight. I haven't seen you in months." He reached for the pitchfork but Lexie, goaded by some instinct of self-preservation she didn't entirely understand, jerked backward. The heel of her shoe caught in a crack and the back of her knee hit the edge of the manger. With a cry she tumbled downward. Tremaine scrambled to catch her but she buckled over the side, landing with a screech in the hay, stampeding the frightened cattle in all directions.

If Lexie hadn't had the breath knocked out of her she might have laughed, but hearing Tremaine's roar of amusement, ringing to the rafters, drove the humor right out of the situation. She scrambled upward, straw clinging to her hair, her eyes alight with vengeful fury, and hurled herself over the side of the manger straight at him.

"Hey," Tremaine laughed, trying to catch his breath. "I—"

She hit him in the midsection and was rewarded with a gasping "oof" as she connected with board-hard flesh. The force of the impact made her arms fly around him, and she pummeled his back with her fists as he sought to pull her off. She wanted to kill him!

"Lexie," Tremaine said through his teeth, his fingers biting into her arms. "Stop it."

"You—you—you're all the same!" she forced out. She didn't ask herself what she meant. She just knew that Tremaine was the source of all her problems, and she'd be glad to scratch his eyes out.

But he wouldn't let her. Steel-strong fingers pushed her back, holding her at arm's length as she squirmed to do more damage. She was as ineffectual as a kitten and the knowledge made her angrier, but apparently not as angry as he was, for he shook her and bit out furiously, "What the hell's got into you?"

"Nothing!" Lexie panted. She twisted and fought and caused him to yowl in pain when she kicked his shin. Then as fast as her rage had surfaced it faded, slipping away like sand through a sieve. But pride wouldn't let her explain her unwarranted attack. Not that she could have anyway. She was a mass of emotions these days, as mercurial and unpredictable as the inclement spring weather.

Tremaine stared at her, his dark hair tumbled across his forehead, his blue eyes slits of cerulean in a lean, hard face. Thick lashes obscured his thoughts, but his mouth was an implacable line of anger. "Your mother wants to see you at the house."

"She's your mother, too," Lexie shot back. "Why do you always say that?"

"She asked me to come get you." He spoke distinctly, as if she were hard of hearing. "She wants to talk to you."

"She raised you, too," Lexie went on heedlessly, striking blindly with arrows she instinctively knew would puncture his armor, wounding deeply. "You don't like being part of this family. You don't like me, and you don't like my mother."

"Lexie, for God's sake—"

She jerked one hand free and pulled his fingers back from her arm. Her skin was red beneath his grasp. She was appalled to feel tears burn her eyelids and she turned away from him, pressing a hand to her lips, wondering what terrible demon had possessed her into being so cruel.

"I'm sorry, Tremaine," she said suddenly. "I don't know what got into me."

"I do."

She glanced back uncertainly, to see him dusting off his jacket with one hand. "You do?"

"You didn't like me bringing up Jace Garrett."

"What do you mean?"

The look he sent her sliced through any flimsy attempt at deception. "I saw you with him last night, Lexie. You don't have to pretend."

Her blush spread to the roots of her hair, and she swallowed back a lump of fear. "Don't tell Pa. Please, please, Tremaine. I'm sorry. He'd be so upset." As quickly as she'd pulled herself away from him, now she reached for him in entreaty, her fingers burrowing into his sleeves. His muscles tightened, but she was too self-absorbed to notice. "I don't want him to know—yet. Let me tell him when I'm ready. Please."

"Then, you'd better get ready pretty quick, if what I saw's any indication of what's going on." Censure deepened his voice.

"It wasn't what you think."

"Wasn't it? How do you know what I think?"

"Well, it wasn't like you and Mary-Anne."

For a moment he was at a loss for words and Lexie pressed home her advantage. "Jace and I want to get married. It was just a kiss. That's all. I want to break the news to Pa at the right time. You know how unreasonable he is about the Garretts." Her soft green eyes pleaded with him, begged him to understand.

She could smell the damp rain on him and the fresh scent of soap. It was warm and intimate, mingling with his own sweat; a pleasant odor that was somehow uniquely Tremaine, making Lexie feel close to him for the first time in memory. Pleased, she held on tighter, though she could sense him drawing away. "Don't ruin this for me, Tremaine. I'm meeting Jace tonight and we're—"

"What? *Tonight?*"

"Yes, we want to . . ." Lexie cut herself off, sensing Tremaine was not the person to tell.

"You want to what?" he asked, his expression grim.

"Nothing. I just need to meet Jace, that's all."

"Like last night?"

Her jaw tensed. "Yes, like last night. Were you spying on me?"

"I saw enough to forbid you to meet Jace Garrett," he ground out.

Lexie's lips parted. *"You* forbid it?" She was incensed all over again. "Now listen to me, Tremaine Danner. You can't tell me what to do. I'm almost eighteen, and I know what I'm doing." At his continued silence she swallowed her anger and shook her head, adding insistently, "I've got to do this my way. I'm meeting Jace, and we're going to plan how to approach our parents."

Tremaine's eyes were hooded in the gloomy afternoon light and Lexie tried hard to peer up and see what he was thinking. But instead her gaze found his mouth and a strange liquid sensation swept through her, surprising her, so much that it almost made her forget what she was saying.

She felt how tense he was then, how rigidly he held himself in control. "Tremaine . . . ?" she asked in a whisper, not understanding.

"Tremaine! Lexington!" Pa's voice boomed out and

Tremaine released her so fast she almost stumbled. She saw her father's straw hat as he sloshed through the puddles to the wooden ramp that led to the barn floor, three feet above the ground. As he climbed toward them, his boots scrunched on the grassy mud that coated the two-by-fours nailed to the ramp for purchase against the incessant Oregon rain.

"Lexie, your mother wants you," Pa said. "Run on up to the house. Tremaine, I'd like to speak to you."

His clipped voice boded trouble. Lexie glanced uncertainly at her father. Had he seen her sneak back to Matilda's stall? One look at his weathered face and she knew that she—or Tremaine—had stepped over that invisible line which separated acceptable behavior from disgrace. Her heart somersaulted. Could he know about Jace? Had Tremaine already told him?

No, she didn't think so. Tremaine, for all his faults, wouldn't have let her think otherwise if he'd already given away her secret.

"Yes, Pa," Lexie murmured, slipping down the wet boards, balanced only by her flailing arms as she half ran, half slid to the ground. She would come back later and check on Matilda, after her father was safely at the house. The fact that Pa had returned to the barn meant her mother must be very impatient to see her indeed—but about what Lexie couldn't imagine.

Her shoes sank into three inches of mud, and she cursed herself for not putting on boots first. She'd been anxious to get out of the house and away from her mother's pile of needlework, and she'd been careful to skirt the worst mud pits—at least on the way to the barn.

Dampness oozed into her toes as she struck out for the house. Guilt-stricken at the appearance of her shoes, and dreading the lecture she was bound to receive, Lexie held her skirts high and tiptoed from one grassy tuft to another. Halfway to the house she stopped. Her bonnet, the one she'd grabbed from its peg in her closet, the one her mother had ordered specially made for her to wear to church, the one Lexie had tossed gleefully onto the hay in the loft—was still in the barn. Eliza Smythe Danner could forgive many things, but Lexie knew she'd be pushing her luck by returning late, wet, bedraggled, and hatless to boot. For insurance purposes, she retraced her steps to the barn.

She was at the bottom of the ramp when she heard her brother's voice raised in anger.

". . . Why the hell can't we tell her? She has a right to know the truth!"

"There are reasons," Pa answered evenly.

"What reasons?"

"It's for her own protection."

"Well, I want her to know how many brothers she really has," Tremaine growled. "It's long past the time she should be told, and I'm tired of lying."

Lexie leaned closer, blinking in the rain. She stepped onto the ramp, her shoe sliding a little on the wet wood.

"What difference does it make, son?" Pa demanded.

"She's grown-up. She has a right to know," Tremaine answered mulishly.

"When the time is right I'll talk to her." There was a short beat of silence, then Pa added, "That's all, Tremaine."

Lexie stood at the end of the ramp, balancing herself. Rain had turned her blond hair to dank locks and at the sound of footsteps coming her way she wheeled around, nearly pitching head-first into the muck surrounding the barn before sinking into it again, ankle deep. Desperate not to be caught eavesdropping, she lifted her dripping skirt and started for the house. But it was too late. Her father caught sight of her before she'd taken three steps.

"Lexington. What are you doing here?" he demanded. He was standing in the doorway, looking as white-lipped and furious as she'd ever seen him.

"I left my hat," she answered, swallowing.

"Then come up here and get it and go to the house."

"Yes, Pa."

She couldn't meet his eyes as she clambered up the ramp, her mind abuzz with questions. They'd been discussing her. They had to have been. But none of their conversation made one lick of sense. What had Tremaine meant about how many brothers she had? She had four: Harrison, Jesse, Samuel, and Tremaine—though he was really only a half-brother. Could there be one she didn't know about? It wasn't possible! Unless Pa had been with someone else.

The idea was so repugnant that Lexie thrust it from her mind. Pa was not that kind of man.

Grabbing her hat, she squelched it on her water-soaked head. Tremaine was standing by the manger, watching her, and she sent him a questioning look. Later she was going to demand he tell her what was going on, but for now she didn't want to risk her father's ire. He didn't get mad often, but when he did "the skies open and pitchforks rain down," as Cook had been known to mutter on more than one occasion.

Lexie scrambled back down the ramp and set off in full gallop toward the house, heedless of the mud that spattered on her skirt. It was too late to salvage it anyway. She would go upstairs and change, toss her clothes in a washtub, then meet her mother. There was no time to dry her hair so maybe she could just keep her hat on, she reasoned.

The Danner house stood at the end of a twisting lane, rising out of an emerald clearing, towered over on all sides by time-scarred oaks and firs. Whitewashed, its square pillars supported a steeply peaked shingled roof upon which stood a widow's walk—"Eliza's folly," as her father so often fondly called it.

Now, Lexie glanced upward, half-expecting her mother to be waiting for her within the confines of the walk's pristine, curving balustrade. But there was no one up there. Her mother, unlike herself, had the sense to come in out of the rain.

Tremaine's horse and buggy were still standing beneath the overhanging portico as Lexie approached the house. Her brows drew together.

How had he seen her with Jace when he'd only just arrived?

Pushing the question aside, Lexie ran for the back outside staircase. She had the more immediate problem of facing her mother—and she couldn't do it, looking like this. Mounting the staircase that led to the hallway on the second floor, Lexie half-hopped, unbuttoning her shoes as she climbed. At the top landing she yanked off her shoes and socks and cracked open the door, listening. Not a sound issued from the warm depths of the house.

Gently closing the door behind her, Lexie gingerly tiptoed toward her room, holding her shoes and socks aloft like a thief. The hardwood floor creaked beneath her feet and she glanced back to see the damage her tracks were making. She was going to have to do some quick cleaning up before Annie found the mess she'd made and reported to her mother.

Lexie's room was at the north end of the hall and around a corner to the right wing. She paused at the top of the double-wide staircase to the first floor, glancing down the scarlet carpet runner which nearly covered the oak steps. The entry hall was empty, the oil-fueled sconces on either side of the door emitting a soft warm glow. She breathed a sigh of relief. She was alone. No sign of her mother.

Lifting her skirts, Lexie's heart nearly stopped when she heard, "Lexington, I would like to see you in the parlor."

Guilt nailed Lexie to the floor. From behind a shadowy arch came a whisper of satin and Eliza Danner appeared, her eyes on her daughter, her face set in an expression that made Lexie's spirits plummet. It didn't help when she commanded in her deceptive soft southern drawl, "Now."

"Yes, mother," Lexie murmured.

"Leave your shoes at the top of the stairs. Annie will clean the hall."

With a sweep of satin she turned away from the staircase, the flames in the sconces dancing in the wake of her exit.

Miserable, Lexie sank onto the top step, setting down her shoes. Her mother had a right to be upset. The shoes had been expensive and weren't meant for farm work. But then why did she buy them for me? Lexie asked herself indignantly. Didn't her mother know she had no use for such things? She'd be happier wearing a pair of her brother's breeches and a work shirt and mucking out the barnyard than sitting in silk and satin and making perfect little stitches all the same size on pillowcases meant for her hope chest.

She's never going to let me become a horse doctor, Lexie thought unhappily, pushing her wringing-wet cotton socks into her shoes. It wasn't the kind of thing a "real lady" would do.

Eliza was sitting in a straight-backed gold brocade chair, her hands folded gracefully in her lap, as Lexie entered the parlor. Feeling like a schoolgirl, Lexie sat on the edge of a footstool, hoping she didn't stain the needlepoint cushion with mud.

A line formed between Eliza's smooth brows as she noticed the disheveled state of Lexie's clothes. "Could you please take off your bonnet?" she asked.

Lexie swept the hat from her head, self-consciously pushing back a clump of wet blond hair.

"Did Tremaine tell you I wanted to see you?"

Lexie nodded. "I was hurrying to get back," she said, aware of the small white lie.

"Lexie, I'm not going to lecture you. I know your heart lies with this farm and all that goes with it."

"You do?"

Eliza stood up, moving smoothly toward the front window. She gazed down the curving lane, as if expecting someone to come. "Yes, I know. And I also know you are fixated on the idea of becoming a horse doctor."

Lexie squirmed a little. She didn't like the way her mother put that.

"Believe me when I tell you that I understand how you feel. But women can't take care of livestock, Lexie. They're not strong enough. No self-respecting farmer would allow a woman to pull a calf or geld a stallion."

"I don't think you do understand how I feel." Lexie's fingers tightened in the folds of her skirt.

"I've made the mistake of letting you do as you please. I should have taken you in hand much sooner."

"What do you mean?" Lexie's eyes rounded with concern.

"I've saved some money—for my children," Eliza said. "For their education. I gave some to Tremaine when he wanted to go to medical school, and I want to do the same for you."

Lexie's heart fluttered. "You're going to send me to school?" She hardly dared believe her luck. She could apprentice with Dr. Breverman in Portland, one of the finest horse doctors around.

"I've already enrolled you in Miss Everly's School for

Young Ladies in Portland. It's a very prestigious school and it was hard to find an opening, but—"

"I won't go!" Lexie was on her feet, shaking.

"Lexington," her mother warned. "Sit down. Miss Everly's school is one of the finest on the coast, if not *the* finest."

"I know what kind of school it is. It's for rich girls who want rich husbands! Well, I don't want that. I've got everything I need right here in Rock Springs."

"That's enough."

The tone of her mother's voice stopped Lexie short. But it didn't cool her panic. "Mother, please," she said desperately. "I can't go to that school. If I can't be a horse doctor, I want to stay here. With you and Pa."

Eliza sighed. "What kind of prospects would you have in Rock Springs?"

"Prospects? You mean marriage?" Lexie's thoughts flew to Jace. "There are lots of young men in Rock Springs."

"Like Jason Garrett?" Eliza turned to peer closely into her daughter's eyes.

Lexie couldn't hide her surprise. The secret she'd thought was so zealously guarded was known to one and all! Tremaine had told after all. She'd been wrong to think he would honorably keep her secret. There was nothing for it but to confess now. "I love Jason Garrett," Lexie said in a trembling voice. "I won't go to that school."

Eliza crossed her arms and looked down her aristocratic nose. Her dress was cream satin, her figure only slightly rounded after four children, her bustline and décolletage still smooth and firm. Lexie had always been a bit in awe of her youthful mother, and now, with drips of water running from her limp hair onto her shoulders, her clothes in a sorry state of neglect, her bare feet cold against the thick, flower-patterned parlor rug, Lexie felt completely stripped of feminine armor.

"One year, Lexie, that's all I ask," her mother said. "You need this, and I need it for you. I feel I failed you somehow."

"No, Mother, you didn't—"

"You will start at Miss Everly's School this September. Rock Springs will still be here when you get back. And if

Jason Garrett is the man you think he is, he'll wait for you. That is all."

Lexie was speechless. Inside, her chest tightened, filling up with disbelief and anger. Her future was already decided. She had no say in her own life, none at all!

Lifting her chin with as much dignity as she could muster, she squared her shoulders and marched out of the room, her bare feet pounding with injustice on the carpeted steps. Tears formed in the corners of her eyes, tears of hurt and betrayal. No one cared what she wanted. No one cared what mattered to her. She was a woman and women had to act in a certain, specified way.

She ran the last few yards to her room, slamming the door behind her and flinging herself across the bed. It was so unfair! She'd worked long and hard with Pa, had done more for the livestock than her four brothers put together. She'd welcomed the responsibility of taking over the stables and had groomed and cared for the horses with a love and understanding that came from the heart. Yet her sex decreed that she be a lady.

In a surge of rage Lexie pulled open her dresser drawer and yanked on a clean pair of cotton socks. Flinging open her closet, she grabbed her boots and shoved her feet into them. She would go to Jace. They couldn't stop her. They could send her away, but they would never destroy the love she shared with Jason Garrett.

With a total disregard for protocol, Lexie ran down the stairs, slammed out the front door, and strode bareheaded through the rain to the stables. The top half of the Dutch door was already open and, seeing her, Lexie's black horse, Tantrum, whinnied expectantly.

"Hi, sugar," she whispered, opening the bottom half of the door. "Let's go for a ride, all right?"

But then Lexie stopped, remembering Matilda.

Distractedly, she rubbed Tantrum's head. From where she stood she could see the barn was dark; her father had taken the lantern and left. Matilda was alone.

"I'll be back," she whispered to Tantrum, slipping past him to the interior of the stables. Near the back of the tack room, against a far wall, stood an iron-banded chest, dust-covered and forgotten. Lexie glanced around and listened. The only noises were the snuffling and shifting feet of the horses.

Lifting the lid of the chest, Lexie pulled out a bottle of carbolic acid and a small coil of catgut. Groping along the bottom with her fingers, she found a small knife, a pair of sewing scissors, and the embroidery needle, stuck in a pink satin pincushion, which she'd pilfered from her mother. Several rags and bandanas were folded in another corner, and Lexie reached deeper, drawing out a box of matches and a blue bandana. No one knew about her private hold; no one ever bothered to look in the dusty chest.

And no one, besides Harrison, knew that Lexie had stitched up minor cuts on the horses, either.

She gathered up all her equipment in the blue bandana, grabbed a lantern from the hook on the support beam and a rope from the tack room, checked outside to see if anyone was around, then headed at a fast pace through the now misting rain toward the barn.

It was dim inside, the afternoon's gloom shadowing the far corners. Lexie walked quickly to Matilda's stall. The Jersey's head was hanging to her knees.

"Hollow horn, my eye," Lexie muttered, lighting the lantern and affixing it to a post. The cow's system had been poisoned with infection.

The several hours Lexie had been gone had made a good deal of difference in Matilda's condition. Now her leg showed definite signs of swelling, the hide around the injury taut and dull. Should she wait and show this evidence of Meechum's ineptitude to Pa? It would certainly be sweet revenge.

No. Lexie's stubborn pride wouldn't let her. Besides, chances were that Pa wouldn't allow her to drain the wound, even if he admitted she was right. He would send for Meechum, sure as shooting. She couldn't take that chance.

Looping the rope around Matilda's head, Lexie tied her fast to the top rail, keeping her deadly horns out of reach. Next she wetted the bandana with carbolic acid and scrubbed Matilda's leg. The Jersey was too dejected to notice. A bad sign, Lexie thought, but it certainly made her job easier.

She doused the knife with carbolic acid, then poised it over the swollen muscle, taking a deep breath.

"What the hell do you think you're doing?" Tremaine's angry voice demanded from somewhere behind her head.

Chapter Two

Lexie gasped in surprise. The knife slipped from her fingers, clattered to the floor. She leaped to her feet, seeing Tremaine emerge from the shadows, his expression forbidding.

A shiver slid beneath her skin. There were times, like now, when she realized how little she knew Tremaine. He was an enigma to Lexie—always had been. Most of her recollections of him were vague—dreamy visions of when she was a small child—but in all of them he was an autocratic, authoritative monster who'd mercilessly run roughshod over his baby sister. Though she'd been only six when he left home, Lexie could still remember her joyous feeling of emancipation. Good riddance! she'd thought, glad that her fifteen-year-old nemesis was leaving Rock Springs for a better school in Portland.

She hadn't missed him at all, having more than enough younger brothers to contend with. As time passed, Tremaine became more a stranger than a member of the household, showing up at infrequent times, staying only a few days. His decision to study medicine had kept him away even longer, and over the years Lexie's memory of the power he'd once exerted upon her faded. She could barely recall how much she'd disliked him.

But now she remembered. Tremaine had a lot to learn about who could boss whom. And he was about to get his first lesson.

"I'm draining Matilda's wound," Lexie said staunchly. "You're not going to stop me."

"You little idiot, you could be hurt. You don't even have her backside lashed down."

"She's too weak to move."

He snorted in disgust. "She'll move plenty when you jab her with that knife."

"You can't stop me, Tremaine. I'm going to take care of Matilda and nothing you can do will make me change my mind."

"Stubborn wretch," he muttered, climbing over the rail. With an economy of movement that Lexie almost resented, he dropped lightly to the floor beside her. He picked up the bottle of carbolic acid and made a sound of surprise. "Where did you get this?"

Lexie hesitated. He wasn't going to like her answer. "From your medical bag. Last time you were in Rock Springs."

He swore beneath his breath, half anger, half a kind of reluctant admiration. "Have you done this kind of thing before?" he demanded. "Don't bother answering. I can tell by the look on your face."

Lexie turned away from him, her gaze on the Jersey. "Is it so wrong, Tremaine?"

"Yes," he said flatly. "You don't know what you're doing and you could be hurt—or killed."

"I know more than Doc Meechum, only no one will listen to me because I'm a woman." Her bitterness seemed to pool around them, a tangible thing, a part of Lexie that Tremaine had never seen before. "The swelling's grown," she added, without much hope of being listened to. "Take a look."

Tremaine gave Lexie a searching glance, then bent down and examined Matilda's leg. Straightening, he ran his thumb across his fingers. "It's hot," he said thoughtfully.

"It's infected."

"I thought Pa said she had hollow horn."

"That's what Meechum thinks and Pa believes him," Lexie said with a sniff.

Footsteps sounded outside the box and Tremaine twisted around. Lexie instinctively moved closer to him for protection. If Pa caught her now . . .

"Harrison," Tremaine said, as Lexie's brother walked into the circle of light, his blond hair shining. Lexie breathed a sigh of relief. Of all of them, Harrison was the best at finding out what she was up to.

"What's going on?" Harrison demanded, peering over the rail. "I came to check on Matilda."

"She's fine," Tremaine said. "Lexie was—er—checking on her, too."

Harrison's green eyes swept the stall, assessing the situation in a glance. "Lexie," he said, his voice a warning, yet full of the understanding he shared with her. "Doc Meechum split her tail and you know that—"

"Don't sing that man's praises, Harrison. Please! You and I both know the only way he cures an animal is by God's will."

Her brother's lips tightened. Though Harrison didn't much like Meechum's practices either, he had more respect for the man than Lexie did. "Meechum saved Kelsey Garrett's horse when everyone thought it would die before morning."

"That was years ago. Think how many animals have died since then under his care!"

Before Harrison could retort, Tremaine interceded. "Matilda's leg is hot," he said quietly.

"Let me see." Harrison, too, jumped into the stall and Tremaine stepped backward, giving him room and nearly pinning Lexie to the back of the stall. His shoulder touched hers and she could feel the heat radiating from his body, could smell his pleasant scent above the dusty barn doors. She breathed deeply, noticing the way his black hair brushed the collar of his shirt.

"It is hot," Harrison said in some surprise. He glanced at his sister. "The leg's swollen."

"It's infected," Lexie said flatly. "It needs to be lanced and drained."

"Is that what you were trying to do?"

"Yes," she answered simply.

"And you agree?" Harrison asked Tremaine.

Lexie stiffened, regarding Tremaine with faintly veiled hostility. He was a doctor and knew more about medicine—any kind of medicine—than either she or Harrison did. But he was also arrogant and mule-headed and she didn't trust him to side with her even now.

"It's swelling rapidly," he said, as much to himself as Harrison. "It's definitely filling with fluid or pus. Yes, it should be lanced."

Eyes shining, Lexie met Tremaine's gaze.

"But Lexie shouldn't do it," he added, dashing her spirits. "It's too dangerous. If you don't want Meechum to do it, I'll handle it myself."

"Could I assist?" Harrison asked eagerly, forgetting Lexie in an instant.

"You can make sure Matilda doesn't twist around and kick me."

Lexie heard no more. She was so incensed she could hardly think. Her first instinct was to flee, but she refused to give Tremaine that satisfaction. Instead she stayed, watching as he made an incision in the knot on Matilda's leg, draining out the offending fluids, rinsing the wound with carbolic acid, then stitching it up with catgut.

When it was over, Tremaine wiped the leg with the bandana, then stepped back. "You make a darn good horse doctor," Harrison observed with a grin. Belatedly remembering Lexie, he glanced at her apologetically. "Well, he does," he said lamely.

Lexie couldn't answer. She felt a pain inside her so huge it threatened to swallow her up. First Miss Everly's School, now this. She couldn't imagine being treated with less respect.

Tremaine glanced at her, his dark blue eyes narrowed in the uncertain light. Forcing her face into an implacable mask, Lexie met his stare evenly. She knew she should thank him for what he'd done, but she couldn't. She hurt too much inside.

Without a word she turned on her heel and left the barn.

* * *

The afternoon had deepened to twilight while she'd been in the barn. A glance at the house revealed warm squares of light shining through the parlor windows. Mother and Pa, and probably Jesse and Samuel, sitting down together as a family. Lexie's chest tightened. She would have liked to be with them, to know what they were saying, even though they might be discussing her unladylike behavior. This was the time of day she enjoyed being with her family the most— but not tonight. Tonight she was going to meet Jace, and though it was long past the time she'd told him she would be at the stream, there was a chance he might still be waiting for her. It was a chance she was determined to take.

She let herself into the stables, grabbed Tantrum's bridle from a peg by the door, slipped into his box stall, and slid the thin straps over the horse's tossing head. Tremaine, home for a brief summer holiday, had given the spirited gelding his name after Tantrum refused to be broken by anyone but Lexie. It had been one of those rare moments in her childhood when she'd realized she loved her older brother, appreciating his sense of humor. But right now she couldn't spare him a kind thought.

"Come on, boy," she said to Tantrum, clucking her tongue as she led him from the box. His ears pricked forward and he shifted restlessly, wheeling around in a tight circle.

She saw his blanket and saddle sitting on the sawhorse right where she'd left them, but in her rebellious state of mind Lexie decided to ride bareback. She drew the gelding to the sawhorse and mounted him, smoothing her hand along the silken fineness of his neck. The door was still open and Tantrum pulled toward it eagerly, but Lexie kept a firm hand on the reins.

"In a minute. Come on now. Be patient." She rode him carefully through the opening, kicking the door shut behind her.

Tremaine was standing outside the stable doors, his black hair damp from the misting rain. "Where are you going?" he demanded.

"Out." Lexie slapped the reins against Tantrum's neck. The horse's muscles bunched for a leap forward but

Tremaine yanked on the bridle. "Let go!" Lexie yelled. "Get out of my way!"

"You little hellcat! It's nearly dark."

"You are not my keeper!"

"No, by God, but someone should be. You're not safe alone!"

"Let go!" She jerked Tantrum's head backward, out of Tremaine's grasp, turning him so hard he half-reared. Swearing, Tremaine tried to hang on but the gelding trampled his foot and with a howl of pain and anger he let go.

"Lexie!" Tremaine yelled, as Tantrum, suddenly realizing he had his head, surged forward at breakneck speed across the field toward the back fence.

Lexie clung to him, not knowing whether to attempt to turn him, or just let him run. He was heading straight for the fence at the back of the barn. Beyond were sweeping fields, leading toward the Cascade foothills and a circuitous route to the Garrett property. Tantrum could jump the fence. He'd done it before. But never with someone on his back.

She had a sense of Tremaine running after her. Praying hard, she buried her face in Tantrum's neck. She was going to risk it. The horse's steps shortened as he neared the fence, his muscles tensing. Lexie held her breath and squeezed her eyes shut. She heard Tremaine's angry yell, felt the horse spring from the ground. For a moment her heart stopped, but then she was sailing upward, her hair streaming out behind her, the wind whistling past her ears. Tantrum's hooves gently brushed the top rail before he landed in perfect stride on the other side.

"Lexie! Damn you," Tremaine bellowed, his voice faint as Tantrum bore her ever farther away.

Jubilation filled her. She laughed, glad that she'd thwarted him. "Oh, you sweetheart," she said to Tantrum, the horse's ears flicking back and forth. "Thank you. Thank you."

Tantrum homed in on their favorite route—running beneath the stand of maples near the stream. Wet branches clutched at Lexie's hair, the night's gloom gathering around them like a cloak. It was intimate and somehow right. She was with her one and only friend, and she was on her way to Jace.

The gelding raced across the sloping fields, eating up the distance with ground-devouring strides, running with a freedom Lexie would soon be denied. But she wouldn't think about that. Not now.

Only when the Danner house was long out of view and the wind-flattened fields stretched endlessly toward the horizon did Lexie finally lift her head, bringing in the reins a bit, slowing the wildly galloping horse. Just because she was in the mood for speed didn't mean Tantrum should work up a lather.

Fighting her, the spirited horse tossed his head, unwillingly slowing to a trot and finally a walk. Lexie sat up straight and glanced behind her, aching inside. She wanted to hate them all but couldn't. They only wanted the best for her; she understood that. But she knew she'd die if she had to go to a school that specialized in corset cinching and coquetry. Her mother couldn't have picked a more dreaded fate.

The silvery stream that marked the westernmost boundary of the Danner property appeared on Lexie's left. She walked Tantrum toward it, thinking back to when Tremaine had seen her with Jace. It must have been where the stream cut near the lane that led to the Danner house. There was nowhere else he could have seen them.

She would have to be more careful in the future.

Tantrum splashed through the crystalline waters. Lexie wrapped her fingers in his black mane as he climbed up the small hill that led to the plateau where most of the Garrett land lay. Giving the horse his head once again, Lexie let Tantrum gallop across the damp knee-high grass, catching onto the trail that angled through the woods on the far eastern side of the Garrett property.

She rode to a stand of cedars whose lower trunks were ringed by a canopy of boughs, perfect for keeping out the rain. She and Jace had met here often.

Sliding from Tantrum's back, Lexie waited, her eyes squinting in the darkness as she searched for Jace. Her heart pounded, both with fear and exhilaration, and her breathing was rapid and shallow.

She swallowed. "Jace?" she whispered.

There was no sound save for the wind soughing through the upper branches. She glanced skyward, to see the treetops dance and shimmy, bending to and fro, as if waving at some far distant traveler.

Lexie waited as long as she dared, then climbed upon Tantrum's broad back, turning him in the same direction they'd come. But she wasn't ready to go home yet. She couldn't face all the recriminations.

With a boldness she'd never dreamed she possessed, she guided the gelding toward the Garrett home. She would call on Jace herself—as a friendly neighbor. There was no harm in that, and it made good sense to keep up relations with the wealthy family.

Jace Garrett raised his whip to the churning bays pulling his carriage, snapping it across their sturdy hindquarters. Surging against their harnesses, the team of horses tried to meet his ever-increasing demands, but Jace was a driven devil. The whip cracked and sang, a sharp accompaniment to the murmuring rain.

"Get on," he hissed through his teeth. Lexie was waiting for him. He'd been late once before, and he'd stumbled all over himself with apologies—an intolerable position to be in, as far as Jace was concerned. Though Lexie hadn't guessed the reason for his tardiness, she was a smart woman. Next time—this time!—he might not be so lucky.

Rain ran down the brim of his silk hat, ruining it. But Jace had been in too much of a hurry to employ one of his drivers. Besides, when he met with Betsy, or any one of his former mistresses, he didn't want anyone to suspect. As far as he knew, his dalliances were a fairly well-kept secret—as unpublicized as his dead father's had once been. Those who knew weren't likely to tell. After all, the Garrett name carried a lot of weight in Rock Springs. Jace could make life difficult for anyone who chose to go up against him.

He set his teeth, wondering how long Lexie would wait for him. Thinking of her brought a smile to his lips. Her innocence sometimes amazed him. The way she kissed him was so soft and sweet. He didn't kid himself that she would be the same way after they were married; no wife ever was. But if all went well he could still have Betsy—or some other discreet, willing female—and Lexie might never suspect. Any way around, he was going to make Lexie his wife. She was everything he needed: beautiful, quick-witted, from a good family—a family possessed of some of the finest acreage around—acreage that abutted the Garrett property.

Jace's eyes narrowed against the drizzling rain. He'd been careful with Lexie. He hadn't rushed her. Anytime she lifted her luscious mouth for a kiss he brushed her lips lightly and carefully, never revealing the lust burning through his veins. There was a kind of excitement in holding back. It made *her* beg him for more! Sometimes he didn't know if he could wait until she was eighteen to make her his, but wait he must. The Danners weren't keen on him already. If he tried to steal her away before they deemed it was proper, he would never achieve the peace so necessary for his future plans.

It was Jace's dream to one day own both parcels of land. That would ensure the Garretts' remaining the wealthiest, most powerful family of Rock Springs—a goal Joshua Garrett, Jace's father, had achieved, one Jace meant to keep.

Ahead he could see the turnout to their meeting place. Jace drew up the panting team and pulled the carriage to a stop. He stepped down and eyed the dripping cedars with annoyance. Cupping his hands around his mouth, he called, "Lexie!"

The wind shook rain off the neighboring trees, dousing him. He swore. "Lexie! Are you there? Come to the lane. It's too wet."

Once again there was no answer, and Jace concluded she'd gone. Swearing again, he climbed back to the driver's seat and drove the horses up the rest of the lane to the Garrett home.

Lexie sat astride Tantrum, who stood stamping and fretting in front of the white fence and gate, which led to the Garretts' formal grounds. She was filled with misgivings. The imposing Garrett mansion was directly in front of her, its shadowed peaks and gables staring and monstrous to Lexie's fanciful mind. Swallowing, she imagined what Lucinda Garrett might make of her unexpected visit; Jace's mother, the matriarch of the Garrett family, was not known for her warmth and understanding.

Lexie glanced downward. Her clothes were bedraggled, wet, and boyish—certainly not the proper attire of a fashionable young lady. Lexie had never wanted to *be* a fashionable young lady, but with the daunting prospect of facing Jace's family, and possibly enduring their scorn and ridicule, she suddenly wished she'd taken more care with her appearance.

You can always leave.

Tantrum tossed his head and snorted impatiently. Lexie slowly dismounted, tying the reins to the ghostly white rail of the fence. The rain had lessened somewhat, but it gathered and ran down Lexie's nose. The wind snatched gleefully at her hair. She longed for a brush. She was crazy to be here, but her desire to see Jace was too strong to ignore.

Hesitating, she bit into her lower lip, staring at the rambling blue stone manor in front of her. The Garrett home was one of the finest in the county; a reflection of the wealthy family that owned it. Even as a young child, Lexie had sensed that the Garretts and the Danners ran in somewhat different circles; a fact that had made Eliza's privileged attitude all the more perplexing.

Squaring her shoulders, Lexie walked up the pebbled path, drawing on her courage. A tenacious wisteria tangled up one side of the porch, its purple petals bruised by the rain. Toward the rear of the house were the servants' quarters, and beyond the main house stood the carriage barn, a smaller replica of the main building. To the west and farther out were the stables, barn, and other farm buildings. Over a distant rise Lexie could just see the roof of the bunkhouse where most of the Garretts' farmhands lived. The Garretts were city people who'd moved to Rock Springs even before the Danners had arrived. But their tastes remained rich and citified and were reflected in the glory of their farm.

Before Lexie could mount the front porch steps, the door suddenly flung outward and Jace's younger sister, Kelsey, came tearing through it, as if the devil himself were on her heels.

"Kelsey!" Lexie called, stopping the young woman dead in her tracks.

Kelsey swiped the back of her hand across her eyes, her teeth set in an obstinate line. "Lexie," she said, bewildered, glancing back over her shoulder.

Kelsey was much younger than Lexie; she was barely thirteen. But even now her beauty was something to behold, and promised a woman of rare and stunning looks. Burnished auburn hair, tinged magenta in the right light, curled softly down her back. Gray eyes, wide and heavily fringed, were huge in her small face. Men had already asked for her hand in marriage, willing to wait until she was of proper age to possess such an unusual wife, but Jace and Lucinda had discouraged all suitors.

Now, however, Kelsey's piquant face was ravaged from tears which formed in the corners of her eyes faster than she could wipe them away.

"What's wrong?" Lexie asked anxiously.

Kelsey inhaled, shuddered, then shook her head. "Nothing," she said bitterly. "Mother is just—upset with me."

Because of Jace, Lexie knew intimately the problems the Garretts had faced this last year. Joshua Garrett, Kelsey and Jace's father, had succumbed to the scourge of diphtheria. He'd left behind a dozen businesses in Rock Springs to manage, and six hundred acres of land to farm. Jace had eagerly stepped into the role of provider and patriarch, but Kelsey hadn't been ready to grow up. She'd rebelled in a myriad of small ways, the latest being her refusal to treat the servants as lesser beings—the way Lucinda wished her to. Lexie sympathized. People were equal. The Danners treated Cook and Annie with respect. But Lucinda was a tyrant who expected her daughter to obey unthinkingly. Jace could get around her. Lucinda had a soft spot only for her son. But with Kelsey she was hard and autocratic, adding credence to the rumor that she was as tight with her affections as her money.

Seeing the girl's tightly clenched fists, Lexie touched her sleeve. "Is there something I can do?"

"No. I just need a little time to myself before Mother or Martha finds me." She pulled herself together with an effort. "What are you doing here? And what happened to you?"

"Nothing." Lexie self-consciously smoothed her skirts. "I was—er—looking for Jace. Is he around?"

The front door banged open behind them, making them both jump. Lucinda's voice echoed loudly, "Kelsey Orchid Garrett, come back here this instant!"

Kelsey started, and without a backward glance bunched her skirts and hurried around the side of the house, taking off on a gallop toward the carriage house.

Lucinda stormed onto the porch in a rustle of black sateen, her rail-thin body as tough and dry as prairie grass. Her aristocratic jaw was thrown forward pugnaciously. "Kelsey, you come back now or forget about supper! No daughter of mine's going to talk that way. If your father were alive he'd whip you within an inch of your life!"

Lexie wished she could melt into the floor boards.

Lucinda seemed to realize for the first time that she wasn't alone. She glanced sharply at Lexie, her blue eyes lit by a fierce light. Collecting herself, she drew up her chest and declared haughtily, "Well, it's Miss Danner, isn't it? What brings you here this evening?"

"I . . . um . . ."

"Come on, come on. Get on with it."

Lexie's throat closed. She couldn't tell her why she'd come; she just couldn't do it. Lucinda Garrett was a woman to reckon with. She had a reputation of achieving what she wanted by pure orneriness. And she would give no quarter and suffer no fools.

"I was just on my way home," Lexie prevaricated. "I was taking a ride and I stopped by to say hello."

"Well, it's a special day indeed when a Danner comes calling on the Garretts."

"Yes, ma'am," Lexie answered self-consciously. Silence lengthened between them. "I was—wondering if Jace was around."

Lucinda's lips turned downward in distaste and she looked properly appalled. "No, Jason isn't here. I don't expect him until later."

"Where is Jace?" Lexie asked before she could help herself.

"In town. We've businesses to take care of, you know. If Jace wants to see you, I'm sure he'll let you know. Good evening, Miss Danner."

She wheeled around, quietly but firmly shutting the door behind her.

Humiliated, Lexie turned blindly back to Tantrum. She was climbing the fence to mount him when she heard the rattle of a carriage. Jace's team appeared around the bend near the woods, his face a blur of white against the blacker carriage.

With a sob of relief Lexie jumped down, running pellmell toward him. Jace had barely pulled the horses to a stop when Lexie was at the side of the carriage, breathing hard. "Jace! I'm so glad to see you. I'm sorry I was late. I've had the most awful day. I couldn't get away before now."

"Whoa, there, Lexie. Slow down."

She wanted to fling herself in his arms, feel him enfold her close to his chest. But Jace wasn't fond of impulsive displays of affection, so she waited for him to climb down, trying to control her emotions.

"What are you doing here?" he asked, his brows drawing together, as he cautiously stepped from the bottom step, grimacing as his right shoe sank into a puddle. "What happened to your clothes?"

"I rode Tantrum bareback. I couldn't wait to see you, and when you weren't at the stream, I decided to come here."

"You came here?" he repeated, surprised. He pushed back his hat to peer into her anxious face.

"Oh, Jace, please," Lexie said, feeling on the verge of tears.

Seeing her despair, he gently took her arm and started leading her toward the porch. But Lexie, feeling unsettled and friendless, disregarded her own better judgment, and threw herself into his arms. Jace froze. "Lexie . . ." he said, a trifle breathlessly.

"Please hold me, Jace," she begged. "Just for a minute."

He complied but she sensed how constrained he was. Not understanding, she clung all the more tightly. Jace, to keep his head, merely waited. But he could feel the pressure of her thrusting breasts and that brought a rush of memories of his last hours with Betsy. Before he could do something he regretted, he gently pushed Lexie away. "I stopped by the stream on my way, but I was late, so don't worry. I—ah—had business to attend to."

"What kind of business?" Her voice was low and despondent, her eyes downcast. He could tell she didn't really care about the answer. She just wanted comfort.

"Oh, this and that." He put his arm around her shoulders and gave her an affectionate squeeze.

Lexie was too caught up in her own misery to pay attention to the weighty pause between her question and his answer. "You won't believe what happened today."

"Why don't you tell me?"

"It's my mother," Lexie burst out with pent-up injustice. "She—she insists I attend Miss Everly's School for Young Ladies!"

Jace suddenly laughed and pulled back to look into her indignant green eyes, one arm circling her waist as he led her toward the house. "Really?"

"Yes." Lexie regarded him with vexation. He wasn't taking this news in the manner she expected him to. "I told her I wouldn't go. I can't! She knows how much I want to be a horse doctor, but she won't even consider it."

"Well, Lexie, I don't think it's such a bad idea. Your mother only wants what's best for you."

She stopped, peering up at him. "Whose side are you on?" she asked despairingly.

He smiled. "Yours, sweetheart. Ours," he corrected himself as he held the door. "But I have to admit, your temper could use a little curbing and maybe a finishing school is just the place for you."

"Jace!"

He chuckled, but at her look of horror, didn't add that he thought Miss Everly's School was the perfect way to keep her busy until they could marry. It would also give him an excuse not to see her, and therefore he wouldn't be tempted to take what she so innocently offered each time they were together. "Come on inside. It's too wet out here to talk. Actually I'm glad your mother brought this up."

Deflated, Lexie followed Jace inside the domed entry hall, waiting in silence as he lightly shook the rain from his silk hat, pulled off his overcoat, and examined his watersoaked shoes. From somewhere toward the rear of the house, Lexie could hear Lucinda berating one of the servants. Jace made a face and gestured toward the parlor. Lexie walked ahead of him, sitting primly on the horsehair couch as he closed the doors behind them and sat down across from her.

Regarding her with a brotherly benevolence that made Lexie feel impatient, Jace remarked, "Miss Everly's School has a wonderful reputation. The finest around."

Lexie stared down at her clasped hands. She felt as tense and frustrated as she had when she'd faced her mother. "I can't believe you just said that. I would rather be boiled in oil than step across the threshold of any finishing school."

"That's a bit drastic, even for you. I know you think you want to be a horse doctor, but—"

"Think I want to be?"

Jace sighed, as if dealing with a particularly dull-witted child. "What kind of job would that be? Even if you were accepted by the farmers around here, you'd spend most of your time in a buggy or wagon, heading from farm to farm, working long hours for what? Half the time the animal would die anyway—and you wouldn't get paid. It's bad enough these days being a doctor, like Tremaine, but a horse doctor . . ." Jace lifted a realistic palm. "It's just not the career for a woman."

Lexie flushed. "I suppose you want a wife who will mend your shirts and cook your meals."

"Lexie . . ." The long-suffering tone of his voice drove her to her feet, but before she could say something she might regret, Jace rose and took her hand. "After we're married we'll have a whole army of servants to tend to our needs. Someone else can mend my shirts."

"That's not what I meant."

With a sigh, he asked, "Well, then, what did you mean?"

"I'm not that kind of woman, Jace. I can't just take care of a home. It's not—it's not"—she groped for the right word—"fulfilling enough. I want to be an animal doctor."

His mouth quirked. "And you want to put Doc Meechum out of business."

"That's right." Lexie was emphatic. It wasn't the noblest of purposes, but then Meechum's supposed expertise was a travesty.

Jace's thumb lifted her chin and his dark eyes looked deeply into hers. "You know, being my wife would entail extra responsibilities. We both want children, don't we?"

Lexie nodded, her heart beating unevenly. Was he going

to kiss her right here? In the parlor of his own home? "Jace," she said in a whisper, half-scandalized, half-delighted.

"I'm going to build us a house, Lexie. On the other side of the property." He waved in the direction of Rock Springs. "One that'll put the rest of them to shame."

This was news to Lexie. "You want to live on part of this farm?" she asked, a bit apprehensively.

"Toward town. I always planned on moving closer in. Six hundred acres is a lot of land between here and there."

"But I thought—I mean, I expected us to build our own place. Somewhere else."

"It'll be our own place. It'll just be on Garrett land. And Lexie, our house will have hot and cold running water, with a bathtub big enough for two." Swept away by his dream, he wrapped his arms around her, squeezing her close, creating a wave of longing so strong in Lexie that her knees felt weak.

"Oh, Jace," she murmured, her emerald eyes glimmering brightly.

"Think of it, Lexie. Just you and me and our own house. The biggest one around. Your parents' home and this one"—he gestured disparagingly with one hand, dismissing Rock Springs' most elegant home in a single motion— "will look like hovels in comparison."

"I don't need that fancy of a house, Jace. I just need you."

"We'll have it all, Lexie."

His mouth was just inches from hers, all he had to do was bend down and kiss her. "But what about Miss Everly's School?" she breathed, her lips parting.

Jace's gaze was locked on her soft mouth. Lexie waited expectantly, longing for his love. His grip tightened and his lips slackened, but then he suddenly let her go and cleared his throat. "How long are you supposed to attend?"

Disappointed, she murmured, "One year."

"Well, that's perfect! We'll get married after you graduate."

Lexie blinked. "Jace, I'm not going to Miss Everly's School! If you want to get married, let's get married now."

"Lexie, be reasonable. It's been less than a year since my father died. I can't just leave Mother to run things alone."

"You can still run things. You'll just be married to me. We

could even live here for a while, until our house was built."
Lexie drew a deep breath. The last thing she wanted to do
was reside under the same roof as Lucinda Garrett, but what
choice did she have? She would never go to Miss Everly's
School. Never. Jace just had to face that fact.

"Your parents want you to wait until you're eighteen."

"But I don't want to wait!"

Jace was silent so long she grew afraid. She'd been too
forward again, she could tell by the way he was looking at
her, his eyes filled with a wariness she didn't fully understand.

Then he suddenly drew her into his arms and all her fears
dissolved. "The truth is, Lexie, I really would like you to go
to Miss Everly's School," he said against her hair. "It would
be good training for you, even if you never use it."

"How can that be good training, then?"

"Look at your clothes. They're hardly fitting for a lady.
Mud-spattered split skirt and cotton waist, boots, no bonnet
. . . I'd like to see you in silk and satin, with a sash and a
bustle and a parasol. I don't want a horsewoman. I want a
lady. And I want that lady to be you."

Lexie regarded him through eyes huge with hurt. She was
speechless. The fervor with which he spoke revealed how
serious he was. But he didn't want *her!*

Footsteps sounded on the plankwood entry floor and the
doors to the parlor were thrown open. Jace dropped Lexie as
if he'd been caught in the act of committing a crime.
Lucinda's thin face deepened into a scowl when she saw
Lexie, then her gaze lit upon her son and her face softened.

"I thought I heard you come in. You're late. I was
worried."

"I had some problems in town," Jace answered in an
off-hand manner. "Walter Pennington was late paying rent
on the mercantile. Pennington's wife's been sick and he
hasn't been paying."

"What about Templeton?"

Jace loosened his string tie. "I'm letting Conrad go
awhile," he said. "We'll see what happens in the future."

Their business talk was of no interest to Lexie, who rarely
visited Rock Springs proper, except with her parents. She

knew Walter Pennington, and she also knew Conrad Templeton was manager and half-owner of the Half Moon Saloon—another of Jace's business ventures, one Lexie's parents didn't approve of for reasons still unknown to her.

Lexie's heart was in farming. When Jace brought the discussion around to Garrett Livery, her ears perked up.

"Tom Benton is as lazy as they come, but he knows horses," Jace was saying to Lucinda. "I'll have to keep him running the place until I can find someone else as qualified."

Lucinda slid a meaningful look in Lexie's direction and said, "Well, we'll talk about this later. Come on in and eat now. Martha's got supper waiting." Her lips tightening, she added, "Kelsey won't be eating with us. She's run off outside again. I sent MacDougal after her." Inclining her head, Lucinda said to Lexie, "Good evening, Miss Danner."

Lexie suffered a thousand humiliations at being so summarily dismissed. Her face flooded with color. "Good evening," she murmured, striding quickly from the room and through the front door. It was very dark by now, but the clouds had moved rapidly toward the east and clearer skies stood out in the inky blackness. Faintly she could see a first star.

"Lexie." Jace caught her arm just as she reached the white rail fence. "Don't leave."

"I'm not welcome here," she said, unlooping Tantrum's reins. "Your mother wants me to go and I'm late anyway."

"My mother's not head of this household," Jace reminded her gently. "Since Father died, I'm the man in charge."

Lexie shook her head but made no further move to mount Tantrum, and Jace touched her damp blond hair.

"Don't worry about my mother. She'll come around. She's just got to get used to the idea of me wanting a Danner. It's not that she doesn't respect your family, but there've been a lot of bad feelings."

"Because your father accused mine of stealing!" Lexie's chest swelled chokingly.

"Let's not talk about that. It's over and done with now." Jace's jaw tightened ominously, but Lexie wasn't looking at him. All she could see was Joshua Garrett's roaring anger over two acres lost to the Danners when Crystal Creek carved a new bed. The stranded Garrett cattle had wandered into the Danner herd and Joshua had bellowed and wielded his rifle like a savage.

Jace suddenly wrapped his arms around her in the protective way she loved so much—and so seldom received. It was Jace's understanding during this unsettled time that Lexie relied on. She needed him, loved him totally. He was the only person who understood her.

"What are you going to do about Miss Everly's School?" he asked.

"What can I do?" she responded bitterly, turning her cheek into his shoulder. "My mother insists I go and since you won't marry me, I have no other choice."

"It'll be worth it, Lexie. I promise." He lifted her chin and kissed her lightly, in the way that always made her ache for more.

Cautiously, she wound her arms around his neck. She didn't really understand what made Jace pull back all the time. When she'd caught Tremaine with Mary-Anne she'd gained the impression that they were both eager for each other. Of course that had been a long time ago, and her memory might be playing tricks on her, but shouldn't Jace be a little more demanding?

As if hearing her unspoken plea, the tempo of his breathing altered. His dark eyes burned with an unholy light. Lexie caught her breath, her lips parting. "Jace?" she asked uneasily. He suddenly dragged her close, so close in fact that she was wedged against him in an embarrassingly intimate way. "What are you doing?!"

"Kissing you like you want to be kissed." Before she could offer up a response, he bent down and covered her mouth with his. It was a kiss like no other he'd given her—a hard kiss, full of burgeoning passion and suppressed desire. Lexie was so stunned she did nothing for a moment, then a deep panic overtook her and she jerked her mouth away, gasping. Automatically, she slapped him hard with her open palm.

The sound of flesh hitting flesh was a cold dash of sanity. Jace tossed her aside as if she were a rag doll and, horrified, Lexie covered her mouth. "I'm sorry," she whispered miserably. "Oh, Jace, I'm sorry."

"No, I'm sorry." He lifted his own hand, his fingertips

gingerly examining the damage done to his face. He sounded more resigned than angry, as if she'd been given a test and somehow failed.

Sensing something important slipping away, Lexie stumbled over her words, hastening to apologize. "You just took me by surprise and I—I wasn't ready. I really am sorry."

He glanced past her, staring distantly in the direction from which he'd arrived. She knew she'd made him angry.

"Jace, I—"

"Mr. Garrett?"

Lexie and Jace both turned at the sound of the newcomer's voice. Old MacDougal, the stooped Scotsman who had been sent to chase after Kelsey, was standing by the gate, worrying his hat between his gnarled hands. "I dinna mean to bother you, but Mrs. Garrett, she was worried about young Kelsey. 'Tis at the barn, she is, tending a pair of wee motherless lambs."

"Bring her to the house," Jace told him flatly. "Those lambs won't make it."

Lexie placed a hand on his arm, appalled. "You can feed them round the clock! There's a chance they might live."

If she'd angered him before, she'd now compounded the problem. With an effort, he said, "Take care of the lambs yourself, Mac. But bring Kelsey back."

When the man had gone, Jace turned to Lexie. "It's almost dark. You'd better be getting home."

"I'll go to Miss Everly's School for Young Ladies if that's what you want," Lexie burst out anxiously, clutching his arm. "Please, don't be angry with me."

"I'm not angry."

Lexie felt like crying. He was lying. She'd alienated the one person who cared about her. "Do you want me to go away to school? Would you—come visit me sometime—if I asked?"

His expression lightened a bit. "Of course I'll visit you. I love you."

His words were music to her ears, yet she still felt vulnerable and frightened. "Do you?" she asked, desperate to be reassured.

"You're going to be my wife."

She could sense his smile behind his words. Eager to

restore peace, she said softly, "I love you, too. I'm sorry if I upset you."

Jace's dark eyes narrowed. "Never mind," he said brusquely. When he reached for her again, she came willingly into his arms. This time his kiss was soft and tender. Lexie clung to him, but before she'd really gotten her fill, he gently pushed her away. "Now, you'd best get back before your father sends the sheriff after you."

Nodding, Lexie said, "Can we meet tomorrow?"

"Hmmm. Maybe." He touched her cheek. "But I've got a lot of business in Rock Springs. I might even stay the night in town." Seeing her expression, he smiled. "Don't worry. I'll let you know when I'm back."

"Oh, please, Jace. Try to come. I need you."

He smiled. Her intensity did his male ego a world of good, especially after the beating it had taken beneath the force of her slap. But Lexie would come to heel. It was just a matter of time.

The door opened and Lucinda appeared like a dark shadow on the porch. Jace could feel her disapproval, knew she wished him to marry a rich Portland debutante. But he wanted Lexie. He burned for her and the Danner land. And once some of this unwomanly rebellion was pounded out of her, she would make a perfect wife.

"Let me give you a leg up," Jace said softly to Lexie, earning him a delighted smile from the innocent, golden-haired vixen.

Encouraged by his loving attention, Lexie wheeled Tantrum around and said respectfully, "Good evening, Mrs. Garrett."

"A lady would be riding sidesaddle," was the woman's repressive reply.

"Goodbye, Jace," Lexie added, wanting to scream out that she would rather die than become a so-called lady, but managing to hold her tongue as she lightly touched her heels to Tantrum's flanks.

Jace stared after her, satisfied.

"Are you going to marry her, son?" Lucinda asked.

"Yes."

"She's trouble. She's wild and willful. Likes animals better than people."

"Mmmm." Jace knew only too well Lexie's less appealing characteristics. He was coldly infuriated at being slapped, and he was still steamed at the way she'd questioned his decision about the lambs in front of old MacDougal. Jaw taut, he said, "Kelsey's at the barn with those bummer lambs. I'm going to have Mac put them down. They're too much trouble to take care of."

Even with Lucinda's disparaging remark still ringing in her ears, a warm feeling enveloped Lexie as Tantrum softly galloped across the waving, moonlit fields. Jace had made it clear how he felt about her. Now there would be no more secret meetings, no more guilt! Soon Jace would ask Pa for her hand in marriage and for that she could even suffer through a year of Miss Everly's School.

The barn and outbuildings were dark when Lexie finally arrived back at the Danner farm. Leaning over Tantrum's side, she unlatched the gate, smiling. It probably wouldn't be wise to let the horse jump the fence again; she really shouldn't have done it the first time.

The gelding's ears were pricked forward and he trotted eagerly toward the stables. But at the door he suddenly shied sideways, nearly unseating Lexie who was attempting to lean down and twist open the latch.

"Hey, there, boy. Shhh." Lexie held the reins tight, managing to finally stop his mincing steps. She slid off his back, pulling him after her toward the door.

The stables were gloomy inside. Groping, Lexie found the catch to Tantrum's box and led the sweating horse inside. She was going to have to rub him down before she went to the house, which was fine with her. The longer she could put off facing her mother and father again, and the prospect of Miss Everly's School, the better.

She reached for the lantern and encountered warm flesh, the flesh of a human hand. A scream formed in her throat, but was stifled after one terrified gasp as the hand grasped the lantern, striking a match to the flame.

Tremaine's harsh countenance appeared out of the darkness, as if conjured by a genie. He stared at Lexie in a way that made her heart pound and her blood run cold.

Before she could move he reached for her, his grip an iron

manacle around her wrists. She backed up instinctively, drawing a fearful breath. She'd never seen him so angry or so intense, yet she knew instantly what he was thinking. There was no excuse for the way she'd ridden Tantrum over the fence. It had been irresponsible and foolish. And the blue flame of anger lighting Tremaine's eyes assured her that retribution was at hand.

Chapter Three

Tremaine glared down at the willful young woman caught between his hands. He wanted to shake some sense into her, by God. She was reckless and wild and asking—no, *begging!*—for trouble. She'd been a source of irritation to him as long as he could remember and now, staring into her wide, shadowed eyes, that irritation was magnified a thousandfold.

He hadn't seen her for nearly a year; he couldn't remember how long it had been before that. From the moment he'd learned she wasn't his sister, he'd mentally cut her from his life. He'd thought it would be so easy.

What a fool he'd been! Lexie, for only God knew what reason, had invaded his very soul. Since graduating from medical school, he'd purposely stayed in Portland, working at Willamette Infirmary, living in a cramped apartment, *anything* just to be away from her! But he occasionally came back, his rare visits short and frustrating. And then seeing Lexie last night with Jace had struck fear in his heart, crystalizing his warring emotions.

He couldn't let her marry that low-bellied rounder.

His hands tightened on her shoulders. He heard Lexie sweep in a soft, frightened breath, and the smoldering dull ache of forbidden longing surged through him. He swore viciously beneath his breath, damning the fates. Lexie might not be his sister, but he had to treat her like one! Why she must be kept in the dark was a mystery, but Eliza and Pa were adamant Lexie not find out the truth.

And it was killing him.

"You and I are going to have a little talk," he said tautly. "Now."

Lexie twisted her arm but his grip was too tight to break. "You're hurting me."

"I'd like to knock some sense into your thick skull," he declared furiously. "That circus stunt you pulled tonight was dangerous. You're lucky Tantrum wasn't hurt."

"I know, I—"

"Shut up," he said softly. "And listen."

For once in her life Lexie did as she was told. She closed her mouth and stared up at him, a mutinous flame lighting her green eyes. Her hair lay wet and dark against her bare head, her skirt was mud-spattered, her boots soaked. The cotton waist she wore was wet and stuck to her skin, offering Tremaine a tantalizing glimpse of smooth, moist flesh beneath.

He paused to take a breath. There was something so elemental about Lexie that it made him feel raw, vulnerable. "You're in serious trouble with Pa and your mother," he said brusquely. "They've been asking where you are. I told them you took a ride on Tantrum because you needed time to think."

She regarded him warily. "You lied for me?"

When she put it like that, he instantly recoiled, dropping his arms in disgust. "You'd better get up to the house. I'll take care of Tantrum."

He turned away, picking up a brush and eyeing the prancing gelding. Tantrum rolled an eye at him and snorted loudly, shifting his hindquarters.

Behind him, he heard Lexie's soft laughter. "He'll never let you near him. He'll kick and thrash."

She followed him into Tantrum's box, her breasts accidentally touching his back when he stopped short to argue with her. Tremaine gritted his teeth and muttered, "I can handle him."

"No, you can't. You'll get hurt."

"Your concern for my welfare is touching, but believe me, Lexie, I won't get hurt."

She tried to shift around him, to take the lead rope attached to Tantrum's bridle from his hands. There was a peculiar moment when her arms and Tremaine's got tangled and he touched the firm skin at her waist. Lexie glanced at him as Tantrum's hindquarters shifted warningly. The gelding slashed backward with his powerful legs, his hooves clanging into the rail, the sound ringing to the rooftops.

"Get out of here, Lexie!" Tremaine bellowed.

"If you'd just let me help," she argued, grabbing the lead rope. "Let go! You're scaring him!"

For an answer Tremaine pushed her up against the side of the box, breathing almost as heavily as she was.

"What are you doing?" she cried, pushing on his chest.

"Don't move. Don't do anything. That horse is a menace and you're only aggravating—"

"Oh, for Pete's sake."

They were so close he could see the dark gold strands of hair at her crown, could count the lashes framing her eyes. Tantrum shimmied around restlessly. Lexie smiled up at Tremaine. "Honestly, Tremaine. Just get out of the box. Now, let me go."

He pulled back slowly and she slid under his arm, touching a flat palm on Tantrum's sweating neck. "There, boy. Relax," she cooed to the nervous horse. "It's only Tremaine. You're all right. Yes, that's right. You're okay." Her eyes on Tantrum, she held out her hand to Tremaine. "Hand me the brush," she said in the same soothing tones. "Then back out of the stall."

Tremaine was reluctant to leave her with the gelding, even though he knew better than anyone how much the animal trusted her. Wordlessly, he handed her the brush, watching her hands as she stroked Tantrum's quivering flesh. The gelding switched his tail and minced back and forth, trying to twist and see Tremaine, who was just out of range.

"You can go to the house," Lexie said. "I'll be there as soon as I'm done."

"Thanks," Tremaine answered dryly. "I'll stick around all the same."

Lexie brushed with smooth, hard strokes. Tantrum's muscles were like liquid velvet beneath his slick, shimmering coat. Tremaine stood perfectly still, mesmerized by the soft fluidity of her motions. Time seemed suspended, and for a moment he forgot his anger and reveled in the sensuality of her movements.

When Lexie was finished she regarded him silently, her brows raised questioningly. "Something wrong?"

"No." He drew a breath. "You have an amazing effect on that horse."

"Tantrum and I understand one another," she said, slipping out of the box stall. There were oats stored in one of the tin-lined bins, and Lexie, knowing she should save the oats for winter, broke one more rule, dumping a scoopful into Tantrum's feedbin.

"You really know how to push things to the limit," Tremaine observed.

She glanced at him. He stood in the center of the room, his arms folded across his chest. The lantern's uncertain light cast shadows over his already lean countenance, magnifying his forbidding air. If she hadn't known he was capable of humor, she would have been frightened by this stern, uncompromising man. But Tremaine had a softer side when he cared to show it.

"Mother wants me to go to Miss Everly's School for Young Ladies," she said, the thought just popping into her head. "What do you think about that?"

Tremaine's lips twitched. "You're kidding."

"I wish I were," Lexie said feelingly.

She could see the grin on his face, and she knew he felt she was getting what she deserved—which only stoked her anger.

"Miss Everly's School, huh?" He rubbed his jaw. "I hear that's quite a place."

Lexie had a few choice words stored up for what she thought about the school, but she bit them back. After all,

Tremaine was growing more approachable and a plan was shaping in her mind. There might be a way out of her predicament yet.

She walked across the wooden floor, stopping in front of Fortune's box, holding out her hand to Tremaine's snuffling stallion. Fortune's affections were easily swayed. He greedily searched her hand for a treat. Stroking his blazed nose, Lexie said over her shoulder with forced casualness, "You know, you could help me."

"Oh?"

Lexie went back to the oat bin, scooping up a handful, then bringing it back to Fortune, who eagerly inhaled the grain. "You could talk to Mother. She listens to you."

Tremaine had the audacity to laugh.

Lexie sighed. "I can't go to that school, Tremaine. I'll die there. I will," she added stubbornly when he refused to take her seriously.

"You sure you don't want a career in the theater, Lexie? Drama suits you."

She reached out and shoved him before she thought. He barely moved, grinning down at her like the tormenting big brother he was. "I'm not fit to attend that school," she muttered.

"You mean you don't *want* to attend that school. You're fit enough."

"That school's for rich young women. I'm not rich." Lexie quelled her anger with an effort and turned to him. She was desperate. And it was true what she'd said about Tremaine's relationship to Mother. He could wrap her around his finger like nobody else. All he had to do was *ask*.

"Lexie, you may need that school more than you know. No woman in their right mind would jump that fence on a horse. Especially a horse like Tantrum." He flung a disparaging glance at the gelding who, apart from a flicking of his ears, now unabashedly ignored Tremaine. Tremaine shook his head, glancing again down at Lexie. "And trying to perform surgery on Matilda? You're not thinking straight."

"Well then, you and Jace have something in common!" she said, glaring at him. "He thinks I should go, too."

Her words had the desired effect. Tremaine stiffened as if

she'd slapped him. The thought reminded her of that awful moment when her hand had connected with Jace's face—the memory so intense it had the power to make her forget her own immediate problems. She fervently hoped Jace had forgiven her. How could she have slapped him? *How?*

"You saw Jace, then," Tremaine bit out.

"We're getting married," said Lexie, tossing her head. Miss Everly's School be damned. She would find a way to get Jace to propose before September yet.

"You're not ready to marry anyone," he said angrily. "You're too pig-headed. What kind of wife would you make?"

Lexie's mouth opened in surprised hurt. She sensed that Tremaine was purposely trying to wound her, but his reasons escaped her. Turning away from his condemning gaze, she said softly, "I'd make a damn good wife. I could make him happy."

Silence fell between them. Tremaine was so still that Lexie squinted at him through the gloom. She couldn't read his expression but she could sense his disapproval, and she sensed the leashed power of him in a purely feminine way. It wouldn't be smart to make an enemy of him. But, oh, if she could only get him on her side!

"You were with Jace tonight?" Tremaine asked in a strangely harsh voice. "Down at the stream again?"

"No, at the Garrett house." Lexie tilted her head and studied him perplexedly. "When did you see me at the stream with Jace, Tremaine? That was last night and you didn't get here until today. I saw Fortune and your buggy parked in front of the house."

"I arrived last night," he admitted.

"Last night? You didn't stay at the house."

"No, I didn't." As if the conversation were working its way into dangerous territory, Tremaine shifted his weight, then reached for the lantern, turning down the flame. "You'd better get to the house. Eliza and Pa are waiting."

"Where did you stay?" asked Lexie, unwilling to give up.

"In Rock Springs." His voice was clipped.

Lexie raised innocent emerald eyes to his. She regarded him with faint puzzlement. "But why didn't you . . ."

Tremaine extinguished the lantern and the stable fell into

total darkness. Lexie could hear his breathing. She blinked, trying to adjust to the blackness.

"We're done here," came Tremaine's disembodied voice.

"I can't see!" Lexie twisted on her heel, her hands in front of her. Annoyed, she said, "I was going to the house. You didn't have to turn off the lantern."

"Didn't I?"

She felt him move past her, a warm shadow stirring the dusty stable air. She heard a click and the door was opened, a cool breeze lifting her hair, moist air dampening her cheeks.

Tremaine stood in the doorway, outlined by the faint moonlight. He waited for her and Lexie walked past him, her heels loud against the plankwood floor, her head held high. She was tired of everyone telling her what to do, plotting against her. Didn't she have any say in her life at all?

She started off toward the house, then realized Tremaine wasn't following her. "What are you doing?" she demanded.

"I've got a few things to take care of," he threw over his shoulder as he headed in the direction of the barn.

"What things?"

"None of your business."

His words brought an angry flush to her cheeks, more because they were spoken with a patronizing edge than the fact that he wouldn't reveal what he was doing.

Lexie looked toward the house, where the lanterns glowed mistily through the rain-dampened windowpanes. Her heart lurched. She swallowed against a dry throat, her boots squelching through the mud as she resignedly headed toward the front door. There was no more putting off the inevitable.

Moonlight fell on her hair, turning it to silver, and Tremaine's unwilling gaze followed after her. A fire smoldered within him. The same fire that had refused to be quenched the night before, when he'd staggered up the steps of Jenny McBride's rooming house, still aflame despite the gallon of scotch he'd drunk at the Half Moon Saloon, trying to smother that burning torrent.

But neither Jenny's soft ministrations, nor the Half Moon's scotch could help Tremaine where he needed it the most. His was a problem that had begun years before, when he'd finally learned the truth about himself and Lexie. And the problem had grown.

Tremaine drew in a breath until his lungs ached, then he expelled it slowly, wondering what in the hell was wrong with him. This desire for Lexie repelled him. It was totally outside the realm of his experience. As far as Tremaine was concerned, women were fine creatures with glorious ways to satisfy a man's pleasure, but they were untrustworthy and fickle and consequently he'd never become attached to any one of their sex for long.

But Lexie had always been there. When they were kids Tremaine remembered her being a nuisance. She'd been the apple of her mother's eye, and he'd been insanely jealous. Though he'd known Eliza wasn't his real mother, he'd wanted her to be. Lexie showing up so soon after Eliza and Pa's marriage had threatened Tremaine's world. Vaguely, he remembered losing one mother; he hadn't been willing to lose another. The solution to Tremaine's eight-year-old mind had been clear: remove the competition.

What began as a small germ soon became a full-blown idea, and as Lexie grew, Tremaine plotted new, imaginative ways to get rid of her. The birth of his brothers didn't lessen his obsession. To his way of thinking, Lexie had to go.

When she was three he put her on his horse and slapped the bay's haunches, sending it racing across the pasture. To his intense fury Lexie dug her chubby legs into the horse's sides, hung onto the reins and laughed, riding around the yard as if she'd been born in the saddle.

He'd gotten a whipping for that one.

Then there had been the castor oil in the jam. He waited for days for just the right opportunity, doctoring one jar which he purposely kept hidden away. The first chance he got with Lexie was alone at the table. He quickly exchanged jars. But then disaster struck. Pa and Harrison walked in at just that moment and decided to help themselves. Everyone had gotten sick. Another whipping had followed and, worse yet, the loss of Eliza's affection. Though Eliza had never said as much, he'd felt the change. His father had never wavered in his affection, but Tremaine could almost remember the moment Eliza had drawn away from him. He'd become an outcast—unloved and unwanted.

It had made him hate the squawling Lexie even more.

When he'd grown older he'd ceased to care about Lexie. He had other brothers—babies who didn't bother him so much. Then he'd overheard a scrap of conversation between his father and Eliza and everything had fallen into place.

They were in the parlor, unaware that he'd come in from outside. Pa was standing by the mantel, looking down at his beautiful wife. "We're a family, Eliza," he was saying in a soothing tone. "One family."

"Yes, but Lexie isn't a Danner." Her eyes were riveted to the yellow paper in Pa's hand. "That wire proves it. If anyone finds out the truth—" she choked out.

"No one will find out. No one knows but you and I."

Tremaine hadn't understood the significance of the paper; he still didn't. But he'd been old enough to understand the import of Eliza's words. Lexie wasn't a Danner! She wasn't Pa's child! Hazily, he remembered that period of his life when they'd drifted from town to town. He could recall Eliza showing up like an answer from heaven with a suitcase full of money. She must have been pregnant then, he realized. She'd been an unwed mother.

This new side of Eliza had made Tremaine regard her with cold tolerance. Not because he cared about her past, but because she'd just proved how complicated and treacherous women could be. It was his first lesson, and it was one well learned. She'd bought respectability. She'd bought Pa.

Unable to deal with these new and awful realizations, Tremaine had shunned the farm, turning unknowingly to the occupation his father had once shared: doctoring. Joseph had been pleased with his choice, able to live vicariously through his son. He'd applauded Tremaine's decision and had agreed that he could leave home for better schooling in Portland. At fifteen, Tremaine had purposely distanced himself from the whole family, returning only at vacation times and during the heaviest work season of the summer. The fact that Eliza chose to bestow a chunk of money on him to pay for his education didn't bother Tremaine in the least. She claimed it was hers and Pa's money, but he knew the truth. He'd treated the money as a loan and had been paying her back ever since he'd been in practice.

There was an unspoken war going on between Tremaine and his stepmother. Eliza never told anyone Tremaine wasn't her son, and Tremaine, for reasons he didn't understand himself, kept the secret. But when he was around Eliza, Tremaine never felt truly at ease. She valued his opinion; he knew that. But the days when he'd wanted her to fill his own mother's shoes were long, long past.

While Tremaine was away, Lexie grew up. One visit she'd been a brat in pigtails, the next she was a young woman. Tremaine had stared at her in wonder the summer he turned twenty-three, watching her help break the wild ponies that Pa had purchased for a song. Lexie had fearlessly, joyfully forced them to heed her tremendous will.

He'd felt a strange heady sensation then—one he'd quickly denied. But it had worsened over the last few years, and Lexie's ignorance of their true relationship, her trust in his "brotherly" feelings for her, had been an aggravation he hadn't known how to deal with.

It wasn't Tremaine's first experience with desire for the opposite sex—Mary-Anne Laytham had seen to those needs fully and completely when he'd been still wet behind the ears—but it was his first experience in having to hide them. Here was Lexie—his *sister* for all practical purposes—and he couldn't keep his eyes off the curve of her muslin skirt as she bent over and examined a horse's hoof, the sway of her breasts as she moved, the sight of sweat trickling through the fine dust gathered on her moist skin.

He hated himself for his feelings and deliberately buried them deep inside, blocking them out. He determined that the less he saw of her, the better.

But later that same summer he came home to Rock Springs to see her riding bareback across the fields on Tantrum, that miserable gelding flying toward him, his black tail streaming out behind him like a flag. Lexie's hair had been a golden banner as she'd ridden to a sliding halt in front of him, grinning hugely. Behind her, the raging fuschia and orange hues of the setting sun were baking the far distant hills.

"Well?" she asked impudently. "I can ride better than you."

"You always could, Sundown," he answered with a smile.

She hadn't heard the endearment—at least not the way it sounded to his own ears. She slid off Tantrum and walked with Tremaine toward the house, her color high, her eyes deep green emeralds, her lips pink and sensual. Inside, Tremaine was filled with a pounding ache.

"What's the matter with you?" Lexie asked, seeing his expression change. Amused, she added, "You look like you could eat nails."

In self-defense, he muttered a total untruth, "You ride that monster like a boy. You don't even look like a woman."

Lexie turned to him, wounded. "What do you mean?"

"I mean, you look and act like a ten-year-old boy," he said through his teeth. "Pa lets you handle the horses because he favors you. He knows you hate keeping house. But sooner or later you're going to have to become a real woman."

It was with a mixture of sadness and relief that he saw the look of loathing cross her young face. "I am a real woman!" she cried, and she dug the toe of her cowboy boot so hard in his shin that he howled like a wolf.

Then she was on him, scratching his face, huffing and puffing and wriggling like a wildwoman. "Stop it!" he demanded, clasping her wrists.

"You take it back!" she yowled. "Take it back or I'll kill you!"

"Damn it, Lexie . . ." he bit out.

"Take it back! Take it back!"

It was Pa who broke up their tussle, bellowing for Tremaine to leave her alone. Even he had a tender spot for the tyrannical woman/child. Tremaine left in disgust.

From that day forward, every encounter with Lexie had been a trial. Tremaine rationalized his feelings. She was a blossoming woman. It was natural for a man to notice. He would get over his interest in her. Still, every time he saw her they clashed. He suspected she hated him. And he was afraid to analyze his feelings for her.

At the railing to Matilda's stall, Tremaine drew another deep breath, leaning his arm over the top bar. The Jersey rolled a dull eye his way, keeping her weight off her bandaged leg, switching her burned tail.

"You'll be all right," Tremaine told her.

But would *he* be all right? His interest in Lexie hadn't diminished; he was honest enough with himself to recognize that now. But she thought they were related! And Pa wouldn't even hear of telling her the truth.

Sighing, Tremaine resigned himself to his role of big brother. He didn't love her anyway. He didn't love any woman. But Lexie was a fire in his blood that raged like molten lava any time he even heard about her and Jace Garrett.

Stroking his chin, Tremaine thought about spending the night under the same roof as Lexie. The idea was intolerable. With a shake of his head he walked back toward the house to tell Pa and Eliza that he'd had to change his plans. Jenny McBride's rooming house was looking better all the time.

Chapter Four

W here do you think you're going, young lady?"

Pa's voice came easily from the parlor, and Lexie, who had been entertaining ideas of sneaking to the sanctity of her bedroom, walked into the room with her head held high. "I was going to bed," she said quietly.

"Without any supper?" This was from her mother. Sitting on the brocade couch in her satin dress, Eliza looked so perfect she could have been a cameo.

"I'm not hungry."

Lexie's younger brother, Jesse, who was dark like Pa and Tremaine, shot Lexie a mocking look, so much like Tremaine's that Lexie felt like screaming. Wisely, Jesse kept his own counsel, too smart to interfere with whatever punishment Pa and Mother chose to mete out.

"Your father and I would like a private talk with Lexie," Eliza said in her quiet, authoritative way to the room in general. "Please leave us alone."

On his way out, Harrison winked at her in commiseration. "Fight them, Lex," he said in an undertone.

Surprised by his understanding, Lexie's lips parted. Then

at her mother's stern glance, she swallowed and folded her hands in her lap. But inside she seethed with rebellion.

Her youngest brother, Samuel, regarded her with thoughtful green eyes. He, too, was dark but, unlike Jesse, he never stirred up trouble. He seemed to want to say something to her, but he passed by her without a sound.

Jesse came last, moving with that sensual swagger that Lexie so detested. Already a handful, he was too much like Tremaine for his own good, she decided. Why were her parents so worried about her? she fretted in vexation. Jesse had already caused them more gray hairs than she, Tremaine, and Harrison put together!

Then Lexie was alone with Pa and her mother. Pa looked uncomfortable, but it was clear Eliza was waiting for him to speak first.

She knows her woman's place, Lexie thought bitterly.

"I'm not going to ask you where you've been. Tremaine explained you needed time alone." He cleared his throat, fingering his hat. "Your mother and I only want what's best for you, Lexie. And Miss Everly's School for Young Ladies sounds like a good idea."

"Your idea, Pa?" Lexie questioned.

"Well, I'm no expert on women," he said by way of an answer. "There've never been many girls born to the Danners."

Eliza made a slight sound of protest and Lexie glanced her way. But her mother could have been carved in marble. Her blond hair was perfect, her slanted blue eyes staring at her husband in such an intense way that Lexie wondered what secrets were behind them.

"Your mother knows what's best for you, Lexie. I don't." With that, Joseph sat back, as if he'd completed a dreadful task and was relieved it was over.

Eliza rose in a sudden shiver of satin. She came to Lexie and clasped both of her hands. "I know you hate this," she said softly. "But I think once it's over you'll thank me."

Lexie swallowed. She did love her mother, and there were moments like these when she felt she could reach her if she just tried hard enough. "I can't be like you," she struggled to say. "I'm not a lady."

"Don't say that. Don't ever say that!" Eliza squeezed her hands. "Do you hear me, Lexington?"

"But I'm not like you!" Lexie cried. Giving up all pretense, she turned to her father. "Pa, please, don't let her do it. I can't go there. I can't." Even her assurances to Jace that she would attend the school died a quick death. Lexie's heart was full of fear. She wasn't meant to attend that school. She knew it!

"That's enough." It was Pa this time. He shook his head, and she knew he was regretting all the indulgences she'd been allowed throughout her childhood. She could practically read his mind. He wished he'd made her spend more time in the house.

Lexie's heart wanted her to flee, but she couldn't. She pleaded silently with her eyes, but her mother was implacable. "Tomorrow we'll go to Rock Springs and pick out some fabrics for your wardrobe. You'll need new dresses—why, you have hardly anything suitable."

"I won't go." Lexie's low voice quivered with rebellion. She drew her hands behind her back. "I won't do it."

"Yes, you will." Eliza's voice was the crack of a whip. High spots of color formed on her cheekbones. "And after one year, if you still want to act like a hellion, so be it."

Lexie was struck dumb. She'd never heard her mother say such a word. Even Joseph looked dazed.

"Now this conversation is over," Eliza said, her southern accent deep and authoritative. "That's all."

Lexie turned desperately to Pa. There was no help there. She whirled on her heel, a sob in her throat. The front door opened at that precise moment, admitting Tremaine, who took in the scene in the parlor with a glance.

"Pa?" he asked.

Lexie gathered her skirts and ran past him. She tore up the crimson stairway runner in the direction of her bedroom. From far below she heard Tremaine say clearly, "I have to go back to Rock Springs tonight. There's something I forgot to do . . ."

Lexie looked despairingly at the corset her mother had left on her bureau. It was a wicked thing, with arched stays and long strings that dangled down. Lexie swallowed, glancing at herself in the wavy mirror. Drawing a breath, she wrapped the corset around her rib cage, attempting to tie the strings behind her back.

Her first effort was clumsy. The corset fitted lopsidedly, looking for all the world as if it didn't want her any more than she wanted it. A grin reluctantly formed on Lexie's lips. She pulled her one good dress from the closet and tried to fit it over the corset. Somehow she managed, fighting back bits of hysterical laughter. When she looked in the mirror again, however, the laughter died.

Even she had to admit it was a rather miraculous transformation. The lavender and pink calico dress cut demurely over Lexie's breasts, but the lift from the corset pushed her soft flesh daringly forward. A frothy ruffle caressed her neck and, when she breathed, the ruffle and her whole bosom quivered in a way that made her lips part in delight.

She stepped back, her hand at her throat, alarmed. There was something unexpectedly seductive about looking like a woman. She hadn't expected to feel it.

"Lexie?" A soft rap sounded at her door at the same moment her mother called.

"I'm almost ready," she said, reaching for her lavender cape. Quickly she connected the hook and eye at her throat. At the last moment she glanced once more in the mirror. Her hair was tied back in a long braid. Unable to stop herself, Lexie coiled her braid into a knot at the nape of her neck. She pinned it there, then stepped away from the mirror, almost afraid to look at herself again.

When she walked into the hall she was breathless. Eliza regarded her questioningly, then smiled, touching the coil of sun-bleached hair. "I like this," she said softly.

Lexie immediately felt foolish. Squeezing past her mother, she hurried outside to the buggy.

The Danners didn't own a carriage; Joseph felt it was too fine a vehicle for farmers. But the buggy was warm and roomy, with extra blankets and soft black-leather padded seats. Pa took his place beside Eliza and Lexie, after making certain they were all tucked in.

"Someone's bandaged Matilda's leg," he said, shooting a

glance in Lexie's direction. "You wouldn't happen to know who, would you?"

Lexie kept her eyes on the rutted mud track ahead of them. "Tremaine."

"The boy's taken up horse doctoring, too, then?" Humor threaded through Pa's voice.

"One profession isn't enough for him, I guess," she said primly. Spying the full-blown grin on her father's face, Lexie sighed. "How is Matilda? I didn't get a chance to look at her this morning."

"She does seem better," Pa answered thoughtfully.

The ride to Rock Springs gave Lexie plenty of time for reflection, something she wasn't certain she wanted to do. Belatedly, she remembered the conversation she'd overheard between Tremaine and Pa. With all the concerns about her future, she'd forgotten what Tremaine had said, but now it came back in a rush. *I want her to know how many brothers she has.*

Shooting a long glance out of the corner of her eye, Lexie studied her father. It was all a bafflement. She couldn't imagine what Tremaine had meant.

But she was determined to find out.

The town of Rock Springs lay in the foothills of the Cascades. It tangled around the base of a sheer rock cliff and could only expand westward—which it was doing in leaps and bounds. Mid-center of town, coursing down the side of a rock cliff, was Fool's Falls. It bubbled into a frothy pond at the base, forming Rock Springs' northern boundary, curling into a stream that ran behind the bank, the feed store, the Half Moon Saloon, and McBride's rooming house.

The town itself stood on a crossroads. The north-south road dead-ended at the falls. It was believed that a hangman's gallows once stood in front of the rushing water; now the land was an empty square.

The east-west road bore most of the bustling town's businesses—and every other store was a shrine to Joshua Garrett, Jace's father. As Lexie rode by, she read the signs: Garrett Tannery, Garrett Blacksmithing, Garrett Mercantile.

Pa stopped the buggy in front of the mercantile. "Mind your feet," he said, helping Lexie down onto the muddy, rutted road. When Lexie and Eliza were safely on the wooden sidewalk, he strode toward Garrett Livery and Feedstore.

"Come along," Eliza said, clasping her daughter's arm.

The town was a beehive of activity. The echoing sounds of hammers could be heard in four different directions from where she stood; buildings were going up before Lexie's very eyes. People window-shopped and met each other on the sidewalks, laughing, happy, glad to see one another.

Thinking of giving all this up made Lexie feel sick inside. What would Portland be like? It was a big city. There was bound to be crime and corruption and God only knew what else. She had a sense of her simple life slipping away from her and her mouth went dry.

First Eliza took her to Rock Springs' one and only bank. It was a two-story clapboard structure with gold-lettered windows, iron bars spaced ominously behind them. Eliza walked up to the teller's cage and said to the mutton-chopped man at the window, "My main account is at Portland Security Bank. Could I wire funds here?"

Lexie stared at her mother's back, stunned. Eliza and Pa had money in a Portland bank? "Mother," Lexie murmured, drawing close to her. "What money?" she whispered.

"Money for your education, dear. I told you."

"In a Portland bank?"

"We'll talk about it later."

Hearing her dismissal, Lexie tightened her lips and walked away, staring at the glass-covered plaques containing old money, which decorated the walls of the bank. It felt as if a door were cracking open; a door into a secret world that she'd either never noticed, or that had been hidden from her. Her mother never ceased to amaze her.

Her mind suddenly jumped to the conversation she'd overheard at the barn between Tremaine and Pa. She silently resolved to ask Tremaine what he and Pa had been talking about at the first opportunity. Tonight, sometime. Eliza had already told her they were having a special dinner to toast her acceptance into Miss Everly's School and that Tremaine would definitely be back to join in.

Lexie was determined to pull the truth out of him, if it killed her.

The mercantile smelled a little of perfume, and a little of formaldehyde, the preservative used in making textiles. Lexie followed after her mother, and Eliza gave her a worried look. "Are you all right?" she asked.

Lexie nodded. She just wanted this day to be over.

"Well, Mrs. Danner!" a voice boomed from behind the counter. A round-faced gentleman appeared, his smile broad. It was Walter Pennington, the man who had been late paying Jace the rent.

"Good afternoon, Mr. Pennington," Eliza said in her soft tones. "It's surely a rainy spring."

"That it is. A rainy spring." He smiled at Lexie.

"Hello, Mr. Pennington," said Lexie.

"You're lookin' awful pretty today, Miss Danner," he said.

"Thank you." Lexie shifted uncomfortably.

It was then she realized that Walter Pennington had been helping someone else and had dropped them as soon as she and her mother had walked in the store. A beautiful woman with black coiled hair stood at the counter. Though still young, she exuded a tarnished, faded loveliness, like a rose just beginning to wilt. Her skin was soft and unlined, but something about her expression suggested she'd seen more of the world than anyone had a right to, and had given up worrying about the miseries of life long ago. To Lexie's amazement, she didn't seem to mind being forced to wait her turn.

Seeing Lexie's gaze, Walter said to the woman, "I'll be with you in a minute, Jenny."

"Take your time."

Her voice was husky and rich. She lifted the top of a jar that contained dried rose petals and inhaled in such a way that her whole bosom seemed destined to rip from her bodice. Lexie watched in fascination. The woman heaved a sensual sigh and replaced the top of the jar.

Eliza was in her element. She showed Walter Pennington bolt after bolt of cloth, creating an enormous stack of ribboning colors cascading over the mercantile's counter. Looking at the pile of material, Lexie wondered how her mother could afford such luxury. Once again came the unsettling feeling that there was more going on than she could grasp.

"What about this taffeta?" Eliza asked, holding out the bolt for Lexie to touch.

It was jade green and had a faint raised pattern of twining flowers. Lexie couldn't imagine where she would wear such fine cloth, but then her future tumbled back with terrible clarity.

"It's nice," Lexie mumbled. She walked over to the patiently waiting woman.

"You're Miss Danner, then," the woman said. "I've met your brother."

"Really? Which one?"

She smiled, and there was a world of knowledge in the way her lips curved. "Tremaine."

"Lexie!" Eliza called sharply.

"How do you know Tremaine?" Lexie asked, ignoring her mother even as Eliza bore down upon her.

The woman glanced incuriously at Eliza. "Oh, we've been acquainted a long time. I own the rooming house at the end of town. He stays there now and again."

Like a door being opened on a long-forgotten world, Lexie remembered, then, a remark Pa had made to her mother: ". . . the woman's reputation is in shreds. Since her husband died, she's been taking in boarders. There've been some cruel rumors. Folks seem to think she's no better than Templeton's upstairs girls . . ."

Templeton's upstairs girls. The Half Moon Saloon. Lexie made a sudden giant leap into adulthood as she understood what that meant. No wonder her mother was grabbing her arm and half-dragging her away from the counter. Eliza would never countenance Lexie's associating with anyone from McBride's rooming house. This, then, must be Jenny McBride—Tremaine's friend.

"Lexie's attending Miss Everly's School for Young Ladies this fall," Eliza said in a loud voice to Mr. Pennington. She didn't actually glance over her shoulder to Jenny, but it was clear to Lexie she was drawing feminine battle lines. Embarrassed, Lexie felt like dropping through the floor.

The rest of their time in the mercantile, Lexie couldn't keep her mind on what she was doing. She was haunted by a vision of Tremaine wrapped in Jenny's arms, enjoying God only knew what kind of sinful pleasure.

Every now and again, while Eliza bought yards and yards of cloth, Lexie would slide a secret glance Jenny's way. She couldn't help comparing herself to the other woman. What magic did Jenny possess that called out to Tremaine? She shuddered. Whatever it was, she hoped it didn't call to Jace the same way.

Mr. Pennington was ringing up their purchases. Jenny stood by, seeming oblivious to the slight of being forced to wait. Lexie, acting on pure feminine instinct, said in a low voice that was still loud enough for Jenny to hear, "Jace is coming by today, Mother. Later this evening."

Eliza stiffened, smiled, and said, "That's nice," then turned her attention back to Mr. Pennington. Jenny gave Lexie a long, searching look.

On the street, Eliza said, "Lexie, don't ever do that again."

"Do what?"

"Alert people to the personal goings-on in our family. I don't want rumors spread." She squared her shoulders. "Come along, we're going to see Mrs. Weatherby."

According to Eliza, Mrs. Weatherby was the only seamstress worth her salt in Rock Springs. Lexie was fast losing enthusiasm for this pursuit, and as she dragged along behind her mother, her gaze swept past the Half Moon Saloon toward the rooming house at the far end of town. She thought about Tremaine's sexuality and experienced a strange feeling in the pit of her stomach. She could see how women were attracted to him. Tremaine was magnetically male, possessing a hard, sensual face and the kind of stripping gaze that seemed to stop women in mid-sentence. He was, she decided objectively, pushing her own realization of him to the very far corners of her mind, quite potently attractive.

Which was why, in very unladylike fashion, Lexie determined she was going to have to speak to Tremaine about the facts of life. Next time Jace kissed her with passion she wasn't going to be caught unaware. She needed to know what was expected of her, and Tremaine was so obviously the right person to ask.

She had a lot of things to get straight with him. She could hardly wait for tonight.

Jace Garrett lay back in the tilted chair, sighing with contentment as the young woman leaning over him kicked a wooden box behind the chair's back legs, propping it up. Simple pleasures, he thought with an inward grin, smelling Betsy's clean soapy scent, feeling the tickle of her long black hair as it brushed his cheek. He indulged his lusty appetite at every opportunity. Oh, he could have had one of Templeton's whores, but why pay for hardened boredom when Betsy was so willing, so pathetically naive?

"I've got you set fast and secure now, Jace," she said in her soft, uneducated drawl.

"Thank you, Betsy," he murmured, eyes closed.

The steamed towel came next, so hot he involuntarily sucked in a breath. Betsy wrapped it around his face, her long fingers delicately touching and testing. He could smell the starch and feel the moist heat. He sighed, his senses replete.

"I've been wishin' you coulda been here last night," Betsy said huskily.

"I've been wishing the same."

The truth was, Jace had been wishing it a lot. A night without Betsy was a night wasted. But then, contrary to popular belief, Jenny McBride was an old-fashioned woman who kept a sharp eye on her tenants. It wasn't that Jenny was conventional. Lordy, no! If *she* wanted a lover, she took one, though Jace personally had never caught her with a man in her bed. Still, she did as she pleased, a continual thorn in Jace's side—as she had been in his father's side before him. Her dead husband had left her the rooming house and she ardently refused to sell it. No amount of Garrett money could buy it from her.

But that wasn't what bothered Jace the most. Jenny, for all her own lack of inhibition, was peculiarly tyrannical about her tenants—particularly the young female type. If she suspected Jace's dalliance with Betsy, a drifting young female who had escaped a cruel, brutal father to wind up half-starved on Jenny's doorstep, it would all be over. Jace would have to give Betsy up, and he was singularly unwilling to do that—until he tired of her himself.

The hot towel was unwound and he opened his eyes to look into Betsy's sweet face. She wasn't as pretty as Lexie, nor as smart, Jace supposed. But she knew what to do to make him cry with ecstasy, something a wife would never be able to accomplish. In Jace's world there were two types of women: wives and whores. He wanted both.

Betsy pulled out the strop and started whipping the shiny-bladed razor back and forth. Jace lay back and closed his eyes again, a smile on his lips. She was no barber, but who cared? It was a treat to be waited on.

Just as he was anticipating the smooth strokes of the razor, he heard the door to Betsy's room creak open. The scent of jasmine perfume was cloying in its excess. "Jenny," Jace said, never opening his eyes.

"Thought I'd find you here, Garrett." Disapproval wrapped around each sharply uttered syllable. "I'm needing a word with you."

"I'm needing a shave. Come back later."

"Fine. If you don't want to talk to me in private, we'll talk in front of Betsy. I hear you're courting one Miss Lexington Danner. Is it true?"

Betsy stopped in her sharpening. Smoldering inside at this unexpected twist, Jace opened one eye and winked at the shattered girl. "Don't you believe everything you hear now, Jenny."

"I just hope you're being honest with Betsy about your intentions," said Jenny flatly, stoking Jace's anger afresh. "You've been fair-warned."

With that she swept out of the room, leaving Jace with a stricken-eyed Betsy Talbot.

Tremaine lay on the cot beneath Jenny McBride's stairway, an alcove cut into the kitchen. His arm was tossed over his eyes and he groaned at the *thunk! thunk! thunk!* of Jenny's footsteps as they hammered into the stairs.

His head pounded with a kind of vile glee. He hadn't had enough to drink, he realized, and now he was paying the price without the oblivion he'd so desperately sought the night before. He hadn't spent the night in Jenny's bed, either. Instead he'd whiled away the whole damn evening right here, smelling Jenny's perfume and listening to her rant about town politics. She was a suffragette in the worst way, and though normally he enjoyed her company, baiting her at every opportunity to get a rise out of her, last night he'd found his attention wandering to more earthy desires. He didn't want to talk. He wanted to take her to bed and relieve the throbbing ache that seemed to follow him around like a dark, taunting cloud.

But though sex was in his thoughts and heart, he hadn't given Jenny any sign of what he was feeling. He couldn't. The trouble was he didn't want *her!*

So Tremaine had sat at Jenny's table, nursed a spreading, cancerous ache, and done absolutely nothing about it—a situation that struck dread in his soul. What, he wondered now, had happened to his rather amoral sexual appetite?

Lexie's image floated in front of his eyes, and he saw her as she'd been last night: wild, tangled, her wet skin showing through her blouse. Fifteen seconds of reflection were all that was needed to assure him all his parts were in prime working order. With a groan of disgust, he turned over and spent another miserable ten minutes trying to erase Lexie's image.

It was Jenny's furious footsteps again pounding on the stairs that finally quenched the flame of desire, dousing it to the same dull, smoldering ache. A moment later Jenny stood in the center of the kitchen, hands on her hips, breathing rapidly, her swelling bosom rising and falling. She slammed a pot into the kitchen washtub.

"What's wrong?" Tremaine asked, sure he really didn't want to know.

"Jace Garrett," she said through her teeth. "When Joshua was alive it was bad enough, but Jace is worse because he's Lucinda's son, too."

Tremaine heartily agreed, but he kept his thoughts to himself. Climbing from the cot, he raked his hands through his tousled hair. Jenny flung him a dark look.

"It isn't fair for a man to look so handsome when he first wakes up," she muttered, though in truth she looked rather luscious herself.

"I'll take that as a compliment." Tremaine smiled lazily and asked, "Have you got any coffee, Jenny?"

"For you, anything. I saw your sister in the mercantile this morning. All you Danners are damnably good-lookin'. Somehow it isn't quite fair."

Tremaine's pulse leapt. "You saw Lexie?"

"Mmm-hmmm." She sent him a curious glance, enjoying his lean powerful face and the aura of leashed power in a purely sensual way. Though Tremaine didn't know it, Jenny harbored secret feelings for him, which she was careful to disguise for she was certain if he knew she cared, she would never see him again. As it was, his visits to Rock Springs were far too rare, and though last night she'd been delighted to see him, his lack of interest had bothered her. Never before had he been so distant. She didn't like thinking that their relationship might be over. "I hear your sister's going off to school."

Tremaine didn't want to talk about Lexie. "That's what I hear, too," he said, accepting the cup Jenny handed him, sensitive to the way her fingers lingered over his. "What's got you so riled about Jace Garrett?" Tremaine asked with lazy amusement. "His price for this place not meeting your expectations?"

She snorted. "That skinflint? He won't pay half what it's worth. The only good Garrett left is Kelsey, and Lucinda has the poor child's life all planned out for her." Jenny stomped through the kitchen door to the screened porch. "Trying to marry her off to Paul Warfield, with all the money he earned cheating folks. What's the woman thinking of?"

"Warfield's mayor of Malone," Tremaine pointed out, his eyes dancing over the rim of his cup.

"The man's a crook!" There was a pump on Jenny's back porch, and Tremaine watched through the window as Jenny pumped furiously for several moments, hauling in the brimming kitchen washtub with strong arms. Placing it on the stove, she stoked the fire.

Tremaine would have offered to help, but he'd learned from past experience that Jenny had certain rules that must always be followed. Rule number one was that she was the master of her own house. She was quite capable of managing by herself.

It was this trait that had endeared her to Tremaine in the first place—that and her cockeyed moral views. Though others in town treated her as a pariah, Tremaine admired her. Each to his own, Jenny always maintained. Except when she felt someone was being cheated.

She was the only woman he truly trusted, and though he enjoyed their on-again/off-again sexual relationship, he was sadly aware it would foil their friendship in the end.

"I should throw that scoundrel out of here," Jenny muttered.

"Who?"

"Garrett! Haven't you been listening?"

Tremaine stopped, his cup halfway to his lips.

"It's not Garrett business ways that are bothering me," Jenny said as she scrubbed furiously at the already spotless china plates. "It's Jace and Betsy. He's using her just like he did the last one. That man wants it all."

"Jace Garrett is upstairs with one of your tenants?" Tremaine sat perfectly still.

"Betsy's giving him a shave upstairs now."

"Which room?"

"Number nine." Jenny paused in her task to regard him squarely. What she read in his face made her breath catch. Tremaine, who seemed to regard life with humor and irony, looked blindly furious. So the rumor about his sister and Jace was true, she realized, and selfishly wished Tremaine would bestow on her some of the passion in his eyes, glittering like blue ice. "Just what are you going to do?" she asked, watching him scoot back his chair.

"Take care of things," was his clipped reply.

Betsy Talbot leaned over the man she loved, cautiously shaving his sideburns, softly humming. "It was all a mistake about Miss Danner, then?" she asked for the third time.

"Mmm-hmm." Jace could almost fall asleep it was so peaceful.

"You're not gonna marry her, then?"

"Didn't I just say she was leaving town? Miss Everly's School for Young Ladies is a long way from Rock Springs."

"But she'll be back, won't she?"

"Unless she finds some Portland man to marry first. Now, hum some more of that tune, honey, and let's not argue."

Satisfied, Betsy began shaving his cheek and chin. She wasn't as dull as she let him think, but she understood what Jace Garrett expected from her. She knew her chances with him were mighty slim. But she had one secret on her side. She suspected there was a new life fluttering within her. Whatever happened, a Garrett wouldn't abandon his own child.

The door opened with a small squeak. This time Jace barely heard it. The somnolence of the room had worked its magic, and he was on the threshold of a very nice dream. For a moment Betsy stopped shaving and humming and that nearly wakened him, but then the razor stroked down his neck and he tilted his head farther back, exposing the vulnerable stretch of his throat.

The razor slid down his chin and stopped. "Betsy?" Jace murmured, wondering why her fingers seemed so hard and tense.

The blade pressed deeply against his throat and Jace's eyes flew open in terror. Tremaine Danner's cold blue eyes bore down on him.

"What the—?"

"Lexie thinks you plan to marry her," Tremaine said in a reasonable voice. "I'd like to hear it from your own lips."

Jace searched wildly for Betsy. She stood on the opposite side of the room, her eyes huge. "You can't just come in here and demand—"

"The hell I can't. I'd better hear your intentions to my sister are honorable," Tremaine said with a humorless smile. "Otherwise I slit your throat."

Jace swallowed, but there was no spit in his mouth. His eyes bulged. "I'm—I'm—"

The blade pressed the tiniest bit tighter.

"I'm going to marry her!" he burst out.

The same moment Tremaine removed the blade, a cry erupted from Betsy's lips. She ran out of the room and Jace glared at Tremaine, his hand cupped protectively around his throat.

"You maniac! I believe you *would* kill me, Danner!" Jace charged. "I haven't made the engagement official because your damn father won't let me set foot on your property!"

"My *damn* father," Tremaine stressed warningly, "knows what kind of man you are. Don't expect a warm reception if you ever get up the nerve to actually ask for Lexie's hand in marriage. I'd venture he'll turn you down flat."

"Lexie hasn't," Jace answered smoothly, pleased by the brief flare of anger in Tremaine's eyes.

"She won't go against my father's wishes."

"She'd run off with me tomorrow if I crooked my finger."

"You're in a mighty vulnerable position to be talking like that," Tremaine snarled, twisting the razor in his hand.

Jace swallowed, discretion being the greater part of valor. His throat felt arched and exposed. There was only so much baiting Danner would stand.

Tremaine would have dearly loved to rip Garrett's tonsils out with his bare hands. He couldn't imagine what Lexie saw in this scum. With a growl of frustration, he flung the razor on the table, then yanked Jace forward until the chair bumped down on its front legs. Instantly Jace sprang to his feet, his pallor purpling with suppressed rage.

"You take your brotherly responsibilities too far!" he spat between clenched teeth.

"I know that Lexie wouldn't take kindly to knowing about Betsy."

He wouldn't tell her, would he? Jace's chest tightened as he searched Tremaine's dark face for a clue to his intentions. No, Tremaine wouldn't disillusion Lexie unless he absolutely had to; Jace knew enough about Danner's principles to call this one right. "Betsy," he said firmly, "was just giving me a shave. If I wanted a woman, I'd park myself in plain view at the Half Moon. Jenny's just being a mother hen."

Tremaine didn't believe him for one instant. Jace's reputation—for all the zealous care he took to preserve it—was far from sterling. But Tremaine was loath to break the news to Lexie.

His temper cooler now, Tremaine remarked dispassionately, "Lexie says she loves you. I hope she's wrong."

Jace's dignity had taken a beating, but he wasn't a man to be easily intimidated. "That would gall you right down to your socks, wouldn't it? Being brother-in-law to a Garrett." He chuckled. "I must admit, I'm looking more forward to the union every day."

"You're a cold bastard, Garrett. I'd look out, if I were you."

"Am I supposed to understand what that means?" For all his blustering remarks, Jace's back broke out in a fine sweat. He'd always been a bit in awe of Tremaine Danner. The man was too handsome and tough and impervious to anything but his own damnable code of ethics.

"It means you'd better treat her right or your head's mine," Tremaine warned softly.

"You're supposed to be a doctor. What kind of threat is that? You're not above the law, Danner!"

But Tremaine had already turned away from him in disgust, and Jace's rising voice was lost on the empty room.

Chapter Five

Matilda regarded Lexie, calmly letting Lexie run her hand down her leg. "The swelling's definitely down, girl," Lexie said, patting the Jersey's sleek neck. "You're almost as good as new."

Straightening, Lexie climbed over the rails out of Matilda's stall. She reached up and unhooked the lantern from its peg. It was dark in the barn, pitch black without the lamp's uncertain light. Lexie picked her way carefully across the hay-strewn floor until she reached the plank down to the ground. Rain dimpled the puddles surrounding the barn and ran off the eaves in small, persistent streams. Lexie sighed. It wouldn't do to ruin these clothes, too. Her mother would kill her for sure. Sweeping her bonnet from the hay bale, she smashed it on her head.

She stepped cautiously onto the wet plank. Her shoes started sliding and she held out her arms, half-running, half-slipping down the ramp. On the ground she checked each soggy tuft of grass carefully before stepping on it until she reached the gravel drive that made a sweeping curve beneath the portico.

Supper was probably nearly ready; Cook had been work-ing all day, Eliza said, making it possible for them to accomplish their trip into Rock Springs and back, and still have time for Lexie's special celebration party. Lexie's shoulders slumped. She had no enthusiasm for this gathering—unless Jace comes by, she thought hopefully, glancing down the lane. She hadn't lied when she'd told her mother he might stop by; Jace had almost said as much last night. But there was no sound of the Garrett carriage in the lane, only a noisy chorus of frogs from one of the pools created by the rain.

Lexie stood beneath the portico, peering through the paned windows into the candlelit dining room. Her moth-er's twin silver candelabras sat at both ends of the long table, their light quivering above a starched peach tablecloth—linen overlaid with Italian lace—a gift from her grandmoth-er, Eliza had told Lexie when she'd posed the question about its origin. Pale peach bone china refracted the light in rich, gleaming sparkles. There were seven place settings, one for each member of the family. If Jace did arrive, Eliza would have to set another place. Lexie prayed he wouldn't let her down.

Pushing open the front door, Lexie delicately shook the water from her cape. She swept the bonnet from her head and checked her shoes. Then she lifted her skirts and climbed the stairs to her room.

There was laughter coming from Harrison's room. Lexie could hear Jesse's sardonic tones and Harrison's more jovial ones. She smiled and thought about finding out what had put them in such good humor, but then she remembered her own part in this occasion and she went to her bedroom to get ready.

Tossing her cape on her bed, she sat down at her dressing table, staring at her reflection in the mirror. She tried on several smiles but none of them seemed quite right. With a sigh, she unwound her braid, brushed her hair, then plaited it once more, letting the golden coil fall over one shoulder. Her dress was still clean and fresh, saved from destruction by her cape, but Lexie pulled another from the closet. This was made of moss green lawn with a delicate design of seed pearls around the neck.

Pouring water from a pitcher into her washing bowl, she rinsed her face, the cold water making her skin tingle, then she pulled the dress over her head. In the mirror her breasts gleamed provocatively above the neckline and, with humor twisting her mouth, she decided she hadn't given the corset its proper respect.

She felt more alert by the time she descended the stairs to dinner. Halfway down the steps, she heard the lilt of her mother's laughter, a noise so rare as to be nonexistent. Eliza was in the dining room and, from the sounds of it, so were Pa and Lexie's brothers. Except for Tremaine.

She was on the bottom step when she heard hoofbeats approaching and for a moment her pulse leapt. Jace! But then through the steaming window she recognized Tremaine's buggy. Fortune was puffing and stamping beneath the portico. The door opened and Tremaine strode inside, soaked to the skin.

"I'm too late," he said, observing Lexie.

Her hand still lay on the curving end of the stairway rail. Unaware what caused the sudden narrowing of Tremaine's gaze, she had no idea how picture-perfect she looked at that moment. "You're not too late," she said. "I haven't joined them yet."

"I need to rub down Fortune and change." He glanced toward the dining room. A wave of laughter swelled upward.

"We'll wait." Lexie was thankful for any delay to the charade of happiness she was going to be forced to play.

"You look beautiful, Lexie."

She swung her startled gaze his way. Compliments from Tremaine were as rare as diamonds. "Thank you," she said.

The sconces by the door drew a glowing circle of light around her. Her hair was soft and golden, her skin firm and supple. The fabric of her dress had a velvety cast and the rustle of her petticoats was like a tantalizing invitation.

For a moment Lexie imagined Tremaine looking at her with intent, burning eyes. Her stomach made a peculiar somersault, the way it did when she dreamed of being with Jace.

Unprepared, Lexie shrank back against the balustrade, sensing her brother's masculinity in a way that alarmed her.

Then Tremaine smiled and she berated herself for being a silly goose. "I'll be back in a few minutes," he said, and was out the door.

Lexie walked across the plankwood entry to the dining room. She stopped short in the doorway, shocked by the sight that met her eyes. Pa was pulling the cork from a bottle of champagne and Lexie watched in amazement as the cork released with a loud *pop* and champagne fizzed over his hands and into a waiting crystal goblet.

She remembered that her father had once been a prominent Boston physician, not a small-town Oregon farmer. Like her mother, there were sides to her father she could only guess at and the realization made her uncomfortable.

"This one must be mine," Pa said, wiping the goblet with one of the elegant napkins. Smiling, he poured his wife a glass, then another for Harrison. Jesse and Samuel were apparently deigned too young.

Lexie had never seen her parents drink champagne before. She wondered why her acceptance to Miss Everly's School was such an achievement.

Seeing her, Pa's smile widened. "Lexie!" he called, motioning her into the room. He poured another goblet full of the frothy liquid.

A silence fell on the gathering. Lexie felt herself the cynosure of all eyes and was slightly unnerved. Samuel looked nonplussed, Jesse seemed almost shaken out of his normal cynicism, Harrison regarded her with a kind of anxious pleasure, Eliza's lips were parted in delight, and Pa, as he held the champagne toward her outstretched hand, said softly, "You're as lovely as your mother when I first met her."

Embarrassment pinkened Lexie's cheeks. "Is the champagne in my honor? I haven't done anything."

"Well, actually, we're honoring both you and Harrison," Pa said, glancing at his wife.

Eliza sipped her drink with an inbred gentility that increased Lexie's nervousness. "Harrison is also going away to study this fall."

"To study?" Lexie asked blankly. She turned to Harrison, surprised that he hadn't told her.

"I just found out," he admitted, frowning into his drink.

"Study where?"

"Dr. Breverman has accepted Harrison to apprentice with him," Eliza said quietly.

The room seemed to sway before Lexie's eyes. Dr. Breverman! The horse doctor! *The one man Lexie would sell her soul to learn from?* Lexie's hand shook and Harrison was there to rescue her untouched glass. Dimly, she was aware of Annie bringing in the succulent leg of spring lamb. She saw a quivering bowl of Eliza's mint jelly placed beside it. The candles danced. Lexie's eyes blurred.

"Harrison's going to Portland to study under Dr. Breverman?" she asked stiltedly.

"It's what he's been wanting," said Pa, uncomfortably.

"It's what we've both been wanting, you mean!" Lexie cried bitterly. "How could you? *How could you?*" She turned blindly, resenting the whispering rustle of her dress, aiming for the door.

"Lexington, I forbid you to leave this room," Eliza said.

Annie stood in the archway to the entry hall, holding two silver pitchers of sparkling wellwater, their outsides dewy with cold. The young maid looked alarmed as Lexie swept past her, nearly knocking her over in her bid for escape.

"Lexie!" Pa bellowed.

"Oh, dear. Oh, dear," Annie murmured anxiously, balancing the heavy pitchers.

Lexie couldn't breathe. She yanked open the front door to find Tremaine scraping the mud off his boots. He glanced her way. "Lexie?" he asked tensely.

She stared at him, her face ravaged, and he made an involuntary move toward her. The moment allowed Harrison to catch her arm. "Don't leave," he begged.

Then Pa was there, standing by her left side. "Lexie, we've gone over this time and again. There's no future for you being a horse doctor." He sounded as sick with disappointment as she felt. "No farmer in his right mind would let a woman—"

"Like you?" she cut him off, her lips trembling. "No farmer like you?"

"It wouldn't be safe and I—"

"What kind of person do you think I am? I'm strong. I'm intelligent. If I were a man, would you let me go to Dr. Breverman?"

"That's a pointless question since you're a woman," Pa answered stiffly.

"You would rather trust a fool like Meechum because he's a man than listen to your own daughter! My sex is my downfall, is that it?" Lexie saw her mother standing in the archway, her features pale and drawn. "Is that it?" Lexie choked out again.

Eliza regarded her headstrong daughter compassionately. "Your father is only facing the reality of your situation, Lexie."

"I won't listen to you anymore. Any of you. I won't do what you want. You give me no credence as a thinking, feeling human being!"

Eliza shook her head. "Lexington—"

"I'm tired of being sheltered and coddled," she said with suppressed fire, her voice gathering strength, her shoulders shaking. "I'm tired of being treated like a *woman.*" She fairly spat the word out.

Tremaine stepped inside the door, closing it softly behind him. He stood close by Lexie, his expression unreadable. All the questions that had plagued her for years—all the questions that had bubbled in the caldron of her mind, waiting for the right time to fulminate—burst forward. "I want to be treated as an adult," she said with only the faintest quaver in her voice. "I don't want to be lied to any more."

"You haven't been lied to—" Pa began, but Lexie cut him off.

"Then what were you and Tremaine talking about in the barn yesterday?" she raged, heedless of the pain she might cause her mother.

Tremaine moved almost imperceptibly, and she heard his breath hiss through his teeth as he inhaled. But Pa was puzzled.

"You were talking to Tremaine in the barn yesterday. You were talking about me and how many brothers I had," Lexie clarified, her words tumbling out, faster and faster. "What did you mean by that? Why don't I know how many brothers I have?"

It was so quiet she could hear the gentle hissing of the candle flames as they encountered molten wax. Eliza's hands moved to the string of beads at her throat, trembling.

Pa looked dazed. "Lexie, you shouldn't have eavesdropped on a private conversation."

Lexie turned to Tremaine. "Will you tell me?"

Tremaine's eyes were very blue. Lexie pleaded silently with him, her stark need cutting through him like a knife. He glanced at his father, then slowly his gaze crept to Eliza.

Lexie counted the seconds. He'd wanted to tell her yesterday. He'd tried hard to convince Pa it was the time. She didn't care what the answer was. She just wanted everyone to quit hiding things from her.

"Yes," Tremaine said steadily.

Eliza made a sound of protest. She looked helplessly at Joseph, who regarded her with solemn eyes. "It's time," he said, sighing.

Lexie waited. Tremaine's gaze was still on Eliza, and she felt the heat of their tense, unspoken exchange. Her heart somersaulted. This was a bigger issue than she'd realized.

The clink of silver being placed around the table reminded them all of Annie's presence. "That'll be all for now, Annie," Eliza called in a strained voice. "I'll let you know when we need you again."

"Yes, ma'am," Annie said, taking her cue and leaving. Her gaze lingered on Jesse's indolent form a moment too long but Jesse gave no notice of her. He, like everyone else, was waiting for some long-buried revelation.

Eliza didn't disappoint them. "I was married before," she said. "Lexie, you're my daughter from that previous marriage."

Whatever she'd expected, it wasn't this. Lexie blinked several times. "Wh-a-at?" she asked in a whisper.

Pa laid comforting hands on her shoulders. "We've kept it from you because we wanted to protect you. I couldn't love you more if you were my own daughter," he said sincerely. "As far as I'm concerned, you are my daughter."

"Well, who is my father?" Lexie asked faintly. "Where is he?"

"My first husband's dead, Lexie." Eliza sounded faraway. "He died before you were born. He was your father."

"What was his name? Why wasn't I told?"

"I'll explain it all later." Eliza's tone said the conversation was closed.

"Did you know?" Lexie asked, turning blindly, swiftly toward Tremaine. She bumped against the hard wall of his chest.

"Yes."

Her throat ached. She wanted to cry and rage but couldn't shame herself in front of her family. Once again her urge to escape overpowered her. She yanked open the door and ran bareheaded through the falling rain. She ran blindly, straight ahead, stopping in a mire of mud and water, her breath catching in her throat. She couldn't think. Couldn't *breathe!* The structure of her life had broken down with one deadly fall of a lethal hammer.

The front door opened behind her. Lexie didn't look back. She bent forward against the rain and nearly fell over, stumbling, mud kicking onto her dress, cold water seeping into her shoes.

She'd only run a few feet when strong arms encircled her. She knew Tremaine by his scent and she fought like a wildcat, a fierce silent struggle punctuated only by her choked breathing and Tremaine's grunts of surprise whenever she kicked vital tissue.

"Let me go!" she panted. "Let me go!"

"Not until you listen to me," he ground out.

"I'll never listen to you! I'd rather die!"

She twisted and writhed and he finally pinned her hands behind her back, dragging her toward the stables. "Let me go!" she cried again. Sobs caught in her throat.

"Lexie, for God's sake."

"I don't want you to touch me! I hate you! I hate all of you!"

"I know how you feel," he said through his teeth but his grip never slackened.

She tried to hold onto the Dutch door but her fingers scraped helplessly on the wettened wood. Tremaine hauled her inside, then released her in one swift movement, slamming the bolt home before she could fight her way back outside. The horses moved restlessly, snorting, hooves stamping nervously. Lexie doubled her fists, then sank onto a hay bale. She hadn't realized she was crying until she felt the warmth mingled with cold on her face.

She heard Tremaine sigh in the darkness. "Lexie," he began.

"Don't say anything. I don't want to hear any more lies!"

"You think this is a lie?"

She buried her face in her hands. No, she didn't think it was a lie. But everything else in her life had been.

Tantrum nickered and Lexie stumbled toward him as Tremaine swore, reaching for the lantern. Lexie threw her arms around the gelding's arched neck. Tantrum shimmied and sidestepped, but Lexie clung like a burr, burying her face against his warm coat, closing her ears, fighting back her lung-choking anguish.

Tremaine lit the lantern and patterns of light sparkled across the stables' shadowy corners. Lexie didn't notice. Her eyes were squeezed shut as tight as she could get them.

Finally, she laid her cheek against Tantrum's sleek hide, drawing a long, unsteady breath. "How long have you known?" she asked brokenly.

"A while. Like you, I overheard a conversation I shouldn't have, and it brought back some memories."

Her face felt hot and sticky. "What memories?"

"Memories of when I was a boy. When Pa first met Eliza."

"You remember?"

"Sort of."

Lexie tightened her jaw. "Were you sent to tell me?"

His laugh was more an uncomfortable appreciation of her savvy than an expression of humor. "I suppose you could say that, although neither of them would have probably chosen me if they'd had any choice. Harrison, Jesse, and Samuel found out just now, too."

"Then tell me. I want to know everything." Her fingers wound into Tantrum's mane.

He sighed. "Would you let go of that damned horse and make me think you're ready to hear it?"

Lexie hated to give up her support; Tantrum was a rock in a swiftly changing sea. But she understood the sense of

Tremaine's words. She wanted them to treat her like an adult, so she had to act like one.

Tremaine's foot was propped on the same hay bale Lexie had forsaken for Tantrum. Now he lifted it and she sat down again, chilled to the bone.

"I guess I was about eight when it all started. My mother fell off a roof and died. Pa started drifting after that and we just existed for a while.

"We were somewhere in the South when we met Eliza—I found out later it was New Orleans. She was alone and she needed protection. Pa married her."

Lexie, who had been staring at the dust and straw littering the floor, glanced up. "Did they fall in love? Pa and Mother?"

Tremaine hesitated. "I think they turned to each other in a time of need," he answered carefully. He didn't add his own belief that love was a highly overrated emotion known only to a select few and that trust between the sexes was rarer still.

With a sigh Lexie rose from the hay bale. In the lamplight her face had more color than the ghostly shade she'd exhibited in the entry hall. Tremaine was not unaware of her beauty. He realized that their relationship was about to take an abrupt turn. He was no longer her brother, and whereas she might easily adjust to that knowledge, he'd been having trouble coming to grips with it for years.

She paced the small scope of the stable floor, turning to him, her hands clasped tightly, her face serious. She was, he thought with wry humor, bewitchingly lovely. And so woefully unaware! It was terrifying to think what could happen to her out in the wide world. Maybe Miss Everly's School was just the thing for an innocent green-eyed beauty who was about to be launched into society.

As if reading his thoughts, Lexie shuddered. "So that's why Mother's been so adamant about me becoming a lady. She wants me to be like her."

"She wants you to have all the things she had to forsake," Tremaine corrected gently.

"Why did she have to forsake them?"

Tremaine ran a hand through his black hair, dragging his

gaze away from the soft, swelling mounds of Lexie's breasts. "I don't know all of it. I know your father was a wealthy southern gentleman and that Eliza inherited a substantial sum of money at the time of his death. The money's in a Portland bank. Your mother met with an investment banker and her money's been invested wisely in several profitable ship-building companies. She's saved all these years to be sure and send you to school."

"And Harrison," Lexie replied bitterly, her own frustration and disappointment swelling up painfully inside her.

"And Harrison, and Jesse, and Samuel. And me," he added as an afterthought.

"Why didn't she want me to know?" Lexie moaned. "Why has it been such a secret?"

"I don't know. I don't think she wanted questions asked."

"Where did she live? How did my father die? Why wasn't I told before?"

She was working herself up to a glorious fury, and Tremaine was glad to see a return of the Lexie he knew. He could hardly deal with the lost and lonely one whose rare tears wrenched his heart. "All I know is that you were named after your mother's hometown. She grew up in Lexington, Kentucky."

"It doesn't feel right," Lexie murmured, struggling to accept all this new information. "I don't know anything about Lexington. Or Boston. Or anywhere but Rock Springs."

"I think that's why Eliza enrolled you at Miss Everly's School," Tremaine pointed out.

"I know why she kept it a secret," Lexie said suddenly, her voice low.

Since Tremaine had his own theories about that, he asked, "Why?"

"Because it would be too hard to explain. She was pregnant when she married Pa. A lady wouldn't want that known."

Tremaine felt it went much deeper than that but kept his thoughts to himself. Who knew what made Eliza Danner tick? He'd puzzled over her for years. All he'd ever come up with was that there was something in her past—some strange secret—that she refused to disclose. Dryly, he said,

"I think your mother could handle that kind of speculation all right. She's tougher than she looks."

"My mother," Lexie murmured. "Not your mother. Your father, but not mine." She exhaled on a choking laugh. "You and I aren't even related, Tremaine!"

"I know."

He watched her face as this fact slowly took root. She was amazed, and slightly repelled. She glanced up at him, wide-eyed. "You aren't my brother," she repeated. "You aren't even my half-brother."

Lexie stepped backward and her heel slipped on a knot in the plankwood floor. Tremaine automatically extended his hand, but she jerked away from him, her fists pulled tautly into her chest. So it does make a difference, he thought, frowning.

"Why didn't they tell us?" she asked.

"I suppose they thought it wouldn't matter."

Lexie shook her head, wisps of blond hair falling free of her braid, gently curling around her flushed cheeks. "It does matter," she said, and he read the swift series of emotions that tumbled across her mobile face. Shock, amazement, fear . . .

"It doesn't have to change anything," he said, struck by the irony of *him* soothing *her!*

"It changes everything," she argued softly, regarding him through green eyes filled with something akin to horror. Before he could ask her to define what "everything" entailed, she'd unlatched the door and headed out into the wild spring rain.

Tremaine stood silently in the center of the stables. "I suppose it does," he said thoughtfully, and followed after her, seeing her collapse against the fence, oblivious to the blinding rain.

Lies, lies, lies. Incredible soul-destroying lies. Pa was not her father! Tremaine was not her brother! How long would they have kept the secret if she hadn't stumbled upon some of the answers herself? Forever?

Lexie's arms lay weak and shaking on the top rail, her forehead pressed against their rain-slick flesh. Water slid in rivulets down her hair and eyes. It was too much to think about all at once. She had to divide it into pieces. Her real father was dead. Her mother hadn't wanted her to know. She and Tremaine were not brother and sister.

A shudder shook her. It was this that affected her most. It crushed down on her, made her stomach quiver, her legs turn to jelly. And yet a part of her had always known.

Looking back through older, wiser eyes, she remembered Tremaine's change of attitude toward her. He'd resented her when she'd been a young child, treating her with all the callous disrespect of a true older brother. Then things had subtly changed. She could almost pinpoint the moment.

It was in the summertime. She hadn't seen Tremaine in a very long time, but he'd come home to help out with the haying. The fields were dry and hot and Lexie had foolishly forgotten to close a gate. The cattle had surged into the clearing, pounding as one straight down the lane toward the cool shade. It took hours to round them all up again, and when it was over it wasn't Pa who gave her a blistering dressing-down. It was Tremaine.

"How could you be so careless?" he demanded furiously. "What a stupid thing to do! You're old enough to handle some responsibility. Why don't you—"

She cut him off by shoving against his chest with all her might. "Shut up!" she screamed. "I'm sorry! I've said I'm sorry! You have no right to yell at me!"

"The hell I don't!" he roared. "You deliberately left that—"

"Deliberately!" she gasped.

"—gate open just to cause trouble. If I were Pa, I'd horsewhip you and make you do all the chores by yourself."

Lexie was so incensed that she stamped her foot and pushed at him again. They tussled, but his superior strength made her efforts pointless, and she stomped off crying, shamed and humiliated. He didn't even try to apologize. He didn't care.

Her anger sustained her all through that next week, especially when Pa deemed some of Tremaine's suggestions worthwhile and Lexie ended up spending long hours laboring with the pitchfork and plow. The only good that came out of it was that she didn't have to stay in the house, sewing and embroidering.

But then everything changed. From the nasty self-serving older brother, Tremaine suddenly became a cold and wary stranger. Lexie literally ran into him that Friday night, slamming into his broad chest by mistake as she ran out the kitchen door on her way to the stables.

"Excuse me," she stated coldly, pushing away. "I've got to go cause more trouble."

When he didn't rise to the bait, she threw him a haughty glance over her shoulder and the inscrutable look on his face made her heart squeeze uncomfortably. From that moment forward, he treated her differently, looked at her differently, and—or so she'd thought—liked her less.

But now she was certain that in the space of those few days, between the fight and that Friday night, Tremaine had learned she wasn't his sister. The look on his face had been a mixture of disbelief and dawning understanding. He became more cautious. Careful. Even gentle. After that, whenever his gaze fell on her, she subconsciously squirmed inside, sensing, but not understanding, the change that was taking place.

Now she knew.

The freezing rain finally penetrated her emotionally overloaded senses and she began to shiver. He's not my brother, Lexie realized, the idea settling deep into her soul.

Thunder rumbled to the east, followed by a crack of lightning. Lexie's throat constricted. For a moment the fields glowed with unearthly light.

"Lexie?"

Tremaine's voice forced an involuntary cry from her throat. She whirled around. Rain dripped off his black hair and down his hawkish nose, collecting on his sensual lips. He was looking at her with concern.

"You're soaked to the skin and shaking like a leaf."

"I—feel—sick," she said, turning back to the fence.

"Let me see—"

"No! Don't touch me. Don't—touch—me." With wings on her heels, she raced through the mud and rain to the safety of the house.

In her room later that night, Lexie stood by the window, arms squeezed tightly around her middle, as she stared miserably out into the darkness. She'd shunned Tremaine and the strange feelings he'd ignited. She didn't want anything to do with him. She wanted Jace.

Lexie drew a long breath and closed her eyes. She was going to marry Jace and she was going to become a horse doctor. If it meant a year away from home before she could realize her dreams, so be it.

At the thought of Tremaine, peculiar and frightening feelings stirred deep inside her. Alarmed, her eyes flew open. Maybe he wasn't her brother, but she was damn well going to keep treating him like one.

Chapter Six

Fall, 1882

Lexie grabbed the tin milk pails, trying to make as little noise as possible as she let herself out the back door and into a still starry, unseasonably warm autumn morning. It wasn't her job to milk Matilda, but there was so little time left before she was sent off to that awful school that she seized every opportunity to show Pa and Mother how much they would miss her.

At the barn she dropped the pails with a clatter and lit the lantern. Matilda bawled loudly.

"Be right there, girl," Lexie said. She grabbed the three-legged milking stool, settled herself beside the cow, clenched her fingers around two teats, and began expertly squirting warm milk into the pail from Matilda's burgeoning udder.

It wasn't long before she heard plaintive mewing. Glancing around, Lexie saw the eager barn cats. With a deft twist, she sent a stream of milk their way, spraying their faces. A mass of gray and black tumbled and hissed as they each fought to be first in line.

Lexie laughed. "Patience is a virtue," she reminded the teeming fur.

"Lexie?" a sleepy male voice asked. "What are you doing here?"

Lexie glanced around. Jesse, her younger brother by two years, stumbled toward her, bleary-eyed and shadow-faced.

"I'm supposed to be doing the milking."

"I know." She turned back to Matilda. It wasn't Jesse's fault that he was so much like Tremaine, but lately Lexie couldn't help blaming him for all her problems. Jesse had been the bane of her existence. He'd been in and out of trouble all summer. Pa had even turned Lexie's responsibility for the stables over to Samuel, bypassing Jesse, because Jesse had been caught kissing Annie—an unforgivable transgression in Eliza's eyes that had nearly gotten the poor girl fired.

Jesse was trouble simmering beneath an indolent exterior. Just seeing him depressed Lexie, reminded her how soon she'd be leaving.

"You want me to take over?" he asked, yawning.

"Why don't you just go back to bed?" Jesse had gotten home well after midnight last night; Lexie heard him stumble in—as she'd heard Tremaine so many times in the past. Harrison was the only one who seemed to have any morals in her family, but she wasn't thinking too kindly of him these days either—the traitor!

"Tremaine's supposed to be coming home soon," Jesse remarked, flopping on his back against a pile of hay shocks.

Lexie's heart squeezed. "What for?" Tremaine had left the morning after Lexie learned he wasn't her brother and hadn't returned all summer.

"A visit, I guess. Are you going to tell him about Jace?"

Her brother's shrewdness caught her off guard. "What do you mean?"

"Oh, come on, Lexie. Jace isn't stopping by all the time just to patch up things between us and the Garretts. Maybe he's got Pa fooled, but I know better. He wants you."

That should have made Lexie feel better, but it didn't. She rhythmically squeezed the milk into the pail, wondering what was wrong with her. Jace had braved her father's Winchester and her mother's cool reserve in order to see her, yet Lexie still felt miserable. "He has yet to ask Pa for my hand in marriage," she pointed out.

"Do you want to marry him?"

Lexie thought about the way Jace still held back every time they kissed. She wished he would be a little more tender. "Yes, I do," she said firmly, though some of her certainty had vanished over the summer and she didn't rightly know why.

"Tremaine will have a fit. Pa and Mother don't much like Garrett, but Tremaine can't stand him."

"What Tremaine thinks doesn't matter a whit to me!" Lexie stated primly.

"What about Harrison?"

Lexie drew a breath and sighed. Her once close relationship with him had crumbled to dust. She couldn't help blaming him for realizing *her* dream. When Harrison left for Dr. Breverman's, he and Lexie had parted on uncertain terms. Now Lexie felt guilty.

"Well, when Tremaine gets here, be sure and let me know. I can't wait to see the sparks fly." Jesse straightened, stretched, and sauntered out to the lightening day.

Lexie finished her task, kicked the stool out of the way, blew out the lantern, and balanced the full pails as she headed back toward the house. She was already sweating and the moon was still glowing brightly.

The day was sure to be hot as Hades and, if Jesse's prediction came true, about as much fun.

The operating room of Willamette Infirmary felt like the inside of a brick oven. Sweat beaded on Tremaine's forehead, while he scrupulously stitched closed his patient's perforated intestines. In the back of his mind he thought of the frothy torrent of Fool's Falls. Tonight, when he got back to Rock Springs, he was going to plunge in—clothes and all.

The nurse was standing by with the sponge. She was obsessively dutiful, dabbing at the open wound every time Tremaine's fingers stilled. It was more annoying than helpful, but Tremaine gritted his teeth and waited as she once more stopped him in the process of stitching the last few bullet holes closed.

"Looks like a goddamn sieve," Dr. Peter Caldwell, Tremaine's assisting surgeon, remarked. "How'd it happen?"

Tremaine was in no mood to be loquacious. "I'd say he stepped in front of a gun," he answered shortly.

Undaunted by Tremaine's answer, Peter said, "I heard it was a union problem. Down at Monteith's shipyards."

"Don't matter what it was," the nurse said staunchly. "Dr. Danner's fixed him now."

"I'm going to close," Tremaine warned, and the nurse sponged like mad. With an inward sigh he waited, feeling sweat trickle between his shoulder blades.

An hour later he was striding down the front steps of the ugly white hospital. Outside the air was thick and sultry. The temperature was already soaring into the eighties and it was barely ten o'clock in the morning.

"Ya ready for Fortune, sir?" a young boy asked, appearing from the cobblestone alley that led to the back of the hospital.

"I sure am, Roy."

The boy nimbly disappeared and was back within minutes, with Fortune already put to the buggy. Tremaine slipped the hospital livery boy a dime and was rewarded with a flashing grin.

"Thank ya, Dr. Danner. Thank ya!"

The buggy was cool from being under the sheltered livery barn roof, and Tremaine sighed with relief as he headed south out of Portland. It would be hours before he was in Rock Springs—hours before he could take that swim.

His lips tightened as he thought about seeing Lexie again. He'd avoided her all summer but he'd promised his father he would come out tonight and pick up her trunk. Lexie would be leaving for Miss Everly's School soon, and Harrison had already joined Dr. Breverman's small class in Portland.

"Come on, get moving," he said to the trotting stallion, feeling the air clear as soon as he was out of the city. But his thoughts were still dark and uneasy. He didn't want to see Lexie again. Especially since Pa's last letter had made mention of how attentive Jace Garrett had become over the summer.

Tremaine wondered if Lexie knew about Garrett's mistress, and if not, when—and by whom—she should be told. He figured Jace certainly hadn't brought Betsy up.

Gritting his teeth, Tremaine worried he would have to tell her himself. He certainly didn't want to. But then he thought of Lexie and Jace together, and he groaned aloud in frustration.

At Rock Springs, Tremaine took one look at Fool's Falls and decided he was too old to make a public spectacle of himself. With sweat dripping down his temples, he got Fortune a drink, some oats, and a short rest, then he headed the buggy toward the Danner farm.

He would take a dip in the hot springs before he showed up at the house. It was better than nothing.

Lexie stood barefoot on the slab of rock that hung above the clear, softly moving water below. Heat rose up around her in waves. When she glanced over the dry fields, the air seemed to move and jiggle. These last few weeks of summer had been some of the hottest she could remember.

She wiggled her toes over the lip of the rock. The green water looked deceptively cool and calm. Lexie looked around once more, then stripped off her camisole and drawers. Feeling the hot, dry breeze sweep across her skin she dove cleanly into the water.

Her first contact was a shock; cold water nearly knocking the breath from her lungs. But as she knifed lower, heat from the hot springs' source turned the liquid around her into a warm, sensual delight. Lexie stayed down as long as she dared, shooting to the surface only when her lungs were swelled to bursting.

She gasped for several seconds, wiping hair out of her eyes. Now the water felt as warm as a bath, ripples of heat eddying to the surface as her feet treaded to keep her afloat. Tantrum stood tied to a nearby cedar, regarding her incuriously. Ears barely moving, he flicked a fly away with his tail.

Lexie dove down twice more. Today, as soon as she could, she'd escaped from the farm and ridden into the Cascade Mountain foothills at the far end of the Danner property. The hot springs had already soothed away most of her restlessness.

A few minutes later she heaved herself from the water onto the same outcrop of stone, turning her face skyward, closing her eyes on a sigh.

Tremaine still hadn't arrived, and it was both a relief and an aggravation. She didn't know how she would act when she saw him again. Would he really react as strongly as Jesse had said?

Lexie flung her arm over her face, breathing hard from exertion. She concentrated on Jace, pushing Tremaine out of her thoughts. Why wouldn't he kiss her—really kiss her? And why did it seem like his business in Rock Springs kept him away from her more and more? Though she was glad he'd never arrived that fateful night last spring when her world had come crashing down around her, she'd since been piqued by the continual business problems that had kept him in town.

Or was it just an excuse not to be alone with her?

Lexie opened her eyes, squinting up at the hazy blue sky. She imagined Jace's lips pressed against hers, hungry, demanding. She'd been afraid of his kiss once before, now she longed for it.

The heat made Lexie feel sleepy. Her eyelids drifted shut. Time passed slowly. She thought dreamily of Jace . . . his black hair . . . his angular face . . . his blue, blue eyes.

She sat up with a start, her body aflame with desire. But it hadn't been Jace she'd been dreaming about! Her heart was thundering, her skin sensitized and quivering. With a moan she thrust Tremaine from her thoughts, then was seized by a sudden terrible ache that stretched from her toes all the way to her lungs, threatening to choke her. Blinking, Lexie wrapped her arms around her knees. Long shadows were stealing across the fields. A dry, brown leaf floated to the ground. Summer was as good as over.

For no reason that she could think of, she bent her head to her knees and cried.

Fortune's tired steps lagged slower and slower. Taking pity on the poor, game animal, Tremaine walked him along the twisting stream, following it up to the Cascade foothills. He'd left the buggy at the lane, out of sight of the house. No one would know he was back until he'd finished swimming.

The last rays of the setting sun were painting a streak of pink at the horizon as Tremaine cut through the granite boulders that led to the hot springs. Fortune's ears suddenly pricked forward eagerly. Tremaine glanced around; the hairs on the back of Tremaine's neck rose; he reined in Fortune abruptly.

Someone was already here.

Silently looping the reins over a branch, Tremaine crept forward slowly. He had a sudden mental image of Jesse and his latest paramour and some of the tension left his shoulders. Was he going to walk into a late summer tryst?

But the vision that met his eyes stopped him dead in his tracks. Lexie, naked as the day she was born, was stretched out on the rocks in the sweet abandon of sleep.

Her chest rose and fell evenly, her breasts soft white globes against the tanned flesh of her chest and arms. Her stomach was a soft hollow, her smooth skin downy and misted with sweat. A small triangular tuft of blond hair capped a pair of the longest, silkiest legs Tremaine had ever seen.

His mouth went dry. His first thought was relief that she was alone; there was no sign of Jace Garrett. His second was that he should be feeling a helluva lot more guilty about staring at her.

But he couldn't help himself. It was as if he'd been starved for the sight of a female body—which was ridiculous, considering his occupation and his own rather indulgent lifestyle. His eyes swept over her, drinking in the sensual delight of her, inventorying every part of her for later, tortuous review.

He wanted her as much as he ever had. More. He felt himself harden instinctively and dragged his gaze away.

For several moments he stared at the darkening blue sky overhead, but all he saw was Lexie. Lexie, Lexie, Lexie. He would have to leave and let her awaken with her dignity intact.

But he glanced back one last time; he couldn't help himself. As if feeling his hot gaze burning into her, Lexie slowly turned her head, sighed, and blinked to wakefulness.

And then she looked straight at him.

"Tremaine?" she asked in a sleep-drugged mumble.

"Sorry to disturb you," he answered, his voice strained.

Lexie stretched sensually—and remembered her nakedness at that moment. Her eyes widened in shock. With a cry of mortification she grabbed her clothes. Tremaine deliberately turned his back, his shoulders beginning to shake with suppressed laughter at the look of maidenly horror that had crossed her face.

Lexie barely noticed. Her fingers scrambled with her clothes. There was a soft rip as she tore the fabric of her drawers in her haste to put them on. "How—how—long have you been standing there?"

Tremaine's back shook. "Long enough."

"And you didn't have the decency to wake me?" she screeched.

He cleared his throat. "Well, I would have, but I couldn't think quite how to do it."

Lexie stared at his broad shoulders in appalled wonder. Her mouth dropped open in affront. He was laughing! Laughing at her! "Very funny," she muttered in angry humiliation, which broke the dam on his control, drawing deep chuckles from his throat.

He turned around just as she'd finished buttoning up the tiny pearl buttons down the front of her sleeveless shirtwaist. Ignoring him, she tossed her head and brushed the dry grass and dust from her split skirt.

"Well, it's your turn to turn around," he drawled and Lexie's gaze flew to his face. His blue eyes simmered with humor and challenge. Slowly, he began removing his shirt and she saw a vee of tanned skin down his front. Dark hair arrowed downward and as Lexie watched, he tossed off his shirt, his fingers working on the buttons of his breeches.

"What are you doing?" she shrieked, whirling around in a panic.

"Going swimming. In case you hadn't noticed, it's hot."

She stood staring across the baking fields, her fists clenched, her heart pounding. She heard the splash of water and hazarded a glance back. Tremaine was under water. His clothes were tossed in an untidy pile, evidence that she wasn't dreaming this incredible interlude.

When was the last time she'd seen him naked? Had she ever? She couldn't remember. Even when she'd caught him with Mary-Anne she'd only managed a glimpse, then had been too embarrassed to do more but run home.

After several long moments Lexie turned toward the hot springs. Where was he? Why hadn't he surfaced?

"Tremaine, if you're playing games with me, so help me I'll kill you," she said through her teeth.

She strode to the lip of the rock and stared down. A splash sounded and his dark head surfaced. He shook water from his hair and smiled up at her. "Care to join me?" he invited casually, water dripping down his arrogant nose and stern jaw.

Beneath the water she could almost make out his bare limbs as he treaded water. "No, thanks."

"Coward."

"Hah!" She folded her arms and glared at him in mock fury. She should be angry with him. Scandalized. Yet, his spirit of camaraderie kept her from feeling anything worse than slightly embarrassed. And, she realized with a start, she was terribly glad to see him.

While Tremaine swam the sun sank lower, until it was just a fiery blaze caught between two mountain ridges. Lexie heard a splash as he heaved himself out of the water and she kept her gaze trained toward the mountains. She didn't move, but neither did she look at him. "It's almost dark," she remarked, pretending absolute nonchalance as he stepped into his clothes.

"You don't have to try so hard not to look," he said.

"What would I want to look for?" She shrugged. "I just wanted to give you some privacy."

His shout of laughter said he knew better. "Come here," he coaxed, motioning to where he stood.

Lexie slid him a wary glance. "What for?"

"Because I asked you to."

Every nerve Lexie possessed suddenly went on alert. Tremaine had never sought out her friendship before, why should he start now? "I like it right here," she said, feeling querulous and foolish, but somehow certain she didn't want to come any nearer.

He lifted his shoulders dismissively. "Suit yourself." He sat down against the bole of a cedar, drawing one knee up and draping his arm across it. His shirt was open at the throat and wet from his damp body. Unwillingly, Lexie was aware of his unconscious, yet blatant virility. Her gaze was drawn to the tight stretch of his tan breeches and she glanced away quickly, femininely aware of her own sorry state of dress.

Tremaine, however, was quite content to look at her as she was. Her hair was tangled into lovely golden layers, some lighter, some darker. It lay against the shoulders of her white eyelet shirtwaist, fanning out across the sun-dried flesh on her arms and neck. Sensing his stare, she gave him a quick, shy smile and he was reminded achingly of their tenuous childhood friendship. "You look beautiful, Sundown," he said before he thought.

Shocked, she gaped at him, then burst into delighted laughter. "Good heavens, Tremaine. I'd forgotten that nickname. Whatever made you think of it?"

"I don't know. The sun's setting. It just reminded me that we didn't always hate each other."

Lexie smiled. "We don't hate each other." There had been moments when she and Tremaine had been friends, she remembered with a rush of pleasure, liking this side of him she so rarely saw. "So what brought you home?" she asked, walking closer to flop down on the grass beside him. "We haven't seen you all summer."

"Didn't Eliza tell you?"

"Tell me what?"

"I'm picking up your trunk and taking it to Miss Everly's School. Pa asked me to come and get it."

"Oh." Disappointment crushed down on her. She'd thought Tremaine might have come just to see her—a foolish dream she hadn't realized she harbored until he'd just shattered the illusion. And why should it matter anyway? she asked herself angrily. Tightening her jaw, she said, "It's only a few weeks away now. I can't believe I'm actually going."

"Maybe it won't be so bad."

"It'll be worse than bad. It'll be intolerable." She lay on her stomach, resting her chin in her hands. "I want to live on a farm and be a horse doctor."

"And marry Jace Garrett?"

Lexie hesitated. "Yes."

This brought silence from Tremaine so she gave him a

searching look. His face was implacable and shuttered. Impatient, Lexie asked, "Well, aren't you going to say anything? Give me some new advice? Try to make me feel better?"

"It's only one year, Lexie."

"But it's not what I want!"

"I *know* what you want," Tremaine answered a trifle testily. "You just can't have everything you want all the time. Life isn't like that."

"Oh, really." She almost smiled. "When did you become such an expert?"

His blue eyes stared impassively into hers. "When I realized how much Jace Garrett is going to disappoint you."

She should have been infuriated. Tremaine's remarks about Jace always infuriated her. But this time all she could muster was mild annoyance. Still, she glared at him.

"Lexie," Tremaine said softly, reaching out to brush a finger across her cheek. "I don't want to talk about Jace right now. Or Miss Everly's School."

She leaned back, away from his touch. "What—do you want to talk about?"

He dropped his hand, drawing a deep breath. "I don't know. Nothing, I suppose." He watched the creeping lavender shadows grow across the ground, sighed, and said, "We'd better get back. Pa'll be wondering what my buggy's doing in the lane."

"Wait." Lexie laid a hand on his arm, halting him in the act of rising. He peered at her through the gathering twilight. "I don't want to go back just yet. I'd like to talk some more."

She felt the tension slowly leave the muscles of his arm. He inclined his head in agreement and sat back down, so close to her that her knee almost touched his taut thigh. Lexie carefully withdrew her fingers from his arm.

"I don't remember ever being your confidante," Tremaine remarked. "What happened to Harrison?"

She snorted in true unladylike fashion. "Benedict Arnold," she muttered and Tremaine's mouth twitched with humor. "I haven't forgiven him yet."

"It's not his fault he wants to be a horse doctor."

"Don't try logic on me, Tremaine. It won't work."

"When has it ever?"

She shot him a look but his smile was disarming, and it did treacherous things to her heart. He was very likable when he was in an approachable mood, she realized. Too likable. Ignoring his moratorium on bringing up Jace, she said, "Tremaine, I need some advice."

"You want *my* advice?" He arched a disbelieving brow. "On what?"

"Jace." She felt color creep up her neck as she considered what she was about to say. But it was as good a way as any to stop the foolish feelings rushing through her bloodstream—and it also addressed an issue that had been bothering her for months. "I have some questions about, well . . . about sex."

"Sex?" His head jerked up in surprise.

"Don't make this hard, Tremaine. I don't have anyone to talk to." She peered up at him, trying to discern his mood. He looked more taken aback than appalled. "I just don't know that much about it."

"Well, Lexie, that's all to your benefit."

"You don't understand." She bit her lip indecisively, wondering how far to take this conversation. Especially considering how Tremaine felt about Jace. Might as well be hung for a sheep as a lamb, she thought, plunging in. "I just don't know what I'm supposed to do now that—Jace and I are almost engaged."

Tremaine made a choked sound. "You don't *do* anything."

"But I get the feeling I'm doing something wrong." She turned pleading emerald eyes on him. "It's just not happening the way I think it should."

"I'm afraid to even ask what that means."

Lexie regarded him soberly, sure now that she'd embarked on a foolish quest. He wouldn't understand. Whatever had possessed her to think he would?

"Have you seen Garrett today?" he asked carefully.

"No. He's been busy in Rock Springs." At Tremaine's grim snort of disapproval, she grew hostile. "I can see there's no talking to you where Jace is concerned!"

"Lexie," he said with unexpected tenderness. "I just don't want you to get hurt."

"I won't be. But . . ."

"But?" Tremaine coaxed, albeit unwillingly.

"I just don't think he wants me enough," she burst out. "He doesn't want to—kiss me enough."

There. She'd said it. Let him make of it what he would. Swallowing, she waited for the recriminations she expected to receive.

Tremaine was utterly silent. He gazed pensively across the night-shrouded pastureland toward the mountains. Gaining courage, Lexie added softly, "When he kisses me, I don't know what to do. I want to kiss him back but I'm afraid to. I'm afraid he'll think I'm too forward. And then when I don't, I get the feeling I've disappointed him somehow."

Tremaine's jaw worked. "I doubt that you disappoint him, Lexie."

"Oh, but I do. He pulls back. I can feel it."

"Well, that's probably good. You're not married yet. You don't need to rush things."

"But that's not the way you are, is it?" Lexie asked, climbing onto her knees and dusting off her clothes.

Tremaine made a sound of disbelief. "I don't think I'm the right person to talk to—"

"Please, Tremaine. I know this sounds so ridiculous, but I need to talk to someone. Don't you see?"

"Your mother is probably—"

"No." She cut him off firmly. "She's not. I can't talk to her about anything."

Tremaine stared into Lexie's smooth, innocent face and wondered how in the hell he got himself into these messes. He could scarcely bear to be around Lexie. In fact, he'd spent the summer away from her to put things in perspective. But seeing her again made reason fly off on wings of heated passion. Though his mind argued with him even now, he could still see her lying naked on the granite outcropping. A liquid wanting uncoiled inside him.

She'd picked a helluva time to hope he might change his mind about Jace Garrett.

Misunderstanding his lightning change of expression, Lexie thought his anger was directed at her. "Tremaine?" she asked uneasily.

"What?"

Something inside Lexie seemed to be forcing her on. She

couldn't help herself. "What do you feel when you kiss a woman?" she asked. "Don't you want to keep on kissing her?"

"Oh, Lexie, stop it." He jumped restlessly to his feet and she scrambled up beside him.

"Well, don't you?" she demanded, unwilling to give up.

"Yes, if it's the right woman."

"And if it isn't?"

"Sometimes even then," he admitted with a bark of humorless laughter.

"Then why doesn't Jace want to kiss me?"

"Guilty conscience?" Tremaine posed, unable to prevent himself.

Lexie frowned. "What do you mean?"

Tremaine sighed, regarding her through narrowed eyes. It was becoming difficult to maintain a poker face. Half of him wanted to laugh at the absurdity of Lexie asking him for advice on sex; the other half wanted to sweep her in his arms and show her what it was all about.

"What would make you want a woman?" Lexie asked suddenly.

"Lexie—"

She gingerly touched a hand to his arm. "Please, Tremaine. Tell me. I need to know. What would make you want a woman?"

He looked down at her fingers lying loosely on his hot flesh. "She would have to be—ah—someone I found attractive," he answered with difficulty.

"Beautiful, you mean?"

"Attractive in some way."

She glanced down thoughtfully, her lashes sweeping her cheek, then met his gaze again. Her emerald eyes were full of an unfathomable need that made Tremaine's chest constrict. "Then she wouldn't have to be beautiful, as long as you liked the person she was inside."

"That's right."

Darkness seemed to close around them. The top of Lexie's head looked unnaturally dark, her skin glowed softly. Desire surged through Tremaine like an unwelcome curse. His pulse began to pound in that deep, age-old rhythm. He wondered how in God's name she couldn't sense what she was doing to him.

But she did sense it, a little. Instinctively. She turned her face up to his, her lips within inches of his. "Do you have a woman in your life right now?"

"No one special." Almost against his will, his hand moved upward, cupping her chin. Her skin was marvelously smooth and his thumb moved over her flesh, starvingly, demandingly.

"Jenny McBride?"

Tremaine swept in a breath. "Who have you been talking to?"

"I'm not completely ignorant, Tremaine."

"Then you'll know Jenny and I are just friends."

"And there's no other woman in Portland?"

Tremaine could have listed half a dozen females whom he saw on an irregular basis. But there was no special woman. "No."

Lexie regarded him with wide, innocent eyes. Only when his thumb slid down her throat to probe at the hollow of her neck, did she ask unsteadily, "Tremaine?"

"What?" Slowly, he bent his head.

"What are you doing?" she asked, drawing back.

"What does it feel like?" he whispered.

Surprised, Lexie made a sound of disbelief. "You're not going to . . ."

"Kiss you?" His mouth twisted as she jerked her startled gaze to his. "I believe I am."

Lexie reared back as far as her body would allow but his fingers plunged into the wild tangle of her blond mane, holding her captive. He pulled her inexorably forward, his dark head descending toward her trembling lips.

She tried to squirm from his grasp. She'd asked for this, she knew it. But he was terrifying her! She opened her mouth to scream just as his lips covered hers, muffling her cry. Her hands fought to push him away, but he held her tight, his mouth claiming hers in a hard, surrendering kiss.

Immobilized, Lexie was momentarily stunned to acquiescence. In that second her senses came alive, awakened by the sweet demanding pressure of his lips pressed to hers. Tremaine seized the opportunity to gather her closer, his mouth moving over hers with inflaming expertise, stroking, touching, finding new ways to fit against her.

There was a roaring in her ears. Her heart pounded like a wild thing. She clung to his arms, feeling the universe tip and sway. Tremaine seemed to expect this sensation because he held on tightly, dragging his hand up and down her spine convulsively, fitting his thighs close to hers.

It was as if the floodgates had opened. She felt a mad desire that had nothing to do with sanity. The nameless yearnings and frustrations she'd felt all summer were culminated here. Now. With Tremaine.

Tremaine!

Realization washed over her in a frigid, dousing wave, just as she recognized the probing hardness between his legs for what it was. She dragged her mouth from his. "Tremaine," she gasped, frightened, pushing her hand against the immovable wall of his chest. His heartbeat was strong, fast, and terrifying.

He drew a breath, his mobile mouth twisting. "Does that answer your question?"

"Yes!"

He released her so slowly that it was an agony she wasn't sure how to handle. She stumbled on her feet, breathing hard.

"If Jace is holding back," he said with grim humor, "there's a reason. And it has nothing to do with you. Believe me."

Lexie covered her swollen mouth with shaking fingers. She'd been kissed by an expert, she realized. And, God help her, she'd liked it! "Tremaine . . ."

He was already stalking toward Fortune, but now he stopped mid-stride and cocked his head in her direction, his expression unfathomable.

"Why did you kiss me like—like that?" she blurted out.

"Because," he answered with stark honesty, "I wanted to." With that he swung onto Fortune's back, twisted the magnificent stallion around, and waited patiently while Lexie scrambled onto Tantrum.

A thousand questions raced through her mind as she

quietly followed Tremaine back to the house. Several times her mouth formed a query, then her gaze would fasten on his rigid back and the words would wither and die before they were uttered. Tremaine had retreated behind his shell of harsh indifference again, and he was no longer her amiable friend.

Amiable friend? Hah! She knew better.

At the stables she watched as he rubbed down Fortune and for the first time in memory, she neglected her own mount. "Tremaine . . ." she whispered.

"What?" he bit out ominously, his shoulder muscles working fast and hard as he groomed Fortune's legs.

Licking her lips, Lexie asked, "Were you just teaching me a lesson? For being so naive?"

"Believe what you want, Lexie," he said on a short laugh. "Maybe we should just forget what happened at the hot springs."

Lexie sighed in relief, yet the emerging woman in her already knew it was futile. "Can we really do that?" she asked softly, beseechingly.

Tremaine stopped his furious horse grooming and rocked back on his heels, sending Lexie a strange half-smile. "No, Sundown, I don't think we can. But don't worry. I'm leaving tomorrow and you're heading to school soon. Pretty soon you won't even think about it."

Lexie wandered back to Tantrum and began by rote brushing his coat. . . . *Won't even think about it* . . . Her brow furrowed with anxiety. An uneasy restlessness stirred in her breast. She wanted to believe him but a deep part of her soul wouldn't listen. That part burned bright and hot, vividly remembering the touch of his lips, the aching wonder of being in his arms.

How, how can I ever truly forget? she asked herself as Tremaine, without a glance back, strode from the stables.

She had a feeling she'd just made a crucial mistake.

Tremaine swiped at the road dust gathered on his face as he tied Fortune to the rail in front of Jenny McBride's rooming house. He hadn't seen Jenny since last spring and he felt he owed her a visit. She was, after all, a friend. And right now he was badly in need of one.

He glanced to where Lexie's trunk was tied to the back of the buggy. It too was covered with dust. Tremaine grimaced as he recalled his restless night and vowed to himself that he would forget Lexie if it took three solid weeks in the comfort of another woman.

As soon as he stepped across the threshold, he smelled Jenny's ubiquitous jasmine scent. There was no one about, however; the downstairs had a quiet, empty feeling.

Upstairs was another story. He could hear the muffled noises of what sounded like two voices raised in anger. With the memory of Jace Garrett fresh in his mind from his last visit, Tremaine strode to the upper landing. But it was women's voices he heard, he realized, and he was about to head back down when Jenny burst from one of the rooms, murder in her eyes.

"Tremaine!" she cried, stopping short.

"Well, hullo, Jenny, I was just—"

His words died in his throat when Betsy Talbot stepped into the hallway, swelled up like an overripe watermelon. Seeing him, she flushed but she didn't hide her condition. Instead, she straightened her shoulders while Tremaine felt shock rip through him.

"Is that baby Jace Garrett's?" he asked in a deadly voice.

"It ain't nobody else's," Betsy maintained, lifting her chin.

"And does the prospective father know?"

Jenny bustled over to him, clasping his arm. "Yes, he knows," she said, trying to hurry him downstairs.

"And I haven't seen him for months!" Betsy suddenly wailed, throwing her hands over her face and bursting into sobs.

Tremaine shook off Jenny's anxious hands and stared at the overwhelming evidence of Jace's perfidy. He'd done this to Lexie. "Gossip must be rampant," he said without humor.

"If you're worrying if your sister knows, don't be!" Jenny said. "Betsy's been doing her best to protect Jace, which is unnecessary as far as I'm concerned," she added heartily, her eyes glaring meaningfully into Betsy's.

"It don't matter if he doesn't come to me. I've got a part of him."

Tremaine inwardly groaned. He'd heard those same words so many times from some of his most pathetic cases. Women who'd given up everything in the hopes the man they "loved" would come to his senses and marry them.

"What're you gonna do?" Betsy asked, as he turned on his heel.

"I don't know. I'll have to think about it."

Fortune's hoofbeats were a calming rhythm but they couldn't quell the fury seething inside Tremaine's chest. He was possessed of the urgent need to strangle Jace Garrett, and all the way to Portland he entertained himself with a dozen different bloody scenarios. He didn't give a damn about Jace personally, but he cared a lot about how Jace's actions affected Lexie. And considering the blooming state of Betsy Talbot's waist, Jace had a great deal to answer for.

Betsy's weeping, whether feigned or real, had gotten to him. "Don't do anything!" she'd begged in anguish, chasing him onto the street, soaking Tremaine's shirt with a flood of tears. "Don't tell your sister about me. It'll only make him hate me!"

"You should have never let that man have what he wanted," Jenny had put in with asperity. "You can't trust a Garrett. Don't you know that by now?"

"I love him," she'd sniffed miserably. "I love him!"

Tremaine had heard all the declarations of love for Jason Garrett he could stand. "He's been spending a lot of time at my father's. Because of Lexie," he pointed out gently.

"Oh, yeah," Betsy cried bitterly. "He wants a lady, like that mother of yours. He don't want trash like me! He won't even admit the baby's his!"

Tremaine wasn't surprised, considering Jace's slimy character. He ground his back teeth together, flexing his hands on the reins. Thank God Lexie was spending a year at Miss Everly's School. Maybe she would finally wake up and realize that Jace Garrett wasn't the man for her.

Chapter Seven

Lexie stared up at the imposing brick building and hid the shiver of revulsion that shook her willowy frame. MISS EVERLY'S SCHOOL FOR YOUNG LADIES was stamped into the iron plaque above the school's front archway, and the building's evenly spaced rectangular windows seemed to gloat with evil.

The place looked like some kind of hellish prison.

Eliza stood on the front steps beside her daughter. Reaching for Lexie's hand, she squeezed it gently. "I hope you like it a little," she said softly. "Please try."

Lexie regarded her mother soberly. Eliza wore a dark blue brocade dress with a silk hat and veil. She looked more like Lexie's contemporary than her mother. Swallowing, Lexie's gaze swept over her own burnt-orange lawn dress. She felt sorely lacking in comparison—choked by the constraining corset, her head itching beneath the mink-brown veiled hat. Heaving an inward sigh, she lifted a gloved hand to the bell.

The door was opened by a shrew-faced maid, who tightened her lips at the same time Lexie tightened her resolve. The maid showed them through the gloomy but spotless entry room, down a chandelier-lit passage to an equally gloomy parlor. The only sign of life in the room was the faded pink roses scattered across the wallpaper.

A dark-haired woman of indiscriminate age and a stony expression glided into the room. "Good afternoon," she said, dismissing the maid with a nod of her regal head. "You must be Mrs. Danner."

"Yes, and this is Lexington," Eliza said.

Lexie executed a short curtsy, growing more panicky by the minute. So this was Miss Everly, she thought rebelliously, staring at the daunting woman, and was therefore shocked when the woman said, "I'm Hildegarde Lawrence. Miss Everly will be right in. Please make yourselves comfortable," she added, gesturing toward the rosewood chairs before disappearing through the door.

"Who's she?" Lexie asked aloud, but Eliza didn't know.

Pa and Samuel brought in Lexie's luggage, the somber rooms seeming to hush their footsteps. They all stood silently in the parlor until a thin woman with gray hair caught in a severe bun and a benevolent smile fixed on her unpainted lips, stepped into the room. "I'm Margaret Everly," she introduced herself. "And you must be Lexington. Welcome to my school."

She reached out a hand, which Lexie accepted. Miss Everly smelled faintly of perfume and cough syrup, and her hand was dry and papery. "How do you do," Lexie murmured.

"Fine. Fine." She nodded sagely and Lexie wasn't certain whether Miss Everly had answered her question or passed judgment on her acceptability.

The gray-haired schoolmistress instructed Pa and Samuel to take Lexie's luggage upstairs, adding to Lexie, "Your trunk's already been delivered."

Tremaine. Lexie's throat felt raw with unnamed misery. It was difficult to pull her mind back to her mother's conversation.

Miss Everly and Eliza discussed future dates and plans, as Lexie stood in silent introspection, feeling the room close in around her. It was a thousand times worse than she'd imagined! This dreary cavern was beyond her vilest nightmares.

Before she fully realized it, Eliza and Pa were saying their goodbyes. ". . . If there's anything you need, please write and let us know." Her mother squeezed her hand reassuringly.

Lexie nodded. "I will."

"I *shall*, Lexie. I shall," she murmured, pulling nervously on her gloves.

"All right, I shall," Lexie said dispiritedly. To her amazement her mother suppressed a chuckle, then gave her a hard hug.

"You'll do fine," she assured her. "By the way, I have a surprise for you."

"A surprise?" Knowing her mother, she was almost afraid to ask.

"I spoke to Jason Garrett and he's coming to Portland this evening to christen your adventure, so to speak. I thought it might be nice for Miss Everly to meet him."

Lexie was speechless. "Jace is coming here?" she asked blankly.

"He wanted to surprise you, but you look so terribly depressed I couldn't wait." She brushed her finger alongside Lexie's cheek. "If all goes well, he'll be here around eight tonight."

Lexie was dumbstruck, as much by her mother's thoughtfulness as the fact Jace was driving to Portland to see her. She would have hugged Eliza back, but the strain on their relationship prevented her. "Thank you," she said, swallowing against a lump in her throat.

Miss Everly, who had discreetly allowed them private goodbyes, reappeared to show Pa, Eliza, and Samuel out. As soon as the door closed behind them, the schoolmistress invited Lexie on a tour through the building. Each room was more ghastly than the last, but Miss Everly was so obviously proud of the house that Lexie murmured words of appreciation. Other attendees were arriving by the hour so Miss Everly handed Lexie over to the taciturn Hildegarde. Hildegarde finished up the tour without a word, showing Lexie the dining room, kitchen, and small outdoor garden.

"The livery's around the corner," she managed to impart as she led Lexie back to the parlor.

"We do get out, then?" Lexie asked with a straight face.

"Yes, miss." Hildegarde's dour expression was totally devoid of humor. "Many times."

Baffled by Lexie's unrestrained fit of nervous giggles, she left Lexie with the crowd of other new recruits. One of the young women was as blond as Lexie, but her face had the smooth plumpness of a pampered angel. She slid Lexie a look out of the corner of her eye that set all Lexie's feminine defenses on instant alert.

Trouble, Lexie thought woefully, vowing to steer clear of this new arrival.

Upstairs in her room, she put her clothes away in one of the twin bureaus pushed against the far wall. Her trunk was sitting beneath one window and Lexie removed the key from her satchel—a gift from her mother—and opened the lock. All the new clothes Eliza had purchased came tumbling out and Lexie carefully shook them and hung them in the closet.

She was nearly finished when she saw the faded Turkish split skirt. She eyed it, frowning. She hadn't packed it and she knew her mother wouldn't have. Miss Everly would no more permit Lexie's wearing it than she would allow a man in her upstairs bedroom. Curious, Lexie picked it up and a piece of paper floated to the floor.

With disbelief, Lexie read Tremaine's scrawling hand: *You might need this yet. Good luck, Tremaine.*

Lexie sank down on the foot of the bed, clutching the garment, perilously close to tears. Then she folded up the slip of paper and put it in her top dresser drawer. She'd managed to push thoughts of what she'd termed The Kiss to the back of her mind during the last two busy weeks. Now, however, they tumbled vividly around inside her head. She didn't even have to close her eyes to recall the devastating harshness of his mouth, the firm feel of his hands, the insistence of his hard thighs. The room seemed to pitch and sway.

"Damn corset," Lexie muttered, her eyes flying open, just as the door to the room creaked behind her.

A red-haired girl with freckles staggered in, heaving a valise onto the opposite bed with a world-weary groan. "I hate them, too," she admitted, "but my parents think I need to wear one to catch a beau. Personally I don't think there's much chance of that anyway. Hello, I'm Ella." She dusted off her hand and stretched it in Lexie's direction.

"I'm Lexie. Are you my roommate?"

"Looks like it." Ella flopped down on the bed and the valise slipped off the edge to land on its catches. The lid flew open and Ella's clothes fairly bounded onto the floor. She sighed. "Oh, for God's sakes."

Lexie liked her immediately. With a silent prayer of thanks that the blond girl she'd seen downstairs hadn't been chosen as her roommate, Lexie sat on the edge of her own bed. "Are you glad to be here?"

Ella rolled an eye in Lexie's direction. "I would rather be a laborer in my father's shipyard."

"Your father owns a shipyard?"

Ella grunted and turned on her side, her back to Lexie. "Would you undo this thing? I can't stand it one more minute. No wonder women faint. I can barely see straight."

Lexie quickly undid the buttons of Ella's dress and untied the long strings to her corset. Sighing with relief, Ella said, "My father doesn't own a shipyard anymore. He sold out to Silas Monteith. You've heard of the Monteiths?"

Lexie shook her head.

"They own a string of the biggest shipyards around and, believe me, they let everybody know it." Ella's dark eyes examined Lexie curiously. "I've never seen you before. Are you from San Francisco? Or Seattle?"

"No, I—" For a moment Lexie wasn't certain how to respond. She was distinctly aware of the differences between her background and Ella's. But then she tossed her head and said, "I live on a farm near Rock Springs."

"A farm? Rock Springs?" Ella's mouth curved in amused surprise. "Where's that?"

"About twenty miles southeast of here."

"Well, what are you doing here?"

There was no malice in Ella's question, just a natural, lively curiosity that Lexie responded to immediately. "The devil if I know."

They both laughed and Ella, who had shimmied her bulky frame from her dress and corset, lay back against her pillow in just her camisole and drawers. It was scandalous, Lexie supposed, but then she'd never had any sisters to share with.

"Maybe this won't be so bad after all," Ella commented. "Except Celeste's here." She made a face.

"Celeste?"

"Monteith's daughter. She got here just before I did. Good breeding should keep me from speaking my mind, but it hasn't worked yet." Ella grinned. "Celeste's a pain in the—" She pointed to her sumptuous derrière.

Lexie had a burning memory of the angel-faced blond and knew instinctively this was Celeste Monteith. But the knowledge skipped away like water over smooth stones. Ella was here, and now Miss Everly's School would be bearable.

Their introduction was cut short by the bell that called them to dinner. Ella shrugged back into her corset and gown, muttering curses under her breath that kept a grin on Lexie's face all through the meal. There were thirty-odd girls, and Lexie's opinion of them wasn't much improved by their petulant actions and shortsighted goals.

"What are your plans, Lexington?" Miss Everly asked down the table.

Lexie, who had decided on meeting Ella to embark on a trip of honesty, said distinctly, "I would like to become a horse doctor."

"A what?" one of the girls asked.

"A horse doctor." Lexie hid a smile and accepted a roll from the passing plate.

"My Gawd," a voice drawled from somewhere down the length of the table.

Miss Everly said in a philosophical tone, "We all come to this school with dreams. Not all will be realized. But one dream will: when you leave here you'll all be changed. You'll have grown. You'll be more than young women, you'll be ladies."

Lexie choked on the dust-dry roll and met Ella's gaze across the table. Ella was amused, but Lexie, catching the horrified looks being sent her way, realized Miss Everly had, in her own misguided way, sought to keep Lexie from ridicule. Celeste Monteith, who as Lexie had surmised was indeed the angelic blonde, opened her blue eyes wide. "A horse doctor!" she announced with a delicate shudder.

Lexie sent her a sweet smile and ground her back teeth together in the process.

Lexie was on the way back to her room when Hildegarde announced flatly to anyone standing nearby, "There's a gentleman caller to see Miss Danner."

Jace! Anxious to see anyone familiar and dear, Lexie raced to the front door. "Jace!" she cried, as he handed the maid his hat and coat.

He looked incredibly dashing, his coppery hair reflecting the chandelier's spangles of light. "Hello, Lexie. Your mother—"

"I know, I know. I'm so glad you came!"

Jace's gaze swept over her, noting the fullness of her breasts, the desperate sparkle in her eyes. Lexie had grown steadily more distant over the summer and he'd been flailing himself with recriminations, worried his gentlemanly conduct had been the wrong tack. Maybe he should have just thrown her down on the barn hay and had his way with her. Maybe that was the only way to treat her.

But now he knew his original plan had paid off. The way her fingers clutched his arm made him want to shout with triumph. He smiled, clasping his fingers down hard over hers. "You are so beautiful," he told her.

The delighted flush that spread across her cheeks made his pulse quicken. "Jace," she whispered, horrified to realize her eyes were filling with tears.

"What is it, darling?"

Lexie shook her head. How could she explain all the doubts she'd been feeling? Doubts *Tremaine* had magnified with one fateful kiss? And she was so miserable here. If only he would take her away from this awful place.

"Lexie." His voice was a harsh rasp. His fingers tightened over hers. She glanced up. His features were drawn and tight.

"What?" she whispered, afraid.

His other hand found her waist and he began to pull her forward. Lexie drew back, suddenly sure she didn't want to be kissed. The thought of his lips finding hers was singularly repelling. When he bent downward, she jerked her head away so that his lips missed their mark, trailing along her cheek.

What the devil was the matter with her?

The dry sound of someone clearing her throat sounded

behind Lexie's head. Miss Everly smiled benevolently. "Miss Danner, it would be more seemly if you waited for your guest in the parlor. I will show him in."

Relieved, Lexie did as the schoolmistress suggested, but she could feel Jace's anger. Several of the other girls were already in the parlor and they whispered together, casting sly glances at Lexie and Jace. There was absolutely no privacy at all—and Lexie was almost glad.

But Miss Everly shooed the other girls from the room, leaving the door slightly ajar after her. It was clear a Miss Everly lady wasn't to be left alone with a gentleman. Even so, Jace grabbed Lexie, startling a cry from her. "I thought you were glad to see me," he said softly. "But you never want to kiss me."

"*I* don't want to kiss *you?*"

"You're afraid of my slightest touch. You know it won't be that way when we're married."

"Yes, I know. But you're wrong, Jace. I do want to kiss you. It's just—you've held back so long and I thought it was because—you didn't want to kiss me."

"You do want me then?"

Jace was looking at her so intently it made Lexie squirm. Yes, she wanted him. She wanted him to take her away from here!

"Why don't you show me?" he suggested silkily. "Maybe then I won't have to hold back."

Tremaine had been right! she realized, as Jace once more imprisoned her in his arms. But when his lips crushed down on hers she felt none of the knee-trembling magic. In fact, she couldn't breathe! She endured his mouth moving back and forth over hers as long as she could, then tore her mouth away, gasping.

Jace's eyes were heavily lidded. "Better," he murmured, and Lexie stared wide-eyed. Didn't he know she'd nearly suffocated? His next words, however, completely drove that out of her mind.

"Have you seen Tremaine?" he asked.

She inhaled sharply. *Did he know?* "Not for a while." She stumbled over the lie. "Why?" Discreetly, she moved from his arms.

"You haven't talked to him?"

"About what?" Her cheeks surged with pounding color as she thought about Tremaine's body pressed against hers.

"Oh, nothing." He seemed somehow relieved. With a hand in the small of her back, he suggested, "Why don't you show me around? I can't stay long. I've got to head back to Rock Springs tonight."

"Tonight? But you won't get home until morning."

"I know. I shouldn't have come all this way, but I wanted to make sure you were settled and happy." His face darkened. "You know Kelsey's causing my mother fits."

Lexie almost smiled. "Yes." Kelsey Garrett had turned into a rebellious young woman, much to Lucinda Garrett's dismay and Lexie's private amusement. Kelsey had taken up shooting a rifle as part of her daily activities. She was determined to foil her mother's plans for her marriage to Paul Warfield, the mayor of Malone. Lexie had heard the sharp report of Kelsey's rifle many times in the last few weeks and she imagined it was driving Lucinda mad with frustration.

"Maybe your mother should realize Kelsey doesn't love Paul Warfield."

"My mother doesn't care. And Kelsey should be glad a man of Warfield's importance is interested in her. He'll have his hands full, though, taming the little wildcat."

"Jace," Lexie began, not liking his tone. "A woman has a right to choose."

"If Kelsey had any sense, she'd choose Warfield," he answered autocratically. Looking down into her troubled face, Jace ran his thumb down her cheekbone. "Like you chose me," he added softly.

Lexie's heart lurched. "Yes," she agreed. "Come on, I'll show you around."

An hour later he was on his way out. Because Hildegarde waited in the foyer, there was no opportunity for Jace to kiss her again—and Lexie was relieved. But sadness crept over her at the thought of being alone.

"Write me?" she begged, as he opened the door.

"Of course," he promised.

The door shut behind him with grim finality. Lexie stood stock still.

"Are you all right, Miss Danner?" Hildegarde asked tonelessly.

Lexie gave her a wordless nod, then gathered her skirts and mounted the stairs to her room.

Inside his handsome carriage, Jace flicked the reins on his team of matching bays. The horses started off on a brisk trot but he knew they were tired. He would have to go to the livery stables and exchange them for a new pair, picking them up on his next trip to Portland.

He squinted against the deepening autumn night, his mouth a thin, resolute line. So Tremaine hadn't told Lexie about Betsy. Jace couldn't understand why, but he thanked the fates all the same. He'd had to avoid Lexie these last few weeks, trying to come up with some kind of plausible excuse for Betsy's pregnancy.

The bitch, he thought callously. He'd be damned if he claimed her bastard as his.

Eliza Danner's request that he visit Lexie on her first day had seemed like a summons to hell. But he couldn't say no. It was an olive branch. A way for the Danners and Garretts to bury their differences. He'd had to accept, sure he was about to pay for his sins.

But lo and behold, Lexie had been glad to see him! She'd reached out to him in that innocent way of hers that sent his blood lusting, left his mouth spit-dry.

The thought of Lexie in his bed was enough to make Jace's pants tighten uncomfortably. Now he half-wished he'd never agreed to her attending Miss Everly's School. But almost as much as he wanted Lexie herself, Jace wanted a real lady. A lady like Eliza Danner. He applauded Lexie's mother's decision to mold her into the same type of woman. Unlike Lexie, he was sure it could be done.

"Gidday yup," he muttered to the failing horses, pulling into the livery at the edge of town. He knew the stable boy in charge from similar visits into the city. "I need a fresh pair," he said.

"Right away, Mr. Garrett."

While Jace's bays were being removed from their harnesses and a smart coal-black pair was put to, Jace pulled a cheroot from his pocket and lit it, letting the thin smoke curl into the biting air. Betsy was another problem. She'd gotten herself pregnant on purpose and it infuriated him.

"If she thinks it'll keep me from having Lexie," he said between his teeth, "she's dead wrong."

"Pardon?" The stable boy looked his way.

Jace smiled thinly. "Nothing."

Fifteen minutes later, he was on his way to Rock Springs. It was a long way back, and he was glad to be on the road. He was also glad to leave Lexie. Seeing her strained his self-control. He didn't want to scare her—he wanted her for a wife. A proper Garrett wife, one worthy of his name and position in the community.

And he'd be damned if either Betsy, or Tremaine Danner, or anyone else, would stop him from having her.

It seemed to Lexie that as swift as the summer had fled, fall was moving as slow and deliberate as molasses in a snowstorm. A month at Miss Everly's School, however, had convinced Lexie there were certain things she could learn after all. Not particularly useful things, but accomplishments that would please Jace nonetheless. She was beginning to learn how to waltz. She'd discovered Shakespeare to be a thoroughly entertaining writer. She'd learned a few French phrases. Sewing was still a problem, as was music, but if it would make Jace happy, she vowed to embroider and sing with the best of them.

Still, time dragged and she lived for the letters Jace sent. He didn't write often, but he managed a letter about once a week. Between his missives and those sent by other members of her family, Lexie bore her homesickness in good grace. Only Tremaine had been silent, which bothered her, especially since he lived and worked in Portland.

One Sunday afternoon, just as Lexie was curling up in a chair to reread *Romeo and Juliet,* a carriage clattered to a stop outside the front door. Lexie peered down from her window and recognized the dark-blond head of her brother Harrison.

She grabbed her skirts and ran down the stairs, earning a tsk-tsk from Hildegarde's tongue as she raced to the door.

"Harrison!" she cried, flinging herself toward him.

"Whoa," he said, holding high a hatbox and another smaller package, before Lexie could crush them in her eagerness to throw herself into his arms. "I take it this means I've been forgiven," he said, smiling down into her laughing face.

"Never. But I'm so lonely I'll deign to put aside our feud for a while." She clung to his arm as they walked inside. "It's so good to see you," she said, her voice catching.

"I'm glad to hear that." He regarded her seriously, his green eyes smiling into her own. "Is it really so bad here?"

"Mmmm." She nodded. "And I don't want to hear how wonderful it is with Dr. Breverman. I can only stand so much disappointment."

"It's wonderful," Harrison admitted, and Lexie jabbed her elbow into his ribs as hard as she could.

Harrison's laughter brought Miss Everly and several of the other girls into the entry room. To their curious glances, Lexie said, "Miss Everly, I'd like to introduce my brother, Harrison Danner."

"Good afternoon, Mr. Danner," said Miss Everly, extending her hand.

Harrison's mouth quirked. "Good afternoon," he answered.

"Harrison has asked me to go for a ride in his carriage," Lexie announced blithely. "Would that be all right?"

"Certainly." Miss Everly smiled benevolently.

Squeezing her brother's arm, Lexie said to him, "I'll be right back."

"You haven't changed," Harrison remarked softly.

"Did you think I would?"

She tossed him a smile, then headed upstairs, walking with a decorum that would make Miss Everly proud. But as soon as Lexie was out of sight, she bounded up the stairs two at a time.

Grabbing her cloak, Lexie glanced longingly at her split skirt. What she wouldn't give to ride bareback. But a ride in Harrison's carriage was preferable to sitting around the dusty alcoves of Miss Everly's School.

Once outside she drew in a deep breath, enjoying the teasing breeze. "Thank you," she murmured with heartfelt appreciation, her eyes closed.

"Don't mention it. I swear, you act like I've broken you out of prison."

"Amen. Where did you get this lovely buggy?" Lexie exclaimed as he helped her into it.

"It's Dr. Breverman's."

She threw him a dark look and leaned back against the elegant, tucked-black-leather upholstery. "Would you like to trade? You can stay at Miss Everly's School and I'll take your place with Dr. Breverman."

Harrison slanted her a look. "Well, I don't know. What's your roommate like?"

Lexie grinned. "She has red hair and freckles and sings worse than I do. Her family wants her to find a husband, preferably a wealthy one, because their fortunes have been in decline the last few years. They had to sell their shipping company and can barely afford to send Ella to Miss Everly's School. But this is her best chance to meet 'the right kind of man.'"

Harrison laughed. "I don't think my prospects are good enough."

Lexie sighed. "I know. Although Mother continually surprises me with the amount of money she's got saved. Do you suppose it all came from my father's estate?"

"I don't know."

They drove to a small corner hotel near the river, not too many blocks from the fashionable Nob Hill area, which housed Miss Everly's School. Harrison held the door for her with a flourish and Lexie adopted a Victorian air. "Thank you so much, Mr. Danner," she intoned. "I am so pleased you invited me out this afternoon."

"My pleasure, ma'am."

They were seated at a window table and Lexie pulled off her gloves. Harrison watched her sardonically. "You may hate it," he observed, "but you really look like a lady."

Lexie shot him a killing look. "What took you so long to come to my rescue?"

"After the treatment I received last summer?"

"Come on. My temper never bothered you before."

To Lexie's surprise he dropped the playful banter and said seriously, "You were shattered, Lex. Everything hit you at once and you wandered around in a daze for months. If

Tremaine hadn't told us to leave you alone, we probably would have taken you to a doctor."

"Tremaine told you to leave me alone?"

"He said you'd work it out." Harrison shook his head. "Since he'd been through it, too, I figured he knew what he was talking about."

Lexie dropped her chin on her hand and stared out the window. A soft, misting fog clung low to the Willamette River and she watched several small boats steam by. "How could they keep it a secret from me? I don't understand why they would."

"Maybe Pa thought you wouldn't love him the same way if you knew he wasn't your real father."

"That's ridiculous." She sighed as the waiter placed a pot of tea on the table between them. Harrison ordered for them and Lexie half-smiled to herself, thinking how much things had changed. "You know, I could have almost guessed that Tremaine wasn't really my brother."

"I know."

Something in Harrison's tone caught Lexie's attention. He was systematically stirring cream into his tea, so systematically in fact that Lexie said, "What's going through your mind?"

Glancing up, he started to deny he was thinking about anything, and then he saw her face. "You wouldn't believe me if I told you," he said reluctantly.

"I might."

He shook his head.

It was clear he wasn't going to talk about Tremaine so Lexie took matters into her own hands. "He hasn't come to see me since I've been here. Nor has he written."

"Tremaine?"

"Yes, Tremaine. He lives in Portland, yet I could be back in Rock Springs for all it matters to him."

"I thought you two didn't get along."

"We don't, as a rule, but when you defected I had to turn to someone."

"*I* defected!" Harrison shot her an outraged glance, but then seeing the laughter in her eyes he said, "So you turned to Tremaine, huh? What's that been like?"

Lexie felt this conversation was turning dangerous somehow, but since she couldn't rationally find a reason to explain her feelings, she said, "He stayed away all summer. I know he never was around much before, but I thought—I don't know—that he would help me more."

Memories sent Lexie's heart quivering, and she narrowed her gaze out the window once more, afraid that Harrison, who had always understood her, would somehow guess what had transpired.

His gaze was penetrating. "I understand Jace came to Portland to see you were settled in."

This was a much safer topic and Lexie grabbed onto it eagerly. "He didn't stay long, though."

"Sounds like the Garretts and Danners are about to become one big happy family. Mother's not against your marrying Jace."

While it was surprising in itself, Lexie thought, she'd long since given up trying to figure out what went through Eliza's mind. "The feud is silly. It should have ended long ago."

"Joshua Garrett's the one who kept it alive," Harrison reminded her. "He always wanted our property and so does Lucinda."

"Well, Jace doesn't, and he's head of the household now. The whole thing's ridiculous anyway. The Garretts have more land than they know what to do with."

Harrison's smile was wry. "That doesn't stop them from acquiring. Look at Rock Springs, Lexie. The next thing you know they'll be changing the name of the town to Garrettville."

Lexie snorted. She'd been wrong. She didn't like this topic any better than discussing Tremaine. "You sound sorry to see the feud end."

His hand dropped lightly over hers. "I just don't want to see my big sister get hurt."

"I can take care of myself," Lexie said steadily. It irked her to know that Harrison, like everyone else, felt her love for Jace could only lead to unhappiness.

Harrison lifted an eyebrow but wisely dropped the subject of the Garretts. He paid the bill, then led her back to the buggy. The breeze had turned into a cold, whipping wind and Lexie shivered a little, pulling her wrap closer around her shoulders. She was pleased by the colder weather. There were less than two months left to Christmas—two months left until her first vacation—two months left until she could see Jace again.

"Would you like to see the hospital where Tremaine works?" Harrison asked as he drove her by Dr. Breverman's offices. A light burned inside the window, and Lexie caught a glimpse of what looked like a small classroom.

"Is it near here?" Lexie asked, her gaze lingering on the swinging sign across the front porch, which listed Dr. Breverman's hours. How she longed to be there with Harrison!

"Not too far. Although it's not in the best part of town."

Harrison slapped the reins across the horses' broad flanks, sending them into a smart trot. They turned north and soon the cobblestone streets became weed-choked, the buildings dilapidated wooden tenements. Laundry, strung from wires between the buildings, flapped wildly in the increasing wind. The stench of urine and garbage made Lexie's nostrils quiver.

"His hospital is here?"

"At the edge of this," Harrison answered with a grim nod.

Lexie breathed a sigh of relief upon seeing the clean, whitewashed one-story building standing next to the river. She could hear the muted shouts and revelry from the saloons and brothels that dotted the waterfront further down. Horses' hoofbeats sounded on the cobblestone roads to the south and west. The river ran smooth and black in the gathering twilight. A ferry boat sat at anchor.

"Do you want to go in?"

Lexie thought about seeing Tremaine and felt an irrational need to flee. Disgusted with herself, she said brightly, "I'd love to."

Inside, Harrison asked the woman at the desk if Dr. Danner was on duty. Lexie, who had always accepted Tremaine's profession with blithe equanimity, glanced around the hospital waiting room and was struck by the responsibility of Tremaine's job. It seemed incomprehensible to her that Pa had once been a doctor, too, yet she could recall the times he'd treated her when she'd been injured and she'd recognized his tender professionalism at some subconscious level.

"Dr. Danner is out visiting patients," the receptionist informed them and Lexie felt a cruel sense of disappointment. "He has many patients who can't come to the hospital."

"Why can't the patients come to the hospital?" Lexie asked Harrison after they'd left Tremaine a message and headed back to the buggy.

"Probably can't afford to pay. This isn't the wealthiest part of town."

Lexie had a vision of Tremaine tending the sick in the confines of their tenements and she swallowed hard. The utter uselessness of her life engulfed her in a wave of deep misery.

As they drove home she stared blindly out at the passing landscape. One way or another she was going to realize her dream, she thought with determination. She would not become a useless ornament like the other girls at Miss Everly's School. She was going to make something of herself. She was going to make a difference. She was going to become a horse doctor.

Chapter Eight

A bitter wind drove against Tremaine's face as he wrapped Fortune's reins around the post outside Jenny McBride's rooming house. Fortune snorted and lowered his head against the pounding force, but Tremaine had no time to see to the horse's comfort. He bounded up the stairs and threw open the front door.

Jenny came from the kitchen, her black hair hanging in a rope over one shoulder, a bowl of steaming water in her hands. "She's real bad," she said tonelessly.

"Get someone to see to my horse," Tremaine answered tersely. "Where is she?"

"Upstairs. In her room."

"What about Marshfield? He's a doctor. Why hasn't he been called?"

"She won't see him. She's ashamed. That's why I sent you that message. She knows you."

Tremaine swore under his breath. His eyes felt scratchy and red from lack of sleep. Twenty hours of straight work and now this. He was so furious with Jace Garrett that he didn't know if he could stand bringing Garrett's bastard child into the world.

Tremaine took the bowl of water from Jenny's hands and resolutely mounted the stairs. It was ominously quiet in the gloomy hallway. Remembering Betsy's room from his last visit, he walked quickly toward it, balancing the water as he knocked softly on the door. A faint moan sounded.

Tremaine let himself into the darkened room. A lantern sat in the corner, throwing flickering shadows over the sparse furniture. Betsy lay writhing on the bed, her fingers tangled in the damp sheets.

He set the bowl of water on the bureau and placed a dry palm against her moist forehead. "Betsy, it's Tremaine."

"Jace," she murmured brokenly. "I want Jace. Please, please . . ."

"Jace isn't here," he said calmly. "I'm going to help you with your baby."

"No, you can't. You mustn't!" She was crying. "I want a midwife!"

Tremaine didn't have the heart to tell her that no midwife could help her now. Her contractions had all but stopped and she was bleeding. He'd seen one other case like this before and despite all his efforts, both mother and child had died.

He examined her quickly and discovered the child was breech and nowhere near delivery. He suspected the baby was already dead.

Jenny came in the room, hovering silently, anxiously, by his shoulder. He turned to her. "Get Garrett," he said grimly.

"He can't help her. He's—"

"Get him anyway."

Jenny read the silent message in Tremaine's ominous face. She nodded and left the room. Tremaine reached into his black bag and pulled out a bottle of laudanum. It was precious little to do for her. But he was going to try to birth that baby himself and he needed her relaxed to do it.

"Drink this," he told Betsy tersely, lifting her head, fairly pushing the liquid past her slack lips. With a silent prayer he set his jaw and concentrated on the task at hand.

* * *

Jace stood at the bar in the Half Moon Saloon, content to watch the farmers, storekeepers, and millworkers of Rock Springs gamble away their livings. It was nothing to him. He had no desire to gamble and less to conspire with the townfolk. His only purpose in being at the saloon was to make certain Conrad Templeton wasn't cheating on the receipts. The Half Moon was a joint venture with Garrett Enterprises, and Jace meant his partner to know who held the reins.

"I've shown ya all of 'em," Conrad said, wiping the bar, but Jace thought the twitch at the corners of the man's mouth, more like a spasmodic shudder than an expression of amusement, declared there was far more to learn.

"You showed me the receipts through September," Jace said mildly. "It's nearly December."

"I ain't got 'em tallied yet."

"Tally them, Conrad." Jace pulled a thin cheroot out of his pocket and sighted down the length of it at the nervous manager. Conrad Templeton paled.

"Yessir," he muttered.

The door to the saloon opened, swirling the smoke from a dozen cigars, sending a chilling, whipping wind throughout the stuffy room. Protests rose from the gamblers at the tables and the whores who were gathered along the upper balcony.

Jace squinted through the smoke to see Jenny McBride, her hair down, her voluptuous curves wrapped in a dark cloak, her hands clutching it as if she had something to hide. His blood stirred and he inwardly swore. He didn't really like Jenny. She was trouble in any phase of his life. She wouldn't sell her land and she'd put all kinds of strange notions in Betsy's head. Jace wished the both of them would just evaporate.

Spying him, Jenny hustled her way to the bar. Jace inwardly groaned, but was enough of a gentleman to straighten as she came beside him.

"What can I do for you?" Jace asked before she could speak.

"Come to the rooming house. Betsy is—having her baby."

She spoke low and intensely. Jace was gratified that she

hadn't made this announcement to the room at large; he was infuriated that she should alert him at all. Worse, to demand that he come!

"Jenny, I have no more intention of coming to your rooming house than of letting Conrad Templeton cheat me out of three months' income."

"Tremaine Danner's taking care of her. He told me to bring you."

Jace froze inside but only for a moment. "You can tell Dr. Danner to go straight to hell."

Jenny sighed and ran a trembling hand over her face. "She may not make it, Jace."

"Then there's nothing I can do, is there?" he answered softly, soberly. He regretted what had happened, but Jace was a man who firmly believed in fate.

"You're really a bastard," said Jenny with loathing, and she twisted on her heel and marched out of the saloon.

Jace waited for Conrad Templeton to return, but his concentration had been sorely tested by Jenny's announcement. So Danner was interfering in his life again. Damn the man. How the hell was he ever going to stand Tremaine being his brother-in-law?

Jace had to spend several long moments remembering Lexie's innocently sensual body—and the acres of Danner land—to convince himself the trade-off was worth it.

Conrad Templeton returned, carrying a black receipt book. His pallor had gone from white to gray. He set the book down on the counter and swiped a hand across the moisture that had formed on his upper lip.

Jace glanced down at the figures with deceptive casualness. He had an agile, intelligent mind and it didn't take him long to find just where Conrad was skimming. Lifting his eyes to Templeton's worried ones, he felt another stirring of cold air whisk through the room. "Conrad," he said silkily, "did you really expect me to overlook these—er—financial discrepancies?"

Conrad's mouth twitched furiously as his gaze moved from Jace's eyes to somewhere behind his left ear.

"You didn't show up." Tremaine Danner's icy voice was dangerously quiet.

Jace felt the menace of those few words right down to his

toes. He glanced backward and encountered a pair of stony blue eyes and a hard, slashing mouth. Tremaine's chin just ached to be smashed with Jace's fist, but Jace was no imprudent fool. If he were to lash out, retribution would be swift and sure. "I was busy," he said calmly, lighting his nearly forgotten cheroot with a gold-plated lighter.

"Too busy to keep the mother of your child from dying?"

Tremaine spoke in a harsh whisper. Jace sat frozen, the cheroot burning close to his fingertips. "Betsy's dead?" he asked dazedly.

For an answer Tremaine grabbed him by his lapels. "Not quite," he muttered. "No thanks to you."

There was no pretense of civility, Jace realized with growing dread. Tremaine's eyes snapped with blue fire. There was a convulsive tension in his fingers that spoke clearly of his state of mind. Jace had never been in a more precarious position.

The room fell silent behind them. In a detached part of his mind, Jace raged furiously that no one—not one individual—saw fit to help him while this driven maniac faced him down.

"Look, Danner," he began reasonably, but Tremaine's hands tightened, and he hauled Jace off his stool in one smooth, deadly motion. The fury in his eyes prompted the gamblers to collectively make silent bets on the outcome of the brewing fight—Tremaine Danner was heavily favored.

"I'd like to kill you with my bare hands," Tremaine snarled. "You're the lowest form of coward I've ever met, and I'll be damned if I let Lexie marry you."

Jace could have pointed out that that was Lexie's choice, not his, but instead said merely, "What about your Hippocratic oath, Doctor? I don't think murder would be—"

"Shut up," Tremaine said softly.

Jace's dignity took a terrible beating as the eminent Dr. Danner dragged him by his expensive wool suit out into the street. He was flung into the frozen mud outside the saloon, which saved his clothes but scraped his cheek. Jace had never been so angered or humiliated. He sprang to his feet, intent on taking Tremaine down a notch or two and damn the consequences.

To his surprise Danner simply leaned against the saloon's

rail, a wry smile on his lips. "You fit in well down there in the street, Jason. Part of the muck and slime."

Jace's eyes gleamed with treachery. "You just earned yourself an enemy, Danner. One you're going to be sorry you made."

"We were never anything but enemies."

"We're going to be brothers-in-law," he said through his teeth. Tremaine tensed involuntarily and Jace, who'd always suspected Lexie was his soft spot, relished this small triumph. "I'm going to marry Lexie regardless of what you say or do. Eliza's for it and so is Lexie. Seems Lexie wants me to make an honest woman out of her," Jace lied with ease. "The last time I saw Lexie she was on her knees, begging me to marry her." Surprised emotion crossed Tremaine Danner's face, and Jace added softly, "You know, I like it when she begs."

Tremaine was on him in a flash and Jace suffered a numbing mist of red pain as he lay at the mercy of Danner's fists. He tried to fight back but he was no match for Tremaine's superior strength and endurance. Danner had always been tough and wild; Jace had wisely given him a wide berth. But he'd goaded him tonight and while he flailed around, hoping to provide some injury, he wondered if Tremaine might not actually kill him.

Then suddenly Tremaine stopped, his eyes glittering with such inhuman fury that Jace's sense of triumph increased. Danner's weakness over Lexie was greater than he'd thought! Laughing inside, Jace wiped blood from his mouth with the back of his hand.

"Get up," Tremaine snarled, yanking Jace to his feet, trying to stand him on his rubbery legs. Dimly, Jace became aware of the group of watchers hovering on the plankwood sidewalk outside the saloon.

"Whad're ya gonna do now?" Jace asked through thickened lips.

Moments later he was sorry he'd asked, when Tremaine dragged him like a man possessed toward the rushing plummet of Fool's Falls. Amidst catcalls and laughter he was shoved under the thundering torrent, battered and tossed, his breath pounded from his lungs. When he finally crawled limply to the side of the pool, spitting and coughing, he saw

Danner standing at the edge of Silver Stream like the dreaded demon he was.

Jace hated Tremaine Danner with a new and violent passion. Hated him. Swearing, sputtering, shivering, he glared at Tremaine's now impassive face. He was going to make the bastard pay. Pay terribly. He thought of Lexie. I've got you, Danner, he crowed to himself triumphantly.

It was time to ask Joseph Danner for Lexie's hand in marriage.

"J'ai, tu as, il a, elle a . . ." Lexie slammed the book shut and closed her eyes, committing to memory the conjugation of the French verb "to have."

"If you go over that one more time I shall have an attack of the vapors and faint dead away at your feet," Ella intoned dramatically. She lounged, as ever, on the bed in only her camisole and drawers.

Lexie smiled wryly. "Why do we have to learn French? I've never met anyone who speaks it, and I'm certainly not going to use it on the farm."

"It's culture, my dear," Ella said in an excellent imitation of Miss Everly's voice. "Women of this area are abysmally lacking in culture. Professor DuLac is knowledgeable in so many areas. Learn from him. Work with him."

Professor DuLac, the only male instructor at Miss Everly's School, was the most self-righteous stuffed shirt Lexie had ever encountered. "I *have* learned," Lexie remarked. "In fact, yesterday I learned how to swear in French as well as English."

"Really?" Ella was intrigued. "How?"

"Sacre bleu," Lexie said, pleased. "It was written on the inside leaf of my book and I asked Professor DuLac what it meant. Direct translation is 'sacred blue,' but apparently it's not the kind of comment a lady would make. Professor DuLac turned purple, right to the crown of his bald head, and then confiscated my book." She held up her leather-bound volume. "This is a new one."

Ella laughed. "Oh, I can't wait to try it out! DuLac is such a pompous ass. Thank the Lord I finally have a reason to enjoy his class!"

"Only a few more classes and we get to go home for winter

break," said Lexie with a happy sigh, tossing her French book on her bed.

"Who cares about home? The Winter Ball is next Friday." Ella reached over and snatched up Lexie's book, balancing it on her head as she walked carefully from one end of the room to the other.

Lexie glanced out the window to the cold, gray day beyond. "Mmmm, that's right," she said distractedly.

The book slid off Ella's head and crashed to the floor with a thump. "Has Jace said he'll come yet?"

"He's too busy," Lexie answered lightly. She didn't want Ella to know she hadn't asked him.

"What about your brother?"

"Brother?" Lexie repeated stupidly.

"The blond one? Or are they all blond? He's certainly a handsome devil."

Lexie was relieved Ella meant Harrison, yet why she should have even considered it might be Tremaine was ridiculous, since Tremaine had never shown up at the school while the students had been there. "You must mean Harrison."

"Are all your brothers as handsome as he is?"

Lexie grinned. "I'm afraid so."

"Good Lord." Ella pretended to faint across her bed. "It's not fair to have such a family. How do you ever find a man to compare?"

Lexie pulled the green taffeta gown with the raised pattern from her closet and held it in front of her. The neckline dipped daringly low. "It's a problem," she admitted, thinking of Tremaine.

"You're not going alone, are you? Good Lord, Lexie, this is our one chance to do the asking!" Ella struggled to a sitting position.

Lexie had been thinking of skipping the Winter Ball altogether. She didn't know any of the young men who came to the school to meet a Miss Everly girl. She'd made a point of steering clear of them. But now she considered Ella's suggestion. "I could ask Harrison, I suppose. Although I don't know how much of a dancer he is."

Glancing at Ella, Lexie was surprised by the spasm of tension on her friend's face. "Ella! What's the matter?"

"Nothing." She drew a long breath and lay back on the bed. "I've just had these pains in my stomach."

"In your stomach? Where?" Lexie was beside her in an instant.

"All over," Ella admitted. "Wait, now. It's passing. I think it's something I ate."

Lexie, who knew nothing of diagnostic medicine but had a keen instinctual understanding all the same, could tell by Ella's pallor and reaction that this was something far more serious. "Maybe we should tell Miss Everly and have her call a doctor."

"No." Ella shook her head stubbornly. Her eyes fluttered closed and she sighed. "She might keep me home from the Winter Ball and it's the only worthwhile event this school sponsors. I couldn't bear living through this year without one taste of freedom and fun."

"But if you're sick . . ."

"I'm not that sick." The faintest glimmer of a smile curved her lips. "Nobody's that sick."

Lexie wasn't convinced. She sat on the edge of the bed beside her friend. "When the horses have stomach ailments, they have to be watched carefully. It could turn into something serious and sometimes, if it isn't treated early on, they have to be put down."

Ella laughed shakily. "Good Lord, Lexie. Are you suggesting I'm a horse?"

"Well, you're acting as thick-headed as one." Lexie smiled. If Ella could laugh, then her condition might not be as serious as Lexie had first imagined.

"If I have to, I'll crawl to that Winter Ball. How often does a 'lady' get to invite a man out? This is the one and only time it'll be proper."

"All right, all right." Lexie tucked the covers over Ella's shoulders. "I won't breathe a word to anyone. We can always dance together," she added with a grin, which drew a sick moan from Ella.

For the next several days Lexie abided by her promise to keep Ella's stomach ailment a secret. But two nights before the Winter Ball, Lexie was awakened in the dead of night by soft whimpers of misery emanating from the other bed.

"Ella?" Lexie asked, groping in the dark for the lantern. Miss Everly's School for Young Ladies had been built before the advent of gaslights, and kerosene lanterns were still used for illumination.

The oak floor was frigidly cold beneath Lexie's bare feet. Another moan sounded from the bed. Lexie lit the lantern with cold-numbed fingers and was alarmed to see her friend doubled over, writhing, and retching into the chamberpot beside her bed.

"Ella!" she cried.

"Help," she choked out. "Help." Her face was a torment of pain.

Lexie didn't wait. She threw on her clothes, pulling on the cherished Turkish split skirt and a cotton shirtwaist. She tossed a cloak over her shoulders and said, "I'll call Miss Everly. I'm getting a doctor."

She buttoned her shoes, hopping on one foot down the hallway. Pounding on Miss Everly's door, she nearly awakened the entire floor before she remembered Miss Everly was spending the night at her sister's home, helping care for her children while the poor woman gave birth to her eleventh child.

"What's wrong with you?" Celeste Monteith complained, poking her head out of her room. Blond hair tumbled fetchingly over her shoulder, and were it not for the perpetual sneer on her porcelain face she would be a very beautiful girl indeed. "You could wake the dead."

"Celeste, Ella's sick and I need someone to take care of her."

The other girl recoiled, wrapping her silken robe more tightly around her small bosom. "Call Hildegarde."

Lexie was thinking fast. "You call Hildegarde. I'm going for the doctor."

"What? *How?* Good Lord, Lexie. What *have* you got on?"

Lexie's feet carried her swiftly down the carved oak stairway. She ran to the front door and was in the process of shifting the bolt when her plight truly occurred to her. Biting her lip, she considered running down the street to the small livery where Cyril, the groomsman for Miss Everly's School, kept horses for them and for several other nearby enterprises.

A woman alone on the streets of Portland? Miss Everly would die of shock!

Lexie cared not a fig for propriety but she wasn't foolhardy. There were dangers a single woman might face in the dark city streets. She hurried to the kitchen, pulled a magnificent knife from the nail above the washboard, and unlocked the back door, stepping into a bitterly cold, moon-washed, clear winter night.

Tugging the hood of her cloak over her head, Lexie clung to the knife in her hand, skirting the main street and moving like a shadow across and through other properties. She climbed one fence and heard the low, bristling snarl of a dog, but she moved valiantly onward.

She reached the livery in remarkably rapid time, appearing in the warm, glowing doorway like a wraith. Cyril, who was sitting on a bucket, half-nodding off to sleep, snapped to attention with a surprised grunt when Lexie spoke.

"Hello, Cyril. My name's Lexington Danner. I attend Miss Everly's School."

"Tarnation, girl!" he sputtered. "What are you doing out here?"

"I need a horse to ride," she said simply.

He looked stunned, even amazed, then suspicious. "Ah'm not authorized to let horses to Miss Everly's students without her permission, miss. 'Specially not this time of the evenin'."

"One of the girls is sick. I'm going for the doctor."

"If'n that's the case, I'll send a message along to the doctor, but you stay right here."

"I'm sorry," Lexie said firmly. "There isn't time. I appreciate your position, but I want a horse." Digging into the pocket of her skirt, she withdrew a handful of shining silver dollars, every bit of cash she possessed. "I'll hire one, if you can't give me Miss Everly's."

He ran his hand through his hair, rumpling it until it stood on end. "It's not right," he muttered, his eyes glued to the glinting coins.

"Take it. All of it," Lexie coaxed. "And give me a horse and buggy I can handle."

"There ain't no buggies. They're all hired out."

She thrust the money into his slackened hand, shoving

past him, examining the horseflesh with a practiced eye that would have given Cyril a start had he known her experience. At the end of the row stood a beautiful, quivering stallion not unlike Tantrum. Lexie chose him.

"Stop, miss!" the groomsman ordered. "That un'll never let you ride him!"

"Show me one that will, then!"

She snatched a bridle from its peg on a nearby post. Cyril rubbed his jaw and shook his head. "Gentle Dawn might do ya," he said, pointing to a petite swaybacked mare who looked half-asleep.

Lexie adjusted the bridle straps to the stallion's head. "I don't have time," she said, snatching a crop from the bench nearby. Holding the crop between her teeth, she climbed up the stable rails and onto the stallion's bare back.

"I can't letcha take him, miss," Cyril said firmly, admiration and concern glowing from his eyes in equal measure. He approached the stallion with caution. "He's too hard to control. It would be suicide."

"Then what's he doing in your stable? Someone must be able to handle him."

"Only a strong man with a will of iron!"

Lexie recalled Ella's twisting pain and said simply, "Move aside. I've paid you. Now I'm going."

Cyril wasn't used to young chits talking back to him, but then neither was he familiar with the way this woman handled a horse. Knowing he was bound to pay, yet equally aware that the girl had overpaid him enough to make the gamble worth it, he opened the box and led the black devil with the young temptress out of the livery. "God looks after his own fools," he muttered as Lexie worked to hold the mincing stallion in check. She wasn't certain whether Cyril meant her or himself.

The black stallion's hooves rustled in the straw on the livery floor, then they rang on the cobblestone street. It was quiet in this section of the city. Gaslights shed watery ribbons of light across the stones. Lexie, whose belief in her own infallibility was waning with each forward move of the stallion's sleek muscles, headed in the direction of the hospital where Tremaine worked. If there was a closer doctor, she didn't know his address. Besides, there would be less explanations with Tremaine. She only hoped he was there.

The stallion moved with an effortless stride, but he chewed and moved the bit, his ears flicking back and forth, as if he hadn't quite figured out his rider. He sidestepped every chance he could, tossing his head, but Lexie kept up a soft, low cooing, gently guiding him down the streets.

As she neared the poorer section of Portland's waterfront, there was more activity in the streets. Several times she heard the murmur of male voices as she passed dark alleyways and saw the red pulsing tips of cigars. Lexie's courage seeped steadily away. Her heartbeat accelerated. Her stomach churned. The knife in her pocket was a welcome companion.

"Hey, there," a drunken male voice called, and she saw a man stumble after her into the street, chasing the stallion. The black horse shimmied and squealed, and Lexie, whose blood ran like icewater through her veins, let up on the reins.

"Go," she whispered and the magnificent horse surged forward with unexpected freedom.

Tears blurred her vision and the horse clattered along the Willamette's riverbank. She clung on and suddenly realized she didn't recognize the area. Her arms ached from the effort of slowing the spirited stallion, and when she finally got him stopped she felt the heave and fall of his magnificent chest.

This street was better than the one Harrison had driven her down, but the unfamiliar buildings warned her she was nowhere near her destination. She walked the stallion steadily, keeping the river to her right. Had she gone too far? Why, oh why, hadn't she paid better attention?

Suddenly a hand snaked out and grabbed the reins. A face leered at her. "Well, well, well," it said. "What have we here?"

Lexie didn't speak. Perhaps, safely hidden beneath her cloak, the stranger wouldn't realize her sex. Silently, she pulled back on the reins in a furious duel with the grinning maniac. He was missing teeth and he reeked of nameless odors, the strongest being a sour ale.

The stallion reared and thrashed. Lexie nearly lost her seat. With more energy than sense she drew the crop and hit her assailant across the face.

"Bitch!" he screamed and Lexie screamed, too. The black stallion wrenched itself free and bolted. Lexie wrapped her arms around his straining neck. Her heart stuck in her throat. She couldn't breathe. She let him have his head until strength returned to her shaking arms.

"Oh, you beauty," she murmured over and over again, aware that, had she chosen a gentler horse, her fate might have been far less favorable.

Long moments later, she carefully guided the stallion, who was tired and in a nervous lather, around a last curve. The river ran serenely by. The streets looked more familiar, and Lexie doubled back, coming upon the whitewashed hospital so unexpectedly that she emitted a cry of relief and thankfulness.

"Can I help you, miss?" a startled voice sounded from Lexie's left.

She glanced down and saw a young man who was more surprised at seeing Lexie than she was at seeing him. She smiled tremulously, realizing his job was to take care of the horses. "I need a doctor," she explained, sliding from the stallion's back. "Could you take care of him for me?"

"That's my job, miss. What's his name?"

"I don't know!" she answered a bit hysterically, then ran up the steps to the hospital.

A different receptionist was on duty. She regarded Lexie with round, wary eyes. "Yes?" she asked.

"Is Dr. Danner in? Please." Lexie drew back her cloak and loosened it at her neck. Her teeth began to chatter as much from nerves as cold.

"Yes, ma'am, he is."

"Could you call him? I have—there's an emergency. I need help."

The receptionist started to speak, then clamped her mouth shut and walked calmly down the hallway.

Tremaine stared down at the dead man lying on the operating table. Five bulletholes in his chest and Silas Monteith swore he'd killed him in self-defense! This was the second man who'd gone against Monteith and got himself shot. The first man had survived. This fellow wasn't so lucky.

"Dr. Danner?"

He turned toward the voice. Standing at the door, the receptionist scrupulously avoided looking at the man on the table. "There's a young woman asking for you. She seems desperate."

"I'll be there in a minute."

Tremaine glanced at the patient another long moment. "Cover him," he ordered tersely to the nurse standing by, then swept up his jacket and headed for the door.

It seemed as if eons passed before Tremaine came striding toward Lexie. Seeing him again was like a blow to the stomach. Her knees turned to water. In his familiar leather jacket and breeches, his dark hair falling forward, his eyes narrowed with concern, his ground-devouring strides reminding her of the sleek, wild stallion she'd left with the livery boy, Lexie wanted to fling herself in his strong, powerful arms.

He stopped short in amazement. "Lexie! What in God's name are you doing here?"

For a moment she couldn't speak. All she could think of was his body hot against hers and the drowning, melting heat of his kiss. The sensual curve of his lips and the blue of his eyes made her remember that moment in a wave of supreme desire.

"Lexie," he said again, his expression changing as he reached for her arm.

She trembled. "I'm—I need help."

That stopped him cold. He regarded her in a way she didn't understand. "What kind of help?" he demanded, gripping her shoulders as if he knew her traitorous legs were about to collapse beneath her.

"My roommate, Ella, has a chronic stomachache. She's been sick for days, but tonight she's in agony."

"Is the pain all over or localized?" he asked crisply.

"Localized."

"Right side or left?"

Lexie thought hard. "Right."

Tremaine glanced over his shoulder, then looked back at her in a gentle way. "Stay here, all right? I need to get my bag."

Lexie nodded. When his hands left her shoulders, however, she had to fight for balance. Tremaine returned momentarily, his black bag in hand. He conferred with the receptionist, then led Lexie to the door.

"Who did you come with?" he asked, looking around with a frown as they stepped into the inky night.

"I came alone."

His brows lifted. "Where's your buggy, or carriage?"

She gestured feebly in the direction of the hospital stables, and Tremaine, his hand firm on her arm, led her toward the lighted interior.

The black stallion had the nerve to nicker when he saw her. Lexie rubbed his nose, glad to see the stable boy had taken such excellent care of him.

"You rode this horse to the hospital?" Tremaine asked in a soft, disbelieving voice.

"Yes."

"All alone?"

The way his aquamarine eyes coolly threatened her brought a dryness to her throat. "Do we have to discuss this now?"

"No." Ordering the stable boy to bring round his buggy, Tremaine swiftly changed from the ominous older "brother" to the clinical doctor. Lexie was glad to see Fortune and stroked the mild-mannered, big-hearted stallion as he was harnessed to the buggy.

They were well on their way to Miss Everly's School before Lexie cleared her throat and said, "I'll have to bring that black stallion back tomorrow."

"I'll do it," Tremaine snapped.

"I know you're mad at me because I came alone—"

"Mad at you?" He turned his darkly handsome head to glare at her and Lexie inwardly shrank. Outwardly, she lifted her chin a fraction and met his gaze defiantly. His drawling "Your talent for underestimation continues, I see" only increased her ire.

Lexie's worry over Ella was all that kept her from launching on a lengthy, and patently untrue, discourse on how she was able to take care of herself perfectly well, no matter the circumstances. Instead she sat by Tremaine's side, biting back her annoyance and enjoying his companionship nevertheless.

He took a different route to Miss Everly's School; a much more traveled one, Lexie realized with chagrin. She would have been much safer on the main streets, but she hadn't been aware she had a choice. Shooting a glance toward Tremaine's grim countenance, she decided to keep that bit of information to herself.

Lantern light quivered strangely from the upstairs windows as Tremaine pulled his buggy to the front steps. Fortune, disciplined animal that he was, simply stood in quiet acceptance as Tremaine and Lexie entered the monstrous brick building.

No one was about on the first floor. Lexie gathered her split skirt in two fists and started up the stairs, never noticing the amusement that lurked around Tremaine's eyes as he noticed her apparel. Eliza might believe Lexie was made for finer things, he thought humorously, but she would never convince Lexie of that.

As Tremaine reached the upper landing, he was aware of an assortment of young, feminine heads, whispering in groups. They looked up at his arrival, their mouths collectively dropping open.

"You're the doctor?" one asked, disbelieving.

What had they expected? he wondered. "Yes."

Lexie's hand found his arm and he was dragged into a room. Once inside he forgot his bemusement at the strangeness of the girls' school and strode directly to the moaning girl on the bed. An older woman with a pinched face was leaning over her. Now she glanced upward, blinking at the sight of him.

"Who are you?" she demanded.

"I'm Dr. Danner," he explained absently, thrusting her out of his mind even before he finished speaking. Lexie had not underestimated the seriousness here, however, he realized, noticing the sheen of moisture on this girl's skin, the shallow, painful breaths.

"We've sent for Mistress Everly," the woman said haughtily, pulling the covers over Ella's perspiring half-dressed form. "She's coming straight here. We should wait until she arrives to take further action."

"Ma'am, you can wait till hell freezes over for all I care," drawled Tremaine, folding back the blanket. "But I'm going to treat this patient now."

"Well, I never!" Hildegarde stumped from the room, thought better of it, and marched back to keep an eagle eye on Tremaine.

And that's your whole problem, Tremaine thought.

Lexie hovered anxiously nearby. She knew it was bad. How bad she expected to read in Tremaine's face, but his expression was implacable. His eyes were gentle and compassionate, however, when he searched Ella's.

"Where's the pain now?" Tremaine asked Ella.

"Right here!" Panting, she pointed to a spot on the right side of her abdomen.

Tremaine parted Ella's camisole from her drawers, ignoring the outraged sucking of Hildegarde's breath between her teeth. Lexie shot Hildegarde a furious look. The woman's sensibilities had no place here.

Ella cried out at Tremaine's touch and Hildegarde was so unnerved that she murmured, "Forgive us, Father. We are mere mortals who cannot appreciate your wisdom and—"

Lexie closed her ears and touched Tremaine's arm inquiringly. He glanced at her, read the unspoken questions in her eyes, and said, "I'd bet on appendicitis, but as to how far the condition has progressed, it's anyone's guess. Her pain's incredibly localized. She can practically put her finger on it."

"Is that a good sign or a bad sign?"

Tremaine said simply, "It's got to come out."

On the floor below, a minor commotion was ensuing. As Tremaine was gathering Ella in his arms, Hildegarde rushed from the room, wringing her hands. "Miss Everly!" she called down the dimly lit stairway. "Upstairs, please!"

It was indeed Miss Everly. She appeared at the bottom of the stairs, her normal fixed smile disrupted, her gray hair hastily tossed into a bun. Upon seeing Ella in Tremaine's arms and subjected to Hildegarde's babbling tale of Lexie's exploits, the headmistress demanded, "Put that child down.

I've sent a message to the school's doctor and he'll be here soon. He knows when one of my girls is feeling poorly."

Tremaine's harsh laughter straightened Miss Everly's already ramrod straight back. "I'm taking her to the hospital, ma'am."

"You most certainly are not," she returned wrathfully. "Ella has been entrusted to my care and her parents—"

"Won't thank you if she dies." Tremaine shouldered his way past her.

Lexie tried to follow but Miss Everly's fingers clawed into her shoulder. "Stop him!" she commanded, her voice warbling with self-righteous indignation. "You brought him in here. Stop him!"

"He's a doctor, Miss Everly," Lexie explained in irritation.

"And a damn good-looking one," a voice said from up above.

Miss Everly rounded on her students, who wisely and quietly shuffled back to their rooms. Then she rushed after Tremaine. "If you do not release her this instant, I shall alert the police, young man! Your abduction is criminal, to say the least. How do I know where you're taking her? *Put her down!*"

If the situation hadn't been so desperate, Lexie would have laughed out loud. When Tremaine turned to glare coldly down at Miss Everly, Lexie had to admire the woman's courage. "You may come with us, if you'd like," Tremaine said in a velvet voice, "but if you utter one word along the way I'll drop you out on the street."

"You are no gentleman, sir!"

"Thank God for that."

Lexie held the front door wide, catching Tremaine's gaze and sharing a silent moment of mirth with him. Miss Everly strode behind them, climbed into her own waiting coach, Hildegarde at her heels, and commanded the hired coachman to take her to Willamette Infirmary. But when Lexie put a foot on the step of Tremaine's buggy, Miss Everly came rushing back to her.

"Miss Danner, it would be in your best interests to return inside. Your reputation has been so tarnished, I can't begin to think how to put it right. You should never have let a strange man into your room! I am shocked and outraged."

"Tremaine is my brother," Lexie said calmly, mentally crossing her fingers at the deliberate misconception. She had a feeling that if Miss Everly knew the truth she would believe Lexie's soul was on a straight path to damnation.

Miss Everly's brows raised. "Your brother?" She collected herself as only a true lady can and said, "Well, I'm most relieved to hear it. But that doesn't mean you can come with us."

Lexie had suffered as much hypocrisy as she could stand. She simply turned her back to Miss Everly and climbed onto the buggy seat next to Tremaine, slipping her arm around Ella. Tremaine slapped Fortune's back and the horse surged forward in a gallop.

Lexie clung to the sides of the rattling buggy. Ella's head lay on her shoulder and the girl shuddered and moaned. "A few minutes more," Lexie soothed, stroking her hair. "Just a few more minutes."

The hospital looked exactly the same: a white building against a star-studded ebony sky. Other buildings loomed dark around it. Tremaine brought Fortune to a stamping halt, twin streams of air shooting from the horse's nostrils. The stable boy took Fortune without a word, and Tremaine carried Ella through the front door.

Once inside Lexie realized she'd been wrong to think nothing had changed. Now the foyer of the building was a beehive of activity.

"A railway accident with a carriage and a shooting at a private home," the receptionist explained breathlessly to Lexie's startled gaze as Tremaine strode down the gaslit linoleum hallway, Ella's limp form in his arms, one of her arms swinging in painful abandon.

Lexie tried to follow, but in this she was thwarted. "I'm sorry, ma'am," a nurse in a volunteer's striped uniform said, as she held Lexie's arm.

"But Ella is my roommate," she protested.

"She's Dr. Danner's patient."

"You don't understand. My name is Lexington Danner. I'm Dr. Danner's—stepsister," Lexie explained anxiously.

"That doesn't mean you can follow Dr. Danner. He's taking that young woman to surgery."

Lexie was forced to sit on a narrow couch beside a man in a knife-edge-creased suit who sat casually elegant, one shoe propped on his other knee. She felt his eyes on her but didn't turn his way. She had no more interest in casual conversation than she did in behaving like a so-called lady.

But her companion had no such qualms. He smiled gallantly and said, "You're Dr. Danner's stepsister."

"That's correct." Lexie groaned inwardly as Miss Everly, along with Hildegarde, stepped into the foyer.

"I thought Dr. Danner wasn't a native of Portland."

Lexie glanced at him, trying to discern his interest, but it appeared this was just small talk. "We're from Rock Springs," she said a trifle shortly.

"Ahhh . . ." He nodded and grew quiet.

At that moment Miss Everly descended upon Lexie, her mouth a line of displeasure and disappointment. Lexie drew in a long breath and prepared herself for the list of transgressions about to be laid on her head.

Maybe she'll expel me! she thought with suppressed joy.

"Lexington," the stiff headmistress intoned gravely. "I'm afraid we're going to have to restate our goals. From now on you and I shall have twice-weekly meetings in my office. A book on etiquette would not be inappropriate."

Lexie managed a weary nod. Her bad luck was holding firm.

Chapter Nine

∞

Victor Flynne surreptitiously studied the attractive young woman seated next to him. Her blond hair tousled fetchingly around her shoulders, and her eyes—the color and sparkle of emeralds—were trained with unwavering dedication on the reception nurse.

Casually, he lifted the scattered remnants of yesterday's newspaper and snapped the pages open. Lexington Danner, he mused. Lexington. Danner. He'd come to the hospital tonight with the hopes of gleaning information about the hush-hush shooting that had taken place this evening at the home of mega-shipbuilder Silas Monteith. But instead he'd met this striking beauty, and her name struck a chord inside his quick investigator's mind.

At that moment a giant of a man with sleek gray hair strode through the hospital doors. "My name's Silas Monteith," he said with gruff authority to the receptionist. "I want to inquire about a patient."

Victor Flynne, whose power to fade into the background was one of his main assets, dipped his felt hat lower over his nose and abruptly turned his attention to the newcomer. For the moment the names Lexington and Danner were shoved aside, filed away to be reviewed later. Victor had bigger fish to fry. Silas Monteith was a veritable goldmine of blackmail possibilities.

With barely constrained anger, Tremaine watched Dr. Peter Caldwell, one of the hospital's staff doctors, drop ether unhurriedly, as if he had all the time in the world. The man seemed oblivious to the unconscious woman on the table. He acted inured to everything around him, his face bored, his methods meticulous and nerve-wrenchingly slow.

"Is she under yet?" Tremaine asked with acid asperity.

"Yeah, she's under."

As if answering Tremaine's question, Ella suddenly turned her head, mumbling, "Whad you say?"

"Pour on more ether," Tremaine gritted through his teeth.

Caldwell shot him a surly look but did as he was told. Tremaine sighed inwardly and flexed his fingers on the scalpel. He understood Caldwell's problem: the young doctor didn't like taking orders from someone not directly employed by Willamette Infirmary. Since Tremaine was only affiliated with the hospital, having never signed on as staff doctor, he was something of an outsider and therefore treated with a reserved kind of respect.

Tremaine's decision had been more a lack of decision—he really would have preferred being a country doctor—and it was this very indifference that made the other doctors resent and mistrust him. Why, they wondered, should he scorn a position most of them coveted? The fact that he was an excellent anatomist and an even better surgeon irritated the already sore wound. It didn't help that he preferred treating patients outside the hospital; people who could not afford a physician's care.

"She's under," Peter snapped again, his jaw tight.

This time Tremaine double-checked, just to be sure, and earned himself a glance of incredible virulence from his contemporary. Ignoring it, he made the incision in Ella's abdomen swiftly and accurately. An infected appendix often started out as a general malaise of the stomach region, but if the pain became localized, so localized that the patient felt capable of putting her finger on it, the surgeon had better move damn quickly. If the appendix should burst, the poisons it spread through the peritoneum were nearly always fatal. Tremaine had never seen a patient survive a ruptured appendix.

Peter came around the table, craning his head to see what Tremaine was doing.

"Get back over there!" Tremaine growled. "God help you if this patient wakes up before I'm finished!"

"Well, hell," Peter muttered, his nape a brilliant shade of crimson. He returned to Ella's head, his back stiff with outrage.

The nurse handed Tremaine instruments and sponges with the unspoken efficiency that indicated long practice. Tremaine thanked her with his eyes as she traded arterial clamps for the scalpel. Thank God he'd finally gotten someone competent.

Once Ella's vessels were closed off, Tremaine searched for the appendix. It wasn't hard to find. Red-hot and swollen, it lay just where Ella had pointed. The scalpel was placed in Tremaine's hand and he deftly removed the appendix, trading the scalpel for a needle and thread. Swiftly and carefully he stitched the incision, undid the clamps, then sewed each muscular layer of Ella's abdomen closed.

"Well done, Doctor," the nurse murmured.

Tremaine, who'd barely had time to remove his jacket before surgery had commenced, grinned at her, his white cotton shirt splattered with blood. "Thank you," he said. Peter Caldwell left the operating room without a word.

Tremaine's thoughts instantly turned to Lexie. He washed his hands, grimaced at the state of his clothes, then threw on his leather jacket. He could change later. Right now he wanted to see if Lexie was still in the waiting room.

She was there all right, hollow-eyed and frightened, her hands clasped between her knees. As soon as she saw him she bounded to her feet.

"Is Ella all right?" Lexie demanded anxiously, her green eyes peering at him in a way that demanded truth.

"She made it through surgery," Tremaine told her gently. "Barring any unforeseen complications, she should be fine."

"Should be?"

"Should be," he said determinedly.

Lexie relaxed, her face glowing in a way that made his heart squeeze. "You operated on her?"

He nodded and at the same moment became aware of Miss Everly, seated primly by the door, Hildegarde sitting beside her. Both women eyed Tremaine with cool distrust.

"Did you remove the appendix?" Lexie asked urgently.

"Yes. Just in the nick of time. It was ready to burst."

She drew a breath through her teeth. "Thank you, Tremaine! Oh, thank you."

"Don't thank me yet," he said with a faint smile, relieved to see how the waiting room had cleared out. Between the carriage accident and the shooting, Willamette Infirmary had been overflowing with emergency patients. It had been all the staff could do to keep up with the rush. Tremaine, who had been on his way out, was long past due on his date. Thoughts of the raven-haired beauty he'd pledged to meet slipped away with only the faintest regret. The warm admiration in Lexie's eyes was worth any later recriminations.

"Dr. Danner." Miss Everly rose stiffly. "I did not realize you were Lexington's brother."

Tremaine would have corrected her, but Lexie rushed into speech, her hand gripping his arm. "When can I see Ella?"

"Maybe as early as tomorrow afternoon." He regarded her thoughtfully. She didn't want Miss Everly to know they weren't brother and sister. As much as it bothered him, considering the older woman's antiquated views, he could readily understand why.

Lexie stifled a yawn and Tremaine said, "Come along, Lexie. I'll take you home."

He silently dared Miss Everly to object, and for once in her life, that worthy woman kept her lips firmly closed.

Dawn was painting faint gray streaks on the horizon as Lexie held out her hand for Tremaine to help her into the buggy. She muffled a cry of amazement and delight at the assortment of blankets inside and the heat emanating from the floor by her feet. The livery boy had set hot bricks inside the buggy at Tremaine's request.

"Whatever possessed you!" she murmured with a sigh of contentment as he tucked a small fur blanket over her legs. "We'll be warm as toast all the way to the school."

Lexie couldn't know about his aborted rendezvous, so Tremaine said lightly, "Who says we're going there right away?"

She straightened with a jerk as he dropped onto the seat beside her, his thigh lightly pressed against hers. "What do you mean?"

"I mean, I'm not taking you back yet."

It wasn't Fortune pulling the buggy this time. It was a fresh horse, a deep black animal with powerful haunches who eagerly tossed his head and fretted at the bit. Knowing how angry Tremaine had been at her earlier, Lexie uneasily wondered what he had in mind. "Am I being abducted?" she asked cautiously.

"Afraid of what that might mean?" His mouth quirked with humor.

Lexie relaxed. At least he wasn't furious. He seemed to have forgiven her pellmell dash through the back streets of the city. "Does saving people's lives always put you in such good humor?" she asked, shooting him a sideways smile.

"Always."

"I've never seen you at the hospital before. Sometimes I forget you're really a doctor."

Tremaine had a sudden burning memory of Betsy Talbot. Never mind that there had been precious little he could do to save Betsy's baby; the circumstances came back in vivid relief. Betsy's tears, her own life hanging by a thread, his fight with Jace Garrett. Tremaine's face hardened. By some miracle Betsy had survived, but it was no thanks to Garrett.

Lexie witnessed Tremaine's change of expression. Her heart squeezed. "What is it?" she asked anxiously.

"Nothing." He couldn't bring himself to tell her about Jace's perfidy, nor his cold-hearted apathy where his mistress was concerned. He would make sure she knew before their engagement was officially announced, but he couldn't tell her yet. Not when she looked at him with those trusting, misty emerald eyes.

"Why did you really bring me out here?" She stifled another yawn and laid her head back, watching the

Willamette's silky waters flowing. They were driving through a parklike area next to the river.

"Because I'm too keyed up to sleep, and I didn't want to be alone."

"So you wanted to be with me?" she murmured. Her head lolled back and dropped on his shoulder, sleep overpowering her. Tremaine glanced down at her golden crown and smiled grimly to himself. *Yes,* he thought. *I wanted to be with you.*

And while she nestled beneath the curve of his arm, Tremaine brought the buggy to a halt at a sheltered spot beside the river, his breath smoking in the frigid air, the yellow glow of a new day's sun gilding the Cascade Mountains to the east.

Lexie stirred and awoke to both delicious warmth and numbing cold. Blinking, her eyes still sleep-drugged, she realized she was seated in an unfamiliar buggy, enveloped by an equally unfamiliar warmth. Blankets covered her up to her nose and only her forehead and eyes were exposed to the chilled December air. Instinctively, she closed her eyes and snuggled back to the source of heat.

Slowly, she became aware that the warmth she felt was an arm draped around her waist, lazily and familiarly. She lay against someone's hip, her head against a broad chest with a steadily beating heart.

Her eyes flew open. She was half-lying on Tremaine. His head was propped against the buggy's canopy and he was fast asleep. At this angle she could see the firm line of his jaw and the beginnings of a new day's dark beard. His lashes swept his cheek, unfairly long and black. In repose, his hawkish nose looked more boyish; his lips thin and sensual; his throat lean and tanned.

Lexie's heart began to thud. Good Lord, what time was it? she wondered. Her gaze darted forward. A blanket had been tossed over the horse that stood silently and peacefully in a small turnout above the river, a stubby rock wall the only barrier to the slowly moving water swirling below.

Tremaine's thigh was beneath her hip. Lexie groaned inwardly. It was a wonder Miss Everly hadn't called out the sheriff to track her down. And if she should ever find out

Tremaine wasn't her natural brother, Lexie would be igno-
miniously tossed from the woman's prestigious school—a
delicious thought she entertained for several moments
before remembering how her mother would take that news.

She glanced back at Tremaine. Something akin to tenderness spread through her veins and for one swift instant she
recalled their kiss. She studied his lips with avid curiosity.
They'd been pressed so hard against hers, yet now they
looked soft and inviting. Soft and inviting? Lexie was
shocked by her naiveté. There was nothing remotely soft or
inviting about Tremaine.

He sighed in his sleep and she swept him another look
from beneath her gold-tipped lashes. There *was* something
touchingly vulnerable about the way he looked, Lexie decided. Something totally different from the Tremaine she
was used to. A thrill of tenderness shot through her and
before she really understood the impulse, she'd laid her
hand on his cheek, then was mortified when his blue eyes
opened and stared steadily into hers.

Something leapt between them, some spark of awareness
that caused Lexie's throat to constrict, her heart to hammer
painfully in her chest. She could see a flame burn steadily in
his blue gaze until his lashes narrowed, hiding their flickering depths.

"Good morning," she said unsteadily. "At least I think
it's morning."

"You fell asleep," he said, and she could feel the way his
voice rumbled in his chest. Trying to extricate herself from
his arms, she was amazed when his grip tightened.

"You fell asleep, too. Tremaine, I have to get back."

"I know." He didn't release her, however. "You're
warm," he said, holding her close.

Lexie hardly knew how to handle this conversation. She
half laughed. "So are you."

He stretched and beneath his leather jacket she caught a
glimpse of spattered, dark red splotches on his white shirt.
"Tremaine!" she whispered in alarm, pulling back his jacket
to see the dried bloodstains. "What happened? Are you all
right?"

To her surprise he grinned like a bandit. "Just a flesh
wound," he drawled.

"Don't joke with me. What happened?"

"I'm afraid that's Ella's blood. I didn't have time to change before the operation and I didn't feel like wearing surgical gear home." He gave her a sideways glance. "And I didn't expect to spend the night sleeping with a beautiful woman."

Lexie immediately withdrew to the other side of the buggy. His remarks made her uneasy. "How am I going to explain this to Miss Everly?"

"Lie," he suggested, stretching languorously in a way that made Lexie supremely conscious of his potent male virility. His stomach was board flat, his shoulders wide and muscular, his legs long, lean, and hard. Climbing down from the seat, he whipped the blanket off the horse's back, then settled in beside Lexie again. His beard-roughened jaw and tousled hair gave him a raffish air that Lexie's senses responded to. Swallowing, she focused her gaze on the sluggish river and concentrated on Jace.

"What lie could I give her?" Lexie wanted to know.

"How about one of the wheels broke down and it took hours to replace?"

"You could have walked me home in the meantime."

"I could have, but I wouldn't."

"Why wouldn't you?" Lexie demanded. "You're supposed to be my brother and, as such, would walk me home."

"Supposed to be?" One of his brows rose in mockery.

"Well, you are my brother," she admitted hastily, flustered. "I think of you as my brother, anyway." This was a patent lie. At his silence, she said hesitantly, "Don't you think of me as your sister?"

"Not really."

Tremaine had long since given up fighting his attraction to Lexie, and in the present circumstances he couldn't see any reason not to let his feelings be known. Her eyes widened like a scared rabbit as he pulled her back to his hard, enveloping warmth.

He didn't give her a chance to protest. He held her face captive between his strong palms and kissed her until she was too bemused to do more than stare at him through desire-hazed eyes.

Flushed, she returned his kisses unthinkingly. She didn't

care that this was Tremaine. She just wanted the feeling to go on and on.

"Lexie . . ." he muttered thickly. "Lexie . . ."

She was powerless against his passion. She wound her arms around his neck and didn't object when he practically hauled her onto his lap. Her legs were wide. She gasped at the feel of him at her most vulnerable spot. His groan of need against her mouth and his tongue thrusting in and out between her lips left her mindless with wanting.

Tremaine had planned to keep himself tightly leashed, but he hadn't expected her to be so willing. He'd only wanted to kiss her. Her fiery response coupled with the feel of sweet, trembling thighs against his manhood was his undoing. Self-control vanished. His hand crept beneath her skirt to stroke the sweetest part of her and Lexie whimpered in surprise and need.

"Tremaine!"

"Shhh." He muffled her cries with his mouth. She struggled until he ceased caressing her. But it was a short respite. Hands at her waist, he settled her firmly over his hips, holding her captive.

Lexie tore her mouth free. "I can't do this! We're in—a buggy. It's not—"

"Lex."

His sober tone stopped her protestations and she looked at him clearly, both horrified and thrilled by the raging passion in those blue eyes. "I want you," he said. "And you want me."

If she'd had time to think, she would have come up with a lie. But he was right. She did want him. And it was such a tremendous surprise that she was too stunned to do more than submit when his fingers slid into her hair, his mouth plundering hers once more.

Her hands slipped over his shoulders and beneath his jacket. She was on fire. She wanted all of him. No matter that this was Tremaine. She wanted *him!*

The storm of kisses he rained on her face and neck had her arching backward, offering him the soft white arc of her throat. "Oh, Lex," he groaned, burying his face into her breasts.

"Do you love me?" she asked breathlessly, naively.

He froze for half a beat. It was more answer than Lexie had expected. She pulled back, staring at him in a new way.

"Do you love me?" she asked again in a devastated voice.

Tremaine hardly knew how to answer. He didn't really believe in love—not the kind she meant. Every woman he'd ever met used the term too loosely. Even Eliza had married his father out of need. To Tremaine's way of thinking, love was vastly overrated. He was formulating a limp response when Lexie shoved herself away from him, scuttling to the far side of the buggy, her chest heaving with emotion.

"I want you," Tremaine tried to explain. "I've wanted you a long time, but you were too young and you didn't know we weren't related. And then there was Jace."

"Who loves me," Lexie spat. "Jace loves me. Take me back to school, Tremaine."

Tremaine would have dearly loved to shatter all her romantic illusions concerning Garrett, but she was too upset already. "I'm not taking you back until you listen to me," he bit out with mounting impatience.

"Then don't take me back! I'll walk!"

She would have leapt from the buggy if he hadn't caught her arm. Her palm swung around but he captured it. Holding her prisoner, he glared into her stormy green eyes. "I'll take you home, but nothing's changed, Lex. I want you, and you want me."

"I don't want any man who doesn't love me."

Her eyes were overbright and Tremaine's heart wrenched. He slowly let her go, and she pulled in on herself, tucking her arms around her waist. He'd made an error. He'd come on too strong. Damn it all to hell, this wasn't what he'd intended!

Lexie was just anxious to put everything back the way it had been. She was frightened, more by herself than by him. "Can we pretend this didn't happen? Please, Tremaine. I just want to forget it."

His brow lifted. This was hardly a solution, but he could tell by her white face it was what she needed to hear. Inclining his head, he turned the black stallion toward Miss Everly's School.

The rest of the trip passed by in a rush of cold wind as the horse pulled them down the cobbled streets. Lexie didn't look at Tremaine. It was late morning, she realized sinkingly, seeing the slanting rays of a watery sun. She should have been back hours ago.

At the door to Miss Everly's School, Tremaine helped her down. His warm fingers enclosed hers for the briefest of moments, but Lexie yanked back as if he'd burned her. She could feel their lingering heat long after he released her.

"You can blame being tardy on me," he said, his breath coming out in puffs of smoke.

"I will. I *shall*," Lexie emphasized. "Since it is your fault."

The door opened on the first knock and Hildegarde stood in the entryway, glaring daggers at both Lexie and Tremaine. She seemed to want to deny him entry, but Tremaine wasn't so easily put off. He grinned at her disarmingly and simply pushed his way inside.

In the foyer, Lexie regarded him apprehensively and Tremaine sighed. "I'm going home to change, then I'm heading back to the hospital," he said. "I'll check on your friend."

She nodded stiffly. "Let me know as soon as I can see her."

"I *shall*," he said with a straight face, then winked at the outraged Hildegarde on his way out.

Lexie shuddered, avoided Hildegarde's suspicious stare, then ran up the stairs to her room.

As it turned out, Lexie had next to no explaining to do. Everyone thought she'd been waiting outside Ella's room at the hospital. Even Miss Everly assumed she'd stayed to be near her friend, and Lexie felt a bit of a fraud. She answered guarded questions about Ella's condition, knowing no more than she had earlier this morning. But no one pressed too deeply for answers. In fact, to Lexie's annoyance, most of the girls were more concerned with an entirely different topic—Tremaine.

They'd seen him gallantly save Ella last night and, from their windows, return Lexie to school late this morning. It was bad enough they were all swooning over Harrison, but now adding Tremaine to the heap made Lexie grind her teeth in frustration. Not that she really cared, she reminded herself. Tremaine was off limits so far as she was concerned. But she was tired of all the girlish sighs and dreamy looks. It was enough to make one ill.

At suppertime, while they sat at the long oak dining table, the downstairs maid delivered the message that Widow Maker, the black stallion Lexie had liberated from the stables, had been returned.

Lexie fastened her eyes on her bowl of soup and ate with unusual absorption. "Thank you, Kate," Miss Everly said in a repressive voice to the maid.

"There was also a message for Miss Danner," Kate added, walking down the table and placing an envelope beside Lexie's plate.

Lexie's heart started to pound. Her name was scrawled in Tremaine's bold hand across the face of the envelope. She felt Miss Everly's silent censure and the avid curiosity of her schoolmates.

"Well, aren't you going to open it?" Celeste Monteith demanded with a malicious smile.

"It's from Tremaine, my—brother," Lexie choked out. "I'm sure it's about Ella."

But was she? Her face flamed at the words that might be written. Tremaine wouldn't dare send something that would scandalize her, would he?

"By all means open it, Lexington," said Miss Everly.

Lexie opened the envelope with slow fingers. She drew out the message, quaking inside, then was relieved and slightly disappointed to read aloud, "You can come visit your friend this evening. I've told the staff at the hospital to expect you."

"This is the brother who brought you home today?" Celeste asked casually, carefully spooning her soup.

"Yes."

"Would it be all right if we all went to see Ella this evening?" Celeste asked Miss Everly with just the right amount of concern tinging her soft voice. "Last night, when Dr. Danner carried her out of here, it was shatteringly worrisome."

Shatteringly worrisome? Lexie's eyes were chips of green ice. Celeste didn't give a damn about Ella. In truth she found Ella loathesome and crude, and Lexie jerked her attention from Celeste's soft, ethereal beauty to Miss Everly's self-righteous face.

"Well, I'm afraid not everyone can march down to the hospital, Celeste. Since Lexington's brother sent for her, *she* may visit Ella." She turned to Lexie. "Please don't be late this evening."

Lexie could almost feel the sharp darts of fury shooting from Celeste's eyes. "Of course," she replied innocently.

She nearly burst out laughing as one of the livery groomsmen drove her to the hospital. Staring out the side of the carriage at the passing buildings, she gleefully remembered Celeste's dark glower and the wrathful, vengeful looks she'd tossed Lexie's way. Hah! For once Celeste had been thwarted in her plans. It was reason enough to celebrate.

Lexie hurried up the steps to the hospital. "I'm Lexington Danner," she told the receptionist who nodded her recognition.

"Dr. Danner told us to expect you," she said, smiling. "Miss Burnham's room is straight down this hall to the right. Number one-thirty-nine."

"Thank you." Lexie paused a moment, then asked, "Is Dr. Danner here?"

She checked her records. "I'm sorry. He's left for the day."

A wave of relief crashed over her. She didn't want to see him again. Ever. She hated him. He'd made expert love to her, then had the arrogance to act as if nothing had changed. Well, damn him anyway. Celeste could have him.

Ella was propped up against several pillows, her face nearly as white as the stiff sheets surrounding her. She smiled wanly at Lexie. "Well, I did it," she said, heaving a sigh.

"Did what?" Lexie pulled up a chair.

"Found a way to miss the only good event that miserable school hosts. I could just die when I think about all of you at the Winter Ball tomorrow night!"

The easy tears of the new convalescent spilled down Ella's cheeks, and Lexie felt a pang of sorrow for her. "It's going to be boring and dull," Lexie predicted, squeezing her fingers.

"No, it's not. Did you know some of the doctors here have been invited? The one who checked me this afternoon is going."

Since most of the wealthy and prestigious families in Portland were annually sent invitations, Lexie wasn't surprised. Miss Everly's Winter Ball was a tradition. Some might scoff at the school's pretensions, but it was still an honor to receive the gilt-edged invitations. No doubt several of the doctors at Willamette Infirmary were from notable families.

"Is this doctor young and handsome?" Lexie asked with a smile, seeking to change the subject.

"He's young. But not as handsome as your brother. Brothers," Ella amended, amused by the tightening of her friend's lips. "Now what did I say?"

"Nothing. I've just heard over and over again about my brothers until I could scream! Celeste's followed me around like a bad smell ever since she clapped eyes on Tremaine, and it makes me sick!"

Faint color invaded Ella's cheeks and her eyes sparkled a bit. "Maybe the two of you could become friends now."

Lexie's answer was a very unladylike epithet that actually provoked a chuckle from the wan figure in the bed.

It wasn't long before Lexie realized she was tiring Ella, so with an excuse that she had to get back, she bade her goodnight and retraced her footsteps down the clean, shining hallway.

There was no accounting for the disappointment she felt. It wasn't like she'd wanted to see Tremaine or anything. Maybe it was realizing how sick Ella had been that had her so depressed. Climbing into the carriage, Lexie listlessly sank back against the cushions while the groomsman clucked to the horses.

"Leaving already?" a familiar masculine voice inquired from the walkway and Lexie nearly broke her neck straining to see Tremaine.

"Stop!" she ordered, and the groomsman obeyed. Tremaine appeared at the side of the carriage and offered a hand to help her down. At her hesitation, his mouth quirked.

"Oh, hell," Lexie muttered, accepting his hand. She could only fool herself so long. "Where were you?" she demanded when she was on the street beside him.

He laughed. He was so devilishly handsome that Lexie concluded it was no wonder Celeste had been smitten. In buckskin breeches, his leather jacket, and a pair of shining brown boots, he was the same Tremaine she'd grown up with, yet he was different.

"Why do you care?"

"I don't." Shrugging, she admitted, "Everyone's been telling me how good-looking you are and I have to admit it's true."

He looked surprised. "Really? And who's been saying such dreadful things?"

"Never mind. If they knew you like I do, they'd realize beauty's only skin deep."

"And what's that supposed to mean?"

"That you've caused me no end of grief during my lifetime and enjoyed every blasted minute of it."

So she'd forgiven him, or at least accepted their attraction for each other. Grinning, Tremaine turned to Miss Everly's groomsman. Soon the carriage was heading down the street.

Lexie's jaw dropped and she stared after it with mixed feelings. She was going to be in trouble again, she realized with a dry mouth. In more ways than one.

"I promise I won't sleep with you again tonight," Tremaine said near her ear.

Lexie drew in a startled breath. "The things you say, Dr. Danner," she murmured uncomfortably.

"That's because I only think of you as a sister."

She glanced sharply at him, but his face gave nothing away. "I don't think I trust you," she said with unabashed honesty, and Tremaine laughed again.

"Good. Don't."

"But I do love Jace," she lied, instinctively protecting herself. Tremaine's dark scowl was his only response as they walked to the livery behind the hospital.

"You are going to take me back, aren't you?" Lexie asked tentatively.

"Eventually. Have you eaten dinner?"

"Yes. You haven't?"

He shook his head. "I just came from a patient and haven't had time."

Lexie realized then why he'd appeared so suddenly. He'd walked from the dismal street where she'd nearly met a horrible fate the night before. "Your patient lives down there?" she asked, pointing to the ominous, darkened tenements lining the narrow street.

"Some of the rooms aren't quite the squalor you see from here. Actually, she keeps a neat home—or at least she did, before she contracted tuberculosis."

"Tuberculosis?" Lexie repeated.

"Consumption," Tremaine explained tersely.

She shuddered. It was a terrible disease and she couldn't imagine living in one of those rooms, gasping for air while your lungs slowly filled with lesions. "I saw those buildings, Tremaine. None of them is fit to be a proper home."

"When did you see the buildings?" he asked, looking down the street from her angle. Other than the corner block, there was very little the eye could view.

Too late Lexie realized she'd given herself away. "Er, well, Harrison drove me through there when he and I came to visit you. Didn't you get the message from the receptionist?"

"It said Harrison had been to see me, but nothing about you." Tremaine threw her an assessing look.

"Well, that's how I knew the way to your hospital." Desperately seeking to change the subject, she added quickly, "I wondered why you never contacted me."

"Lexie, you didn't ride through these streets last night, did you?" Tremaine asked with sudden understanding.

He was much too astute. She threw him a bright smile. "You're changing the subject. Why didn't you come see me? For a while, I thought you were avoiding me."

"I was," he stated flatly, surprising her, then added in an ominously calm tone that nevertheless sent shivers down her back, "If I thought for one minute you rode that monster through here I'd wring your lovely neck."

"I—I don't know what you mean."

He swore pungently and grabbed her arm. "This isn't Rock Springs, you little fool. Do you *know* what could happen to you?"

"I'm not a child, Tremaine," she answered through her teeth.

"Ella might not have been the only one lying in a hospital bed today!" he raged furiously. "Damn you, Lexie. You could have been raped, or murdered, or both."

"I'm perfectly capable of—"

"No, you're not," he cut off autocratically. "You've proven that over and over again."

Her nostrils flared in outrage. How had she ever entertained tender feelings for him? He was just as arrogant and infuriating as he'd ever been. "Tremaine, if you don't start treating me as a woman, I'll slam my fist into your eye."

"Which is such a 'womanly' action to take. So far Miss Everly's School hasn't had much effect on the more irritating aspects of your personality."

Lexie drew a deep breath. His hands were on her shoulders and she knew he would have liked to shake the living daylights out of her. Worse, his touch was starting those passionate sensations she seemed powerless to deny. She tried to shake him off but he held her motionless. Daring him with her eyes, she said testily, "I had a knife."

"A *knife?*"

"From the kitchen. It was in my pocket and I had the crop, too."

Tremaine stared at her in fascinated horror. "Good Lord," he murmured.

Lexie glared at him. It didn't matter that his anger stemmed from concern for her welfare. She was tired of being pushed and pulled by her entire family. And she was tired of trying to understand *him*. "Why," she asked recklessly, bringing their argument back full circle, "were you avoiding me?"

"Because damn it all, Lexie, you drive me to drink."

She laughed, beautifully and tauntingly. Tremaine couldn't appreciate the humor of the situation and merely tightened his hold on her. It was torture to be with her. Especially when she claimed to still love Jace Garrett.

"Am I really so bad?" she accused now, her mouth trembling with amusement.

"Worse," he ground out.

"Oh, Tremaine. I'm alive and well. I'm sorry I came to the hospital through those tenements. I honestly didn't know any other route to your hospital. I plead ignorance. What more do you want?"

Desire burned through his veins at her innocent question. She was more of a woman than he'd guessed, he realized. This Lexie was different from the hot-headed girl last spring. This Lexie knew when the game was up. And she knew how to be a pretty, tantalizing winner. "I ought to throw you over my knee and pound some sense into you," he muttered.

"I'd like to see you try."

"Don't tempt me," he said with tense meaning, dropping his hands.

Lexie immediately stepped away. There was no sense in pushing him. "Let's have dinner," she suggested. "Maybe food will cure your temper."

"I doubt it," Tremaine answered feelingly, but he followed Lexie down the street.

The small restaurant was cozy and cheerful. Lexie sat across from Tremaine, drinking tea while he made short work of a plate of beef, potatoes, and preserved vegetables. She knew there was more on his mind, but it was as if he'd purposely capped his feelings. He was like a block of wood and, perversely, she felt like chipping away at him.

"I received a letter from Jace," she said, gratified by the faint tensing of his muscles.

"Jason Garrett is not my favorite subject."

She'd noticed the growing animosity between Tremaine and Jace, even though she didn't fully understand it. It was two-sided, however. Jace was just as reluctant to discuss Tremaine. "I thought about inviting him to Miss Everly's Winter Ball but I didn't."

"Really." Tremaine seemed to think that over. "Why not?"

"I'm not sure." Lexie drew a quick breath. She didn't want to reveal her true feelings about Jace. He was the only protection she had. Taking a sip of tea, she asked, "Why do you hate him so much? I swear, it's worse than ever between you two."

Tremaine tossed his napkin on his plate, shot her a strange look, then sat back in his chair. "Do you really want to know?"

Lexie felt warning bells go off at his tone. "Yes."

"All right, I'll tell you." He pushed back his plate, leaned his forearms on the table, and said, "I don't like the man's business practices. He practically terrorizes the Rock Springs merchants into bending to his will. I don't like his attitude. All he wants is power. I don't like the way he treats his family. Lucinda may be hard to deal with, but she's his mother. And Kelsey's being ripped in half by both Lucinda's and Jace's needs.

"Furthermore, I especially loathe the way he treats you," Tremaine went on flatly. "He wants you in his bed but he doesn't care a damn about you. He doesn't care about any of his mistresses. Ask Betsy Talbot. She nearly died giving birth to his bastard."

Lexie's face had slowly drained of color. Now a crimson tide swept up her throat and cheeks, spreading with every one of Tremaine's tersely uttered words. Though she wasn't as fond of Jace as she'd let on, Tremaine didn't know that. He was cruelly, systematically assassinating Jace, and Lexie didn't want to hear it.

Tremaine watched her rising color dispassionately. "You're a possession, Lexie. Nothing more. Jace may want you in bed, but he wants the Danner property more. If there was any way he—"

Her hand cracked against the side of his face. She hadn't known she was going to slap him until she did. Tremaine just watched her with stony eyes, his taut jaw the only evidence he even felt the livid mark now glowing on his cheek.

"Liar," she whispered bitterly.

"I didn't think you really wanted to know."

His arrogance knew no bounds. "You're just saying all these awful things because *you* want me!" she declared recklessly.

"If I thought it would help, yes, I would have lied about Jace before. But as it stands, I don't have to. I'm telling you the truth. Grow up, Sundown," he said gently. "I could tell you things that would make your hair turn white."

"I was going to ask you to come to the Winter Ball tomorrow night," she choked, "but I'd rather die than be seen there with you!"

He regarded her grimly and she had no idea what he was thinking. She didn't care. His attack on Jace was horridly unfair.

"I'll take you home," he said moments later, and Lexie, because she had no other choice, nodded her head curtly and walked stiffly ahead of him out the door.

Chapter Ten

A headache pulsed at Lexie's temples as she watched the whirling couples float across the dance floor. She attributed the pain to Kate's brusque ministrations to her hair and wished she'd simply braided it. Instead, her golden mane was painfully pulled straight back from her head and wound with several silvery ribbons to cascade down her back in a luxuriant wave. Catching sight of her reflection in one of the hall's windowpanes, Lexie reluctantly had to admit she did look elegant. A few feathery wisps of blond hair had been left to softly caress her forehead and tiny diamond earrings—Ella's—twinkled prettily at her earlobes.

Kate had brushed Lexie's cheeks with pink powder but Lexie hadn't needed the rouge. She was hot, burning up from the heat of the crowd, and as such her cheeks were flaming with hectic color. All around her there was a din of talk, laughter and general merriment. As usual, Miss Everly's School for Young Ladies' Winter Ball was a roaring success.

Lexie sipped desultorily from her glass of punch. Hours

ago she'd shed the jade green cloak which matched her dress. Now she stood near the crystal punch bowl, watching the colorful kaleidoscope of whirling dancers through distant eyes. She had not once been asked to dance. Unknowingly, she projected an image of cool, haughty disdain that had scared off her potential partners. She wouldn't have cared anyway. Her fury at Tremaine had taken the edge off the evening, and all she wanted to do was live through this wretched ball and go to bed.

Touching a finger to her aching temple, she turned to one of the other girls who, like herself, had been waiting like a shriveling wallflower for someone to approach, and asked, "What time is it?"

The girl, a nearsighted, somewhat homely young lady who was far more anxious about her neglected state than Lexie, said, "Somewhere around ten o'clock, I imagine."

Lexie sighed. It was too early to beg off. She gritted her teeth and resolved to last until midnight.

A storm had been gathering inside Lexie since Tremaine had unemotionally ripped apart Jace's character. She wouldn't believe him. It couldn't be true about Betsy Talbot. Jace would never, ever do that to her.

A small voice inside Lexie's head questioned why Tremaine would invent such an outlandish lie, but she closed her ears to it. To hell with Tremaine. He was just a self-serving, arrogant blackguard. Lexie's fists clenched. She wanted to kick and scream and beat on his broad back. He deserved to be boiled in oil.

She fumed silently for several moments. Maybe the rack was a better item of torture, she thought malevolently. How she would love to slowly stretch him apart until he cried for mercy! She could just imagine his straining muscles and his choking, imploring pleas as he begged her to release him. Tremaine, helpless, was a delightful vision.

"May I have this dance, please?"

She straightened abruptly, having been only subconsciously aware of the man by her side. He was young and not unattractive, and he was talking to her.

"I—uh—yes, of course."

Leaving the homely girl staring wistfully after her, Lexie

walked onto the dance floor and into the young man's arms. "My name's Peter," her partner introduced himself.

"I'm Lexington," she answered.

"I know. I saw you at the hospital."

She gave him a hard stare. "Do I know you?"

"I know your stepbrother, Dr. Danner."

Caught off guard, Lexie asked stupidly, "How do you know he's my stepbrother?"

"You said so yourself. I heard you tell the receptionist several nights ago, when you came in with your friend Ella Burnham."

She'd forgotten blurting out that information. Well, it didn't matter. Even if Miss Everly found out there was nothing she could do about it now. "How did you happen to be at the hospital?"

"I'm also a doctor," he said modestly. "Dr. Peter Caldwell. I've worked with your—uh—Dr. Danner."

Something in his tone made her realize he was not over-fond of Tremaine himself. She instantly warmed to him. "Really. Then you know how exacting and insufferable he can be."

When Peter threw back his head and laughed, Lexie felt people staring at them. "I like you better and better, Miss Danner. I could dance with you all night."

For nearly an hour, Peter kept to his word, monopolizing Lexie and keeping her on the dance floor through song after song. Eventually, however, another brave soul tapped on Peter's shoulder, and Lexie, breathless and overwhelmed at her sudden popularity, was promptly swept into his arms. She was totally unaware that Peter had simply done what most of them had been wanting to do, namely ask her to dance. Upon witnessing Lexie's warm reception, they'd waited for a chance to spin her across the floor themselves.

Her breath was coming in gasps and her feet actually hurt by the time her last partner led her from the floor. Immediately, ten other young men stood by attentively. Gratified, but totally worn out, Lexie shook her head and politely thanked them one and all, and then she scurried for the safety of one of the sheltered alcoves near the back of the tremendous hall.

There were gilded handles on the french doors that led to

a wrought-iron balcony. Lexie tried one and was pleased to find it cracked open. Frigid air, promising snow, swirled around her, cooling her cheeks as she reveled in this exciting and totally unexpected turn of events. Never in her life had she felt beautiful and wanted. She'd always felt Jace's attention to her was some kind of gift. But now other young men were actually seeking out her company, a heady sensation that nearly superseded her fury at Tremaine.

Until she walked back to the dance floor and saw the blackhearted devil himself lounging against a white column, eyeing the room with the faintest amusement, as if the whole affair were funny indeed.

A fresh surge of rage burned through her like molten lava. He hadn't seen her yet. *Good!* It was unbelievable that he'd come to the dance! He'd done it just because she'd told him she didn't want him here!

Peter was once again at her elbow. "Another dance, please?" he asked charmingly.

"I'd love it."

It occurred to Lexie as Peter escorted her to the floor that Tremaine might not know how to dance. When would he have learned? For the first time she was fervently thankful for Miss Everly's training. She could perform a passable waltz and, though she'd told herself dancing was a frivolous waste, now she saw it as a way to socially ruin Tremaine.

Peter expertly whisked her around the perimeter of the floor, so near Tremaine that she could almost reach out and touch his black suit. It infuriated her that he looked so devastatingly handsome. His dark skin was a perfect foil for his snowy-white shirt. The black jacket stretched lovingly over his strong shoulders. His face wore an expression of mild tolerance, as if he were the lord of the manor come to spend time with his loyal subjects.

Lexie wanted to kill him.

Her hand was clasped within Peter's fingers, her other resting delicately on his shoulders. Lexie smiled at him and scrupulously avoided Tremaine's eyes. She wanted to meet his gaze, but she knew the mockery she would find in those stripping eyes. Let him see her first. Let him make the first conciliatory move. She'd be damned if she even looked his way.

After several trips around the dance floor, she was certain he'd had more than enough time to find her and was about to beg off when the orchestra took a break. Gratefully, Lexie let Peter lead her to the punch bowl, where Miss Everly smiled benevolently at all the young couples.

Accepting a cup of cranberry punch, she glanced casually and surreptitiously around the room. Tremaine was still leaning against the pillar but he was no longer alone. Celeste was saying something to him that had him grinning like a satyr.

"Lexington, are you all right?" Peter asked solicitously, taking the cup from her nerveless fingers.

"I'm perfectly fine." She dazzled him with a smile that made Peter gaze at her in wonder.

Inside a slow poison was sliding through her veins, infecting her reason. It was jealousy, pure and simple, but Lexie didn't view it as such. Tremaine's interest in Celeste was just another example of his supreme lack of taste, his faulty judgment. He could no more pick a reliable woman than he could see Jace for the decent man he really was.

When the music began again, Lexie watched as Tremaine led Celeste to the dance floor. She shook her head to Peter's offer of another dance, intending to watch Tremaine's ignominious fall from grace as he contemplated a waltz.

He glanced her way, then, and lifted one brow in silent greeting. So he had seen her. Lexie simply glared at him.

His hand splayed across Celeste's narrow back, nearly covering her gold silk gown. Vaguely, Lexie wondered what had happened to her partner, then noticed the young man with the vacant eyes and perpetually bored sneer standing on the sidelines. *No treasure there,* she thought in reluctant sympathy.

To Lexie's chagrin, Tremaine moved Celeste around the hall's marble floor with admirable grace, looking strong and elegant and thoroughly attractive. Somewhere he'd learned to dance. She supposed it was inevitable—and it made her recognize the huge gaps in her knowledge of him.

It was at that moment that his blue eyes sought hers. Lexie lifted her chin, meeting his gaze defiantly in their silent battle of wills. But he scrutinized her with slightly puzzled eyes, as if he didn't know quite what to make of this formally clad Lexie, until Celeste touched her finger to his chin, drawing his gaze back to hers.

Lexie barely noticed when Peter guided her back to the dance floor, pulling her into his arms, and gently leading her through another waltz. She felt as if she were gliding on ice, everything slippery, unfamiliar, and cold. Swallowing hard, she wondered if she were coming down with something, then her heart nearly stopped when Tremaine's resonant voice asked from behind her, "May I have this dance?"

Peter's reaction broke through Lexie's daze. His eyes flared with resentment and he said with heavy sarcasm, "Be my guest, Dr. Danner."

Lexie was summarily transferred to Tremaine's arms and Peter stalked off to the sidelines. She blinked, feeling oddly out of sync, then was brought to earth with a bang at Tremaine's drawling, "Dr. Caldwell and I don't see eye to eye."

"Is that a fact? You really know how to make friends, don't you?"

He had the audacity to laugh. "It's a talent."

"Where did you learn to waltz?"

"Well, let's see. I think it was while I attended medical school. There was a certain young woman whom I longed to meet. She loved to dance, ergo I learned to dance."

Lexie tipped her head back, viewing him through gold-tipped lashes—and felt her head spin so violently she straightened immediately. "Did you dance with her?"

His smile of recollection was full of unspoken secrets. "Yes."

"Why did you come here tonight?" she demanded testily, mad at herself for being affected by his remarks.

"To see you."

"You're gate-crashing. I rescinded my invitation."

"Your vocabulary's come a long way from the farm," he murmured with a laugh. "You sound just like your friend, Miss Monteith."

He couldn't have said anything designed to inflame her more thoroughly than that! "Celeste Monteith is no friend of mine," she sputtered.

"Now, if you just added a few 'goddams' and a liberal amount of 'hells,' that would sound more like the Lexie I know and love."

She was momentarily distracted by his teasing comment about love, but then she remembered what a joke it was. "You shouldn't have come here. How did you get in? You didn't have an invitation."

"Oh, but I did. Celeste was kind enough to send me one in care of the hospital."

Lexie nearly stumbled. "What?" she hissed.

Tremaine pretended total innocence. "Didn't I tell you? Yours wasn't the first invitation. In fact, I think it's high time I gave her some of my attention."

"I truly hate you," she said with no inflection whatsoever.

He gave her a sidelong glance as he pulled her to the crowd of people near the door. Celeste was watching them through murderous eyes. He leaned down and said quietly, "You're only mad at me because I told you the truth about Garrett. Maybe I was too blunt, but I'll wager you've thought some of those things yourself and just won't admit it."

"All I've thought over is how truly jealous and despicable you are."

"Jealous?"

"You don't like anyone who shows me the slightest attention. You never have. I think it's a flaw in your personality. You can't stand being second best."

"You know, I'd never thought of it that way," he responded coolly. "I think you're right."

Celeste grabbed onto Tremaine's arm as they approached and looked up at him meltingly. "I thought you'd *never* get back to me," she moaned.

"Just dancing with little sister," he said mockingly, the barb plunging deep into Lexie's breast. With a nod at Lexie, he guided Celeste onto the floor where her arm crawled around his and his hand rigidly held the small of her back, pressing her tightly against him.

Lexie hoped Miss Everly would swoop down and pry them apart.

Peter was there with more punch. "I hope you like scotch?" he said with a grin full of evil mischief.

Lexie gazed at him blankly, for all she could see were images of Tremaine and Celeste. "Scotch? I don't know. I've never tried it."

"I'm afraid you just did. I confess to doctoring the punch. It's tradition, you know. Miss Everly is a confirmed teetotaler, so all of us invitees make certain there's a supply of alcohol on hand." He leaned forward confidentially. "It's why the Winter Ball is so popular."

It did seem to Lexie that the room had acquired a dangerous new edge of gaiety. The thought of liquor made her stomach revolt, but she accepted the glass of punch anyway. "I'll drink it as long as you keep your hands to yourself," she said with a bold pseudo-sophistication she hadn't known she possessed.

Peter quickly crossed his heart and held up one palm. "On my honor, ma'am."

Why was it, Lexie wondered dismally as she sipped the scotch-laced punch, that she could handle men like Peter, but she couldn't handle Tremaine? It was befuddling and more than a little irritating, and as Lexie finished her drink, she said, "Wonderful beverage, scotch. Thanks, but no, I don't want any more."

All she wanted, as it turned out, was to drop her head on her pillow and sink into oblivion. She wanted to forget the entire evening. With an effort, she focused on the fact that she would soon be going home to Rock Springs for Christmas break.

"It's midnight," someone said, and Lexie straightened.

"That's my cue to leave," she remarked, but her legs felt decidedly wobbly.

"Be careful," said Peter. "Remember, that wasn't your first glass of scotch."

"How many have I had?" she asked, slightly aghast.

"I'm not sure. A few." He lifted his shoulders apologetically.

She tried to mentally calculate how much alcohol she'd actually consumed, but the task proved too great for her dulled wits. She'd been so absorbed by Celeste and Tremaine that she'd drunk the punch without even tasting it. "Shame on you, Peter," she scolded.

"I know." But he looked anything but repentant.

Tremaine and Celeste materialized in front of them. Lexie had an impression of Tremaine's blue eyes peering down at her, a frown creasing his brow. "What's wrong?" he demanded.

"Who says anything's wrong?" Lexie smiled up at him, and was seized by a nearly uncontrollable desire to laugh, one which took all her willpower to fight.

Before she knew what was happening, Tremaine had her cloak and she was whisked through the door into the frigid winter night. A numbing, drizzling rain was now pouring down from the eaves of the massive stone building that Miss Everly had rented for the dance.

"Are you drunk?" he asked in amazement.

"Good Lord, no. Although I've been infarmed— informed—that the punch was doctored, Doctor." Hearing herself, her lips twitched with mirth and a chuckle escaped despite the hand she pressed to her quivering mouth.

Tremaine shook his head. "Come on. I'll drive you back."

"What about your date?" Lexie asked, stealing a look at him through half-lowered eyes as they waited for the groomsman to bring his buggy around.

"I don't really have a date. Celeste had already invited someone else first. She can catch a ride home with him."

"She won't like it," Lexie predicted in a singsong voice, wagging her finger in front of his nose.

"That's her problem," he said, helping her inside the buggy and swinging lithely in beside her.

"Ladies should never drink scotch," she announced airily, swiping rain from her hair as the buggy lurched forward, throwing her off balance so she fell backward.

"You're really going to think so tomorrow."

The ride back was little more than a blur and, before she realized it, Lexie was swaying on her feet in the center of Miss Everly's parlor, blinking in consternation. "Where is everybody?" she asked, looking around the barren room.

"At the dance. Do you need help up to your room?"

Lexie focused on him, trying to revitalize some of the anger she'd felt earlier. "Why would I need help to my room?" she asked suspiciously.

He laughed. "So you won't fall flat on your face."

"I am *not* drunk."

"Oh really?" He drew her into his arms until her hands were trapped against his chest, her legs brushing his. Alarmed, Lexie pulled back. "Don't . . ."

"Don't what?"

"Don't kiss me again."

"I'm afraid you're going to have to stop me all on your own . . ."

Lexie clung to his lapels, her head whirling. His mouth plundered hers. For a moment she felt as if she were standing outside of herself, watching. Her mind was fuddled. She felt the sweet touch of his lips and responded. Then she remembered all the terrible things he'd said about Jace. Her heart ached.

"Jace . . ." she murmured.

Lexie was fast losing touch with consciousness. A steel arm surrounded her, lifting her. She was carried upstairs, limp and wanton. She felt the soft bed against her back and then . . .

A cold whipping wind brought her to instant wakefulness. With a start she found she was lying on her bed, fully clothed, her jade brocade dress crumpled beneath her.

Fragmented images crossed her mind. Tremaine's kiss. His strong arms carrying her upstairs. A softly whispered goodnight.

Had Tremaine been with her, or had it been a dream?

Shakily, Lexie climbed out of bed and went downstairs in search of a glass of water. She drank thirstily in front of the kitchen washbasin and tried to calm her rioting stomach. If she'd dreamed it, why did her mouth feel as if she'd been kissed hungrily, *starvingly?* Why did her lips feel swollen, her skin sensitized, the secret part of herself throbbing from some nameless ache? Why was there a melting, liquid sensation playing havoc with her lower limbs?

"Too much liquor," she moaned on a shudder, tossing the remainder of her water into the washbasin. Swearing off alcohol for the rest of her natural life, she carefully mounted the stairs and returned to bed.

The buggy rattled over the cobblestones, and rain beat persistently against its drum-taut roof. Tremaine stared through the thick darkness and fought a losing battle with desire. He'd told himself after the night in the buggy that he would have to move more slowly. He didn't want to frighten her. He'd planned a chaste, good-night kiss, but then she'd hung onto his lapels and stared up at him through limpid emerald eyes, her mouth parting provocatively.

Instead of Lexie dressed in a rustling, shimmery green gown, he'd suddenly seen her as she'd been at the hot springs: bare and beautiful, her sun-dried hair a tangle of gold, her body glistening with sweat, her limbs long and seductive.

His resistance shattered, he'd bent his head and captured her lips, his hand pressing into the small of her back. She fit easily and perfectly against him, igniting him with primitive desire.

Her lips opened sweetly, naturally, innocently, under the power of his. The strain of his hold on her forced her breasts to peek over the top of her bodice. Groaning, hating himself for his lack of control, his hand slid agonizingly upward, cupping one ivory mound through her dress.

His tongue plunged into her mouth and she responded with a soft moan. His fingers rounded her breast, caressing her perfect skin. She clung to him, her eyelids fluttering, and it took all his willpower not to toss her onto the couch and press his overheated body against her. He was gripped by a passion so desperate he could scarcely think, consumed by a dangerous, licking fire that threatened to burn down his paltry resistance and sear bare an open path for his desire.

He held her quivering body close and let her feel his need.

And she sighed and murmured, "Jace . . ."

Sanity returned then, brutally swift, excruciatingly painful. She thought she was with *Garrett!*

Now Tremaine laughed bitterly, savagely snapping the reins so that Fortune, poor beast, redoubled his efforts. Even after he'd told her about Betsy, she still fancied herself in love with that bastard! God, women were foolish creatures. Grinding his teeth, he vowed never to see Lexie again until he got over this consuming desire. He'd been right to avoid her so long.

All he had to do was get through Christmas.

Chapter Eleven

Eliza stood slim and straight, a lone figure on the widow's walk, her cloak whipping around her in the December wind. She waved and Lexie felt a lump grow in her throat. She'd thought Christmas would never come. As Pa pulled the buggy to a stop beneath the portico, her gaze swept the frost-crusted fields, the whitewashed house, the stables, the barn.

"I've missed it all," she said achingly.

"We've missed you, too, Lexie," Pa answered, helping her down. "Sugartail's about to foal. Doc Meechum's already had a look at her," he muttered, almost apologetically. "He assures me that everything's fine with her, but after the last one, I'm not so sure."

Lexie banked down her automatic antagonism at the mention of Meechum. "Sugartail's dropped lots of healthy foals. One stillborn shouldn't make a difference."

"Why don't you have a look at her?" Pa suggested, his lips fighting a smile.

Lexie's heart warmed. "I might at that." She pushed open the front door, then stood dazzled in the entryway. The sconces had been lit even though it was still afternoon, albeit a gloomy one, and wreaths of cedar were wrapped around the stairway banister. The house smelled of cedar and cinnamon and in the parlor, at the edge of Lexie's vision, rose a twenty-foot Christmas tree.

It was Jesse who greeted her first, and she surprised a flash of amazement on his darkly handsome countenance. "Lexie?" he asked as he came into the foyer.

Mischief entered her sparkling eyes as she moved forward in a rustle of midnight blue sateen. "Good afternoon, Jesse," she murmured formally, extending both hands.

His deep blue eyes narrowed. "By gum, girl," he drawled, in a perfect imitation of Cook. "Ya up and done it, din't ya?"

They convulsed in fits of laughter and Samuel, who'd come to stand behind his brother, said in pretended shock, "Why, she even *looks* like a lady!"

"Very funny," Lexie said affectionately, dropping all her good intentions and hugging them each in turn. To hell with being a lady if it meant she couldn't express her feelings.

In the midst of this reunion Lexie saw her mother begin to descend the stairs. There was an unsteady smile on Eliza's lips, and Lexie well understood her mother's worry at seeing what changes had been wrought.

Lexie walked to the bottom of the stairs, smiling. Eliza's gaze was admiring. "You look so beautiful," she said. "I hope you're not totally miserable."

"Not totally," Lexie allowed. "After all, I only have six months left."

Eliza's gaze anxiously searched her daughter's face. Seeing the lurking humor in the corners of Lexie's eyes, her own mouth twitched just a little. "The Lord does grant us His blessings," she murmured sardonically, and everyone, including Eliza, laughed.

Lexie had to hide her homesickness behind a pair of over-bright eyes, rather than make a complete fool out of herself. Miss Everly's School for Young Ladies wasn't nearly so awful as the wrench of being away from home. But there were only a few months left. She would survive.

"Where's Harrison?" she asked.

"He won't be able to come," Pa supplied unhappily,

hauling in Lexie's valise and carrying it upstairs. "Your Dr. Breverman knows how to work a man, it seems."

"That's not the half of it," Jesse put in before Lexie could respond. "Breverman's moving to Denver, and Harrison's going with him."

"Denver?" Lexie's heart sank. "Why?"

Jesse shrugged. "Ask Pa. Harrison told him Breverman's been planning to move for a long time. Harrison's sticking with him until he's learned all he can."

"We'll just have to make do without him, then," said Eliza briskly, effectively turning the conversation.

"And—Tremaine?" asked Lexie, her tone light.

For the first time since she'd greeted her daughter, Eliza's face molded into its cool reserve. "We're not certain when he'll arrive, but he's in Rock Springs."

"And up to no good," Jesse added irrepressibly, earning a long look down his mother's aristocratic nose.

"What does that mean?" Lexie asked, certain she didn't really want to know.

Jesse guided Lexie's arm toward the parlor, throwing a wicked glance over his shoulder before remarking, "I believe Mother thinks Tremaine needs a year at Miss Everly's School. His lack of protocol is shocking."

"As is yours?"

They stood together in front of the Christmas tree. Popcorn and silvery tinsel wound around its fragrant limbs. Tiny brass candlesticks were tied with scarlet ribbons on the feathery Douglas fir branches. Small embroidered doilies threaded with satin dangled softly, turning in the breeze when Lexie and Jesse had walked in the room.

"My behavior these days is above reproach," Jesse informed her with a sly smile.

She arched a disbelieving brow. "What has Tremaine done?"

"He spends a great deal of time at Jenny McBride's rooming house. He is, and I quote, 'not acting as a responsible gentleman.'"

Lexie had a quick mental vision of Jenny McBride's beauty. Feeling as if she were suffocating, she asked, "You mean, he has a—woman there?"

"Among other places, I'd guess. He's bound to have a mistress or two in Portland." Seeing her tense face, he asked, "Shocked?" as if suddenly cognizant of her tender, feminine feelings.

She was shattered! "Nothing Tremaine could do would shock me," she answered swiftly. She kept her attention directed at the shimmering tree, ignoring her now amazed brother. Jesse was too much like Tremaine for her to ever feel truly close to him. Yet, like Tremaine, he tended to seek her company now and again.

"Look, Lex . . ." he began uncomfortably.

"I don't really feel like talking about Tremaine anymore. Tell me what's been happening around here. Pa says Meechum took a look at Sugartail. Do you think she'll be all right?"

"What's going on with you and Tremaine?" he asked astutely, frowning.

"N-o-th-ing." Lexie stretched the word out, avoiding Jesse's knowing gaze. She suddenly wished Harrison were around. She could talk to him. He understood her.

"Come on in to dinner," Pa said before Jesse could launch another attack. She seized the excuse with relief, sweeping into the dining room, where Annie was just putting the final touches on Cook's sumptuous meal. Gritting her teeth, she plastered a tight smile on her face and ignored the silly, heart-throbbing misery eating away at her whenever she thought of Tremaine and Jenny McBride.

Jenny McBride gazed wistfully at Tremaine's prone form lying in exhausted sleep across her table. She was dog-tired, too. The life of a country doctor was one of ceaseless hours, drudgery, and despair. The joys and triumphs came much too infrequently.

Why had she thought this would be the way to bring him back to Rock Springs?

Measuring out spoonfuls of freshly ground coffee, she decided she'd been wrong. She'd wired Tremaine about the virulent influenza sweeping Rock Springs and the nearby town of Malone in hopes of spending a few days with him. Once the work was done, she figured, there would be time for pleasure.

But the work had never been done. From the moment Tremaine had appeared at her door, she'd been swept into the demanding job of doctor's aide—it had been either that or be dumped unceremoniously on her own rooming-house porch. Now she shuddered, recalling some of the worst cases. Even her pragmatic nature hadn't been able to stand the terrible suffering—especially the children's. Tremaine had worked unflaggingly, however, and his unfailing humor and expertise had left Jenny feeling something near hero worship. On those occasions when the victim's family didn't want her sort inside their home, Tremaine had bluntly told them they had no choice.

She sighed. She was in love with the rebel.

Pouring coffee, she eyed his sleeping form. Somehow, someway, she was going to make him return that love. She just had to figure out what—or who—was keeping him out of her bed.

He stirred, opened his eyes, and regarded her blearily. "Coffee," he muttered, automatically reaching for his coat.

"Where are you going?"

"Back to Malone and then home. It's Christmas Eve," he muttered.

Sensing he was about to leave without so much as a hug goodbye, Jenny sought desperately for some way to detain him. "You'd better sit down," she said with deceptive casualness. "There's something you should know."

"What?" He hardly heard her.

"Since Betsy left town, Jace Garrett's set his sights on a lovely young blond woman who lives upstairs. He's visited her a time or two."

Jenny felt a tweak of conscience at the lie. It was true that Jace had been looking at the blonde, but then Jace couldn't keep his eyes off any woman. Seeing the slow fury building in Tremaine's incredible blue eyes, she opened her mouth to tell him the truth. But Tremaine slammed his chair around and sat back down.

"My sister thinks that bastard's in love with her," he growled.

"I know." Jenny loathed Jace, too. Not as much as Tremaine, but Jace Garrett had a way of getting under her skin. Still, she wasn't certain she should let Tremaine beat the living tar out of him for imagined crimes.

"It doesn't seem to matter what I tell Lexie," he muttered in frustration. "She still thinks she loves him."

"Maybe she does."

"No." He was positive. "She doesn't." Checking his pocket watch, he groaned. "Never mind. Tell me about Garrett later. I've got to get going. If the Harthorn kid gets worse, send for me. I don't trust Marshfield to take care of the boy. I'll be at my parents' as soon as I'm finished in Malone."

He left before she could utter another word.

The day dawned gray and dismal; the worst Christmas Eve in Lexie's memory. By noon a pale sun had appeared, throwing weak shadows along the frozen ground, but it hadn't dispelled the gloom. Lexie stood with her arms over the rail fence, watching a ewe and her new lamb getting to know each other. The ewe was licking her trembling, knobby-kneed infant, and the bleating youngster was butting its head against its mother's udder.

She hadn't seen Jace yet, though she'd received a message from him inviting her to Christmas Eve dinner. Sometime soon she was going to have to tell him the truth of her feelings. She didn't love him. She couldn't marry him. For some reason, even though she doubted Jace loved her either, she sensed he wasn't going to take the news well.

Sighing, she rubbed her cheek against the back of her hand. Tremaine hadn't appeared at the farm at all. He was, according to Jesse, still living a life of decadent pleasure in Rock Springs with Jenny McBride. Lexie, who had always prided herself on being decent and fair, found herself hating the infamously wicked Mrs. McBride with an unreasonable passion. Never a prig, she couldn't help herself from mentally shredding the woman's character into ribbons, then wondered with a sick heart why it should matter so.

"Lexie?"

She turned to see Pa walking toward her, his Winchester held lightly between callused palms. "Something wrong?" she asked.

"No, I'm just cleaning it. It's not loaded." He propped it

against a fencepost and looked down at her. "You look like you belong here."

"I do. I wasn't made for Miss Everly's School," Lexie remarked, a brisk breeze drawing blond strands of hair across her face.

"I know. I think I realized it as soon as you left."

She was touched by this admission. For so many years he'd fought the path which had been so right for her. "I'll finish, though."

"I know that, too. You're not a quitter."

Joseph Danner stood in companionable silence beside his stepdaughter and ignored the knot of worry in his gut. He thought of the letter he'd received so long ago and the new one that had arrived yesterday. Cleaning the Winchester had been an automatic response. He felt trouble boiling on the horizon. As soon as he got his hands on Tremaine, he was going to have to enlist his help.

Lexie glanced at the man she'd always regarded as her father. She didn't care that some mysterious man she'd never met had begat her. Pa was the only father she would ever know.

"You know I love your mother very much."

Lexie was surprised. She hadn't asked about his feelings, yet now that he'd admitted them, she felt a wash of intense relief. "I've wondered," she said simply.

Afternoon shadows were striping the fields when Pa regretfully left to do chores. Lexie slipped into the stables to tend the horses. Though they were Samuel's responsibility now, she couldn't help babying them. Upon spying her, Sugartail nickered, her unusually white speckled tail switching nervously to and fro. Her belly was stretched out and down, her back drooping under the weight of her imminent foal.

"Think you'll drop on Christmas Eve?" Lexie asked her, rubbing the velvety pink nose. A white blaze ran crookedly between the mare's huge dark eyes.

Tantrum nickered impatiently and Lexie returned to his stall. He slammed his head against her shirtwaist and searched her hands for oats. Finding none, he snorted and tossed his head in disdain.

Slowly Lexie removed one of the crisp red apples from her

pocket that she'd snitched from the cellar. "This what you're looking for?"

Tantrum snatched the ruby-red apple from her hand and chomped it down.

"That animal's so spoiled he's become a nuisance," Tremaine's voice said dryly from somewhere behind her head.

Lexie's pulse leapt. She whirled around to see him lounging in the doorway. At the sight of him she was jolted by such violent longing she could scarcely credit her feelings. He looked so wonderfully lean and male, his jaw darkened by several days' growth of beard. There was a deep tiredness around his eyes and he lifted his arms and stretched sensuously.

Lexie suddenly remembered where he'd been—and with whom. She dragged her gaze from the soft buckskin breeches, straining over taut thighs, and tried to block out the memory of his lazy smile.

For several moments she couldn't find her voice but when she did, she said scathingly, "How was Rock Springs?"

"Rock Springs?"

Lexie gave him a fulminating look, to which Tremaine lifted one surprised, black brow.

"Jenny McBride?" she reminded him acidly.

To her dismay his smile broke into a wide grin. "Oh . . . her."

Infuriated, Lexie concentrated on Tantrum, alarmed at the slight tremor in her hands as she stroked the gelding's tossing head.

"Who told you I was in Rock Springs?"

"Jesse. And Mother."

She could feel his eyes on her back but didn't trust herself to turn around. But it didn't matter. He crossed to where she was standing, one lean hand absently reaching past her shoulder to rub Tantrum's long nose.

Lexie could smell his leather jacket and the crisp, wintry scent of him. She drew in her shoulders and shuddered, though the stables were warm from the heat of horseflesh.

"Cold?"

"No."

"You're shivering."

"No, I'm not!"

She ducked under his arm, throwing him a haughty look. Tremaine's disgusting grin was still in place. "You're shivering because of me," he said, amused. "And here I thought you didn't care."

"Go to hell."

He laughed, pleased by this unexpected twist in their relationship. Lexie might still profess to love Jace, but her reaction gave her away. "If it makes you feel any better, I promise not to pounce on you."

"Oh, really?" She tried to stoke up her anger, but it was nearly impossible. "And that's supposed to make me feel better? Maybe your—er—sexual needs have already been satisfied."

Instead of making him angry, her words elicited a hoot of laughter. "By God, you *are* jealous. You know, you almost had me believing you still cared about Garrett."

"I do!" Lexie's eyes snapped. "You're insufferable, Tremaine. Get this straight—to me, you're still my brother. That's all."

"Want me to prove you wrong?"

The lazy threat shot a thrill into Lexie's heart she could have done without. He was right, damn him. She didn't think of him as a brother. Lord, no. "All right," she amended hastily. "I don't think of you as a brother. But I still love Jace."

Nothing could have ruined Tremaine's mood quicker. Just when he thought progress was being made, she threw Garrett into his face. He scowled.

"Jace is coming here this evening to pick me up," she added quickly. "I'm having supper at the Garretts'."

The truth was, Lexie hadn't decided whether to accept Jace's invitation or not. She didn't want to be with him. But now she saw it was a way of killing two birds with one stone: telling Jace she couldn't marry him, and escaping Tremaine.

"Are you going to the Cullens' tonight?" she asked when the silence between them had become unbearable.

"No, I think I'll stay here." He was terse.

"You're going to miss a great party."

Tremaine regarded her impassively. "Since when do the Cullens have a great party? I could choke on that godawful mess they call oyster stew."

Lexie couldn't help smiling. "It's delicious and you know it."

"It bubbles and steams in that black caldron Mrs. Cullen keeps over the fire, and she stirs it with an evil grin on her face. She looks and cackles like a witch. No, thanks. I'll stay here with Sugartail and let the rest of the family eat that brew."

Lexie suddenly longed to be at the farm with him. They would be alone—maybe for the rest of the night. The Cullens' Christmas Eve bash tended to last until the wee hours, and more often than not her family stayed over. But being alone with Tremaine would definitely be playing with fire!

"Have you ridden this beast to the Garretts' yet?" he asked in a deceptively casual voice, scratching Tantrum's chin.

Tantrum tossed his silky head and had the nerve to actually snap at Tremaine's hand. Lexie grinned at Tremaine's dark glower and Tantrum's unrepentant rolling eyes. "He doesn't like you much."

"Who? Tantrum, or Jace?"

"Either one."

The way Tremaine gazed down at her made Lexie's breath catch. She should leave—*now*. If she didn't, she could be sure the scene in the buggy would be replayed, Jenny McBride or no.

In the interest of self-preservation she tried to push past him. Her hand connected with the hard muscles of his chest. She stopped cold, intensely aware of him. *My God*, she thought with sudden understanding. *I want him. I want Tremaine!*

His eyes had deepened with desire. He clasped his hand over hers. Lexie felt the seconds tick by, her heart in her mouth.

The sound of an approaching vehicle brought her to her senses. She jerked away from him and ran out of the stables. Old MacDougal was perched atop Jace's approaching carriage. As Lexie hurried to the house, the coach's door opened and Jace stepped down, smiling widely.

"Are you ready?" he asked.

She nodded. "Just give me a few minutes." She couldn't help glancing back. Tremaine was standing outside the stables, cold hostility radiating from him as his gaze centered on Jace.

Lexie ran in the house, gathered her cloak and reticule, and hopped in beside Jace before she could be tempted any further by Tremaine.

The diamond ring sparkled in the fading sunshine, glimmering lustrously against the black velvet case. Lexie stared down at it in amazement.

"I thought we would make our engagement official," Jace said with a smile in his voice.

Lexie was so stunned she was speechless. She should have expected this. Hadn't they planned to marry? But Jace had always been so distant she just hadn't dreamed he would give her a ring for Christmas.

She glanced at his handsome face, then stared blankly across the Garrett grounds, leaning against a porch post for support. He'd waited for this opportunity all through that long, tense supper, she realized. No wonder she'd felt his eyes on her while she suffered Lucinda's sharp comments.

"Something wrong?" Jace asked a bit tersely. In that moment he knew Tremaine had told her the truth about Betsy. He went cold inside.

"I can't—accept this." She swallowed. "Jace, I'm sorry. I don't think I love you anymore."

"That bastard," he muttered almost admiringly. "He's turned you against me."

"Who?" Lexie asked, but she already knew.

"Your loving brother, Tremaine."

Lexie drew a deep breath. "He told me about Betsy Talbot, if that's what you mean."

"Betsy was a mistake. It's over now. It was something that happened long before—"

"Don't." She cut him off. "I don't think you love me either. Sometimes I've even thought you wanted me just to needle Tremaine."

"I've wanted you for you, Lexie."

"And a piece of the Danner property?"

Jace wasn't inclined to honesty, but this moment required nothing less than the truth. "Maybe."

"Jace, there's something you should know. Tremaine isn't my brother. He's my stepbrother."

Lexie didn't know why she told him; she'd certainly kept her relationship with Tremaine a secret to anyone else outside the family. But it had suddenly seemed imperative that he know. She didn't expect the reaction she got, however. His face turned gray. His eyes became black pits of vengeance.

"So that's it!" he snarled. "That's why he's been so hellbent on keeping us apart! He wants you for himself. Do you want him, too?"

Lexie flushed. "Tremaine isn't the reason I can't accept your ring!"

"Then why bring him up?" he demanded furiously.

Why indeed? Lexie was momentarily stopped short. Before she could gather her wits, Jace suddenly grabbed her, crushing his mouth down on hers in that way that made her feel she was suffocating. She had to fight to free her lips. "Stop it!" she demanded coldly.

"Well, I think I've waited long enough," he muttered, dragging her toward the barn.

Lexie was both frightened and amazed at his audacity. "Let me go, Jace. What do you think you're doing? Who are you really angry with, me or Tremaine?"

"Do you know what that bastard did to me?" Jace threw Lexie inside the barn, slamming the door shut behind him. "He beat me up in the middle of Main Street, then tossed me in Fool's Falls. I've still got the bruises."

Lexie was too concerned with her own safety to pay much attention to Jace's words. She couldn't believe she was in this predicament! Her gaze darted around the cobwebby corners of the barn, searching for escape.

"Come here, Lexie," he coaxed.

She shook her head, thinking rapidly. Tremaine had humiliated Jace and now he meant to have his revenge. "Jace, be serious," she said calmly. "You can't mean to hurt me just to get back at Tremaine."

"I'm not going to hurt you, Lexie. I'm going to compromise you. Then you'll have to become my wife."

Her mouth dropped open as he advanced on her. "Jace, even if you rape me, I still won't marry you."

"Yes, you will. You'd be ruined, disgraced, tossed out of Miss Everly's School. You'd never be a lady."

She was too astounded to be truly scared. "Do you think I would care? If it were a choice of losing my respectability, or being forced into marriage with you, I would choose the former. I don't love you, Jace."

She wasn't certain he would truly carry through his threat, but she didn't take the time to find out. She stepped back into the shadowy depths of the barn, reaching behind her. Her hand encountered an unlit lantern.

"Don't come any nearer," she warned.

"Have you slept with him yet? You always were eager, Lexie. It was hell trying to hide my desire. Now I see that was a mistake."

"Get back . . ."

His eyes gleamed. "No, you must still be a virgin. Well, good, Tremaine will have to take the leftovers." He reached for her then, his fingers digging into the soft flesh of her upper arms. His mouth groped for hers.

Lexie didn't have time to think. She swung the lantern so hard it clanged against the side of his head. Jace fell to the ground. Lexie stared down at him in horror. He didn't move.

She bent over him and searched for a pulse, her fingers trembling. She nearly wept with relief to feel the steady beat. He was just unconscious.

He stirred and groaned and Lexie leapt to her feet, racing for the door. Her arms were weak and shaking as she lifted the bolt. A man's shadow confronted her and she screamed.

"Hey, lassie," old MacDougal said in concern. "Are ye all right?"

"Oh, Mac," she cried hysterically. "Jace's hurt." She glanced back to see him staggering to his feet. "Please help him."

Then she ran as fast as she could across the moonlit grounds, climbed the fence, and headed across the fields to the Danner property.

Chapter Twelve

Doc Meechum staggered to his feet, wiped his arm across his brow, and patted Sugartail fondly, his hand slapping the air twice before he found the mare's flanks. "She'll be fine. Due soon, though."

Tremaine eyed Meechum doubtfully. The man could hardly focus. He reeked of gin and looked as if he'd lived in the same clothes for a month. Tremaine had to admit Lexie was probably right about Meechum's ability as a horse doctor.

"Hell of a time to be workin'. Christmas Eve." Meechum shook his head and made a grab for one of the stall rails. Tremaine helped the drunken man to his buggy, then went back to the stables. Like Meechum, he thought Sugartail was about to foal; unlike Meechum, he thought there might be complications.

Settling into the straw outside her box, his back against the opposite stall, he draped one hand across his knee and leaned his head back, closing his eyes. Instantly he saw Lexie running toward Jace's carriage. He had to stop fooling himself. She thought she wanted Garrett, and she was just stubborn enough to marry him no matter what.

"Damn it all to hell," he muttered furiously. Why couldn't he have just told Lexie he loved her and ended the matter once and for all? She would have slept with him willingly, then, and Jace Garrett would have been just a bad memory. But some latent nobility had prevented him from lying to her. The truth was he cared too much about her to deceive her.

And look what it got you.

He was going to have to forget her. There was no other solution unless he offered false proclamations of love and asked her to marry him. But if he didn't, she would marry Jace, and he would rather lie to her than see her bound to that scoundrel.

With a growl of frustration he considered his options.

The moon was round and full, painting a ghostly white glow over the crusty ground as Lexie walked the last few feet across the hardened mud to the gate. She laid her arms on the top rail, panting. Part of her wanted to laugh hysterically. How had she ever fooled herself into believing she loved Jace?

She slipped the catch on the gate, then noticed yellow light spilling out from the crack between the top and bottom half of the stables' Dutch door.

Tremaine, she realized. Then, *Sugartail!*

She ran through the door, forgetting about Jace in an instant. Tremaine was in Sugartail's stall, his broad back turned her way, his gaze fixed firmly on the pregnant mare who was standing backward in her stall, her hindquarters strangely rigid.

As Tremaine glanced up, Lexie asked anxiously, "Has she foaled yet?"

"No. But the afterbirth's already out."

"Oh, no . . ."

She moved to the stall just as Sugartail's flanks convulsed in a hard contraction. The mare paid scant attention to either Lexie or Tremaine. Her eyes were dull and glassy.

"The foal won't survive," Lexie said around a lump in her throat. "It might already be dead. This is what happened last time."

Tremaine didn't answer her. He laid his hand on Sugartail's straining hide, his face a mask. Lexie hadn't a clue to his thoughts, nor did she care anyway. She could have cried aloud at the unfairness of losing Sugartail's foal. The mare's offspring were always beautiful and spirited. Lexie had broken more colts and fillies than she cared to count, but Sugartail's were always her favorites. Tantrum was out of Sugartail.

At that moment Sugartail's side protruded outward, and Tremaine said with more excitement than Lexie would have credited, "It's still alive!"

"We've got to get it out fast," Lexie answered quickly.

"We'll have to pull it."

She jerked her gaze to his and found him assessing her with those hard blue eyes. "I'll do it," she told him, shouldering past him. There was no time to waste with hot water and sterilization. The foal had to be pulled down the birth canal before it was asphyxiated.

Tremaine didn't argue. "Then I'll help," he said, rolling up his sleeves as Lexie flung off her cloak and touched the mare's sweaty coat. In that tense moment Sugartail emitted a half whinny so pitiful that Lexie automatically glanced back—in time to witness a tiny hoof and leg slip from the birth canal.

"Tremaine . . ."

"It's turned wrong." He was terse and controlled. "Get back, Lexie."

"What are you going to do? You don't have time to turn it. It'll suffocate."

"I know."

Lexie dug her fingers into his arm, her face taut and pale as she looked up at him through the flickering lantern light. "Tremaine, it can't possibly survive. The air'll be squeezed out of its lungs before—"

"I know, Lexie. I know!"

"Let me do it."

"Damn it, Lexie." He slammed her against the railing, his hand at her throat. "Shut up."

She could only stare at him, hollow-eyed. A moment later he released her, regarding her wordlessly for a long, deep moment. They both knew it was too late to try to turn the poor foal. There was nothing left but to pull it out.

"What do you want me to do?" she asked in a strangled voice.

"I'm going to try to bring the other leg out, then I'm going to yank hard, as hard as I can. We don't have much time."

She nodded, her heart pounding terribly. "I'll help."

"Lex, I don't know if you're—"

"I'll help," she hissed through her teeth.

He didn't argue further. Turning, he ran his hand down Sugartail's haunches but the horse didn't protest. Quickly, efficiently, he reached inside and worked to find the other back hoof and leg. Dry-mouthed, Lexie sidled next to him, shoulder to shoulder. She slid her hands above Tremaine's, wrapping her fingers around the foal's tiny legs. Seconds ticked by.

"When I say three, yank with all your strength. *All* your strength. Do you understand?"

He spoke hard and fast. Lexie nodded jerkily. "One," he muttered between his teeth. "Two." Lexie's fingers tightened and she could feel Tremaine's shoulders stiffen. *"Three!"*

Lexie strained with all her muscles, bowing backward. The foal was yanked from the birth canal, slipped from her hands, dropped with a crashing bounce against the straw-covered floor.

Lexie fell back against Tremaine, stumbling. His arms encircled her. No fluid gushed. It was a dry birth. "Is it all right?" she asked, trembling. "Is it all right?"

She knew it couldn't be. She stared at the huddled form on the floor of the box stall. Sugartail had already turned, the effects of the birth not stopping her from snuffling the small foal, licking its damp, furry hide. She whinnied and Lexie thought her heart would break.

A tiny hoof moved. "God almighty," Tremaine murmured in awe, his breath stirring her hair.

Lexie clambered away from him. She stood tense and afraid, watching the little filly with the same fiery intensity Tremaine had come to respect and admire in her. If she could have willed the filly to survive, she would have.

But she didn't need to. The foal raised its heavy head and looked around dazedly, already trying to pull its legs beneath it.

"My God," Lexie breathed, dragging a breath into aching lungs. "Oh, Tremaine." She turned shining eyes on him, her mouth a curve of pure happiness. "I think—I don't know how—but you did it!"

"We did it," he corrected her, smiling.

"Sugartail did it," Lexie amended with a laugh. "I don't think she'd like us to forget her part!"

"I imagine she won't thank us later when she begins to feel the result of our efforts."

"No, I guess not. But she's okay. And the filly is gorgeous!" Oblivious to everything but her consuming delight, Lexie hugged Tremaine's waist. She didn't notice how the uncomplicated gesture turned him to stone. She was riding high on a crest of joy and jubilation.

But Tremaine was instantly, terribly aware of Lexie. His blood pumped madly. The elemental drama had worked a kind of primitive magic. He was consumed with the desire to bury himself inside her. He wanted to pull back her hair and ravish her mouth with hard, burning kisses. He wanted to drag her to his unyielding contours. He wanted to soothe his throbbing ache in her pliant loveliness.

His hands found her forearms, blindly, and he tightened his hold. "I can't wait until Pa gets home," Lexie was babbling happily. "He was so worried, and he had a right to be. I don't know if Sugartail should foal again. This may have to be her last. I don't think my heart could stand another birth like tonight's. I—" She broke off suddenly, peering up into his face. "Tremaine?"

"Lexie, if you have any sense at all, let me go," he said stonily.

Amazed, she stepped back. Her face flushed. Without another word Tremaine strode out the door. He headed straight for the back porch and the pump. The water would be icy cold, numbing, painful. He hoped to God it would cool his blood.

Steam rose from the claw-footed porcelain tub sitting in the center of the bathing room as Lexie poured in a potful of boiling water. The tub was already half-filled with room-temperature water, the water Annie had pumped earlier in the day.

Lexie dropped her wrapper in a silken pile, stepping into the delicious water, sinking for one luxurious minute into the warm depths, fighting to keep her mind on nothing but the sensual feel of heat and solitude and buoyancy. She wanted to bask in the triumph of Sugartail's perfect little filly.

Her self-indulgence lasted the space of ten heartbeats, before she remembered Tremaine's cold words in the stables. Cold words stemming from hot need. Instantly her body reacted and she suddenly longed for him in a way that embarrassed her. Emitting a frustrated sigh, she opened her eyes, reached behind her to the carnation-scented bath salts on the vanity, and picked up the sponge.

She scrubbed herself furiously with the puffy gold-colored sponge, trying not to think. But her skin was sensitized beyond bearing. How, she wondered dismally, could Tremaine melt her with a few harsh words when Jace's touch made her skin shrivel with loathing?

Swearing softly to herself, she finished bathing and stepped from the now tepid tub, hastily toweling herself off, throwing her wrapper around her still damp body. In the fogged mirror of Eliza's vanity, she saw her pinkened flesh and the blue bruise at the base of her throat, where Tremaine had pinned her against the stall rails.

Tremaine. Her heart flipped. He was somewhere outside. He hadn't returned from the stables and the house seemed strangely quiet. Shivering, Lexie mounted the stairs, pausing halfway up. Where was he? He hadn't left without telling her, had he?

Above her, through the paned french doors leading to the widow's walk, Lexie could see the silvery moon. She had no idea what time it was but she knew it was well after midnight. Pa and Mother and Samuel and Jesse were undoubtedly spending the night at the Cullens'.

Wondering if she could have somehow missed Tremaine, she walked to the door at the opposite end of the hall from hers, rapping softly. "Tremaine?" she called. When there was no answer she twisted the handle.

His room smelled like leather and buckskin. On the oak dresser sat his black medical bag. With a pang Lexie remembered the day she'd sneaked inside this very room and pilfered the carbolic acid and catgut from his bag. It seemed such a long time ago.

Retracing her steps, she was almost to the stairs when she heard the kitchen door bang shut. Below her, Tremaine's distinctive footsteps rang purposefully across the plank-wood floor toward the den.

Lexie heard the clink of glass against glass that meant Tremaine was helping himself to Pa's liquor supply. Curious, and still smarting from his harsh words, Lexie descended the steps, walked barefoot into the arched opening to the dark pine-paneled room. She stopped short.

Tremaine stood in front of Pa's hand-carved, mahogany liquor cabinet, bare to the waist, clad only in his boots and buckskin breeches, the latter soaked with water stains. He was just closing the diamond-paned doors upon a row of crystal decanters. He turned upon hearing her enter, his blue eyes cool and impersonal. Lexie's gaze slid away to the remaining decanter on the sideboard, whose amber liquid was in serious decline—if the brimming glass next to it was any indication.

"You're drinking," she said.

"Your powers of observation never cease to amaze me," he agreed equably. "Want some?" He was already reaching for the cabinet door. "I'm drinking whiskey, but as I recall," he added with faint humor, "you prefer scotch."

"I don't prefer anything. Why are you—dressed like that?" She gestured helplessly to his bare broad shoulders and muscular chest.

Tremaine was intent on pouring her a drink, however, and didn't see her movement. At her trailing voice he glanced around. "What's wrong with the way I'm dressed?"

"What happened to your clothes?"

"I took off my shirt to wash. Here." He strode toward her, pressing a cool glass into her hand. Staring down at her shimmery dark blue wrapper, he lifted a brow and said, "I could ask the same of you."

Lexie drew the silk cover more closely to her neck. "I took

a bath in the tub. But you didn't come in. You were outside."

He nodded. "That's right. I used pump water."

"Pump water!" She stared at him as if he'd lost his mind. "But it's freezing. Whatever possessed you to do that?"

He shrugged. "It seemed like a good idea at the time." Tossing back half his drink, he grimaced as the burning fluid raced down his throat.

His mood was hard to discern, leaving Lexie vaguely discomfited. "I don't understand you at all."

He gave a short bark of laughter. "Well, that makes two of us. Was there something you wanted?"

"No."

"How was your dinner at the Garretts'?"

So that was it. Lexie drew a breath and, remembering how Jace had looked sprawled across the barn floor, she smiled to herself. She was unaware that Tremaine misinterpreted that secret smile to mean something entirely different. "It was a disaster. Lucinda had her eagle eye on me all evening, and Kelsey looked as if she wanted to be anywhere but where she was. The mayor of Malone was there."

"And what about Jace?" he asked in a dangerous voice.

Lexie couldn't help enjoying his jealousy. At least it meant he cared. "Jace gave me an engagement ring."

He glanced sharply at her hands, saw they were bare, then stared down into his glass. By the implacable set to his jaw, she knew he wasn't going to ask where the ring was, and that made her angry enough to bait him.

"What? No comments on how I ought to run my life? No words of caution about my future husband?"

He lifted dangerously simmering blue eyes to hers. "For all I care, you can do anything you damn well please, Lexie."

"Then my marrying Jace Garrett doesn't bother you?"

"If you can't see Garrett for the man he is, then your marriage will be a match made in heaven." Tremaine swallowed the rest of his drink and turned to the cabinet for another.

Lexie was furious. She might be naive when it came to the opposite sex, but it didn't take a master of deduction to see that Tremaine was emotionally involved, whether he wanted to admit it or not. "Whom would you rather I married?" she asked, sipping the pungent scotch. The fiery liquid stole her breath and she nearly choked.

"I don't give a goddamn what you do," he said chillingly. "Just leave me alone."

"Fine." She set her drink down on the sideboard. She'd had enough. Tossing her head, she said coldly, "I don't give a goddamn what you do either. Good night."

His hand shot out and grabbed her as she tried to leave. Lexie's temper flared, her every muscle tensed. She glared at him, green eyes sparkling with suppressed anger. But her breath lodged in her throat at the hunger in his gaze.

She calmly pulled on her arm, but the pressure of his grip didn't lessen. "Whatever's upset you, it has nothing to do with me."

"Oh, hasn't it?" he asked silkily.

"No."

He laughed softly without humor. "You are the worst liar I've ever met. It has *every*thing to do with you—and you know it."

Her heart started to pound in irregular beats at the cold anger emanating from him. She'd asked for this, she realized. She'd deliberately baited him, forced him to confront her. It had not been her most inspired idea, she realized belatedly, her gaze fixed on the wall of his chest.

Tremaine's blue eyes glittered with a dangerous flame but he made no sudden moves. It slowly dawned on Lexie that he was fighting for control of his emotions—which she found unnerving to the extreme. She hadn't meant to push him so far.

But then he suddenly released her, and where she should have felt relief she was crushed with disappointment. "Good night," he said, striding out of the den. She heard the front door crash closed behind him.

Lexie stood frozen for the space of two heartbeats. She'd be damned if she would let him just walk out on her when she was boiling for a fight! Cinching her silken wrapper, she yanked open the door behind him, half walking, half running across the moon-drenched ground behind his purposeful, shadowy figure.

She caught him at the barn. He'd just lighted a lantern

when she appeared at the open door, winded. "I wasn't through talking!" she declared furiously.

"Christ, Lexie! What are you doing?" He glared at her as if she were a bothersome child.

"You didn't give me a chance to explain about Jace."

"I don't want to hear about Jace."

"All I wanted to say was—"

"Shut up, Lexie, and go to bed. You'll freeze to death out here."

"Me? You're the one without a shirt. If you'd just listen to me—"

"I'm dead tired," he cut her off. "I've been up over thirty hours already and I just want to put you out of my mind."

"Tremaine—"

"I want to take you to bed," he said bluntly. "Get out of here unless you feel the same way. Now."

"Wasn't Jenny McBride enough for you?"

It was a mistake to taunt him. He was across the barn floor in two strides, pinning her against the wall. Lexie's impulsiveness was her bane. The flame of anger lighting his eyes said she'd crossed the limits this time.

"I have not been with Jenny McBride," he said through his teeth.

Her heart soared. She couldn't help herself. Of course, she didn't believe him. Why should she? But, well, maybe it was true and if that was the case . . .

Her tumbling thoughts were abruptly cut off when his hands plunged into her silken blond tresses. "What are you doing?" she demanded, dry-mouthed.

"Oh, for God's sake, Lexie. You know," he muttered, bending his head to capture her lips in an earth-shattering kiss.

She thrilled to the feel of his warm lips. Still, she had to remember just what Tremaine wanted from her. There was a big difference between lust and love.

Reluctantly, she tried to twist away but his mouth was expertly persuasive. His hand invaded her heavy mane, holding her head back, lifting up her face. Her lips trembled against the force of his. She pressed on his chest to thrust him away, but his icy cold skin diverted her attention. He *had* washed himself with the pump water.

"Tremaine," she murmured on a soft breath against his hot mouth.

For an answer he redoubled his efforts, holding her more possessively, his lips insistently shaping and fitting hers to his own needs. It was as if he wanted to blot out her voice. His kiss was so forceful, so hot and demanding that Lexie went numb. She forgot, for an instant, that she was intent on pushing him away. Dazedly she felt a now familiar wanton tingling sweeping up her legs, settling between her thighs.

At her lack of resistance his hard grip on her scalp lessened. He drew back to look at her through heavy-lidded eyes, his breathing short and shallow.

"I think you've made your point," Lexie managed to choke out. "I'll go now."

"Oh, you will, will you? And leave me like this?"

She wanted to misunderstand, but the pressure of his probing manhood was impossible to ignore. "I don't know what you mean," she said and he laughed, the sound grating on her pride.

There was the faintest amusement in his eyes as his head bent to hers once more. This time the pressure wasn't quite so intense. His lips were mobile and persuasive, slanting across hers with sweet possessiveness, stoking flaming needs within her. Lexie's breath came short and fast. Her hands clutched his bare arms for support, her fingers digging into the sinewy muscles.

He wrapped one arm around her, tautly, holding her so tightly that her chest felt constricted. His belt buckle dug through the shimmering silk wrapper into her abdomen. His thighs were pressed against her shaking legs. He moved to plant a series of fierce, wet kisses across her mouth and face and neck.

Wave after wave of liquid longings stormed through Lexie's veins. His tongue thrust its way past the barrier of her teeth, teasing and taunting and plunging into the sweet, dark warmth of her mouth. His hand ran convulsively down her back and up again, his tongue deepening its insidious demands.

Lexie's legs were water. Her knees wobbled. Tremaine wedged her against the rough wall, pressing his hips to hers in a way that had her writhing against him. She was too mindless to be embarrassed. The feel of his hard masculinity, throbbing insistently through the barrier of their clothes, was intoxicating.

He reached for the tie on her wrapper and Lexie made an involuntary whimper of protest.

"Don't," he commanded in a throbbing whisper near her ear, his breath hot and sweet. "I've wanted you too long."

Lexie tried to speak, but his mouth closed down on hers again with raw, dizzying hunger. His hand slid down her spine, drawing tight, insidious circles against the small of her back. Her flimsy wrapper twisted taut against her breasts, outlining their fullness. The loose tie binding the thin fabric together unwound with a shameful lack of resistance, exposing a gap of skin from neck to toe.

Tremaine's hand moved inside the fabric, sliding along her hip, and she clamped down on his fingers, her eyes wide. This was more than she'd bargained for.

His smile hurt. "Let me."

His hand moved upward, slowly wrapping around one ivory breast. Her head lolled back, her eyes closed, a moan was wrung from her throat.

"You're not going to marry Jace," he growled, plundering her mouth once more.

Some distant part of her mind rebelled at the autocratic way he was treating her. First Jace, now Tremaine, felt as if he could somehow force her into bending to his will. Lexie struggled but her movements seemed to make him more intent on branding her as his own. The worst part of it was her traitorous body was responding in ways that were beyond belief. When his mouth worked down her throat, closing over the stiff peak of one nipple, she gasped in pleasure.

Her hands dug into his hair. Her mind reeled. Her skin quivered beneath his mouth. Her throat was a trembling, white arch that Tremaine's tongue licked and moistened.

Wordlessly, he pulled the wrapper from her shoulders, letting it slide to a pool at her feet. Lexie swallowed, shivering, alarmed at how far things had gotten out of control. She was going to have to stop things now.

"Tremaine—I don't think—that is—I can't do this."

"Because of your intended? Why let that stop you? It hasn't stopped Jace."

Angry, she tried to push him away, to bend and retrieve her wrapper, but his hands circled her bare waist, pulling her intimately forward. He glared down at her.

"I'm not going to marry Jace," she hissed. Lexie's face was flushed. "That's what I've been trying to tell you, but you're too damn interested in seducing me into submission to give me a chance!"

"You told me he gave you an engagement ring," Tremaine reminded her, unrepentant.

"I gave it back to him."

She finally had his attention. "Why?" he demanded.

"Isn't it obvious? I don't love him. He doesn't love me."

"Then why did you let me believe that—" He cut himself off on a swift intake of breath. "You were trying to torture me," he said in dawning amazement.

Lexie was embarrassed. She *had* wanted to nettle him about Jace. "I just didn't like the way you were acting. You were the one who brought up Jace."

Tremaine glanced down at her ivory shoulders, his mouth twitching as he realized what had prompted her actions tonight. Well, two could play that game. "I thought you loved him. It seems to me you said as much more than once."

She kicked him. She couldn't help herself. Here she was torn between passion and fury and all he could do was laugh!

Tremaine barely noticed. He pulled her to him, crushing her close, kissing her ruthlessly, fighting back laughter. His hands slid over her back and bare buttocks.

"Lexie, nothing's changed," he said, dragging her against him to prove his point. "You'd better get out of here if you expect me to be a gentleman."

He handed her her wrapper and bemused, Lexie put it on. She made the mistake of meeting his gaze and she saw the way a muscle in his jaw tensed.

He stalked toward the other end of the barn; she could hear his boots thudding on the ladder that led to the loft.

Lexie drew a shuddering breath, torn. She should leave.

Go back to the house, to the warmth of her own bed. Curiously, she didn't feel cold. It was then she realized a soft Chinook wind was blowing from the west; a phenomenon that raised the winter temperature, sometimes into the seventies.

She followed after Tremaine, climbing the ladder to the loft. She stopped at the edge, to see Tremaine on his back, sprawled across a blanket spread on a thick mound of hay. Another blanket lay folded beside him. Moonlight streamed blue-white through the slatted vent under the eaves, striping the surrounding hay.

"What are you doing?" she asked.

"Sleeping."

"In the barn?"

He slowly levered himself upward, draping one arm across his upraised knee. "I don't want to sleep in the same house with you. I don't think I could. You should be glad. You're safer there alone."

Lexie sat on the hay-strewn loft floor, dusting off her hands. "You seem to think I've been in danger of losing my virginity. That's not true. I can take care of myself."

"Oh, really? Well, let me give you a little piece of advice. If I'd really wanted you, I could have taken you and there's very little you could have done about it. Remember that next time you're alone with a man—any man."

Tentatively, she sat down on the floor, tugging her wrapper closely around her. She kept a careful distance between them. "I was alone with Jace tonight and I fended him off."

"What do you mean?"

She glared into his handsomely rakish face. "Jace tried to have his way with me tonight when I told him I wouldn't marry him. I had to hit him over the head with a lantern to escape."

Tremaine let out a string of invectives that singed Lexie's ears. "Well, don't leave me in suspense," he drawled nastily. "What happened?"

"I hit him on the side of the head and he went down without a sound. Unfortunately, he was rousing by the time I left. I think he's going to survive."

"Too bad. The bastard. I'd like to kill him!"

"So it's all right for you to want me, but not Jace?"

"Yes!" he growled, tossing aside all his better intentions and reaching for her again. He wanted to brand her as his own and to hell with the consequences.

Lexie turned, but he was too quick. She squirmed in his grasp, but it was no use. He was much too strong for her. She laughed nervously as he half-pushed down on the blanket. "Stop it, Tremaine. You don't really expect me to . . . to . . ."

"Yes?" He was grinning like a maniac.

"To take this any further!"

For an answer his arm curved sinuously around her waist as he sank down beside her. She opened her mouth to—what? Scream? There was no one around to hear her. He stared at her through lazy, amused eyes. Finding her voice, Lexie said crisply, "Pa and Mother will be back any time."

"They're spending the night at the Cullens'. You know they are." He kissed her neck, softly, slowly, sliding open her wrapper once more.

It was one thing to flirt with danger; another to live it. Lexie sensed Tremaine was just teasing her, but she also knew she was on the verge of making love to him.

Lexie drew back, placing her hands on his shoulders. She thrust with all her strength but he was immovable. His skin was sleek; his muscles hard. After several seconds she gave up.

When his lips caressed her throat, she gave in with a soft sigh, her hands winding around his neck.

"You're lovely," he said huskily. In the moonglow her limbs looked long and white. Her heart pounded and she squeezed her eyes tightly closed.

"I think I must be out of my head. I can't believe I'm lying here like—like this—and letting you kiss me."

"Kissing you is just the beginning."

She peered up at him. "You wouldn't do anything I didn't want you to, would you?"

Her innocence amused him. "No."

"Well, I don't want to kiss you anymore."

"Okay. Then touch me."

"What?"

Tremaine grabbed her hand and pressed it to the hard muscles of his chest. She tried to yank back, but the crisp hairs beneath her fingers and the strong beat of his heart imprisoned her more thoroughly than iron chains. His own hands explored her satiny flesh, running up and down her body until she was twisting and gasping.

"Still don't want to be kissed?" he asked softly.

"Damn you." She pulled his face to hers, fitting his mouth hungrily over hers, thrilling to the feel of his plundering tongue. His hand encircled her breast, his thumb rubbing hard over her nipple.

Tremaine was no proof against such a ready invitation. "Oh, Lexie," he moaned. "Lexie, I want you." His mouth closed over the taut peak his thumb had teased and readied.

Lexie jumped in startled resistance. My God! His mouth was on her breast and he was sucking with fierce dominance, drawing the nipple deeper into his mouth with each movement of his lips and tongue. Her fingers delved into his black hair, digging hard. She gasped and writhed as piercing stabs of desire shot through her.

Then she felt his mouth move downward, his tongue sampling the softness of her belly. She was shivering all over, unaware that he was deliberately stoking the fire of her desire, unaware that he meant to have her burning for him.

With a sudden twist he was pulled away from her, but Lexie had barely blinked her eyes open to see why when the sight that met her eyes made her freeze. Without the slightest shame, Tremaine was pulling off his boots and breeches.

This was going too far! "No!" she gasped, closing her eyes, but not before she had received an alarmingly thorough view of his potent, male body.

"No?" His tone was amused as he sank down beside her once more, gathering her heated flesh into his hard embrace.

"Tremaine, you're drunk. You must be. And I'm—"

"You're what?"

She swallowed, mesmerized by the desire flaming in his eyes. "Going to be dreadfully sorry."

His gaze suddenly narrowed on the blue bruise near her collarbone and he swept in a harsh breath. "Garrett?" he demanded in a soul-chilling voice, gently touching the tender skin.

Lexie flushed. "Uh, no. You did that. In the stables."

The look on his face was indescribable. There was regret and pain and disbelief. He was thunderstruck. "God, I'm sorry, Lexie," he muttered, shaken.

The honesty and tenderness of his response made her realize she loved him. Pure and simple. Even knowing he didn't return that love. His shock at hurting her was real and touchingly vulnerable.

She lifted her lips to his on her own, raining soft, innocent kisses across his cheeks, his eyelids, the sensual curve of his mouth. Someday he might return her love.

"Lexie," he groaned, and now it was Tremaine who sought to pull away.

Lexie had had enough waiting. And her body was hungry for his. She wound herself around him, shattering the last vestige of his resistance. But when his fingers dipped lower, covering the soft triangle between her legs, she clamped her legs together in shock.

"Do you know how long I've wanted to do this?" he muttered against her mouth, never removing his fingers. "Do you?"

She shook her head, alarmed at the flowing moistness he could induce so easily.

"Do you want me?" he asked softly, persuasively.

She couldn't answer.

"Do you want me?" he persisted.

"Y-es."

It was her sweet honesty that broke his control and made him give up his tender torture. He moved over her, poised, and as he stared into her innocent, trusting face he felt a moment of indecision. He wanted her—God, how he wanted her—but what right did he have to ruin her?

Her skin was flushed and dewy with sweat. As he fought for control he felt her warm wetness flow over him. He ground his hips against hers, wringing a moan of pleasure from her. Her head was thrown back, her fingers holding shyly to his buttocks, asking for something she couldn't name. It was Tremaine's undoing. With a groan he muttered, "Don't be afraid."

She was petrified, but unable to stop. Lexie could feel his probing maleness. His hands softly tormented her and she moaned and twisted, seeking a closer union. Tremaine slowly entered her, pushing slightly deeper into her tight warmth with each stroke. Finally, when there was nothing else he could do, he drew back and plunged deep into her willing softness. Lexie cried out in pain.

"I'm sorry, darling," he whispered hoarsely as Lexie automatically froze in preparation for another thrust. All she could think about was that he called her "darling." It kept her from realizing what she'd done.

He kissed her gently. The tenderness in his gaze banished some of the shame and remorse already flooding through her veins. His lips grazed her temple and her ear, finally coming to rest on her trembling lips.

He was still buried deep within her and when he moved she stiffened. But there was no more pain. Expecting him to leave her, she was amazed and overwhelmed by the feel of him plunging deeper inside her, then easing back, plunging a little farther the next time. Sweat dampened his forehead from the concentrated effort to hold back and give her pleasure. Lexie's lips slackened as his efforts began to have their desired effect. Something was happening inside her. Her hips arched to meet his. She emitted a little whimper of need. Spiraling sensations radiated like liquid heat from the core where his flesh stroked hers.

"Lexie, Lexie," he rasped in anguish. "I can't wait—"

His words sank into her brain and she reached a shuddering ecstasy at that moment, crying out at the feeling of pure pleasure that engulfed her. Tremaine thrust deeply inside her with sweet, savage force and she instinctively wrapped herself around him. He gasped her name at the peak of his own climax and Lexie, still stunned by the pleasure he could give her, was stirred at the power of moving him so.

He rolled onto his side, bringing her with him, and she heard his labored breathing. "Lexie," he murmured again, cradling her close. He sounded as astounded as she was.

"I love you," she murmured in a heart-wrenching voice. "I love you."

His mouth extinguished any more words. He sheltered her in his arms. She didn't know that he couldn't bear hearing her vow her love again. Too many times in the past he'd heard those hollow, empty words flow from feminine lips. He knew Lexie didn't mean them. She was only seduced by their lovemaking.

"Shhh." He pulled her atop him and let his hands slide down her back.

"But I do."

"This is not," he said deliberately, "the time to use your mouth for talking." And he covered her lips with his own and began the glorious business of making love all over again.

Chapter Thirteen

∽⟨✦⟩∼

Lexie turned over in bed, vaguely aware of a tenderness between her legs and at her thighs. She opened her eyes and watched pale afternoon sunlight stream through the window across her comforter. It's Christmas, she thought with surprise, then with a torrent of memory: *Tremaine!*

His familiar scent lingered on her skin. She brought the covers to her chin, shaking as she recalled the events of the night before. She'd lain in his arms—no, *participated* in his fervent lovemaking!

"Oh, God," she murmured, burying her face in the pillow.

She didn't know how long they'd been together when the coldness of the barn had finally penetrated. Tremaine had folded her in her silken wrapper and carried her to her bedroom. Lexie had been so bemused she barely remembered. But she remembered now.

It took about thirty seconds of reflection for Lexie to bound out of bed, galvanized into action. If anyone found out . . .

Quickly, she brushed her hair and washed her face, pulling a muslin dress over her head, taking a moment to examine her reflection. She looked just the same. The same slightly tilted nose. The same green eyes. The same honey-blond hair. No one would know that last night she'd become a woman in every sense of the word.

Guilt and shame washed over Lexie in equal measure as she scurried down the backstairs to the kitchen. No one was about. Everyone was sleeping in, she realized with resounding relief.

She stared at the laid-out fixings for Christmas dinner. Soon Annie and Cook would arrive to prepare the meal. Everything was the same! She clapped a hand to her mouth and forced back a hysterical trill of laughter.

A crashing wave of weakness rolled over her as she recalled the way Tremaine had cried out his pleasure.

Oh, Lexie, Lexie. I want you . . .

Her heart lurched painfully. A sound on the stairway brought her back to the present. Her parents were home. Someone was up.

"Lexie?" It was Samuel's voice, bleary with sleep.

"Go back up to bed," she said briskly, appearing in the archway that led from the kitchen to the main hall. Samuel was standing on the stairs, looking younger than his fourteen years. "Nobody's awake yet. We won't celebrate Christmas until this evening."

"Pa's up. He never went to bed. He went to the stables to check on Sugartail."

"You sure he didn't come in? You might not have heard him."

Samuel ran a hand across his eyes and yawned. "Nah, he's still out there. I'm getting dressed and going to join him." He clomped back up the stairs and left Lexie standing in the kitchen archway.

Lexie hurried after him to the sanctuary of her bedroom. She sat on the coverlet, twisting her hands in her lap. Be calm, she told herself. Think. It's not the end of the world.

She braided her hair for something to do, pinning it at the back of her head. Every time she thought about Tremaine's lovemaking, her stomach flipped over and her heart ached with desire and dread. Every time she moved, she felt the remnants of his stormy passion.

She clutched the bedpost and half laughed in disbelief. She loved him. She'd realized that sometime last night. She never, ever wanted anyone else to make such lush, wonderful, poignant love to her. She wanted Tremaine. Only Tremaine.

Unable to stand her own company, Lexie ran downstairs in time to see Samuel racing toward the stables. Her heart pounded. Where was Tremaine? What would he say to her when he saw her? How would he react?

She had determined to go in search of him when Pa and Samuel came walking toward the house. Jesse was with them, too, and it was clear he was in disfavor. Pa was bellowing at him.

". . . too damn young to be tom-catting around. Next time you spend the night out, don't bother coming home at all."

Jesse's face was coolly mutinous. "Does that apply to Tremaine, too? Or only to me? I notice he's not around."

Lexie's heart nearly stopped. Seeing her at the door, Pa set his jaw and didn't answer. "Where's Tremaine?" Lexie asked, unable to help herself.

"Rock Springs," answered Jesse as he strode past her. "Apparently Jenny McBride came to the house last night and got him. He left Pa a note."

Jesse and Samuel headed toward the kitchen. Lexie stood frozen. Jenny McBride? *Jenny McBride!* She looked at Pa, who was removing his boots with the bootjack.

"Are you all right?" Pa asked, examining her colorless face with concern.

Lexie managed to nod. "What did—Mrs. McBride want?"

"I don't know," he answered tersely.

But Lexie understood. Choking on her humiliation, she ran upstairs. Tremaine had lied to her! He'd teased and cajoled and made her believe he cared about her, then he'd gone back to Jenny.

She pressed her hands to her cheeks, fighting down a wave of nausea. She closed her eyes and cried inside. How could she have thrown everything she valued away on the hope that Tremaine would come to love her? His actions today showed her the real truth of the situation. She was simply another woman to him.

Tremaine slid off Fortune's back and wearily walked the stallion inside the stables. He tried to shake off his lingering depression, but the Harthorn child's death haunted him. There'd been precious little he could do, yet the boy's small body lying still and cold on the bed was a memory he would rather forget.

Jenny had been with him. She'd coaxed him into going back to her place, but Tremaine had stood silent and unresponsive in the middle of the kitchen. Even when she wrapped her arms around him, he hadn't moved.

"Why don't you stay?" she'd invited.

He'd shaken his head. "I can't."

"Why not?"

Tremaine had thought of Lexie. All he wanted was to lose himself in her. "Because there's someone else in my life," he'd told Jenny as gently as he could.

Now he just wanted to be with Lexie again. He hurried to get Fortune in his stall and stiffened when he sensed someone else in the barn. His father was leaning over the rails to Sugartail's stall, smiling.

"She's a beauty, isn't she?" Joseph said.

Tremaine nodded. How would he feel when he learned about him and Lexie? Tremaine sensed it was not going to be well-received.

"Cullen said you've been working in Rock Springs. Some families were sick with influenza." He cleared his throat. "Was that why Jenny McBride stopped by today?"

Tremaine suddenly realized what his father was getting at. "I didn't spend Christmas with Jenny, if that's what you're asking. The youngest Harthorn boy died today."

"I'm sorry, Tremaine." Pa was shaken.

"There was nothing anyone could do."

Joseph dropped a hand on Tremaine's tense shoulders. "It's not easy being a doctor sometimes. You look done in, son. Maybe you ought to catch some sleep before Christmas supper."

"Christmas supper." He thought of seeing Lexie, sitting at the table, and knew he couldn't hide his feelings from Pa any longer. "There's a girl I'm interested in," he said at length, feeling his way.

"Seriously interested in?"

He nodded.

Joseph's face slowly broke into a grin. "Well, good. Now Jesse can't throw your dubious assignations in my face. You planning to marry this girl?"

"Pa, it's Lexie."

He stared in disbelief. "Lexie? Our Lexie?" Seeing his son's implacable face, he panicked. "You can't marry Lexie. Everyone thinks she's your half-sister!"

"But she's not, is she? We'll just have to let the world know the truth."

Joseph was stunned. Tremaine, hoping the discussion was more or less closed, picked up a currycomb and began tending to Fortune. The sooner he could be with Lexie, the better.

"We can't let the world know the truth, Tremaine!"

"Why not?" Tremaine brushed Fortune's coat with smooth, hard strokes. He wasn't going to let his father's opposition stand in his way.

Joseph reached over and grabbed his arm, his fingers digging into his flesh. Surprised, Tremaine stared at him. His father's face was deathly pale.

"Pa?"

"You don't understand. People will start asking questions. The truth will come out." His words tumbled over one another, faster and faster. "Everyone will ask questions."

Tremaine's brows drew together in angry puzzlement. "Since when do you care what people think?"

"Since when it involves Eliza!" Joseph bellowed. "If Eliza's past comes out, she could go to prison!"

"What?"

"Eliza killed her first husband," he choked out, clutching Tremaine as if his own life depended on it. "And if certain people learn the truth, she could be prosecuted for murder!"

Lexie paced the confines of the parlor. She'd stopped flaying herself over her own naiveté and was now trying to determine what to do. She would confront Tremaine. She deserved some kind of explanation. There had to be an explanation.

Jesse, dressed in a dark suit that made him look older and forbidding—and an awful lot like Tremaine—came into the room. He glanced at the Christmas tree, then his gaze fell on Lexie.

"What's wrong?"

"Nothing!"

"You've been nervous as a cat all day."

"I've got something on my mind." She swept past him to the windows, staring out at the deepening twilight.

"Tremaine's at the stables with Pa. He came back about half an hour ago."

Lexie's heart leaped to her throat, nearly suffocating her. She swallowed, threw Jesse a measuring look, then decided she didn't care what he thought. Gathering the rustling skirts and petticoats of her gown, she ran out the front door.

Tremaine searched his father's eyes for some sign that he was joking. Fortune's warm breath steamed gently in the cool December air. "What the hell are you talking about?" he asked softly.

Joseph sighed and ran a hand through his silvering hair. "Eliza hit Ramsey Gainsborough, her first husband, over the head with a poker. She killed him straight out."

Tremaine stared in amazement. "My God, you're serious."

"She killed him," he repeated dully, nodding, as if to convince himself as well.

"Why?"

Joseph's face tightened. "Because he was forcing her into bed with him—like he did every night. It was self-defense."

The color drained from Tremaine's face. Images of how he'd spent the night with Lexie paraded across his mind. He could scarcely keep his mind on what Pa was saying. Dazedly, he muttered, "If it was self-defense, she's innocent."

"Gainsborough's friends will never believe it was an accident. That's why Eliza ran away."

"Why didn't you tell me this before?"

"Eliza and I felt there was no need."

"You mean *Eliza* didn't want it known! My God!" He threw down the currycomb with such force that Fortune jumped, startled. "She killed her husband."

"And he deserved it," Joseph insisted. "Lexie's father was a powerful, sadistic rapist. He married Eliza for her family name, then he used and abused her, treating her no better than an animal."

Tremaine said nothing. He couldn't believe what he was hearing! Nor could he see that it had any connection to his wanting Lexie.

"She told me the whole story years after we were married. She couldn't even speak of it at first. Gainsborough dragged her upstairs and threw her on the bed. She crawled to the floor. She was by the hearth. She grabbed the poker and when he came for her, she hit him over the head."

Tremaine swore, softly, in disbelief.

"Even though Gainsborough's dead, she still hates him with all her heart," Joseph finished.

Tremaine let himself out of Fortune's stall. "So what has this got to do with me and Lexie?" He strode toward the back of the stables, near the tack room, and stared blankly through the square glassless window to the open fields beyond.

"I don't want Lexie to know what a cruel man her father was," Joseph went on. "I don't even want her to know his name. It's as much for Lexie's protection as Eliza's. Gainsborough was very powerful. Too powerful. He had friends on both sides of the law."

"That's no reason to keep the truth from her! Besides, it's been years."

"Gainsborough's friends aren't the type that forget. If they could locate Eliza, they would find a way to send her to prison."

In one of those blinding moments of perfect clarity, Tremaine suddenly understood why his father had given up his practice to live in obscurity in Rock Springs. It was for Eliza. It had all been for Eliza. Eliza, who was southern born, possessed of a hundred useless feminine skills and pursuits, unable to fit into a small Oregon town of pioneers. Now he knew why he'd never felt comfortable around her, why he'd never been able to let her fully step into the role of motherhood even though he'd wanted her to! She was a fugitive, and she'd turned his father into a fugitive too.

"No one must know Lexie is Gainsborough's daughter." Joseph's tone was stern. "No one. Everyone must think she's mine."

"The family already knows differently," Tremaine argued hoarsely. He hadn't really thought in terms of marriage but he suddenly knew Lexie was the woman he wanted to share his life with. It was impossible that Eliza's secret could stop him. He wouldn't let it!

Joseph drew a deep breath. "I wasn't worried last summer. It had been so long. But then I got the letter."

Tremaine stared at him, hollow inside. "What letter?"

"It arrived a few days ago. Someone claiming to be a relative wants to know if I'm the Joseph Danner who came around the horn on the *Bonnie Lynne* in '64."

Icy dread settled around Tremaine's heart. He felt a stab of primal fear. "Someone wants to find you—or Eliza."

Joseph nodded. "Eliza killed a powerful man. Gainsborough's friends want vengeance against her. What better way to hurt her than to use her daughter—*Gainsborough's daughter*—against her?"

"You're sure the letter isn't from a relative?"

"Reasonably sure. It's—ah—not the first one I've received. But the other one was a long time ago."

A misty memory of the day he'd overheard Joseph and Eliza discussing Lexie's true parentage floated across his mind. There had been a letter in Pa's jacket pocket.

"You've got to tell Lexie," Tremaine said suddenly. "You've got to warn her."

"Eliza would never stand for it."

"Hang Eliza," Tremaine snarled. "If Gainsborough's men are still searching for her, they'll eventually find her."

"Not if we keep the secret within our family. No one else knows about Eliza's past. Everyone thinks Lexie's my daughter. We're safe as long as we don't tell anyone."

Tremaine shook his head. "It's too late. Lexie knows the truth. She sees no reason to keep it a secret. She's told people."

"Well, she'll keep it a secret from now on," Joseph declared, worry turning his voice to anger. "But you can't marry her. Ever. Jace Garrett's not my choice for a husband for Lexie, by any means, but he's safer than you are."

Tremaine's head snapped up. "Jace Garrett's a conniving snake! Besides, Lexie's already turned him down."

"Well, be that as it may, you'll not marry her, Tremaine. You can't. You'll put Eliza *and* Lexie in jeopardy if you do."

Tremaine stood with his back to his father, his hands clenching and unclenching. His mind was spinning in terrible, frozen circles. "You can't hide this!"

"I must," he said on a weary sigh. Clouds gathered in his blue eyes. "I know your feelings for Lexie run deep. I've seen the way you look at her when you think no one's watching. But you've got to forget her. Let her marry Jace and have a trouble-free life. It's what's best for her."

"You don't understand," he choked out, vivid images of Lexie's supple body filling his mind, her soft cries echoing in his ears.

"You might love her, son. But if you do, you'll leave her to Jace."

Tremaine didn't speak. Love her? *Love* her? He wasn't prepared to admit to loving anyone. But his feelings for Lexie were as close to love as he'd ever gotten.

"I wrote back and lied," Joseph went on. "I said I came on the spring wagon train a few years later. I don't want anyone finding Eliza."

Tremaine nodded. He turned blindly toward the door. "What's the return address on that letter?"

"It came through the Victor Flynne Investigative Agency in Portland. Why?"

"I'll check it."

"Pa?"

Tremaine froze. Lexie stood in the golden lantern light spilling through the doorway. She wore the dark green dress she'd had on at the Winter Ball. Her hair fell loose to her shoulders; her green eyes slid him a look full of hurt and questions.

For a moment Tremaine had the urge to tell her the full truth. To hell with Eliza and her first husband's powerful friends. He wanted Lexie. He wanted her now. But some of his father's pleas had struck home. He had to know more before he could jeopardize her future.

"We're just coming back to the house, Lex," Pa said gravely, shooting a glance at Tremaine.

"No." Tremaine's voice was a harsh rasp. "I'm leaving."

"Leaving?" Lexie's face paled.

He couldn't have wounded her more if he'd told her straight out that he'd used her. His lips thinned in anger at the sight of his father's frightened face. Damn it all to hell. He was going to hurt her no matter what he did!

"Tremaine . . . why . . . ?" Lexie asked in a small voice.

He shoved past her, closing his ears to her gasp of anguish, lashing himself for the bitter tears that swam in her green eyes. Until he settled this thing with Victor Flynne, he would never convince Pa the danger was past.

He waited outside in the shadow of the barn until Lexie walked back to the house. Her head was bent, her arms wrapped around her middle. But as he watched her she lifted her chin in that defiant way that wrenched his heart. He watched until the front door closed behind her, the frost-kissed wreath swinging on its hook from the force. This was the most hellish mess he could ever imagine. He strode to where his buggy stood forlornly at the side of the stables.

"Lexie, there's something I want to ask you."

Lexie lifted her eyes from her plate and looked at Pa.

"Your mother and I would like you to keep the truth of your parentage a secret. It would be simpler for all of us if no one started asking questions."

She was so miserable she could hardly think straight. "Why?"

He cleared his throat, fiddling with his fork. "We're a family and I'd like to keep it that way," he said lamely. "I've already talked to Tremaine."

Lexie's fingers dug into the linen tablecloth. Inside she was screaming. "Tremaine—still wants people to think— he's my brother?"

Pa nodded.

"He wants to hide the truth?"

Frowning, Pa nodded again.

Lexie's throat closed. Tremaine was behind this! He'd made a mistake and now didn't have the courage to face it.

Fresh tears scalded her throat but she willed them away. "I won't say anything," she answered bitterly.

"Lexie, what's wrong?" Eliza asked with concern.

Lexie picked up her fork and stabbed her meat. "Nothing," she choked out. "Not a single damn thing."

Fortune's bridle jingled as he tossed his dark head and whinnied at the sight of other horses standing at the Rock Springs hitching posts. As if in tandem with his dark thoughts, the weather had dropped thirty degrees overnight. No more Chinook wind. Now the wind whistled off the mountains to the east, wickedly cold. His hands were raw and red as he snapped the reins. He'd been riding around so long and so aimlessly that it took him by surprise that he'd reached the town.

With a muttered curse he pulled the buggy up in front of the nearest hitching post. He wanted the company of a woman. He wanted to wipe out Lexie's memory. He wanted to drink himself into a stupor and forget who he was.

He stalked blindly through the frigid darkness, toward the lights and flickering tinsel glinting through the steamed windows of the Half Moon Saloon. A light dusting of corn snow fell on his shoulders, peppering his face.

Conrad Templeton greeted him with the indulgent pleasure of a man who'd already imbibed too much spirit. He clapped Tremaine on the back and said in a happy, unsteady slur, "Good tidings to you, my man. Lemme pour you a draft."

Tremaine was in no mood for beer; he wanted a bottle of whiskey—maybe two. But he let the happy barkeep bring him a foaming draft nonetheless. He sat with it at a small table, staring into space.

Doc Meechum stumbled up to the bar, attempting three times to pull some coins from his dirt-crusted pants before they spilled out, pinging against the floorboards, falling into the cracks. Swearing, he bent to pick them up, spied Tremaine, and said, "How's that there mare you got? She won't have no problem. Gotta stop by tonight. Told your dad I would."

Tremaine didn't enlighten him that he was a day late and dead wrong on his professional diagnosis.

The door opened and Jace Garrett strode in, a white bandage covering his temple. Tremaine's black mood was somewhat improved by the sight of Garrett's injury. He lifted his draft in an unspoken salute to Lexie.

Garrett's gaze fell on him in that moment. His face flushed dark red and he strode to Tremaine's table. "You won this round," he said flatly. "And you can have her."

A spasm of pain crossed Tremaine's face before he could hide it, and Garrett looked at him with new interest. "Something wrong in paradise?"

"Get the hell out of my sight," Tremaine muttered.

Looking immensely cheered, Garrett met up with Conrad Templeton, who fell all over himself to please his boss. Tremaine stared bleakly into his mug.

One of the Rock Springs whores moved over to his table and rested an inviting palm on his shoulder, sliding him a look from knowing eyes. Lifting her brows, she waited for his answer. She was small and dark-haired, her small breasts pushed up over a rustling black sateen bodice.

Tremaine, very deliberately, stuffed several bills down the front of her dress. She smiled and he saw her teeth were brown and broken. Lexie's beautiful white smile, sneaking past soft pink lips, crossed his vision.

He left without another word.

Chapter Fourteen

⁓

Spring, 1883

"Which do you think I should wear?" Lexie asked, holding up a royal blue velvet waist and skirt in one hand, and a rich chocolate brown lawn dress in the other.

Ella, lounging against Miss Everly's meager feather pillows, squinted over the top of her English literature book and asked, "Whatever happened to that gorgeous green dress? The one you said you wore to the Winter Ball?"

"I don't like it much." Lexie turned her back to Ella, hiding her expression. Deliberately, she hung the chocolate gown in the closet, hoping Ella wouldn't pursue the subject.

Ella's book snapped shut and Lexie inwardly sighed. "What do you mean you don't like it? It's the best dress you own."

Lexie's gaze automatically sought out the lovely jade taffeta, but she stared distantly beyond. She couldn't explain how that dress reminded her poignantly of her feelings for Tremaine.

"Well, then I'd pick the blue," Ella said. "It's kind of matronly, but it's a pretty color."

"Matronly?" Lexie stepped into the skirt, then fastened

the woven silk frogs that marched up her left shoulder of the shirtwaist, ending at an ecru lace cambric collar. She lifted her chin. "I defy you to call this matronly!"

Ella's mouth curved. "Okay, on me it would be matronly. On you, it's rather nice."

Lexie picked up her mother-of-pearl brush and quickly brought her hair to a crackling shine. "The truth is, I wish I didn't have to go to this party."

"Are you kidding? Having Celeste invite you to the Monteith home is an honor. The other girls are practically apoplectic with envy."

"But you aren't."

Ella sighed in contentment, stretching backward, her red hair a mass of short unruly curls. "Celeste can't stand me and the feeling's mutual. She wouldn't dare invite me. I'd embarrass her somehow."

"Oh, you would not." Lexie started to braid her hair, then gave it up in disgust. She didn't have time. Celeste's driver would be at the school any minute.

"Yes, I would. I'd do something absolutely horrid on purpose." Ella grinned with sly satisfaction. "I understand there's a duck pond on their property. Wouldn't you just die to see Celeste floundering in the water with the honkers and quackers?"

Lexie collected her black velvet cape, her eyes laughing at Ella in spite of the misery that clouded them most of the time. "I'll keep it in mind," she said dryly. "Why in God's name did she invite *me?*"

"Because since you came back from Christmas vacation, you've knocked all the men who want a 'Miss Everly Lady' off their feet. There isn't one dandy among them who wouldn't give a wing of Daddy's mansion to make you his wife. Where did you ever learn to flirt like that?"

Lexie stopped short, her hand on the knob. "What do you mean?"

"I've seen you at some of the dances—or when someone else's date comes to call. You've got that cool little smile and that way of talking. It drives men crazy." Ella looked thoughtful. "As a matter of fact, I could use a lesson. I haven't found that wealthy husband yet and I'm running out of time."

"I don't know what you're talking about." Lexie was growing uncomfortable. She thought back to her attitude over the past few months. Had Tremaine changed her so drastically? She'd tried so very hard to put him out of her mind.

"Celeste likes having you around. You draw men like honey to a bee."

Lexie ran down the stairs and waited on the front stoop. Celeste had gone home for the weekend and had promised to send a carriage around to pick Lexie up for the party her father, Silas Monteith, was throwing in honor of Celeste's eighteenth birthday. Lexie's birthday had come and gone without much fanfare. Her parents had sent gifts and love; Jesse, Samuel, and Harrison—from Denver—cards. If Lexie had needed further proof that Tremaine wished to forget their night together, his lack of acknowledgment on her birthday had been the crowning blow.

The carriage driver helped Lexie to her seat, and she sat with her hands folded tautly in her lap as they jerked forward and began rumbling down the street. She wasn't going to think about Tremaine. She wasn't. It didn't matter to her that their night together had only meant a few tawdry hours of pleasure to him.

She looked out the side window, distantly watching the passing Nob Hill homes as the carriage driver headed west. The Monteiths' home was on the farthest edge of the fashionable residential district, its sloping grounds surrounded by towering firs and the rolling, mountainous hills on Portland's western rim. But her thoughts were on Tremaine—always Tremaine.

He'd shut her out of his life and gone back to Jenny McBride. That was a fact she couldn't ignore. He might be embarrassed, she realized, over deflowering a woman he'd once thought of as his sister, but that was a paltry excuse for leaving her without so much as a word of goodbye!

Gritting her teeth, she hardened her heart—as she'd hardened it a thousand times already. It was God's own miracle that she wasn't pregnant, but for all Tremaine cared, she could be living in shame, forced to bear it alone.

It takes two, you blackhearted bastard! her heart cried out in pain. She ought to hate him. She ought to strangle him with her bare hands the next time she saw him. But why, oh why, did the thought of seeing him again bring a flutter to her heart, and a throbbing ache in the region of her lower limbs?

Drawing a long, shuddering breath, she folded her painful memories into that secret corner of her heart—the corner reserved for Tremaine alone—and with a visible snap of her head and squaring of shoulders, she pushed him out of her mind for the rest of the ride.

Victor Flynne swirled his brandy in the crystal snifter Silas Monteith had grudgingly offered him. He gazed out the window of Silas' opulent office, watching carriages turn into the torch-lit drive and pull up to the front steps of his home.

"You're going to have to get out of here, you bastard," Silas hissed through his teeth. "I don't want anyone seeing you." He slammed the strongbox lid shut; the door to the safe followed with a hollow thud.

Victor smiled to himself and sipped his brandy. "Don't worry."

"Here's your goddamn five thousand." Silas slapped a thick pile of bills on the windowsill and glared furiously down at him. "Don't come back again."

"That isn't our arrangement, Silas," Victor reminded him. "What do you think these people would say if they knew you'd shot a man in cold blood? Maybe they're not for unions, but murder's murder. You'd be cut out of Portland society quicker than lightning."

"It was self-defense!"

"My information says it was murder—and my information just happens to be the truth. That man was a unionizer and you were afraid your shipbuilders would listen to him. So you killed him."

Monteith was purple with suppressed rage. "I'd rather be a dock worker than pay you another filthy dime," he snarled.

"Ahh, Silas . . ." Victor shook his head. "Your reputation is far too precious for you to take such a stand. The pillars of Portland society are a puritanical lot. You'd be cast out like yesterday's garbage. I'd venture to say . . ."

Victor trailed off at the vision of pure loveliness stepping from the running board of the latest arriving carriage. Blond hair the color of cornsilk, high cheekbones, a wide, sensually curving mouth. "By God," he murmured. "Lexington Danner."

"I'll not pay another cent!" Silas roared, working himself into a fit. "Keep after me, and you might find yourself hanging from a rope tied to some lonely tree!"

Victor was unruffled by Silas' threats; he'd heard them all a hundred times before. For all his bluster, Monteith was wary of Victor's incredible informants and connections. Victor Flynne was almost as accepted as Silas amongst Portland's wealthy class. Only a handful knew of his underhanded business dealings—and most of them, like Silas, had found out the hard way.

"Do you know anything about that girl?" Victor asked with deceptive casualness.

Monteith glowered though the mullioned windows, his eyes assessing the beautiful blonde who was now gathering her skirts to walk up the porch steps. "No."

"That's Lexington Danner. One of your daughter's classmates, I believe. She has an interesting history. You wouldn't believe some of the things I've uncovered."

Victor's inner smile widened, but then he remembered his meeting with Lexington's stepbrother. Tremaine Danner had caught up with him in the lobby of one of Portland's finer hotels and coldly demanded to know what Victor wanted from one Joseph Danner.

Victor had been instantly wary of Dr. Tremaine Danner —the same Dr. Danner who had tried to save the man Silas Monteith had shot. Unlike his father, however, Tremaine didn't skirt the issue at all. He wanted to know who had contacted his father and why. Luckily, Victor had lied convincingly, telling him a woman from Kentucky had lost her cousin's trail in Portland; the reasons were no more sinister than that. Whether Tremaine believed him or not, Victor still didn't know. Whatever the case, Victor needed to get the rest of the facts on the Danner secret and fast.

Silas Monteith broke into his thoughts with a harsh, "Get the hell out of here, Flynne."

Victor sighed, handed Monteith his glass. "I might need a favor from you soon."

"I won't help you in any way!"

"Yes, you will." His voice was steel. "You're friendly with some Portland bankers. I want to know about the Danner finances." His gaze narrowed. "Eliza Danner has money somewhere."

"Eliza Smythe Danner?"

"You know her?" Victor asked eagerly.

"Hell, yes. She's one of the biggest investors in my shipbuilding business."

Victor was ecstatic. What a piece of luck! "I want to know all about the Danner family. Everything you can learn. Silas," Victor added, sensing he'd pushed the man to the end of his tether, "there's more ways of paying blackmail than just by money."

Monteith closed his mouth and eyed his wily tormentor shrewdly. His businessman's mind saw the possibilities in this new option, but all he said was, "Goodnight, Victor."

Flynne gave a short bow and let himself into the hallway. The guests were gathered in the main ballroom and no one noticed him leave—until he nearly ran into the one woman he'd hoped to avoid.

Lexie, who had stepped into the nearest room to catch her breath before facing the lively crowd, almost collided with a man in a light brown suit as she reentered the foyer. "Excuse me. I'm sorry," she said hastily. "I wasn't looking where I was going."

"No harm done." He smiled and would have gone around her, but the door opened again, and he had to wait for the newest guests to dispose of their cloaks and hats and find their way to the ballroom.

Those crucial moments gave Lexie a chance to really look at him. "Have we met?" she asked hesitantly. There was something distinctly familiar about him.

"I doubt it. You, I would remember." He strode out the door and down the stone steps, raising a hand for his carriage.

Lexie was left to stare after him. She was certain she'd seen him somewhere before, but for the life of her, she couldn't remember where. He was not the kind of man to stand out in a crowd; indeed, he seemed to melt into the surroundings. But the cut of his suit was expensive, his overall air one of subtle wealth. She felt certain they'd met before.

"There you are, Lexie!" Celeste cried, appearing in a cloud of peach silk from the double doors at the end of the hall. Music followed after her and she grabbed onto Lexie's arm, nearly dragging her toward the ballroom. "We're desperate for young women here tonight. Most of Daddy's friends are old warts with rotten teeth and oodles of money. Please, help me! I know you'll think of something to say to them!"

The familiar-seeming man was forgotten as soon as Lexie was swept into the ballroom. The floor was black and white marble tile. Three chandeliers were suspended from the domed ceiling. Lexie couldn't help marveling at the Monteiths' ostentatious home.

"This is Sir Henry Simonson," Celeste introduced breathlessly, wrapping Lexie's hand through the man's arm. "He's been waiting for a dance partner all evening. Sir Henry, I'd like you to meet my friend, Lexington Danner." Celeste left before Lexie could utter a word.

Embarrassed, Lexie eyed her companion. There were no warts and his teeth looked fine, but he was an emaciated old codger with a baggy chin and eyes that seemed wont to caress Lexie's shape.

"Miss Danner," he said, covering her hand with a papery dry palm. "Would you care to dance?"

Lexie would rather have eaten worms. She painted on a smile and nodded, swallowing as he led her onto the floor beneath the center chandelier, his lascivious gaze following the curve of her breasts beneath the blue velvet shirtwaist.

She was glad the damn thing buttoned all the way to her throat.

Little Billy Greaves grinned wickedly at Tremaine and wiggled the fingers on his right hand. Two had been chopped off at the first knuckle; one at the second. The cleaver had just missed his thumb.

"They's good, Doc. See?"

"You're lucky to have anything left at all, Billy," Tremaine remarked sternly. "I wouldn't be stealing again anytime soon."

Billy's lack of response drew a sigh from Tremaine. The boy was probably already at it. He had no father, and his mother showed the same boredom toward her son's welfare as she did to everything else in her world. Tremaine had never seen a more apathetic creature. She did nothing more useful than sit around their smelly tenement and eat whatever Billy could pilfer. The fact that an enraged butcher had chopped off his fingers didn't seem to move her in the least.

Knowing it was a pathetic stopgap, Tremaine pressed two quarters into Billy's palm. "Get a job," he urged the nine-year-old boy.

"Ah will!" He bobbed his head enthusiastically, amazed at his good fortune. "Ah will!"

Tremaine walked to the door. From another room he heard the wet, wracking coughs of the one friend Billy had—a young woman whose husband had left her when he'd learned she had consumption. Tremaine knocked softly on the door.

"Who is it?" came the rasped inquiry.

"It's Dr. Danner, Grace. I just wanted to see how you were doing."

The door opened a crack. She was bent over, her young face lined and ravaged by a disease that would surely take her before summer arrived.

"I'm better today," she said, opening the door wider. Billy, who had been hovering behind Tremaine, now squeezed beneath his arm.

"Ah'm going to get some food," he said matter-of-factly. "Ah'll get you some, too."

"No, Billy. You can't—" She was cut off by another cough that nearly doubled her over, but she slapped away Tremaine's automatic move to help her.

"It's all right," Billy said. "Dr. Danner give me money." With the lithe swiftness of a river rat he slipped around Tremaine again and was gone.

"You shouldn't have," the woman said.

"And how do you expect me to sleep at night?" Tremaine smiled, helping her back to the dusty couch near the fire. "What else can I get you?"

"Nothin'." She patted his hand for all the world as if she

were comforting him. "You get some sleep. You look plumb tuckered out."

Fifteen minutes later, Tremaine strode somberly down the building's garbage-strewn front steps, breathing deeply of the tangy river-scented night air. He walked quickly toward his buggy, paid off the street urchin he'd hired to watch it, then climbed into the driver's seat. His mind was numb. He'd spent the last few months mired in this dreadful corner of East Portland. No one else at Willamette Infirmary had wanted to. Only Tremaine, who had his own demons to battle, cared for a fight that was lost before it was begun.

Something crackled in his pocket as he guided Fortune toward the ferry dock, which would take him back to the west side. He thrust his fingers inside and encountered a stiff vellum envelope. Celeste Monteith's invitation.

Tremaine sighed. He was tired, and it was late—too late to attend the party. Besides, Celeste had written in her flowery hand that she'd invited Lexie too. Tremaine had to avoid her at all cost.

Lexie. Just the thought of her made him feel tight and hot inside. He'd tracked down Flynne in the hopes of learning more about Eliza's past but the man had stonewalled him. Tremaine had spent the better part of the last four months fighting his feelings for Lexie, while wondering if the threat to her and Eliza was even real.

Half an hour later, he was driving through the eastern-most section of Nob Hill, on the way to his rooming house. To the north the masts of sailing vessels could be seen along the waterfront. The closer Tremaine got to them, the closer he came to the bawdiest, most raucous section of town. A man had to be careful not to be crimped and forced into a voyage he wasn't ready for if he chose to walk those streets alone at night.

Tremaine let himself into his rooming house and climbed the stairs. He opened the door to his room and stood in the center of the apartment. It wasn't really home. He'd never intended to practice in Portland as long as he had. He'd always intended to go back to Rock Springs.

From the view of his third-floor window he could see the brothels and piers along the waterfront. Willamette Infirmary was within walking distance. Miss Everly's school was deep within Nob Hill's sheltering walls. And Silas Monteith's house was only half an hour away . . .

A wave of uncontrollable longing swept over him. "Damn it all to hell," he growled, stripping off his clothes. He had to see Lexie. She would most certainly hate him, but he didn't care.

If she wasn't at the party, he would track her down at Miss Everly's School.

Lexie swirled beneath the chandeliers, light glancing off their glistening tiers to sparkle in her hair. She was dying! Her face was flushed and perspiration trickled down her back. She should have listened to Ella and worn the emerald taffeta; the velvet was much too hot.

"So you attend school with Miss Celeste," the gentleman who was her current dance partner remarked.

"Yes," said Lexie, breathlessly.

"A fine school."

"Yes."

Her vision was a blur; her ears were full of music and a general din of chattering voices. She was thirsting for punch and was about to beg off when the small orchestra on the dais finally trailed off in a weak finish of their last number.

Lexie excused herself from the portly gentleman and made a beeline for the punch bowl. An ironic smile played on her lips. Celeste's reason for inviting her was now painfully apparent; Lexie handled the lascivious older men, Celeste the well-heeled younger ones. There had been no chance for Lexie to dance with some of the dashing rogues who stood along the sidelines. Celeste made certain their attention always came back to her.

Not that Lexie really much cared, but it galled her to be duped and used by Celeste so dreadfully. And she was tired of the vicious looks being sent her way by the lightfooted old codgers' grim-eyed wives. What had ever possessed her to agree to come to this party?

You needed to get away from your own thoughts, a voice inside her head reminded her. The gaiety of an evening out—like so many other evenings she'd spent the last few months—was all that kept her from thinking of Tremaine.

The memory of her night with him seemed burned on her brain; nothing could erase it. Yet recalling it was a torture too great to bear.

"Miss Danner, please excuse me," a deep voice intoned. "I've been a terrible host. I haven't had a chance to meet my daughter's best friend."

Lexie's head jerked around, her hand sloshing a bit of punch onto the white linen-covered serving table. "Best friend?" she repeated on a smothered giggle.

"I'm Silas Monteith," he said. "Would you care to dance?"

The man before Lexie was burly and square, with sleek silvery hair, a hard chin, and disinterested eyes. She suddenly remembered seeing him at the hospital when Ella was sick—and in that moment she remembered the familiar-seeming man she'd met earlier as well. He'd been in the reception area. He'd learned her name and asked where she lived. Why, she wondered somewhat uneasily, had he pretended not to know her tonight?

"I'm really kind of thirsty," Lexie murmured softly. "Could we just wait this one out?"

"If you wish." He smiled, the effort seeming to stretch his lips. "Celeste told me she was inviting someone from school but I had no idea you would be such a beauty."

Lexie sipped her punch, seizing the small distraction to hide her expression. She'd taken an instant dislike to Celeste's father. "Thank you."

They stood in relative silence as couples swished by to the strains of an intricate piece. When the music ended there was a smattering of applause. Lexie clapped politely.

"Please, let's dance," Mr. Monteith urged as the next song began. His fingers around her arm were insistent.

Lexie would have given anything to melt into nothingness but there was no way she could insult her host. With a smile nearly as phony as Monteith's, she let him lead her to the dance floor and take her into his arms.

His hand was sweaty as he clasped her palm. Lexie had to fight the urge to snatch hers back and wipe it on her dress. Swallowing her revulsion, she fell into step.

"Celeste tells me you're from Rock Springs," Monteith commented. He held her a proper distance away and for that Lexie was thankful.

"That's right. Born and raised there."

"It's a farming community, isn't it?"

Lexie slanted him a look. He seemed genuinely interested, almost too interested. The man fairly hung on her every word. "Mainly. There's not much industry yet, but Rock Springs is growing by leaps and bounds." She glanced around, wondering where she could escape to as soon as the music stopped.

"I was thereabouts once," he reflected. "And then, of course, I've had business dealings with your mother, Eliza."

"Really?"

"She's an investor with my shipbuilding company."

Your mother met with an investment banker and her money's been invested wisely in several profitable shipbuilding companies . . .

Tremaine's words came back with a painful jar. So Eliza had invested with Monteith. How ironic. Lexie didn't think she'd trust Monteith with a nickel.

At that moment there was a slight commotion from the direction of one of Silas's older friends. The man had imbibed a bit too much and had stumbled and crashed into the couple dancing next to Lexie.

Monteith pulled Lexie away from the shouts of laughter and general confusion. Lexie would have chosen that moment to end their dance but Monteith held her tight in his arms and said, "Lexington's an unusual name. Are you named for Lexington, Kentucky?"

"Uh . . . yes . . ."

"Is that where your mother's from?"

Lexie hesitated. She was growing uncomfortable under all his questions. "Yes."

"She must be from a very wealthy family, having so much of her own money."

"I suppose she is," Lexie murmured, finding his curiosity in very bad taste. To her relief the song finally came to a close. "If you'll excuse me, I really need some fresh air."

Lexie was so intent on escape, she nearly tripped on her long skirts in her haste. It wasn't until she was almost to the opened balcony doors that she recognized the tall man standing near an empty alcove.

Tremaine's blue gaze stripped right to her soul.

Lexie's heart nearly stopped. On a strangled gasp she made a dash for the doors. She felt Tremaine's gaze following her as she stepped into the cool spring night and gulped air. *What was he doing here?*

"Lexie," he said behind her.

Goose bumps rose on her flesh. Her shoulders stiffened. She glanced desperately around for some means to leave the balcony, but apart from a two-story jump to the back lawn, there was no avenue of escape.

She felt him directly in back of her. He had the unbelievable nerve to clasp her upper arms with his strong fingers. Lexie swallowed another gasp and wrenched herself free, whirling to face him. "Leave me alone, Tremaine," she hissed.

"I've been trying to."

"Well, you've been doing an excellent job until tonight!"

"It's been hell."

This admission stole her breath away. She couldn't bear to meet his gaze. For months she'd ached for him, hating herself for wanting him even after he'd coldheartedly used and left her. To hear from his own lips that he'd suffered hit her like a blow to the stomach.

She dragged her gaze from his beloved face. Did he have to be so damnably male? One look into those turquoise eyes and she felt a powerful, primal longing that made her want to fall into his arms.

"Go away," Lexie said almost pleasantly, though her voice shook ever so slightly. "Because I don't want to see you ever again."

He sighed. "Fair enough. I suppose I deserved that."

"You deserve that and much, much more," she assured him, her pride returning in a rush of glorious fury. She glanced upward, her green eyes sparking. "You left me!"

"I know."

"You didn't even bother to see how I felt, how I *survived* that next day! You were in too much of a rush to meet your lady friend in Rock Springs to even bother with me!"

Tremaine's brows snapped together. "Jenny? That's not—"

Lexie didn't wait to hear any excuses. The way he said that woman's name was enough to make her forget every bit of poise and sophistication she'd learned at that godawful school. She doubled her right fist and slammed it into his stomach, reacting with the outrage of a younger sibling rather than the cold fury of a woman scorned.

Tremaine bent over, gasping and laughing. "For God's sake, Lexie," he managed to say, but she was on him like a prizefighter, beating on his shoulders and back and head.

"You're—a—miserable—blackhearted—coward!" she panted, then found her arms pinned behind her by a very angry man. "Let me go, damn you!" She writhed and twisted but he held on with grim determination.

He pushed her to the edge of the balustrade, his blue eyes lit by a cold, furious light. "Shut up a minute and let me think!"

"You've had months to think. *Months!*" To her fury, tears scalded the back of her throat, burned her eyes. "So, your conscience finally got the better of you and you decided to face me," she added scathingly, hiding her feelings as best she could, "Well, I don't care, Tremaine. As far as I'm concerned, *you don't exist!*"

"Does this feel like I don't exist?" he snapped back, squeezing her arms so tightly she felt they would break. "Damn you, Lexie," he bit out under his breath. "You really try my patience."

Lexie narrowed her eyes. Her whole body was trembling, her breasts heaving with outrage and injustice. "I try your patience? You seduced me, then left me for your—your—"

"I seduced *you?* Who was it that followed me to the barn, dressed in a silk wrapper, and wouldn't leave even when I ordered her out? Who was it who wound herself around me when—"

Lexie thrust against his chest with all her might, closing her ears. "Don't say it! Don't say it!"

"Why not? Because you can't stand hearing the truth?"

Lexie turned her face away to fight back the tears battling against her pride. She couldn't answer him because he was right. It was her mistake for believing he cared about her in a special way.

Slowly, he released her wrists. She could feel his gaze on her but she refused to meet his eyes. "Why did you come here tonight?"

Tremaine drew a breath. "I'm honoring my invitation."

Lexie blinked, embarrassed. "Invitation?" He showed her the vellum envelope and she said bitterly, "Celeste seems to have a penchant for sending you invitations."

"I don't give a damn about Celeste. I came because she wrote on the invitation that you would be here. I need to talk to you."

"I don't want to talk to you," whispered Lexie painfully, pulling away from him.

"Lexie. Wait. Please."

"I can't." Blindly, she walked back inside the stifling ballroom. She headed in the direction of the punch, then stopped. She needed to get out of here.

Turning, she walked straight into Tremaine's chest. "Oh, Lexie . . ." he murmured, folding his arms around her.

Her head jerked up, startled. But they could have been one of the dancing couples; no one paid them any attention.

Against her will, she felt the hard muscles of his chest; the steel strength of his arms; the warmth of his brandy-tinged breath. A pulsing wave of desire turned her legs to quivering liquid. His grip tightened as he felt her weaken.

"You left me, Tremaine," she said again. "You left me."

"I had to, Lexie. Or the same thing would have happened again."

It took her brain half a beat to understand. She nearly choked. "You flatter yourself!"

"We would have slept together again at the first chance if I hadn't left. I couldn't risk that."

Lexie was horrified at his highhanded arrogance. "You're —awfully sure of yourself!"

"Can you deny it?" He drew away to look into her eyes. It was impossible to lie with those sharp blue eyes assessing her so thoroughly. Lexie swallowed and said nothing at all. She would have slept with him again. Lord help her, she wanted to *now!*

She tried to squirm away from him, but he led her to the dance floor, jerking her tight against his masculine shape as they began to waltz. If she'd been hot before, she was burning up now.

"Lexie," he added in a low voice that made her throb with awareness. "I've spent the last few months in a state of constant rage and frustration. All I could think about was wanting you."

"Oh, right. That's why you told Pa you didn't want anyone finding out we weren't related."

"I didn't tell Pa that. It was his idea."

She couldn't stand one more lie! Lexie's emotions were crashing inside of her. Her skin felt sensitized from his touch. Wanton desires raged through her, and she remembered his legs wrapped around hers, the sweet pressure of him thrusting her against the blanket.

She shook her head. She couldn't be his mistress—and he'd already made it clear, by his actions, that that was all he really wanted.

"Lexie, listen to me," he muttered through his teeth.

"No! You may not worry about your reputation but I've got to worry about mine! I'm not going to make that mistake again."

His eyes darkened stormily. "Was it a mistake?"

"Yes!" she hissed.

"You felt something that night, Lexie. Admit it. You never would have slept with me if you hadn't felt something."

"All I felt was loathing and disgust!"

Tremaine stared bemusedly into her flashing green eyes, then threw back his head and laughed. Lexie, for all her weeks of hating him and blaming herself, could almost see the humor of the situation. Almost.

"Well, I guess I'll have to work harder at making certain you feel something more positive."

Lexie missed a step and trod on his toe. Tremaine's infuriating arrogance made her absolutely crazy, but the thought of sleeping with him again sent her blood singing through her veins.

"Forgot the waltz already?" he said near her ear. "Remember, one-two-three, one-two-three—"

"I know how to waltz!" Purposely, she ground her shoe into his toe again, then narrowed her eyes at his unabashed grin. But she couldn't deny that she loved him. As much as she'd tried to kill that love, it still existed. And her heart felt lighter than it had in months.

A reluctant sparkle of mirth glinting in her eyes, Lexie

met his gaze. Her breath caught at the deep desire simmering in his like a blue flame.

"Dr. Danner!" Celeste trilled out in delighted triumph. "There you are! And here I was afraid you might have mislaid my invitation." She swept toward Lexie and Tremaine in a rustle of silk and satin and shimmering diamonds. Her fingers clutched Tremaine's arm. "A dance?" she asked coquettishly. "It's my birthday."

Lexie, needing a moment to gain perspective, said quickly, "Tremaine would love to dance with you. I'm afraid my waltzing is still amateurish."

"Then we'll have to have another lesson," Tremaine said meaningfully, but Celeste was already tugging him toward the dance floor. "Don't go anywhere," he warned Lexie, meeting her gaze over Celeste's blond head.

As soon as they were engulfed by the glittering crowd, Lexie ignored his edict and headed for the door. Tremaine could make her forgive him without offering one word of apology. He could make her forget all about Jenny McBride. He could make her forget the way he'd walked out on her.

"Miss Danner!" The shout of joy distracted her for a moment, and Lexie could have groaned when she saw Dr. Peter Caldwell appear on her left. "I've been trying to dance with you all evening."

"Have you?" Lexie glanced anxiously over her shoulder.

"Yes, but you've been awfully busy." His tone held a note of reproval, as if he thought she'd been purposely choosing her dance partners and ignoring him in the bargain.

She saw Tremaine bearing down on her, Celeste a burr on his sleeve. "Then dance with me now," Lexie said in sudden decision, flinging herself into Peter's surprised arms.

"By all means," Peter grinned.

Lexie managed to maneuver away from Tremaine, but all too soon the music ended. Without a word to Peter she made another dash for the door, only to feel Tremaine's hand close possessively around her wrist.

"Leaving so soon?" His tone was polite, but Lexie glanced back to see the anger that filled his eyes.

"Yes, I can't stay any longer."

Sensing Tremaine was about to desert her, Celeste said

quickly, "Then you won't mind if I monopolize your brother for a few hours, will you, Lexie? I'm about to expire from thirst." She waved herself with one hand, drawing a long breath that had her breasts nearly spilling over her dangerously low-cut bodice. "Tremaine, could you get me a drink, please? No, wait, I'll come with you."

He hesitated, then, as if he'd come to a long-dreaded and painful decision, Tremaine nodded, moving away from Lexie. She sensed he'd given up on her. It was a distinctly unpleasant notion.

"Wait!" she cried. "Please, I'd like something, too." Tremaine turned back slowly, his eyes narrowed and cautious.

"What would you like?" he asked politely.

You, she thought desperately, and as their gazes clashed she saw his eyes darken with emotion, as if he'd heard her.

Celeste was tugging insistently on his arm and he said to Lexie, "I'll be right back."

Lexie expelled a pent-up breath, feeling decidedly weak. *What have you done?* a frightened voice inside her head asked. She was afraid to answer it.

Celeste and Tremaine returned a few moments later. Lexie accepted the glass of punch from Tremaine's fingers.

"Mind if I borrow your brother for a few moments?" Celeste asked with a sly smile.

"Tremaine is not my brother," Lexie answered flatly. She'd be damned if she perpetuated that lie any longer. "He's my stepbrother."

Tremaine grabbed Lexie's hand, steering her toward the other end of the room, leaving Celeste standing open-mouthed behind them. "You shouldn't have told her," he muttered, taking the cup from her fingers and placing it on a small sideboard.

"And why not?" Lexie demanded as he dragged her unceremoniously out of the room. "What difference does it make now?"

Tremaine couldn't answer her. It was up to Pa to tell her about Eliza. He pulled her toward the door.

"Where do you think you're taking me?" she demanded as his long strides had her half-running behind him through the front door.

"Away from here."

A cool April wind fanned Lexie's hot cheeks. "Without so much as a goodbye to our host?"

The look he sent her burned right to the soles of her feet. "If I don't get you home soon, I'm afraid I might be forced to take you in my buggy."

"Take me in—" Her mouth dropped open. She glanced quickly from side to side, afraid of eavesdroppers. "I can't believe you just said that!"

"Can't you?"

The footman brought Tremaine's buggy to the front steps as Lexie pondered that. Tremaine lifted her inside, then climbed up beside her. Lexie tried to collect her wits. "I'm not your lover, Tremaine. You can go back to Jenny McBride—"

"Get this through your thick skull. Jenny McBride's not my lover," he said through his teeth, cracking the reins against Fortune's broad hindquarters. The stallion leapt forward, the buggy jolting Lexie so that she had to hang onto the sides.

"Don't lie to me, Tremaine," Lexie sputtered, clasping the seat as they bumped down the Monteiths' elegant curving drive. "You went to her Christmas Eve, after you'd made love to me! Jesse told me!"

The buggy pulled onto the road and Tremaine reined Fortune into a fast walk. "Jesse has an incredibly one-track mind," he bit out furiously. "Jenny came to the house that night to tell me one of my patients, a little boy, had taken a turn for the worse. I asked her to come get me if he didn't improve. I spent the rest of the night and half of Christmas day with him."

"I don't believe you!"

"I'm not in the habit of lying."

"Can you honestly tell me you and Jenny McBride have never been lovers?"

There was a long, telling silence and Lexie knew the answer before he gave it to her. "No, I can't tell you that," he admitted. "But it was over long before I made love to you."

The way he said that—so boldly, so factually—made Lexie die a thousand humiliations. She had slept in this man's arms, had let him pleasure her as only a husband should pleasure a wife. His bland acceptance of what to her had been a shattering life pinnacle made her choke with mortification.

"Then why didn't you come back?" Lexie asked in a small voice when they were well south of the Monteith estate.

"There were a lot of reasons." Tremaine drew a deep breath. "The main one being it wasn't the right time for us."

"And now it is?"

She could see his jaw tighten even in the dim shadows of the buggy. Lexie shivered and looked away. There was more here than he was willing to admit. Much, much more. And much of what went unsaid had to do with Jenny McBride. Despite his claims, he'd been in her rooming house and he cared about her. Lexie wouldn't be played for a fool. She'd already suffered enough heartbreak. Tremaine still had feelings for Jenny.

The buggy drew up in front of Miss Everly's School. Lexie climbed down before Tremaine could help her. How dare he come and shred the thin fabric of her new life?

He was right on her heels, and when she reached the threshold he touched her lightly on the arm. "Lexie, you can't ignore the way things are between us."

"What way, Tremaine? *What way?*"

For an answer his hand cupped her jaw and all her fury dissolved in a white-hot blaze of desire. A muscle jumped in his jaw. "This way," he said softly, and kissed her so hard she had to clutch the sleeves of his jacket to keep from falling.

When he finally drew back she was breathing hard. "Why have you avoided me so long? Why are you here now?"

"I'm here because I don't give a damn about anything but being with you."

The door suddenly opened behind Lexie, and Miss Everly stepped into the warm April night. "Dr. Danner," she addressed him politely.

Lexie thought about all the miserable moments she'd spent the last few months. She couldn't stand to go through that all again—not even for Tremaine. With wings on her feet she fled into the school and up to her room, surprising Ella, who was half asleep across her bed.

"What in creation has got you so stirred up?" she demanded.

"Tremaine!" Lexie spat. "I hate him. I *hate* him! He's not my brother, he's my stepbrother. And he's ruined me!"

To her shock, and Ella's dawning comprehension, Lexie burst into a flood of tears.

"So that's what all the pathos has been about these last months," Ella said wisely.

"I never *ever* want to see him again!"

"How has he ruined you?"

Lexie flung herself on her bed and stared up at the ceiling. "He made me fall in love with him."

Ella shook her head in mock pity. "The cruel bastard. He ought to be boiled in oil."

"Amen," Lexie muttered, but all she could remember were his strong arms holding her tightly, his low voice warning her they would be together again.

Chapter Fifteen

❦

It was an august group of Portland dignitaries who assembled in the Portland Park Blocks for Lexie's graduation day. They sat straight and proper in a row of chairs on a raised platform, the June breeze blowing and crackling against the pink paper curtain that hid the podium's understructure. The scent of roses wafted through the air like a song, strong one moment, sweet and distant the next. The ground smelled damp and musky from yesterday's rain.

Lexie's hands were folded in the lap of her blue-sprigged lawn dress as the mayor's wife stood in the center of the dais, effusing over the importance of young women in society today. As far as Lexie could see, a certificate from Miss Everly's School guaranteed only a proposal of marriage from the son of one of Portland's finest families. Half the class was already engaged and planning weddings as early as next week.

Not one of the graduates was planning a career.

Ella, at the end of the row, caught Lexie's roving eye and winked. Even Ella, good friend that she was, had no plans other than to find a husband. But Lexie couldn't give up her notions of marrying for love. The thought of picking out a husband with an eye to his bankbook made Lexie shudder with revulsion. Besides, she loved only Tremaine.

She turned her face to the itinerant June breeze and closed her eyes. First the mayor's wife, then someone else, droned on and on. At last Miss Everly stood to speak and there was a smattering of applause from the back. Pa and Eliza were seated in the last row, and Lexie could picture her mother lightly applauding.

"I've never had the pleasure of working with a more dedicated and serious group of young ladies in all my life," Miss Everly opened, smiling benevolently.

Lexie glanced skyward, half-expecting God to strike Miss Everly down for the outrageous lie. Ella caught Lexie's look and coughed into her hand several times, fighting back laughter.

". . . Portland's finest," Miss Everly was going on. "Ladies in every sense of the word . . ."

Lexie inwardly groaned, closing her ears. Only a few more hours and she would be done with Miss Everly's School forever. Tomorrow she and Pa and Mother were heading back to Rock Springs. Her parents didn't know it yet, but Lexie planned on taking over responsibility of the stables again. She felt that, given enough time, she could convince them to let her become a horse doctor. She'd paid her dues. In time they would realize she would never change her mind.

Miss Everly finished to resounding applause and then the ceremony was over. Lexie stood, glancing around for her parents.

Pa was standing toward the rear of the seats. Across the sea of feminine heads, he winked at Lexie. She winked back. In his hands were gifts from Jesse, Samuel, and even Harrison, who'd mailed a package to her from Denver.

There was nothing from Tremaine.

"Are you ready to go to the reception?" Pa asked her when she met up with them.

Lexie glanced around the park, half-hoping Tremaine would be there, knowing he wouldn't. Her throat tight, she murmured, "More than ready." She followed him and Eliza to their waiting buggy.

There was more pomp and circumstance awaiting them at Miss Everly's School. A huge tiered cake sat on a crystal platter in the parlor. Silver carafes served tea and lemonade. A sea of people wove in and out of the rooms, offering congratulations. The continued merriment wore on Lexie, and by the time her parents finally left for their hotel she had a crashing headache.

Celeste chose that moment to approach her. "Where's Tremaine?" she asked. "I thought for sure he'd be here tonight. Didn't he come to the ceremony?"

Lexie set her teeth. Celeste had purposely snubbed her, ever since finding out Tremaine was her stepbrother. Now, as if sensing the rift between them, Celeste was slyly pouring salt in the wound.

"He's busy," Lexie said shortly.

"Too busy to celebrate his *sister's* graduation?"

"Too busy to waste time watching a bunch of silly females twitter and giggle!" she snapped.

"Well!" Celeste was affronted. "Listen to Miss High-and-Mighty herself."

"Get out of my way." Lexie strode out of the parlor and toward the front door. She needed air. She nearly collided with Dr. Peter Caldwell in her haste and stood blinking at him, surprised.

He looked slightly embarrassed. "Hello, Lexie. Is Celeste here?"

She groaned aloud. Peter's hands were full of yellow roses and a gold-foil-wrapped box with a brilliant blue ribbon. Celeste had told everyone about Peter's offer of marriage but Lexie hadn't believed it until now.

She stepped into the star-studded night and breathed deeply. Her parents' hotel was just around the corner but she didn't feel like seeing them tonight. Tonight she wanted to get over the peculiar melancholy that had stolen over her.

There were several buggies parked along the street and more than a few carriages. She stood for several long moments before she realized she recognized one of the horses.

"Fortune," she whispered, her heart giving a strange little kick.

Lexie crossed the street without a second thought. The

boy guarding the coaches suddenly appeared and eyed her warily. "You want something, ma'am?"

"Where's the owner of this buggy?"

He stared silently at her. Impatiently, Lexie dug into her skirt pocket and dropped several coins in his palm.

"In the hotel, ma'am," he supplied quickly, as if the faster he betrayed Tremaine's whereabouts, the less trouble he would be in.

So he'd come to see Pa and Mother, huh? Without even a word of congratulations for her? Lexie's anger sparked and she strode to the hotel like an avenging angel.

She was nearly to the front door when a hand snaked out from the shadows and grabbed her arm. "Are you looking for me?" Tremaine's voice asked.

"Let go of me!" Lexie demanded, frightened. "Did you have to scare the living daylights out of me? What are you doing here, lurking in the shadows?"

"I was just going inside. What were you doing snooping around my buggy?"

"Wondering what you were doing!" she retorted furiously, but her anger was ebbing. He was holding her so closely she could see the humor touching his lips and the glint in his eyes. "Are you going to the hotel to see Pa and Mother?"

"I've seen them." His tone was abrupt. "I was just about to tell them goodbye."

"Goodbye?" Lexie's heart lurched. "What do you mean goodbye?"

"Ah, Sundown." He cupped her cheek in his hand, and Lexie barely had the presence of mind to step back. "We had a small argument and I just wanted to settle it before I left."

"An argument about what?"

Tremaine looked down into her lovely, worried face, and sighed with frustration. He'd spent the last month torn between frustration and duty, wanting Lexie, knowing his father would never forgive him for having her. Tonight he'd tried to straighten all that out, but Pa had still been adamantly against telling Lexie the truth. Eliza had sat in frozen agreement.

"We argued about you, if you must know," he said gently. "I told them some things they didn't want to hear."

Lexie could scarcely believe her ears. When she thought of

all the things Tremaine could have said, she blushed. "Like what?"

"I didn't tell them about that," he assured her, amused. "Lexie, I quit the hospital today. Marshfield's been writing me about moving into Portland, and since that leaves Rock Springs without a doctor, I thought I'd start a practice there."

A warm feeling flooded her. Then she remembered how she'd reacted the first time he'd mentioned moving back home. A guilty apology was actually forming on her tongue before she realized the real reason he was coming home: Jenny McBride.

"Well, I'm sure that'll be convenient for you," she said with brittle coolness.

"Oh, for God's sake," he snapped and suddenly yanked her arm around and dragged her across the street.

"What do you think you're doing?" she demanded.

"Lexie," he said, stopping beside the buggy and turning her around to face him. His hands gripped her upper arms and he glared down at her. "I don't know how many different ways I can say this: Jenny McBride's a friend, that's all. There's been no woman these past few months but you."

Slightly mollified, she murmured, "There's no reason I should believe you."

"Is there anywhere you have to be for the next few hours?" He was impatient.

"No-o-o . . ."

"Then get in. I've got some work to finish up, but I wanted to at least say congratulations."

He didn't give her time to argue. He was already striding to his side of the buggy. Lexie could have been miffed at his highhanded attitude, but she was much too eager for his company. She climbed into the buggy beside him. Silly as it was, the fact that he'd wanted to see her on her graduation day kept her warm and happy inside for a long, long time.

The Willamette flowed by like a dark whisper as Tremaine helped Lexie down from the buggy. A plank-and-log ferry moved toward them smoothly, lanterns rocking gently, leaving quivering trails of yellow light on the black water.

Lexie stared across the wide, placid river. "We're crossing to East Portland?" she asked, surprised.

"There's someone I've got to check on," Tremaine responded. "I've been taking care of some of the poorer families over here and they need to know I'll be leaving." He sighed heavily and walked to the edge of the riverbank. "I hope Marshfield, or someone else at the hospital, thinks about checking on them."

Lexie came to stand beside him. Huge horse-powered spindles pulled the twin ropes of the ferry, dragging it inexorably to the opposite shore. They sailed across the glasslike water, heading downstream until the ropes stopped their movement, guiding the ferry toward the eastern shore.

Lexie glanced around. There were several other rigs aboard the huge raft. Horses snorted anxiously and Lexie wondered how often Tremaine made this trip.

She stole a look at his forbidding features. His eyes were hooded. The wind tossed his black hair across his forehead. She longed to reach out and erase the lines of worry that bracketed his mouth. There were so many questions she wanted to ask, but she sensed this was not the time. Tremaine had a job to do, and he wasn't in the mood for explanations right now. After he visited this mysterious patient, she would be able to find out why he seemed to push her away even though he said he wanted her.

The front logs of the ferry bumped lightly against the wooden pier. Horses and buggies clattered onto the dock and up the rutted banks on the opposite side. Tremaine and Lexie were just leading Fortune off the ferry when a young fellow darted between the wheels of one buggy and the horse of the next, trying to sneak aboard.

"Hey! You!" the ferry master bellowed. "You can't ride for no fare, you bleedin' stowaway!"

"Billy!" Tremaine said in surprise.

The lad stopped short. Lexie saw a dirty-faced boy of around ten, with straggly brown hair and bright suspicious eyes.

"Dr. Danner?" the boy asked, sliding around the back of the buggy, keeping out of the way of the grossly fat, sweat-stained ferry master who had given chase and was thundering toward them. "Ah came to git you! Grace is real sick."

Tremaine collared Billy before the ferry master's hamlike hands could reach him. "The boy's not going across," Tremaine said to the panting giant, handing the man their fare. "He's coming with us."

"The little bleeder's stole passage before! He should be jailed, that's what! You care to pay for them times, too, mister?" The ferry master licked his lips. Rather than arguing, Tremaine tossed him some more money.

"What's wrong with Grace?" Tremaine asked tersely as he, Billy, and Lexie led Fortune up the riverbank. "I was just coming to see her."

Billy reached up to stroke Fortune's neck and Lexie's heart jerked painfully. Two of his fingers were gone.

Her gaze flew to Tremaine for an explanation, but his whole attention was on Billy.

"She's real bad," the boy whispered in a scared, awed voice. "She don't move except for the coughin'. I'm afeared she's gonna die."

Tremaine's lack of encouragement made Lexie realize young Billy wasn't making more of the situation than there was. Tremaine wasn't offering false hope; his dark, somber features bore witness to his own fears.

Lexie instinctively sidled close to Tremaine. The wind threw his black hair in front of his eyes as they reached the main road. "Who's Grace?" she asked. "His mother?"

"A friend. She has consumption."

"Will she . . . ?" Lexie licked her lips, unable to finish.

Tremaine's arm stole around her shoulders and he folded her into his chest for a moment before urging her and Billy to climb into the buggy.

Lexie hesitated, forcing Tremaine's dark head to turn her way, his blue eyes questioning and impatient. "I'm sorry," she said around a lump in her throat.

With a groan, Tremaine's hands plunged into the thickness of her mane and he crushed his mouth to hers. Lexie gloried in his unexpected assault. The heat of his breath filled her mouth, the warmth of his tongue inflamed her. *I love you,* she thought, her heart aching painfully. Her hand crept up his neck. She would have loved for him to keep on kissing her forever. Tears welled in the corners of her eyes. She wanted him so much.

Reluctantly, Tremaine drew back, a shudder passing through his tall frame. Billy was already scrambling into the buggy. With a strong heave, Tremaine set Lexie up beside him. Soon they were lurching up the last few feet of track to the road.

The smells of the river were soon replaced by the stench of garbage and sour milk as they wound through the rows of ugly tenements. A skinny child appeared out of the gloom as soon as Tremaine pulled his rig up in front of one particular building, and, as if this transaction had taken place a million times before and required no words, the boy silently took Fortune's reins.

Tremaine grabbed his medical bag, then pulled Lexie down, clasping her hand with a fervency that spoke more clearly than words. She sensed how he felt about this part of town, how he despised the ever present poverty and filth.

She followed him up a narrow foul-smelling stairway, Billy at their heels. At the third-floor landing Tremaine rapped lightly with his free hand against the panels of a chipped and peeling door.

Billy had no such qualms. He thrust open the door and barreled inside. Tremaine, with Lexie's hand still clutched tightly in his larger one, followed into the dim, candlelit room.

A woman lay on a narrow, dusty couch, her eyes glassy and unseeing, staring fixedly at the cracked ceiling as if there were some message written there. Before they could cross the room, she doubled over in a spasm of coughing that left her weak and retching, only to flop back on the couch with a shudder and stare once more at the ceiling.

"I brung the doctor," Billy said to her, pathetic in his anxiety.

The woman didn't respond.

Tremaine finally released Lexie's hand. He walked over to the woman—Grace, Lexie remembered; Billy's friend— and rested his palm against her cheek. "Can you hear me, Grace?" he asked.

A rattling wheeze sounded from her throat. "I have seen the Lord and He is merciful," she whispered.

Tremaine set his medical bag down beside her. He glanced back at Lexie. "Are you all right?"

She nodded. "Is there something I can do?"

"Take Billy back to his mother. She lives across the hall."

Lexie gently touched Billy's arm, but he could have been carved in stone. Carefully, she twisted him toward her but his young face was rebellious—and full of tortured pain. Soundlessly, Lexie guided him toward the door, but once they were in the oppressive hallway he seemed to gather his wits.

"Ah haf to go to work," he said.

"Work? Tonight?" Lexie attempted to move him toward his own door but his feet were planted firmly on the grimy floor.

"Dr. Danner tol' me to git a job. Ah got a duty at the livery."

He was gone before Lexie could offer another word of protest, clattering down the stairs as if the devil himself were snapping at his heels. Thinking of the sick, dying woman in that dirty room, Lexie understood his need for escape.

She let herself back inside and saw Tremaine sitting in a chair beside Grace, holding her limp hand. A bottle of laudanum stood in evidence on the floor next to Tremaine's chair. There was precious little else to do.

Lexie, quiet as a churchmouse, walked through the door to the next room, closing it softly behind her. It was pitch-dark save for a sliver of light spilling through the cracked window. The room must have been the woman's bedroom, yet there was no bed. Closing her eyes, Lexie leaned against the wall, then slid silently to the floor. There was nothing left to do but wait.

Sometime in the dark, Lexie awakened from fitful slumber to find Tremaine sitting on the floor beside her, his head against the wall, his eyes closed. "Tremaine?" she asked quietly. He opened his eyes and stared down at her. She couldn't see his expression, but she could feel his weariness as if it were a tangible entity. "Is she going to die?"

"Probably sometime this morning," he rasped.

Lexie, whose heart was full of love for him, laid her hand

against his rough-hewn cheek, feeling the prickly edge of his beard. He dragged her into his arms, his face buried in the scented glory of her hair.

When he kissed her it was with the fervent passion of a man who wants to block reality. Lexie dropped all pretense. She wanted him just as desperately. His mouth moved on hers, hard and demanding, and her lips parted wantonly. She whimpered softly when his tongue dove into her mouth, plunging in and out.

Not a word was spoken. His hands were rough with need. He pulled her leg over him and she was astraddle him, a highly exciting position that took Lexie's breath away. She could feel the hardness of him and she ached between her legs in response.

"Lexie," he groaned, his kisses maddeningly elusive as he tried to drag his mouth from hers.

"Please, Tremaine," she begged. Her pride was in tatters already. She had nothing to give but herself.

"Oh, God." He clamped down on her thighs and held her rigidly against him. "This is not—the time—and place," he gritted.

Lexie closed her ears. She wanted him too desperately to listen to reason. He strained against her and she wriggled, gasping when his hands moved beneath her skirts, his thumbs daringly rubbing the juncture between her thighs. She wanted to rip off her drawers, for even their delicate barrier was too much.

Another time she would have been ashamed at her abandon. For now, with death looming like the jaws of hell, she wanted to celebrate life. "I love you," she whimpered against his hot mouth.

For Tremaine those three little words were a cold dash of sanity. His heart wrenched. "Lexie . . ." he groaned, dragging his mouth from hers.

But she wouldn't give up. Her tongue touched his lips innocently, experimentally. Her grip on his shoulders was full of tormenting need. He understood that need; he'd been faced with the cruel reality of death too many times not to have felt it himself. He'd even used women to help assuage the awful helplessness of it.

But he couldn't now. Not here. Not with Lexie.

A fit of convulsive coughing from the other room finally made Lexie give up her assault. With a long, shuddering sigh, she pulled herself away from him, gazing at him soberly.

Tremaine, from long practice, wearily climbed to his feet to see what modicum of relief he could offer Grace, if any.

Fortune clipclopped tiredly along Nineteenth Street toward the West End Hotel. Faint gray fingers of dawn crept over the fashionable villas and town houses. Lexie sat quietly next to Tremaine, feeling gritty and limp from lack of sleep. She'd thought she might collapse from emotional exhaustion, but the memory of Tremaine closing Grace's eyes and muttering a soft prayer was too powerful to forget.

Tremaine touched her thigh. "We're here," he said, reining Fortune to a halt. The stallion stopped instantly, snorting what could only be viewed as a sigh of relief.

"I'm still awake," said Lexie, gathering her skirts.

"Here, let me help you."

Lexie waited until he came to her side of the buggy. Instead of taking her hand, he placed his palms around her waist and hefted her easily to the ground. For a moment his touch lingered, and she looked up directly into his aquamarine eyes.

"What about Billy?" she asked.

Tremaine reluctantly let her go. "I'll make sure he's all right. I've got to get back and take care of Grace's burial anyway." He drew a breath. "Someone has to."

They didn't speak of Billy's mother; both of them knew she would do nothing more useful than offer a goodbye toast to the woman who had meant so much to her son. This bothered Lexie terribly but, as Tremaine had pointed out earlier, there were some things one just had to accept.

Lexie was still pondering the sober truth of Billy's plight when she walked into the hotel lobby and nearly ran into Miss Everly. Pa and Eliza rose from the settee where they'd been seated—Pa looking worried sick, Eliza white and pale.

Lexie stopped short so quickly that Tremaine, who had been following behind, collided into her. His hands dropped lightly on her shoulders, steadying her.

"Miss Danner," Miss Everly greeted Lexie frigidly, her arms crossed around her middle. Gone was the benevolent smile.

"Yes?"

"It has come to my attention that you have not been honest about your relationship with Dr. Danner." Tremaine slowly lowered his hands as Lexie's heart sank. "Celeste Monteith told me, just yesterday, that you are not truly related. When you did not come home last night, I assumed you'd spent the night in the hotel with your parents. However, now I find that you and—" Here she shot a withering look at Tremaine "—your *step*brother have been out all night with no chaperone. I am sorry, but as I just told Mr. and Mrs. Danner, I have no choice but to rescind your diploma."

Lexie's embarrassment turned to wonder, then to incensed outrage. How dare this woman pass judgment on her? Her conscience tweaked a bit at the knowledge of the pleasure she'd shared with Tremaine, but Miss Everly had pronounced her an unfit lady for such a minor infraction that Lexie was filled with burning injustice.

"You may keep your diploma," she stated evenly. "I wouldn't want it now anyway. How do you live with yourself, Miss Everly? Your piousness must be a great burden to you!"

"Lexie!" her mother gasped.

"I'm not through," Lexie swept on, ignoring the chuckle of male amusement she heard from behind her head. "Tonight I watched Tremaine offer peace and encouragement to a woman during her last hours. She died about an hour ago. If you cannot reconcile my conduct to your own moral code, I'm afraid I have no interest in being a Miss Everly Lady."

Two high spots of color stained Miss Everly's cheeks. "Well," she said after several minutes. "Well."

Lexie could feel Tremaine's shoulders shaking with suppressed laughter. In a tone so low that only she could hear, he said, "Very nice delivery. You didn't swear once."

Lexie had to quell the urge to stomp on his foot, along with the equally unforgivable need to shout with laughter. She felt she'd been freed!

"I suppose allowances must be made once in a while," said a rather flustered Miss Everly.

Pa, a smile threatening the corners of his lips, came forward to take Lexie's arm. "I suppose they must," he agreed, shooting a glance at his son. "Come on, daughter. Let's go home."

Tremaine's hand lingered on her arm. "I'll see you there later," he said, softly. Then he was gone.

Chapter Sixteen

Jace Garrett settled more comfortably into the leather cushions of Conrad Templeton's chair and crossed his ankles on the Half Moon Saloon's manager's desk. Scratching a match across the bottom of his shoe, he lit a cheroot and eyed Conrad, who was standing by the office door and wearing an uneasy smile, with tolerant amusement.

"Sit down. Sit down," Jace invited expansively.

Conrad did as he was bidden, albeit reluctantly. Jace couldn't understand the man. Since they'd reconciled the books last Christmas, Conrad paying back in full—with only a modicum of interest tacked on—the amount which had mysteriously disappeared, their relationship had been a friendly one. Why Conrad still felt so uncomfortable Jace couldn't imagine.

"I ought to tell you," Templeton said now. "There's a man in the saloon who's been asking questions about the Danners. Lots of questions."

Anger flickered inside Jace. He didn't want to think about the Danners. Since Lexie's rejection, he'd been nursing his injured pride with any woman who was willing. He'd even gone so far as to make another play for Betsy Talbot, but that bit of baggage had actually turned him down flat! She'd been too long under Jenny's suffragette influence, Jace concluded darkly, and had then had the good fortune to collar some horny lumberman just down from the hills and talk him into marrying her. She'd left Rock Springs soon after and, since Jenny kept an eagle eye on any poor woman who should arrive in town alone, Jace had been forced into the humiliation of paying for the Half Moon's whores.

"He can ask any damn questions about the Danners he wants," Jace snapped irritably. He climbed to his feet, walked to the window on the back side of Conrad's office, and threw open the sash. Instantly he heard the rush and tumble of Fool's Falls, and the chatter of the stream as it flowed along the rock wall beyond the back of the saloon. The noise reminded him of Tremaine's ignominious treatment of him last winter and he swore under his breath. But it was a hot June night so he left the window open. Thinking of Lexie made the night even hotter, he reflected bitterly.

"I don't like him in here," Conrad muttered. "His questions are strange."

"Like what does he want to know?"

"The layout of the farm. How many children are in the family. If Joseph Danner has any other occupation besides farming." Conrad shrugged.

Jace was growing intrigued in spite of himself. "Show him in here," he said in sudden decision. The fellow's interest in the Danners might be worth investigating after all. Jace was still smarting over being made to look a fool. What he wouldn't give to find some way to get even with Tremaine.

The man Conrad ushered into the room was rather nondescript and Jace lost enthusiasm almost instantly. Whoever he was, he couldn't be anyone important. But the cut of his slacks was expensive, the way he held himself remarkably refined. And the amused slant to his mouth said he was used to getting his own way.

"What's your name?" Jace asked abruptly after Conrad left.

"Victor Flynne," was the smooth reply. "I've been rather anxious to meet you, Mr. Garrett. I believe we have a common goal."

"And that is?"

Flynne smiled, his teeth straight and even. "We want something from the Danners."

"Sit down, Mr. Flynne," said Jace. "And start talking."

Jenny McBride fanned herself with one hand and considered the dismal prospect of her future. She'd been a widow for over five years and a lonely woman for even longer. Women's rights were fine, but she would be the first to admit life was pretty empty without a man sharing her bed.

Hot, she stepped through the screen door to the back porch of the rooming house and grasped the handle of the pump. A spray of water gushed out and Jenny dipped in her hand, running the water over her face and throat.

The pounding crash of Fool's Falls beckoned her and she walked along the bank of the stream, behind the false-fronted Rock Springs businesses. Nearing the Half Moon Saloon, she recognized Jace Garrett's voice drifting from the open window of Conrad Templeton's office.

Jenny grimaced. She didn't like Jace any more now than she had last winter, though he'd been a bit more human since Lexington Danner broke their engagement. *That* had been a fortunate day! Jenny hoped Tremaine would stop by the rooming house and regale her with all the intimate details, but she'd seen neither hide nor hair of him since Christmas.

How was she going to get him back? she wondered forlornly, more convinced than ever that he had a woman in Portland. No one of Tremaine's looks and sexuality would be living a life of celibacy. And he'd said as much anyway. Selfishly, she'd hoped it wouldn't last.

Words sounded above the crash of the falls; words from the Half Moon's open window. ". . . Danner . . . Lexington, Kentucky . . . will pay handsomely . . ."

Jenny didn't recognize this new voice, but her interest quickened at the nature of the words. She stole closer to the window, trying to catch a glimpse of the man speaking.

He was sitting in a chair, smoking, one knife-creased leg thrown over the other. Jenny had never seen him before but his conversation was shockingly illuminating.

". . . Danner came to Oregon on the *Bonnie Lynne* in '64.

He brought his wife, Eliza, and his son Tremaine, who was then about eight years old."

"Well, he's about thirty now, so that fits," Jace remarked testily. "Get to the point."

"I believe Eliza Danner was pregnant when they arrived. Do you happen to know the birthdate of Lexington Danner?"

"Sometime in February." Jace's chair squeaked as he shifted impatiently.

"Well, then that fits. I believe Mrs. Danner was pregnant during the voyage."

"What the hell has this got to do with anything?" Jace growled.

The stranger coughed in light sophistication. "Let me backtrack a bit, Mr. Garrett. It's come to my attention that you have a distinct rivalry going on with members of the Danner family, specifically Tremaine Danner. There have been numerous recountings by the town members of when Dr. Danner—uh—tossed you into Fool's—"

"I have no love for Tremaine Danner," Jace cut in harshly.

The other man hesitated, eyeing Jace shrewdly. "If I were to give you information that might prove embarrassing for Dr. Danner—maybe even dangerous—would you be willing to tell me all you know about the Danners as a family?"

"Why do you want to know?"

"I have a client who wants to know. A very wealthy client," he added meaningfully.

Jace sat perfectly still, thinking. "If you could compromise Tremaine Danner, I would give you the information for free. But you're going to have to give me something pretty special."

"What if I were to tell you that the Danners are hiding an interesting family secret?"

Jace leaned forward intently, waiting.

"I believe Eliza Danner was married before—to a southern gentleman of some prominence. I believe she smashed her first husband's skull with a poker, then ran for her life. Along the way, she met up with a drifter—one broken-down Boston doctor by the name of Joseph Danner, who had a young son in tow. I believe she talked Joseph Danner into marrying her within a week of when they left—sometime in the summer of '64."

"She killed her first husband?" Jace repeated, shocked.

"Not only that, but she was already pregnant by him. Miss Lexington Danner is not Joseph's daughter." The man smiled a knowing smile. "And neither is she Tremaine Danner's sister. I understand the illustrious Dr. Danner is rather protective where Lexie's concerned."

Jenny gasped. Her fingers dug into the wooden slats of the building. Tremaine and *Lexie?* The news hit her like a blow. She felt the blood rush from her head.

"I already knew they weren't related, Flynne," Jace murmured. He was staring stupidly at the stranger. "But I didn't know about Eliza."

"Do you also know that Dr. Danner lusts after his would-be younger sister? I think only the threat of exposing Eliza's crime keeps him from having her."

"Go on," Jace said, when the stranger stopped to puff on his cigar.

He leaned forward. "Things are about to change, Mr. Garrett. And when that happens, Miss Lexington Danner will find she's not the daughter of an Oregon farmer, but the heiress to a fortune far beyond even yours." The man's eyes narrowed in appreciation at the staggered expression on Jace's face. "You had better mend fences with the lovely Lexington right away, or lose her to your most detested rival . . ."

Jenny heard no more. With her skirts bunched in her hands, she sprinted back to her rooming house. She would send a wire to Tremaine. As soon as possible.

If Jace was about to make his play, she was also about to make hers.

The breeze whipped bits of grit and hay into Lexie's eyes as she swept out the barn. Still, it was better than running a household or sewing, two occupations her mother was bent on her learning. She would go completely mad if she were forced to play the role of a lady much longer. She'd been so certain things would fall into place once she was home, but

Eliza refused to let her run the stables, work in the barn, or help out in the fields. She was obsessed with molding her daughter into a lady.

With a snort of disgust, Lexie threw down the broom and unbuttoned the top three buttons of her shirtwaist, wiping off the dewy drops of perspiration. She was hot and frustrated and miserable. The first week she returned she'd expected Tremaine to show up anytime. But now that week had stretched to two. Was he still winding things up in Portland? Or had he changed his mind about moving to Rock Springs after all?

She walked out into the blistering June heat. She ached for him. More so now than ever. She'd told him she loved him. She'd given him everything a woman can give. But she instinctively sensed there was a barrier between them that she couldn't overcome, no matter how hard she tried. Why wasn't he here if he supposedly wanted her so much?

Uneasy with her own thoughts, Lexie walked toward the house.

Pa's buggy stood in front of the portico, the bay gelding harnessed in front switching his tail nervously. Suddenly wanting to escape, Lexie ran to the buggy just as Pa came out the front door. "Are you going to town?" At his nod, she said in a rush, "I want to go with you. I can't stand just waiting around here all day."

"Waiting for what?"

"Oh, nothing," she said lamely, and was glad when he didn't pursue the subject.

Rock Springs lay like a dull gem in the late morning sun, its only glitter from Fool's Falls. Tremaine wiped the dust from his lips and drove down the dirt road to the outskirts of town, parking in front of Jenny's rooming house. It had taken him longer than he'd expected to make certain the hospital wouldn't just forget the people on the other side of the river. Even with Jenny's terse, cryptic wire burning a hole in his pocket, he hadn't been able to speed up the process.

But now, thirty-six hours after he'd received her message, he was finally here. And what, he wondered reflectively, pulling the crumpled paper from his pocket, did it mean?

There's trouble brewing. Family problems. Come as quick as you can. Quicker.

The last time Jenny had summoned him so urgently, it was for Betsy Talbot's miscarriage. For some reason this strange message seemed more ominous.

He rang the bell of the rooming house, but when there was no immediate answer, he let himself inside. Dust motes swirled and his footsteps echoed down the hallway. At the kitchen he stopped short. A pot of beans was parboiling on the cookstove, adding more moist heat to the sweltering day. Other than the muted sounds upstairs, this was the only sign that someone was home.

Tremaine sank onto the cot in the alcove, uneasy. But the round-the-clock hours he'd worked finally took their toll and he fell, sprawled across the narrow bed, into exhausted slumber.

Lexie stood in front of Fool's Falls, the mist of water cooling her flushed cheeks, trying to slow down her galloping pulse. The trip to town had been a mistake. A terrible, mind-numbing mistake. Tremaine's buggy was parked boldly in front of Jenny McBride's rooming house; Fortune looked like he'd been gathering dust there for some hours.

They're just friends, Lexie reminded herself. *They are no longer lovers.*

She drew in a long breath, amazed at herself. How had she ever become so insecure?

She glanced upward. The sun was straight above her. Pa would be done with his errands soon and start wondering what had become of her. With more resolve than courage, Lexie walked behind the shops, following the stream toward the rooming house near the end of town. She would confront Tremaine. She was tired of all the wondering.

Jenny McBride set the sacks of staples from Garrett's Mercantile on the slatboard counter, then turned and surveyed the sight that met her eyes. She hadn't realized how much she loved Tremaine until she'd found him draped so inelegantly over her cot. Amused, she prodded his sleeping form with her toe, but all he did was groan and slap at her.

"It's afternoon, you lazybones," she said, grinning. As she

watched his deep, even breathing, a feeling of profound tenderness stole over her. She leaned down and placed her hand against the side of his cheek. He muttered something unintelligible.

Jenny McBride had waited far too long for the man she loved to show her any love in return. Taking his chin between her strong hands, she pressed a warm kiss to his lips. "If you won't come to my bed, I'll have to come to yours," she told him reasonably, and she fitted her body directly on top of him.

At that moment, Lexie looked through the open screen door of Jenny McBride's rooming house. For half a beat she didn't believe it was Tremaine. But the arms wrapped so tightly around Jenny's petite shoulders were achingly familiar, the leg thrown possessively over her drawn-up skirts one that had held Lexie pinned the same way.

Jenny's laughter spilled into the relentless sunny day. "Slow down, Dr. Danner," she said in sublime amusement. "If I'd known you were going to be so ready, I would have got back sooner."

"Jenny . . . ?" Tremaine's voice was a sensual slur. His hands slid over her sumptuous derrière. Icy reality shot through Lexie's veins.

She pressed her hand to her mouth and stumbled away from the porch. Lies. It had all been lies! That was no kiss of friendship. And in the middle of the day! They couldn't even wait until evening!

A cry of anguish lodged in her throat, suffocating her. She had to get out of Rock Springs. She'd waited for Tremaine too long as it was.

She wasn't going to wait anymore.

Chapter Seventeen

Lexie sat perfectly straight in her chair. Dinner was over and Annie was clearing the plates. If she'd been asked what she'd eaten, she wouldn't have been able to recall.

"Harrison won't be back until August," Pa was relating with regret. "I picked up a letter in town today and I left it in the buggy. I'll get it for you."

"Did he say why he can't come home?" Eliza asked, as Pa scraped back his chair and went to get Harrison's letter.

"Just that he's busy with work."

Busy with work. Lexie swallowed, wishing she could say the same about herself. She watched the flickering candles but images of Tremaine and Jenny undulated inside the dancing flames. He'd lied. They were lovers still. But why should she care when he'd never professed to caring a whit about her!

"What's troubling you, Lexie? You've scarcely eaten a bite."

Lexie jerked rigidly to attention. Eliza was staring at her in perplexity, waiting for an answer. Samuel and Jesse were looking at her, too. Lexie opened her mouth to speak—then was surprised at what she said. "I want to go to Denver and study with Dr. Breverman."

"We know that, Lexie," her mother answered tiredly.

"As I know I can't. Because I'm a woman." Lexie looked down at her hands. Tears were filling her throat. Before she could embarrass herself, she pushed back her chair, folded her napkin on the table, and walked out of the room.

Upstairs, she wandered outside to the widow's walk. She was as useless and simpering as the worst of the girls from Miss Everly's School. What had happened to her gumption over the last year? Had learning all that coquetry, etiquette, and fine dancing turned her into the kind of woman she despised most?

A shudder rocked her willowy frame. She'd been waiting around like a lovesick cow, waiting for her life to begin when Tremaine came riding up to profess his undying love. Well, it wasn't going to happen.

And she had to get away.

A plan began to form in her mind, one which she'd oft considered, and just as many times tossed aside. She had no money, no connections, but she had a powerful, driving need and that need was what finally won the battle of her conscience.

In her room, Lexie packed a large reticule. As soon as the house had quieted for the night, she slung the bag over her shoulder. Wearing the faded and worn split skirt, a white sleeveless shirtwaist, and a black cloak to cover herself, she scratched out a note of farewell, assuring her family they would hear from her soon. Placing the note on her pillow, she sneaked downstairs to the kitchen. Cook was nowhere in sight. A plate of cornbread sat on the counter, and Lexie stuffed several crumbly pieces into the pockets of her cloak. She grabbed a handful of sugar cubes from the sugar bowl and added them to her booty.

At last, Lexie fully considered the wisdom of running away. A woman alone, at night, with no protection, was asking to be raped, plundered, or killed.

Lexie stood perfectly still in the hallway. She could tell Pa and Mother and at least one of her brothers were in the parlor. Stealthily, she slid into Pa's den and removed one of his pistols from the glass guncase. This she hid in the pockets in the folds of her skirt, then retraced her steps to the kitchen and the back door.

Under the shadow of a moonless night she ran on winged feet to the stables, a dark wraith intent on secrecy. But when the Dutch door creaked open, she heard the unmistakable sounds of someone already inside.

Lexie froze, but Jesse's voice demanded from the gloom within, "Who's there?"

"It's me. *I,*" she automatically corrected herself. "What are you doing here in the dark?"

Since she'd already been found out, Lexie lit a lantern. Jesse was standing in front of the tackroom door, his shirt unbuttoned, his lean chest heaving. The flush on his dark face made her realize she'd caught him doing something he shouldn't.

It was as if all Tremaine's transgressions were visited on his younger brother, and Lexie was instantly incensed. She flung open the door to the tackroom and Annie, white-faced and ashamed, straw dangling in her black hair, was buttoning her shirtwaist as fast as her trembling fingers could work. "Miss Lexington," she quavered wildly. "Please, don't say nothin' to your ma. She'd sack me, sure enough."

Lexie simply turned on her booted heel and walked straight for Tantrum's stall. The gelding nickered a welcome and snuffled her hand for a treat. Automatically she fed him the purloined sugar.

"Lex," Jesse said quietly, standing beside her. "What are you going to do?" It was then he noticed her bulging reticule and dark clothing. "Are you *leaving?*"

"Yes."

"Alone? You can't be serious. It's not safe."

"Jesse, if you want your secret kept, you'd better forget you saw me tonight." She slid the bridle over Tantrum's head, tugged a saddle onto his broad back, and drew the cinch.

"I won't let you do it." He grabbed her arm when she tried to lead Tantrum out of the box. "Where are you going? Rock Springs?" he demanded tersely. "Who are you meeting?"

"Do you have any money?" Lexie asked thoughtfully, ignoring his furious grip. "I need a loan."

"Christ! There's no talking to you!" His aquamarine eyes swept Lexie's set face. "Here," he said shortly, pulling a wad of bills out of his pocket, the money he'd earned from selling some of Pa's lambs. "Take it. But I'm coming with you."

"No, you're not." Lexie moved past him and out into the black night. She mounted Tantrum while Jesse was still swearing and arguing with Annie. Like a whisper, she was gone before he could find her.

Rock Springs was only an hour away, but Lexie, knowing Jesse would be hard on her heels, veered Tantrum off the rutted road and into the brush. It would take longer, but no one would find her. And she didn't plan on staying in Rock Springs tonight anyway.

Tremaine stared fixedly at Jenny McBride. "What did you say this man's name was?" he asked softly, dangerously.

"Flynne."

He swore roundly and raked a hand through his hair. "Why didn't you tell me earlier?" he boomed out furiously, scraping back his chair in one furious motion.

Jenny stirred cream into her tea in precise little circles. She was hurt. Tremaine had thrust her from him as soon as he'd realized whom he was with. She'd known then, for a fact, his heart belonged to another woman—and she sensed that Flynne's warning was fact: Tremaine loved Lexington.

"I didn't tell you earlier because you were such a beast," she stated flatly. Her womanly pride had taken beatings before, but this one was particularly devastating.

"Damn it all to hell, Jenny. I'm sorry. But this is important. Tell me about Flynne!"

"Because your *sister* might be in danger?"

Tremaine stared at her, realizing in that dreadful moment that she already knew the truth. "Flynne told you?" he asked softly. "He knows?"

"Yes."

Tremaine exploded with a vicious swear word, one that singed even Jenny McBride's well-seasoned ears. Realizing she'd lost him already, Jenny drew in a heavy breath, resigned to her role of best friend. Quickly and accurately, she recited the conversation as she remembered it.

Tremaine's expression changed from incredulous fury to ashen worry. "My God," he muttered, suddenly sure that his father's nebulous concerns had been right. "I've got to get home," he said blankly. As an afterthought, he gave Jenny a quick kiss on the forehead, then was gone.

She drank her tea in utter loneliness. She'd played her part, and now it was time to think about the future. A future that did not include Tremaine Danner.

Lively music spilled from the Half Moon Saloon onto the dry and dusty street. The night was so dark that the lamplight only cut rectangular squares through its inky thickness, leaving the center of Main Street a ribbon of perfect blackness.

Jace Garrett stood by his carriage, thoughtfully puffing on a cheroot. He eyed that patch of blackness unseeingly, for his vision was turned inward. One thought chased around in his mind like a dog circling after his tail: Lexington Danner was an extremely rich woman.

It hadn't been so long ago that she'd been in love with him, Jace reminded himself. Tremaine was a problem, but Victor Flynne had intimated that he might be out of favor with Lexie. God! How he would love to bring down the estimable Dr. Danner! His mouth curved cynically. What a pleasure that would be.

A rattle and bump at the western edge of town caught Jace's attention. A carriage was approaching, lamplight sneaking through the curtains on either side of the windows. It was an elegant carriage, its lacquered finish now obscured by the prevailing dust. The team was strong, sturdy, and handsomely groomed. Whoever it was had money to spend, and plenty of it.

The carriage passed in front of Jace, along that strip of blackness. Dark as it was, Jace was certain he'd never seen the carriage before. His curiosity heightened when the vehicle churned right through Rock Springs, heading southeast. There was nothing in that direction but farms and filthy lumber towns. And his property and the Danners.

Jace was still staring after the coach long minutes later. His own vehicle seemed shabby by comparison and he could hear old MacDougal's snores as the man nodded over the reins. Jace prodded him angrily. "Someday I'm going to hire a driver worth his salt," he muttered furiously.

MacDougal came to with a snort. "Aye, Mr. Garrett," he said, wiping a hand across his drowsy eyelids. "It be home, you want?"

"Aye," Jace answered cynically.

Hoofbeats sounded and Jace saw a dark rider appear from behind the mercantile. A black cloak obscured the man's features, but a hot breeze lifted the hood at that moment, revealing long blond hair. A woman!

"Just a minute," said Jace, and he stepped from the plankboard sidewalk into the gloomy center of the street. The horse and rider approached, the horse shying at the sight of him. As black as the night was, Jace saw the woman's face clearly as he exclaimed, "Lexie!"

"Get out of my way, Jace," was her taut reply.

"Where in the hell do you think you're going at this time of night?"

He would have grabbed the reins, but she jerked Tantrum's head back and wheeled him in a tight circle. "None of your business!"

And then Jace knew that the wheels of Victor Flynne's plan were already in motion. Nothing else could have forced Lexie out alone. "Let me help you," he offered.

She laughed. "I wouldn't accept your help if you were the last man alive."

"You're running away from something. Lexie, I know what it is. Victor Flynne was here a few days ago."

"I don't know any Victor Flynne."

"Well, he certainly knows your family." She was sidestepping the horse around him so Jace played his trump card. "He knows Joseph Danner isn't your father."

That caught her attention, but she didn't seem unduly worried. "It's no shattering secret," she remarked unconcerned. "Now let me pass!"

"He also knows your mother's a—"

The blast from a rifle perilously near their ears caused Tantrum to rear up and scream in surprise. Lexie slid to the ground and rolled, choking on dust but unhurt. She scrambled to her feet and was actually glad for Jace's strong arms, throwing her to safety near his carriage. Old MacDougal wrestled with Jace's own bolting team, holding them back with all his strength as they quivered and sweated and whistled in fright.

It was a gambling fight, Lexie realized as she laid a calming hand on the nearest of Jace's horses. Two men stood outside the front of the Half Moon Saloon. One held a rifle, aimed at the sky; the other watched warily, his hands held in front of him.

"Never a dull moment," Jace drawled.

"Tantrum," Lexie said, glancing back. The spirited gelding had raced out of town, heading west.

"You want to find him?"

Lexie stared into the face of the man she once had thought she loved. He was hardly her idea of a savior, but then beggars could not be choosers. And old MacDougal was a friend Lexie knew she could count on.

With a curt nod, she preceded Jace into the carriage, scooting as far across the seat as she could. Jace lit the lanterns above the open windows and MacDougal turned the team west. Sitting across from Lexie, Jace suddenly leaned forward. Lexie instantly drew back against the cushioned seat.

"Jace," she said warningly.

"You have dirt on your face. I was just going to wipe it off." His white handkerchief hovered in front of Lexie's face. She snatched it out of his grasp, regarding him coolly.

"You malign me, Lexington." He shook his head gently.

They were well out of town when MacDougal suddenly shouted. Lexie leaned out the window. Tantrum was standing by the side of the road, his sides heaving. As soon as the coach came to a stop, Lexie bolted for the door.

Tantrum was in a lather. He rolled his eyes at her, mincing away, but Lexie was able to grab hold of the bridle reins. She jumped when she heard Jace behind her.

"How far are you going?" he asked conversationally.

Lexie, though she would rather cut out her tongue than reveal her plans to Jace, had decided she was going to Denver. She could catch the train at the Portland depot and be in Denver within the week. "I'm going to Portland," she told him in a half-lie.

"Portland! My God, girl. It'll take you all night!" He threw a disparaging glance at Tantrum. "You must be out of your head. You can't ride that beast to Portland all alone. Have you even thought what could happen to you?"

Yes, Lexie had briefly considered the danger. But she had a gun and though she was no markswoman, like Jace's sister, she was handy enough if need be. "I'll be all right," she told him flatly.

To her fury and surprise, Jace bodily lifted her up and hauled her toward the carriage. Kicking and screaming, Lexie connected with vital tissue, causing him to swear. He threw her inside and glared at her, holding the door so she couldn't get out.

"Now listen to me. We'll tie Tantrum to the back of the carriage. I'll take you to Portland myself. You may hate me, Lexington, but I'll be damned if I'll have your dead body on my conscience!"

"Let me out, Jace, or I'll kill you," she said through her teeth. "I swear I will."

"You little she-cat," he said in wonder. "Whatever made me think anyone could make a lady out of you!"

Realizing he would stand there all night if need be, Lexie flung herself into a seat. If the truth were known, she actually preferred riding with Jace to the thought of facing the dark night alone. But she didn't trust him one bit.

Jace, seeing Lexie had subsided for the moment, went to gather up Tantrum. With vague thoughts of ravishing her somehow on the journey ahead, he reached for Tantrum's reins. The gelding snorted and stampeded away, leading Jace on a merry chase. After ten minutes, he was furious and Lexie was convulsed with laughter. Finally, he managed to lash Tantrum to the back of the carriage and climbed in beside Lexie once more.

"Are you going to be reasonable now?" he demanded. To his intense amazement she pulled a pistol from somewhere in the folds of her skirt and aimed it at the space between his eyes.

"As long as you play by my rules," she answered agreeably.

For the first time in a long, long time, Lexie was happy. Miss Everly's School was behind her; her home and family a bittersweet memory; Tremaine a terrible ache she was determined to get over.

She was on her own now, making her own decisions. And she loved it.

Chapter Eighteen

The farmhouse was ablaze with lights when Tremaine pulled to a stop under the portico. He leapt from the buggy and strode through the front door and into the foyer. Raised voices sounded in the parlor and he unerringly headed in that direction, stopping short at the doorway.

Jesse stood to one side of the room, his face dark with rebellion. Pa was facing him with fury sparking in his blue eyes. The few times Tremaine had seen his father angry came back to him and the memories were unpleasant ones. Joseph Danner's anger was slow in coming, but magnificent in its fury when it arrived. Though shorter than Jesse, Joseph gave the impression of towering rage and Jesse, no fool he, stood poised on the balls of his feet, meeting this onslaught with caution and potential flight.

Eliza sat on the couch, her hands twisted tautly together. Samuel, dark-eyed and watchful, sat in the corner chair. Only Lexie was missing.

"What the hell's going on?" Tremaine asked calmly, his own fears slipping to the background at this scene of family discord. There was no sign of Flynne, no reason to be alarmed.

Eliza, from her place on the couch, rose to her feet, her face weak with relief at the sight of Tremaine. She came toward him, touching his arm, and the gesture was so thankful and tender that Tremaine's sense of unease returned. "It's Lexie," she said softly, her voice trembling. "She's taken Tantrum and left."

"*What?* What do you mean *left?*"

"Jesse was the last one to see her and it took him a while to come forward," explained Eliza.

"I followed her." Jesse's voice was taut, his eyes still on his father's white-lipped face. "But I lost her somehow, so I came back."

"And took your own sweet time in the telling of it!" Joseph growled. "Have you lost all your senses, boy? Lexie's out alone on a horse heading God knows where! *Why didn't you come forward sooner?*"

Tremaine stepped between his father and his brother. "It sounds to me like Jesse did what he thought was best. Now, I'll go—"

Joseph reached around Tremaine, grabbing Jesse's collar. "I've had enough of you acting like a rutting bull! Don't think I don't know what was going on between you and Annie. She came into the house in a dither, blushing like a schoolgirl, straw in her hair. You didn't go after Lexie. You were with Annie using the only part of yourself that's good for—"

"Joseph!" Eliza's voice was strident. "If he says he followed Lexie, I believe him."

Jesse deliberately pulled his father's hand from his shirt, a muscle in his jaw pulsing. Tremaine was fed up with the histrionics. "Where did she go?" he asked quietly, dropping a restraining hand on his father's shoulder.

Jesse turned to Tremaine, regret flashing across his handsome face. "I don't know. She didn't follow the road. I would have caught her."

"You mean she just left?"

"About two hours ago."

Tremaine felt a pang of real fear. Two hours! He would

have met her on the road to town if she'd traveled that way. What had possessed her to take a roundabout route?

Now Tremaine understood his father's alarm. But it wasn't Jesse's fault that Lexie had left. "Why did she leave?" he demanded of the room at large. With vague thoughts of Victor Flynne somehow being responsible, he practically shouted, "What the hell happened?"

"She was upset when I saw her," Jesse offered after several tense moments. "She asked me for money. I gave her what I had and told her I was coming with her, but she took off before I could get a horse out of the stables. By the time I hit the road I couldn't even hear her hoofbeats."

Tremaine whirled on Eliza, who stood beside him like a pale statue. "What happened before that? Did she give any hint at where she was heading?"

"No." Eliza shook her head slowly, her beautiful face drawn and lined. "She was distant at supper. Joseph brought up Harrison's letter and then she left the table. That's the last I saw of her."

"What was in the letter?"

"It's not that," Pa disabused him, reining in his anger. "Harrison just can't get home until the fall. That's all I said."

"Tremaine?"

He'd forgotten Samuel sitting quietly in the corner. Now Tremaine glanced inquiringly at his youngest brother. Samuel stood and said soberly, "Lexie still wants to be a horse doctor. I think bringing up Harrison bothered her."

"She's given up that idea," Eliza quickly argued. "She's spent a year at Miss Everly's School!"

Tremaine stared at Samuel. Samuel had a knack for understanding human nature that always surprised him. Eliza sensed it, too. Her face grew pale with anxiety. "You don't think . . ." she began fearfully.

"She can't get far tonight," Tremaine said in sudden decision. "Damn it all to hell," he muttered, his torturous thoughts contriving terrible scenarios where bandits, outlaws, and thieves pounced upon her in the night. There was an ugly element which terrorized the road between Rock Springs and the larger cities, springing unexpectedly, thieving and plundering and raping. But Lexie knew that. What had driven her to take off on her own?

Tremaine strode from the parlor to the foyer, pausing, assembling his scattered thoughts. He needed a fresh horse and something to eat on the way. There was no time for a bath or a change of clothes. He stepped into the moonless night and thought darkly that Lexie couldn't have picked a better time to run off.

"I'll come with you," Jesse said from behind him, the front door closing after him.

"No, stay here. There's trouble coming and I want Pa to have some help."

"What kind of trouble?"

Tremaine would have dearly loved to explain because Jesse, for all his faults, deep down possessed the same family loyalty and honor that he did. Pa had been wrong to chastise him; Jesse had done what he could. But Lexie—the wretch! —was too independent to control.

"I don't have time to explain," he said tersely. "Ask Pa about a man named Victor Flynne who sent him a wire last Christmas. Tell him Flynne's been in Rock Springs asking questions and bartering information. Jace Garrett knows Pa isn't Lexie's father. And he knows about Eliza—tell Pa that."

Jesse grabbed his brother's rock-hard arm as Tremaine sought to stride toward the stables and collect a fresh mount. "What's Flynne got to do with it?"

"Nothing good," said Tremaine soberly.

He was halfway to the stables when he heard the rhythm of hoofbeats and the heavier crunch of carriage wheels approaching from the lane. Intent on his task, Tremaine only threw a glance over his shoulder at the grand coach that swung around the last corner and pulled to a smooth stop beneath the portico's glowing yellow lanterns.

Jesse was there to greet the lacquered carriage, and Tremaine, his senses on sudden, anxious alert, stopped in his tracks. He swore beneath his breath. Was this Flynne's doing? Who else would arrive so late in such an ostentatious vehicle?

He thought of Lexie, alone, galloping on some wide

stretch of uninhabited road, and ran the last few yards to the stables. The only horse worth its salt for speed and stamina was an eight-year-old gelding named Napoleon. Tremaine threw on a bridle and saddle and led the eager horse through the door and into the sultry June night.

He saw Eliza standing on the widow's walk, her hands wrapped around the rail. She was staring down at the coach. Three men had alighted, their features indistinguishable in the gloom. Abruptly, Eliza walked back inside and through the window Tremaine could see her descending the scarlet-carpeted stairs.

Tremaine led Napoleon to the small gathering beneath the widow's walk. An elderly gentleman whose left hand leaned heavily on an ebony cane with a mother-of-pearl handle, was remarking on the elegant portico.

"Beautiful," he said in a resonant voice with a deep southern drawl. "Reminds me of a Kentucky plantation home I once lived in."

Jesse stood in front of the door, looking for all the world as if he were about to deny the man entry. Seeing Tremaine, he reminded the man gently, evenly, "You didn't give me your name."

Tremaine glanced at the two other men. Each was sturdy as a tree trunk and had a face that could have been carved in stone. Their eyes were hooded and cold. One man wore a belt with a gleaming silver buckle. *Gunmen,* Tremaine thought, feeling suddenly naked without the Colt .45 he'd carried around like a second skin when he was a kid. He'd never liked guns as an adult and consequently rarely carried one. Now he knew a moment of icy premonition: These men were killers.

"If you tell your mother ah'm here," the older gentleman advised in a friendly voice edged with steel, "she'll introduce me."

Tremaine couldn't leave. As urgent as it was to find Lexie, he smelled trouble—an odor his brother sensed in equal measure, if Jesse's deep hesitation was any indication. "Go get Eliza," Tremaine suggested quietly. *And a gun,* he added silently, hoping Jesse was as astute as he suspected.

Jesse's narrowed gaze shifted from one man to another. He backed up, but didn't have time to open the door before

Eliza came gracefully through it, her lavender skirts flowing gently around her ankles.

"What is it?" she asked in her quietly rippling voice, squinting to the three men who stood just outside the rings of lamplight.

The elderly gentleman stepped forward. There was a smile on his face, but it was little more than a grotesque grimace. The left side of his mouth didn't lift; the muscles were slack. It gave him the appearance of a leering ogre.

Eliza took one look at him and went white. Her eyes filled with horror, then rolled to the back of her head. A whimper slipped past her lips. She fell so quickly that Tremaine just caught her before her head crashed against the cement steps.

"Who the hell are you?" he rasped in alarm, holding Eliza's limp body in his strong arms.

"My name is Ramsey Gainsborough," he introduced himself, his eyes narrowed on Eliza's unconscious form. "You sir, are holding my wife!"

Lexie couldn't keep the gun at eye level for very long. The tiresome ride took its toll on her muscles. Her eyelids kept fluttering downward, her lashes sweeping her cheeks, though she willed herself to stay alert. But it was warm in the carriage and, halfway to Portland, she sighed and laid the gun on the seat beside her.

"I've never thought you were a gentleman, Jace," she murmured, laying her head against the backrest and eyeing him through half-shut lids. "It would make me happy to prove that wrong."

Jace, for all his burning lust, had a deep, chivalrous nature at times that surprised and bothered him. It was in his mind to throw Lexie down on the seat and toss her skirts over her head. Only two things prevented him: one, old MacDougal would never let him take Lexie without raising some kind of fuss; two, he had the strangest desire to earn her respect.

"Did you really love me once, Lexie?" he wanted to know.

She smiled tiredly. "No, I don't think I did. But if you'd been as honest with me then as you seem to be now, I might have."

"Damn you," he said without heat, and sent his burning stare out the window to the deep night.

When Lexie fell asleep he collected her gun, but made no attempt to touch her.

The parlor was a scene of tense expectation. Joseph Danner stood beside the couch, protectively watching over a still unconscious Eliza. Eliza's chest barely moved, and twice Joseph leaned over her to check her breathing. Samuel was back in his chair by the window, but his dark gaze burned with wrath. In an older man his intensity would have been awesome—even at thirteen Ramsey Gainsborough's men watched him carefully.

Jesse lounged against the fireplace, one arm leaning negligently across the enameled mantel. But his indolence was belied by the cold blue fire flaring in his eyes. His fingers straightened and clenched, straightened and clenched.

Tremaine saw them all in a swift, encompassing glance, weighing his options. His restraint was like a tattered tapestry, slowly unraveling with each tiny pull of Gainsborough's words. And though he was sick with worry for Lexie, he was glad she wasn't here. This man, he told himself, in startled astonishment, was her father!

"Well," Gainsborough remarked, his lazy southern drawl much like Eliza's. Casually, he pulled a Havana cigar from the silk-lined breast pocket inside his jacket. "It seems my resurrection has caused my dear wife to swoon. Do any of you gentlemen possess a match?" he asked politely.

Joseph stiffly pulled one from the pewter stand on the oak end table. He handed it to Gainsborough and said quietly, "What do you want?"

Gainsborough smiled his grotesquely wicked smile. "Ah'll not mince words, Dr. Danner. "What ah want is retribution—payment, if you will, for the agonies ah suffered at this woman's hand. Look at me. My left hand is nearly useless. Ah am forced to walk with a cane. The muscles in my face do not do the bidding of my brain. And why?" He sent a venomous glance toward Eliza. "Because my wife hit me over the head with a poker and crushed a part of my skull. Then she left me for dead." He slowly lit the cigar, letting his words sink in. "Yes, Dr. Danner, ah want retribution."

Lexie, Tremaine thought sickly. *He wants Lexie.*

"There is another member of the family missing, I believe." Gainsborough looked expectantly toward the curving staircase. "Miss Lexington Danner. Is she upstairs?"

"Lexie's visiting friends," Tremaine stepped in. The guncase was in the den. He wondered how he could get past the burly blockade of Gainsborough's men without arousing suspicion. Their gunbelts were at their sides. He had no doubt the pistols were loaded and ready. He also knew they would shoot first and ask questions later. He'd met Gainsborough's type—and the kind of men he employed—before.

"When will she be back?" Gainsborough asked.

Tremaine answered the man's cold smile with one of his own. "Later."

"Ah hope this is not another lie—like the one you gave my man last Christmas."

"Victor Flynne?" Tremaine guessed.

Gainsborough eyed him shrewdly, sensing that, of the entire Danner family, Tremaine was the most dangerous. If Flynne's information could be believed, the eldest Danner son was half in love with Lexington and, though that made him an even more formidable enemy, it also betrayed a vulnerability he planned to capitalize on. "He sent you all a wire, asking if you were the same Danner family who had come to Oregon on the *Bonnie Lynne.* You denied it. But Victor's a diligent, thorough man. Ah might never have found you if it hadn't been for his persistence."

Eliza stirred on the couch, her eyelids fluttering. "Joseph . . ." she cried out softly, anxiously.

"Right here." He wrapped her trembling hand within the warmth of his rough one.

"There's nothing for you here, Gainsborough," Tremaine said flatly.

"Oh, but you are mistaken. Ah want my wife back. And ah intend to have her."

"You filthy, sadistic rapist," Joseph suddenly growled. "Eliza struck you in self-defense! I wouldn't let you have her for any reason."

The insults caused Ramsey Gainsborough to flush a dark, unbecoming red. "My wife is my property! If ah want the adulteress back, there is nothing you can do about it!"

Joseph was on his feet in an instant, but Tremaine was ahead of him, blocking his way. The gunmen's hands lay poised over their pistols, but Tremaine's eyes met Gainsborough's. "Eliza will never leave willingly. Surely you know that."

"Ah intend to prosecute for attempted murder. The lady also stole a king's ransom from me."

"It was her money," Joseph snarled.

"It was my money. Ah am her husband!" Gainsborough bellowed and the gunmen raised their pistols directly at Joseph Danner.

"Wait!" Tremaine commanded. He judged the distance between himself and the nearest gunman. He could take one, but the other fellow's six-shooter was bound to spray enough bullets to kill or injure his father. "If it's money you want, we're willing to discuss financial restitution."

The man's laugh was ugly. He stared with loathing down at Eliza's fragile beauty. "It's you or your daughter, bitch," he said, then added, *"My* daughter. Make a decision."

It was at that moment Tremaine realized how much he cared about his stepmother. He would have laid down his life for her if it might help. But Gainsborough was threatening Lexie, too. And Eliza, pale as death, knew it.

"I'll go with you," she said quietly. "How much time do I have?"

Joseph exploded in fury. He lunged for Gainsborough. Tremaine didn't wait, he threw himself at the nearest gunman's legs, knocking him over, pinning him before he could get his hands on the deadly pistol. Jesse was a flying streak beside him, but he was too late. The gunman with the silver buckle shot once, with perfect aim, and Joseph Danner dropped to the ground. Jesse connected with his arm, but the man swung around, cracking his six-shooter against the side of Jesse's head. Samuel was on Gainsborough, kicking and punching. Eliza screamed, and Silver Buckle yanked her from the couch, pressing the cold barrel against her temple. "Stop," he ordered through his teeth.

Silence prevailed. Eliza's eyes were closed, her captor's arm squeezed across her heaving chest. Pa lay in a pool of spreading blood.

Gainsborough threw a now passive Samuel off him and glared at Tremaine. "Let Pete go," he demanded, straightening his jacket.

Tremaine did as he was told and Pete went to stand by his employer, hands on his gun, his dark glare murderous. Jesse lay perfectly still.

Jesse's groan galvanized Tremaine into action. He stooped over his father and was relieved to see that the bullet had merely cut a chunk of flesh from his upper arm. "Get me the tablecloth," he ordered Samuel, ignoring the strangers. He ripped off his shirt and tried to staunch the bloodflow as Gainsborough staggered to his feet.

"Come back here, boy!" he called, but Samuel kept right on going. Silver Buckle looked askance at Gainsborough, and for a moment Tremaine held his breath. But Gainsborough shook his head and Samuel was allowed to leave.

"Jesse," Tremaine asked, still bent over his father. "Jesse, can you hear me?"

"God," was his miserable reply.

"Let Eliza go," Tremaine said flatly. "We won't fight you."

She was flung unceremoniously on the couch. In a shaking voice she said, "If you leave my family alone, I'll do whatever you want."

Gainsborough heaved a misunderstood sigh. "That's all ah want. Ah am not interested in bloodshed."

The hell you aren't, Tremaine thought furiously, but Eliza, who had always chosen her own path, said with total conviction, "We'll leave tomorrow, if you want."

Samuel came back with the pale peach linen tablecloth and Tremaine ripped it into strips. He bound his father's arm and applied direct pressure, staunching the bloodflow. Joseph's face was ashen, but his breath whistled in and out of his throat.

Gainsborough chuckled, and the sound sent icy premonition down Tremaine's nerves. "Ah would rather stay and get to know my daughter a little, maybe even convince her to ·

287

come back to Kentucky with us. Ah've heard she's a lovely thing." He sighed and settled into the cushions, for all the world as if he were planning to move in permanently.

"Make sure Jesse's all right, then show Mr. Gainsborough Pa's liquor cabinet," Tremaine said to Samuel, earning him a look of shocked amazement from his younger brother. "Do it," he hissed, and Samuel, stiff with unspoken resentment, helped Jesse to a chair and led the now grinning Ramsey Gainsborough to the other room. Pete's burly form guarded the door.

Tremaine was thinking fast. He needed help and he needed to find Lexie. He had to get a message to the Cullens. The Garretts were closer but Jace Garrett was as much to blame for this situation as anyone. Tremaine had to deliver the message to the Cullens himself and, if possible, alert the sheriff.

Pa's hand crept up Tremaine's bare arm. "Find Lexie and keep her away," he beseeched in a faint voice that only Tremaine could hear.

"I will."

But how? And how could he leave his family unprotected? He glanced at Jesse, then at Samuel, who had just reentered the room. Lastly, his gaze met Eliza's and in her eyes was the whole family's answer: Lexie must be kept from Gainsborough's evil plans at all cost.

He determined he would leave tonight—somehow—and follow Lexie's trail. By fair means or foul, he would protect her. And he would make certain she remained ignorant of what was happening at the farm. For Lexie, he realized grimly, would sacrifice herself to save the others.

Tremaine would rather commit murder himself than leave her that choice.

Chapter Nineteen

Lexie had only catnapped, too tense and worried to rest peacefully. Upon awakening, her fingers crept across the carriage seat to find her pistol was missing and, she realized sinkingly, searching the carriage through lash-veiled eyes, in Jace's possession. The gun was in his hand.

Jace was still staring through the window but now Lexie could plainly see the angles of his face; dawn was breaking. She reckoned they must be close to Portland. She was glad for Jace's protection, but anxious to get rid of him all the same, considering how little she trusted him. He mustn't know where she was heading.

He stretched and glanced her way. Lexie feigned sleep for long moments while he studied her, and she had the distinct feeling he didn't know what to do with her. "You're not asleep," he said, breaking the silence.

She would have felt a lot safer with the pistol in her hand. Stretching, she made a great show of yawning, then lunged for the gun. Jace was surprised but not totally unprepared. He tussled with her until Lexie's hair fell free around her shoulders and she ended up across his lap.

"You touch me, Jace, and I'll kill you," she hissed coldly.

Jace looked down at the tempestuous beauty in his arms and threw caution to the wind. "Oh, hell," he muttered and pressed his lips to hers.

Lexie froze. It was incomprehensible to her that she'd ever longed for his touch. She struggled until her hand was free, and then she slapped him long and hard. The crack echoed in the morning stillness.

Jace growled and tossed her down on the carriage seat, his eyes lit by a dangerous flame. "What does it take to turn you into a lady?" he demanded through his teeth, his patience gone.

"More than the likes of you," she answered recklessly.

His mouth slanted fiercely over hers and bile rose in Lexie's throat. She groped along the seat, filled with jubilation when her fingers encountered the cold barrel of the pistol. Jace was hard at work trying to tame her struggling limbs. Lexie fought calmly, coolly, deliberately. She shoved the pistol against Jace's most vital tissue and said reasonably, "If you want to remain a stallion, I suggest you move away—slowly."

"Christ! Lexie!" Jace froze.

"Get off me," she muttered, and he did as she suggested.

His face was flushed; his breathing ragged. "What's wrong with you? You're more man than woman these days! Didn't Miss Everly's School teach you any manners? You used to be reckless, but now you're as hardened as any waterfront whore!"

Those words hurt. Lexie swept in a choked breath but didn't relinquish her hold on the gun. "Tell old MacDougal to drop me off at Miss Everly's School," she said.

"Fine," Jace spat and, when they turned onto the street, added coldly, "Get the hell out."

He practically dumped her on the curb, as anxious to be rid of her as she was of him. Lexie barely got Tantrum untied before he yelled to old MacDougal to drive away. The kindly Scot gave Lexie a wink of encouragement before he snapped the reins on the bays. The carriage lurched away and Lexie was left on the empty cobblestone street.

As soon as he was out of sight, she mounted Tantrum and

walked him quietly along the street. Her heart was heavy as she considered what to do. She needed money for her train fare. The few bills she'd borrowed from Jesse weren't enough.

She would have to sell Tantrum for the rest of the money.

Portland was waking up as Lexie wound her way through Nob Hill to the once grand home owned by Ella's family. The gardens had already suffered from the Burnhams' financial losses; weeds were tenaciously springing up in clumps across the ragged lawn.

The staff had apparently been cut back considerably as Lexie rode through the gates without anyone stopping her. She tied the weary Tantrum to a porch rail, then rubbed his nose for a few minutes before she faced Ella. She would be asking a lot of their friendship.

Lexie raised the tarnished brass knocker and let it fall twice. The hollow *clang-clang* echoed through the sleeping household, and it was several moments before a middle-aged woman in a black dress opened the front door.

"Well, missy?" she demanded, looking down her nose at the sorry picture Lexie made in her grimy white shirtwaist, black cloak, and ripped split skirt.

"Is Ella home? Please tell her Lexington Danner is here to see her."

The maid sniffed and slammed the door in Lexie's face. Lexie sighed. She could hardly blame her. A few minutes later the door was flung open again and Ella, her eyes still heavy with sleep, grinned at her friend. "It's all right, Jane," she threw over her shoulder to the maid. "Lexie's another Miss Everly graduate."

"Oh, Ella, I'm so glad to see you!"

For the first time since she'd seen Tremaine with Jenny, Lexie felt near tears. Her eyes burned and when Ella said, "Well, come on in and tell me about it," she wanted to throw herself into her friend's arms and bawl her eyes out.

"What in heaven's name are you doing with *that?*" Ella asked with delicious horror.

The pearl handle of the pistol was revealed sticking out of the pocket of Lexie's skirt. "For a cool drink and a bath I'll tell you all about it."

"Done." Ella collected her arm and dragged her upstairs.

When Lexie was gratefully immersed in warm water up to her chin, inhaling the lovely rose-scented steam rising off the water from the bath salts, a glass of lemonade sitting on the needlepoint stool beside her, she broached the subject that had been weighing most heavily on her mind. "I need money, Ella, to go to Denver and be with my brother, Harrison."

Ella was sitting crosslegged on the feather tick that covered her bed. "So you can become a horse doctor and avoid marrying some rich old pervert to increase the family's declining fortunes. I envy you," she said with none of her usual irreverent humor.

"Ella! You're not getting married, are you?"

"I'm afraid so." She smiled wearily.

"You don't sound like you—love him."

Ella snorted. "I don't. He's older than my father. But he's rich, and since Silas Monteith cheated my father out of his money, all that's left is a good match between his 'Miss Everly' daughter and someone wealthy."

"Cheated! What do you mean?" Then realizing what her friend was saying, Lexie cried, "I can't believe you're standing for it!"

"Can't you? There is a mortgage on this house that will not be met unless Emmett Grangewood marries me. I'm not pretty like you, Lexie. I can't attract the young and handsome wealthy men."

"But your parents can't make you!" Lexie cried out. This was a subject dear to her heart. "You've got to fight, Ella! They can't make you marry someone you don't love!"

"No one's making me." Ella was quietly sober. "I made this decision myself." At Lexie's uncomprehending look, she added, "I have three younger sisters and four brothers. None of them will have my advantages. My mother's pregnant again. And my father can't find suitable employment. He's not a laborer; he's a bankrupt businessman. Every job he takes is, he believes, beneath his station."

Lexie regarded her in horror. Ella's problems were vastly worse than her own. She felt like a bit of a fraud. But then she remembered Jenny McBride stretched out across

Tremaine and she tightened her resolve. She couldn't bear to be around him anymore.

"You said you needed money," Ella reminded her. "How much?"

But Lexie could have no more asked Ella to buy Tantrum than she could have sprouted wings and flown. "Do you know anyone in need of a horse? I brought my gelding, Tantrum. I thought if I could sell him I could earn enough money for the trip to Denver and the entry fee for Dr. Breverman's classes. Then I could get a job to pay for the rest."

"Why don't you try Silas Monteith?" Ella suggested bitterly. "He's got a ransom in horseflesh at his stables. He might buy your horse. It's either that, or sell him on the open market."

Lexie couldn't bear the thought of haggling over Tantrum's worth to some unknown buyer who might, or might not, treat the gelding right. "Why do you say Silas Monteith cheated your father?"

"Because he only paid half the price for my father's shipbuilding company. When my father complained, Monteith's toughs beat up two of my younger brothers. Curt's broken arm never did set right."

Lexie was horrified. "I can't sell Tantrum to him!"

"Oh, he'll take good care of your horse. Probably give him to Celeste as a present."

Lexie shuddered. "There must be another way."

"There isn't," Ella sighed fatalistically. "When you finish your bath I'll go with you to the Monteiths' . . ."

Lexie's secret hope was that Ella would be proved wrong and that Silas Monteith wouldn't want Tantrum. But when the blustery cheat spied the spirited gelding, he offered Lexie a sum that staggered her. Still, she would have refused, had Ella not jabbed her in the ribs.

"Please don't sell him to anyone else," Lexie blurted out when the transaction had been completed and Monteith's stable hand was leading the recalcitrant Tantrum away. "At least for a while. I'd—like a chance to buy him back."

Monteith's cool gaze made Lexie shiver, but then his lips

drew back in a humorless smile. "I doubt I'll be selling him for a few months."

On the way back to Ella's, Lexie was consumed with remorse and grief. She dropped her head upon the leather cushions and closed her eyes. Her throat was hot. Her eyes burned.

Ella's hand dropped comfortingly over hers. "Don't leave for Denver yet, Lexie. Stay with me a few days and think things over. I could use a friend right now, too."

Silently, Lexie nodded, unable to trust her voice.

Tremaine pushed open the gate to the Burnham property and wondered at the signs of neglect. He was bone-tired and frustrated, not to mention sick with worry about what was happening at home. But Cullen had agreed to keep a watch on the house, and Tremaine had notified the sheriff about Gainsborough's visit, so there was nothing else to be done. Cullen had promised to send a wire to the Portland Western Union office if there was any more fighting, or if the situation deteriorated, so Tremaine was free to pursue Lexie.

Lexie. Tremaine's jaw tightened as he walked up the flagstone path to the front porch. Where the hell was she? He'd tried the railway station first but no one remembered a winsome blond woman riding a black gelding. The station master had assured Tremaine that if she'd gotten on the train, he would have noticed. And Lexie wasn't hiding at Miss Everly's School; the place was closed for the season and Tremaine had convinced the caretaker to let him search.

Lexie had to be in Portland. Tremaine hoped to hell she was staying with friends.

Tremaine rapped on the door, sweating in the mid-morning June heat. Thank God Ramsey Gainsborough had sanctioned Tremaine's suggestion to search for Lexie. What he didn't know was that Tremaine had no intention of bringing Lexie back to the farm. When—and *if*—he found her, he was going to do his damnedest to keep her away. Gainsborough's interest in his daughter was even stronger than his interest in Eliza. And it made Tremaine's skin crawl.

He rapped again, more loudly, and the Burnhams' front door swung inward. A middle-aged maid sporting a sour look on her face eyed Tremaine's dust-grimed appearance with disgust. "Well?" she demanded.

"Is Miss Ella Burnham at home?"

"Who may I say is calling?" She sniffed.

He almost smiled. "Tell her Tremaine Danner wants to see her."

The woman flounced off, but a few minutes later Ella appeared. "Dr. Danner," she said, greeting him with unusual circumspection, inviting him inside.

"Have you seen Lexie?" he asked without preamble.

"You mean recently?"

"I mean in the last few days," he clarified sardonically.

"Is she missing?"

"Miss Burnham, have you seen her or not? I don't have time to waste. I need to find her."

"I'm sorry, Dr. Danner. I can't help you."

Her voice held such real regret that Tremaine gave her a long look. Did she know about him and Lexie? It was possible. He was on the verge of asking her when a very pregnant, tired-faced woman entered the room. "Ella, could you get me some tea?" she asked in abject weariness. Spying Tremaine, she said, "Oh, I'm sorry. I didn't know you had a guest."

"Dr. Danner was just leaving," Ella said to her mother. Her heart was beating fast. For just a second, she'd wanted to go against Lexie's wishes and tell him the truth—that Lexie was right upstairs! She felt in her heart that Lexie's place was with Tremaine, yet Lexie refused to discuss him.

She saw Tremaine to the door, struggling with her conscience. Watching him climb into the saddle and ride away, she knew an irresistible urge to call him back. She'd never believed much in romance, but she knew Lexie loved this man. Why was it so impossible for them to get back together?

Lexie was waiting on the stairs, pale-faced. "I saw Tremaine leave," she said. "Do you think he suspected I was here?"

Ella shook her head. "You should have told him, Lexie."

"No."

She sighed at her friend's sharp tone. "God sakes, Lexie, did something happen between you and Tremaine? I mean, besides the fact that you found out you're so right for each other."

"Nothing happened between him and me. Nothing that matters," Lexie choked out, then fled upstairs before Ella could decipher that mystifying remark.

In Ella's room Lexie threw her clothes and personal items back inside her reticule. If Tremaine was this close to finding her, she had to leave town now. Fifteen minutes later she was arguing with Ella on the porch. "You don't have to drive me," Lexie was saying stubbornly. "I can walk. But I've got to leave. Right now." She threw her arms around her friend and whispered, "I'm sorry."

"Oh, for crying in the night," Ella muttered with a return of her old spunk. "I'll take you to the train station myself. But I think you're making a big mistake."

"I've made bigger ones," Lexie retorted grimly.

The Monteiths' palatial manse was a far cry from the now tattered elegance of the Burnhams' home. Though Tremaine was certain Lexie wouldn't willingly seek help from Celeste, there was a small chance she'd been forced to. Celeste might be spoiled and selfish, but she was wealthy. It was clear Ella's family couldn't help finance Lexie's trip to Denver—and Tremaine was certain Denver was where Lexie was headed —without digging into their own bare coffers. Celeste had invited Lexie to her spring party and though Tremaine, without conceit, recognized Lexie had been the lure to get him to come, it wasn't impossible that Lexie had chosen to seek the Monteiths' help.

A wail of rage and pain sounded from somewhere to Tremaine's left as he walked up the pathway toward the Monteiths' front door. He stopped short, scanning the area. On a small verdant rise beyond the stables, Celeste was standing on the ground, her riding cap hanging by strings down her back, her blond hair swinging wildly as she held onto her mount's bridle reins with one hand, whipping the poor beast for all he was worth with the other. The riding crop whined through the air twice, snapping against hide. The horse reared up and slammed a hoof into Celeste's shoulder before tearing off across the fields, dust kicking up behind its heels.

"By God—Tantrum!" Tremaine exclaimed, stunned. He sprinted toward Celeste, who was just picking herself off the ground, impotent tears of rage and pain running down her face.

"I'll kill you—you—bastard!" she screamed after the running horse. Seeing Tremaine, her face turned beet red and her cries became feminine whimpers. "Oh, Dr. Danner, thank the Lord you're here. That beast attacked me! I think my shoulder's—broken." She crumpled into his arms in a dead faint.

"Stand up, Celeste," Tremaine bit out sarcastically, standing her on her feet. "You're not hurt."

"My shoulder!" she cried.

"You're goddamn lucky Tantrum didn't take a mind to crush you for beating him like that! He's not known for his even temperament. Let me see your shoulder."

Huge, fat tears filled her blue eyes. Chin trembling, she unbuttoned the top three buttons of her dress and demurely pulled the gown over her left shoulder. A bruise was just beginning to purple.

"You'll live," Tremaine pronounced tersely, running his fingers over her collarbone and scapula. "In fact, I'd say you got off luckier than Tantrum did."

"That brute tried to bite me!" she declared, incensed.

For the first time in days Tremaine felt like laughing. "He tries to bite everyone but Lexie. Where is Lexie, anyway? I need to speak to her."

Celeste instantly reverted to her normal wiles, lowering her lashes for a moment. It occurred to her how advantageous this situation was. For months she'd been trying to get the handsome devil to look her way. But he only had eyes for Lexie. Celeste had had to settle for second best—and Peter Caldwell wasn't half the man Tremaine was.

The problem was, she was desperately in need of a husband. Peter hadn't offered marriage yet. And she was two months pregnant already.

She felt the strong warmth of his hands on her shoulders, a plan uncoiling in her scheming, fertile mind. If she ripped her dress and rubbed some dust on her lawn gown, then ran screaming to the house, maybe her father would think Tremaine had stolen her honor. Silas Monteith might force him to marry her! What sweet revenge that would be on Lexie, whom Celeste had begun to hate with a passion since her humiliation at her father's party. And though Tremaine had also been a source of her pain, dropping her like a waterfront whore the instant he saw his *sister*, she was willing to forgive and forget.

"Celeste?" Tremaine's blue eyes were watching her closely and she felt a moment of fear for a plan that might backfire. But Celeste was desperate.

She jerked away from him, ripping at her bodice until the sound of tearing cloth rent the air. She ran as fast as her short legs could carry her, as fast as her layers of petticoats allowed, only to feel Tremaine's strong arm encircle her waist and yank her off her feet.

"What the hell are you doing?" he bit out.

She opened her mouth and screamed, long and hard. Tremaine set her on the ground and stared at her as if she'd lost her mind. In a few moments gardeners and servants surrounded them and Celeste burst into a flood of tears.

"He—he—he tried—to—to—" she blubbered, her face in her hands.

"Oh, for God's sake," Tremaine muttered, pushing through the growing crowd. He didn't have time for this. Silas Monteith himself stormed from the house to join their scene.

"What's all this about?" he roared.

"He tried to rape me!" Celeste screeched, pointing at Tremaine.

Monteith turned on Tremaine in a rush of rage. Tremaine eyed the older man coldly.

"Look! Look what he did to me!" Celeste displayed the darkening bruise, which was now a livid purple-red against her white skin.

The glance of pure loathing Tremaine sent her nearly froze her blood. Even her father seemed to hesitate, which infuriated Celeste. What would he do when he learned she was pregnant? She shuddered to think. Riding that monster horse had been a fool's way to lose the baby, she realized now. It would be much better to marry right away.

"Come into my office!" Silas snapped fiercely, and Celeste's heart gladdened to see Tremaine, whose shoulders had stiffened antagonistically, do as he was bidden. In her own shallow way she truly cared about Tremaine—certainly more than the rutting young buck she'd let take her to bed, only to find he already had a wife and four children! She'd been so hurt and wounded that she'd almost thrown away the diamond and ruby necklace he'd given her. *Almost.* Common sense had come to her rescue at the last moment, and it was now safely upstairs in her jewel box.

But that was nothing to the prize she was sure to have now!

"Have a seat," Monteith ordered gruffly.

"I would rather stand." Tremaine's feet were apart, his hands folded behind his back. If he had to, he would fight his way out of Monteith's house. Each moment that ticked by kept him that much further from finding Lexie. His temper was seething.

"My daughter has accused you of assaulting her person, Dr. Danner," Monteith declared. "I hope you have an explanation."

"I didn't assault her."

"That's it? 'I didn't assault her'?" His beefy hand doubled into a fist and he slammed the desk with amazing force. "Then how the hell did she get that bruise!"

"From Tantrum," Tremaine answered shortly. "How did you come by that horse? Tantrum belongs to my sister, Lexington."

"I'll ask the questions!" Monteith roared.

"I did not assault your daughter. I've already given you more of my time than was necessary. Good day, Mr. Monteith."

Tremaine turned to leave, but Monteith lunged at him from behind the desk, grabbing his arm. It was a fool's move and when Tremaine glared down at him, Monteith slowly unhanded him. "You've humiliated my daughter in front of the servants, and, by God, you'll marry her now or give me one damn reason why I shouldn't force you!"

"You want a reason?" Tremaine snarled in a low, ominous voice. "Try murder, Mr. Monteith. I saw that union man you shot. Five bullet holes in the chest doesn't look like self-defense to me. You shot him over and over again while he just stood there, taking it."

Monteith was so shocked that his eyes were dark pits in a pale, round face. "Prove it!"

"I will." His smile was chilling. "As soon as I marry your daughter, so we can enjoy the fruits of your labor while you rot in jail."

Tremaine's idle threat was even more effective than he'd suspected it would be. Monteith was like a stone pillar. He couldn't seem to function. "Where's Lexie?" Tremaine asked in a quiet, dangerous voice.

"I—" The burly man inhaled a deep breath. "I don't know. She sold me the horse and left with her friend, Miss Burnham."

"Ella Burnham?"

Monteith nodded, his color returning as he weighed the strength of Tremaine's threat. "Now, listen here," he blustered. "I was found innocent of all charges . . ." But Tremaine was already out of the room and striding to the front door.

He nearly ran over Celeste, who was hovering in the hallway. She rushed to her father's office. "You let him leave!" she wailed accusingly. "You let him leave!"

"Shut up!" Silas Monteith bellowed. "The man's no rapist."

With a cry of thwarted anguish, she whirled around and tried to catch Tremaine. But he was already astride his mount, a rolling cloud of dust swirling in his wake.

"She's gone," Ella said half an hour later, so sincerely repentant that Tremaine curbed the desire to shake her until her teeth rattled. "I dropped her at the train station."

"She's on her way to Denver?" Tremaine didn't try to mask his rage.

"Yes. I think so. Dr. Danner, I'm sorry, but Lexie didn't

want you to know where she was going. She doesn't—" Ella broke off and sighed.

"She doesn't . . . ?" Tremaine prompted.

"She doesn't trust you." With the finesse of a steamroller, Ella sent up a silent prayer to the powers that be, stating bluntly, "Ever since you two shared a bed she's been a wreck! She's in love with you, you fool! But she thinks you don't give a damn about her. She thinks you feel an *obligation* to her. You've never given her any indication of how you feel, and she already thinks she's only half a woman from the way that bastard Garrett treated her. And then to actually see you in bed with your mistress, why, it's—"

"Hold on," Tremaine interrupted curtly, stunned by her volley of recriminations. "I don't have any mistress."

Ella placed a firm fist on her plump hip. "The hell you don't, man. What about that McBride woman? Lexie saw you and her together, if you know what I mean. No wonder she's run off!"

"I haven't been with Jenny!"

"Not much you haven't. She *saw* you together at her place."

Tremaine was speechless. He was stunned that Ella knew so much about him and Lexie, astounded that she had the nerve to upbraid him for his actions. But more than that he was growing cold and sick with the certainty that Lexie had somehow witnessed Jenny snuggling up to him on her cot. He groaned inwardly. He'd hurt Lexie in so many ways, when all he'd wanted to do was protect her.

Ella was staring at him with all the fire and scorn of a wronged woman. Taking his life in his hands, he kissed her forehead soundly. "Thank you," he said with solemn gratitude.

Ella gazed after him in wonder. She sighed. If the old reprobate she was marrying could show an inkling of the kind of gallantry Tremaine Danner possessed, life wouldn't be so bad after all.

Chapter Twenty

The train whined and wheezed as it slowed, its wheels slipping and grinding to an earsplitting stop. The tiny mountain town was little better than a train station, hotel, and mercantile. As Lexie stepped from the puffing train, she could see the whole place in one sweeping glance.

Her reticule stuffed securely under her arm, she walked along the weathered plankboard sidewalk to the Katieville Hotel. She was tired, hungry, and filthy. It was too bad there wasn't time for a bath, but the train was due to pull out again in an hour. She would have to settle for a meal and a quick face-wash in the ladies' washroom.

A pitcher of water and a porcelain bowl sat on the counter and Lexie poured cold water into the bowl. She dipped a towel into the liquid and quickly wiped the grime from her face and neck. At least now she was in the Rockies. It wouldn't be too long before she reached Denver.

When she was finished, she left a coin on the counter and thanked the washroom attendant. Refreshed, she walked down the narrow hallway in the direction of the hotel dining room.

The familiar figure lounging negligently against the archway nearly stopped her heart. Tremaine! Lexie could only stare openmouthed.

"By God, I've struck her speechless," he drawled.

"What are you doing here?"

"Looking for you."

He stepped toward her, for all the world as if he owned her, and Lexie, furious, decided to set matters straight. She pulled her pistol from her pocket, letting him see she wasn't to be trifled with.

His blue gaze grew incredulous as he saw the pistol, barrel pointed toward the floor but trembling violently in her hand nevertheless. "You've got a *gun?* Good Lord, Lex! You don't even know how to use one."

"I'm a quick learner." If she'd had the nerve she would have leveled the barrel at his chest, but her experience with Jace in the carriage, though gratifyingly victorious, had left her with little taste for bluffing her way free with a gun. Not only that, if the hotel owner should spy her she would likely be arrested.

Still, the memory and humiliation of finding Tremaine with Jenny made her burn for retribution.

"Put that away." Tremaine couldn't believe his eyes. Lexie had always been wild, but he thought she'd learned something from that fancy finishing school. Strangely, this reversion to her former self pleased him, though he wasn't eager to test her skill with a pistol.

He held up his palms in surrender and Lexie returned the pistol to the pocket of her skirt. "How did you find me?" she asked.

"Ella said she dropped you off at the train station. When I got there, your train hadn't left yet, so I boarded it, too."

Lexie blinked. "You mean you've been on the train all this time?"

"Yep."

"Why didn't you say something before?"

"Because I just didn't."

Lexie gazed at him helplessly. He was as dusty and travel-worn as she felt, yet he still possessed that indefinable male vitality that made her foolish heart squeeze and send echoing vibrations down her limbs. But then she remembered all his lies. With an effort she dragged her gaze from his and examined the floral pattern of the hotel carpet beneath her feet. "I'm going to Denver."

"I know."

"I won't let you stop me," she warned belligerently.

His answer to this was a tolerant smile that made her want to throw herself against him, kicking and pounding. Why, oh, why, did she have to love him? It was impossible to let him weave in and out of her life, slowly destroying her respectability, yet she was powerless to do anything else. If only he loved her just a little, not like a sister, but like a woman.

And if only he hadn't lied about Jenny McBride.

Lexie didn't realize what a profound effect she was having on Tremaine as well. He felt like a man drowning. Her blond hair was tied in a rope over her shoulder, and soft wisps framed her face and stuck to her moist skin. Her lips were pink and soft, a sensual invitation that stirred his blood. Her eyes were full of green fire and joyful wonder, as if seeing him was something so miraculous she couldn't believe it was true. His heart wrenched.

"I'm not going back to Rock Springs," Lexie stated positively. "I'm going to Denver to become a horse doctor." She glared at him. "You can't make me go back."

"Have I said I wanted to?"

"No, but why else would you be here?"

Tremaine regarded her from between narrowed lashes. Though he wasn't about to tell her the situation at home—*that* would send her back to Rock Springs quicker than the speed of light—it was definitely time for a little honesty. "Because I wanted to see you."

Lexie hardened her heart. His hooded eyes gave nothing away and it was damn near impossible to guess his feelings. "You could have seen me any time you wanted in the past few weeks. I doubt you would chase me to Denver unless you had a good reason."

"Ella led me to believe that you had—uh—mis-understood me. I thought it was time we cleared a few things up."

Lexie flushed. "You don't have to feel sorry for me, Tremaine. I can take care of myself."

Tremaine sighed hugely. He guided her toward the hotel stairs and a private alcove. "Lexie," he said with weary patience, his tone causing her to glance up warily just as his head bent to hers. "Shut up."

He was going to kiss her! Automatically, she turned her face away, infuriated that he thought he could tame her into submission by a mere kiss. What an incredibly arrogant male trick!

His mouth never made contact with hers but, undaunted, Tremaine began an assault on the downy curve of her jawline, right below her ear. Lexie made a pitiful sound of protest. Her hands were taut against his rigid forearms; she intended to push him away, but the sweet pleasure of his mouth gently tasting hers stopped her cold.

"Lexie, Lexie," he murmured, gathering her to him in an intimate way that left nothing to her imagination.

She was not so naive anymore. She knew where this was leading, even if he didn't. One hand was stealing down her back, moving perilously close to her buttocks. Lexie's face flamed. Lord, they were right out in public, in front of God and everybody! She squirmed against him. "Tremaine!" she hissed.

His answer was a groan of pure anguish, his hands holding her to him in a thoroughly arousing way. Her knees turned to water, when he moaned, "I ache for you, Lexie. I've ached so long."

"Like you ache for Jenny McBride!" she cried, thrusting her hands against his chest.

This time his mouth crashed down on hers with unerring accuracy. Lexie clamped her lips shut in a vain attempt to stop his sensual battery. But Tremaine persisted, sliding his bottom lip over hers, his tongue touching, testing, flicking, probing, daring her to remain unmoved.

Liquid desire was a demon in her veins. The edges of reality blurred. Against her will, she pressed herself closer to him, her hands tightening and clenching the fabric of his shirt, little moans of frustration issuing from her throat. Her mouth opened wide for his glorious invasion and Tremaine seized the opportunity to plunder what she gave.

I love you. I love you. I love you, she thought incoherently.

He brutally pulled his mouth away, breathing hard, but

his hands still held her pressed against him. "We can't stay here," he muttered unevenly.

Lexie was half hypnotized by his heartbeat. She would have willingly done whatever he asked.

His soft laughter jarred her well-being, but then the shaking breath he drew gave her a sense of supreme power. "Come on," he said gently, holding her to him as he led her toward the stairs.

Her foot on the bottom step, Lexie balked. "Where are we going?"

"Upstairs. I have a room."

"A *room?*" She was appalled at his treachery. He'd meant to seduce her, and she had fallen into the trap so easily, so quickly. Oh, how she hated herself! "Sorry to disappoint you, Tremaine," she said through her teeth, "but I'm leaving in less than thirty minutes!"

His blue eyes darkened in frustration. "The hell you are! You're staying with me." Seeing her pain and fury, he remembered what she thought she'd witnessed. "Lexie, I never slept with Jenny McBride. I haven't slept with another woman since that night with you."

"I saw you, you wretched liar! Ella told you, didn't she? Oh, I could kill her! Let go of me! I'm sick of your lies!"

"I'm not lying. I was bone-tired and sound asleep that day. Jenny slipped herself in beside me, thinking I might be receptive to a little lovemaking."

"And you were loving her right back!" Lexie reminded him harshly, pride scalding the back of her throat.

"Only for a moment. Until I woke up fully and realized I was with her, not you."

"What pretty lies. You think I'll believe them?" Lexie's body was quaking with emotion, and she was powerless to stop herself.

His patience snapped. Tremaine wasn't used to explaining himself to anybody, least of all a recalcitrant woman. "Damn it all to hell, Lexie," he muttered, and with complete and utter arrogance, he half dragged her, half carried her, up the flight of stairs.

"I'll never forgive you for this!" she hissed, but Tremaine was past listening to her. He pushed open the door to his room, flung Lexie inside, then turned the lock behind him.

She glared as he stalked toward her.

"This is not happening to me," she said in disbelief. "You can't seriously think I'll stay here with you."

He lifted an implacable eyebrow, grabbed a wooden chair, placed it between her and the door, straddled it backward, and waited.

The train whistle sounded and Lexie dashed to the window. She tugged on the sash, swore, and finally pushed it upward. The filmy lace curtains fluttered in the mountain breeze. The sky was as blue as the gentians flourishing in the hilly meadows at the edge of Katieville. And the drop to the ground was a bone-breaking thirty feet.

She swore pungently beneath her breath. Tremaine laughed. "Come here, my love, and stop talking like a railroad man. It's hardly fitting for a Miss Everly—"

"Oh, shut up and let me think."

The truth was, the way he'd said "my love" had disarmed her, and Lexie, certain she would regret it a thousand different ways, was beginning to enjoy this interlude with the man she loved. But she'd rather die a horrible death than admit as much. She had to think, and think hard, to save the rags of her respect.

"Lexie." Tremaine's voice had grown alarmingly quiet.

She stiffened her shoulders and refused to look at him. Her every sense was attuned to him and, when she heard him move, she whipped around wildly, ready to make a dash for the door. But he'd only shifted position in the chair, and the amused look on his face at her abrupt move infuriated her.

Then she remembered the pistol. Deftly she reached into her pocket only to find it gone!

"Looking for this?" he asked innocently, pulling it from the pocket of his buckskin breeches.

"You slimy, miserable, blackhearted, cheating—"

"Bastard?" he offered helpfully.

"I truly hate you."

"The last time we were together"—he glanced meaningfully toward the bed—"you said you loved me."

"Well, I wasn't thinking straight then," she flared. "That was a terrible moment in my life! You had just—used me—and I—"

The chair suddenly banged against the door with such a harsh, furious clatter that Lexie gasped. Tremaine had thrown it. Before she could move, he strode over to her and encircled her wrists with his hands. "Used you?" he repeated in a dangerous tone. "I used you?"

Lexie had the grace to blush. "Well, I suppose I was partly to blame," she admitted tautly.

"And it just kills you to admit it. Well, to hell with reasoning with you." His hands slid sensuously up her arms, causing goose bumps to rise in their wake, and rested lightly on her collarbones, his thumbs rubbing across the lacy cotton of her shirtwaist. "Kiss me, Lexie," he ordered softly.

"Of all the nerve! Whatever you want, you'll have to take," she challenged boldly.

His eyes glittered dangerously. Without another word he captured her mouth again. Lexie closed her eyes and shuddered inwardly. She realized belatedly that she'd tendered just the invitation he'd been waiting for.

He was ruthlessly determined, sinfully persuasive. Lexie felt the heat of his marauding tongue on her lips and in the deep recesses of her mouth. He kissed her expertly and thoroughly, eliciting a response she continued to fight even when she knew the battle was already lost.

"Lexie," he whispered, his mouth now leaving flaming kisses on the arch of her throat. Dimly, she realized that he was no detached seducer; the timbre of his voice declared he was just as affected as she was.

Her heart lifted. This was what she wanted! She opened glazed green eyes and met his wordless gaze. This time when his mouth moved persuasively over hers she responded, lifting her face to his gentle plunder. Her hands stole around his neck and lost themselves in the silky richness of his hair.

"God, Lexie," he murmured, shaken.

They seemed to sink to the bed as one. She'd forgotten how much she wanted him, but now she seemed to ache in a hundred different places. She felt the whisper of her shirtwaist and skirt against her skin, the quick, expert unlacing of her drawers, the cool removal of her chemise. She was undressed and unabashedly naked beside him before she really gave the matter any thought. When she did think about it, she lifted her hands protectively to cover her ivory breasts.

"Don't." The breath-stopping tone of his voice made her drop her hands.

"Aren't you"—she licked her lips nervously—"going to take off your clothes, too?"

"In a minute." He smiled, then kissed her so reverently that Lexie could only lie still beneath him in passive bemusement. His tongue drove into her mouth, filling it, then withdrawing. His hands caressed her breast, squeezing the nipple, bringing it to a hard button. Lexie whimpered, but instead of releasing her, his fingers moved downward and slipped into the heat of her, matching the action of his tongue, plunging and withdrawing.

Lexie was no proof against his sensual invasion. She gave herself up to him, her head tossing to and fro on the pillow, her hands reaching for him, drawing her to him. Feeling her surrender, Tremaine lay on his side, pulling her toward him. Lexie's eyes were slumberous jade gems as she gazed at him with love. He inhaled swiftly.

"Help me," he suggested in an oddly restrained tone. At her uncomprehending look, he brought her fingers to the buttons of his shirt. She undid them quickly, pulling the shirt over his broad shoulders, marveling at the smooth, hard texture of his muscles.

She tried to pull his mouth down to hers but he emitted a sound that was part laughter, part groan. "What about the rest?" he asked.

"The rest?" she repeated blankly.

This time he drew her hands down to the buttons of his breeches. Daringly, hardly aware of what she was doing, Lexie touched the straining evidence of his manhood through the soft buckskin. Tremaine's arms tightened around her. Thrilled with this unexpected sense of power, Lexie undid the buttons and explored him some more.

Her tentative, innocent touch drove him wild. "Lexie," he muttered on a strangled laugh.

"What?"

His blue eyes were slits when they gazed down at her. Her own eyes were filled with suppressed laughter. Tremaine almost laughed. She knew what she was doing, the little minx!

"Don't I please you?" she asked, running her hand over his flesh in a silky, sinuous movement. For an answer he threw her on her back and she had just drawn in a breath of laughter when his knee was wedging itself between her legs.

"Yes, you please me, as you well know," he growled. "God, where did you learn to be so bold?"

"From the man I love."

She hadn't meant to tell him again but the words sprang from her heart. Tremaine's touch grew incredibly gentle, his mouth moving down her heated flesh to cover one rosy nipple. Lexie moaned and arched, her fingers digging into his back. He moved with a tormenting slowness that had her twisting and turning and softly crying his name.

When he entered her it was with infinite patience, tortuous gentleness. Moaning, Lexie arched her hips, her hand pulling his hips to her. Tremaine slid into her welcoming warmth and moved slowly, rhythmically. The pace was too slow for Lexie, but Tremaine refused to be cajoled to move faster no matter how frantic with need her clawing fingers were, no matter how exciting her soft whimpers were, no matter how pleasurable her thrusting hips were.

"Tremaine," she gasped, her face fevered and flushed. "Love me. Please, love me."

And then he plunged into her, full length, wringing a strangled cry of pure pleasure from her throat. Lexie hit her tumultuous climax so quickly and so thoroughly that Tremaine, who had always prided himself on offering pleasure before taking pleasure himself, felt his own throbbing release only seconds later, her name torn from his lips in an agonized gasp.

"I love you," Lexie whispered again, chest heaving, forehead damp with sweat. Tremaine pulled her onto her side, their passion spent, but his only answer was an infinitely tender kiss that left her curiously unsated, hungering for words to match his actions.

Late evening sun slanted through the window, marking the bed with elongated rectangles. Tremaine, propped on his elbow, stared down at Lexie's sleeping form for several moments. Exhaustion had taken its toll; she was sound asleep, her breathing slow and even. Her ivory skin was burnished a golden yellow by the setting sun and, amazingly, he felt himself harden again, just watching her.

Silently, he slid from the bed and pulled on his clothes. He didn't have much time and there were things to do. The train had gone hours ago, but Tremaine was still uneasy.

He crept out of the room on silent feet, wondering if he looked as thoroughly sated as Lexie did. Smiling to himself, he ran a hand through his unruly hair and checked to see that the evidence of his desire wasn't visible to all and sundry. Satisfied, he strode downstairs to the hotel lobby.

"Is there a telegraph office in town?" he asked the man at the desk.

"The only wire service is from this hotel, sir," he answered proudly, handing Tremaine a notepad and pencil.

Tremaine quickly scratched out a message to Cullen and paid the man for his services. If there was trouble, Cullen or the sheriff could send a wire in return.

"I'd like a bath, too," Tremaine said as he turned away.

"I'll send the maid within the hour, sir."

Tremaine strode back upstairs. Until he heard from Cullen there was nothing to do but keep Lexie busy. A most pleasurable occupation.

Lexie stretched languorously, her skin rubbing against the cool sheets. She sighed, oddly satisfied, then buried her face in the feather pillow.

From somewhere in the dim periphery of her mind she heard the soft splash of water. A bath. How she longed for a bath! She opened her eyes to unfamiliar striped wallpaper and an arched white ceiling with a milk-glass light in the center. It was nearly twilight, dusk darkening the corners of the room.

Lexie yawned and then sat bolt upright at the sight that met her eyes. Across the room Tremaine was deep within the steaming waters of a wooden bathtub, his blue eyes full of amusement as they encountered her widening stare.

Lexie blinked, thought about the wondrous lovemaking they'd shared, and demanded flatly, "How come you get a bath and I don't?"

"Oh, I won't be selfish." He lifted dripping arms wide, inviting her to join him.

"The tub's too small," she argued, frowning at the almost instant excitement sweeping through her at the mere idea of sharing a bath with him.

"Depends on how you use it."

"What does that mean?"

"Come on over here and find out."

Lexie climbed from the bed, wrapping the sheet around herself as she did so. She walked toward the tub, peering down into its shadowy depths, then was embarrassed at the sound of his mocking laughter.

"If I stood up you could get a better view," he offered helpfully, his hands on the edge of the tub.

"No, I can see just fine!" Lexie stumbled backward, tripped on the sheet, swore again, and nearly fell.

Tremaine chuckled deep in his throat. "Your language is deteriorating by the minute, Miss Danner."

Her eyes shot green fire at him. She regathered the sheet and tilted up her chin, taking a step nearer. "My language is the result of living with too many brothers who have no sense of propriety and decency. My tender sensibilities were bruised by their rough and uncultured vocabulary. I'm afraid I will spend the rest of my life trying to undo the damage they've caused me."

"I *shall* spend the rest of my life," Tremaine corrected her, reaching out a wet hand, grabbing hold of her arm, and dragging her into the water, sheet and all.

Lexie shrieked. Tremaine laughed. She flailed her arms and he untangled the sheet, swearing goodnaturedly. When he finally had her lying across him, naked, he kissed her faintly freckled nose and carefully lifted her above him— then slowly lowered her into a sitting position on top of him, her knees bent over the side of the tub.

"You wanted a bath," he reminded her, when her mouth opened in protest.

"You've done this before," she accused.

"No. But I've had it in mind a while."

"Well, this isn't my idea of a bath," said Lexie righteously, struggling out of the water. Tremaine's hands bore down on her hips until she sank down upon him.

She was instantly aware of the changing status of his desire; she could feel him grow hard beneath her, and, God help her, a thrill of raging passion consumed her.

"Lex," he muttered, his eyes darkening. His hands found their way to the globes of her breasts, wet and warm. His fingers played with her nipple until she was bending over him, panting, crying out at the hot moistness of his mouth as he claimed one rosy tip, pulling it between his teeth.

She squirmed and water sloshed over the sides of the tub. Tremaine guided her over his burgeoning shaft, thrusting into her, impaling her upon him. But it was Lexie who had the power. She raised and lowered herself upon him, defying his attempts to slow the pace, and was gratified when he closed his eyes and stiffened beneath her, groaning deeply as he poured himself into her.

Moments later he was hauling her out of the water and positioning her on the edge of the bed. Alarmed, Lexie asked, "What are you doing now?"

"Paying you back for *using* me like that," he answered, smiling wickedly.

"Using you!" she sputtered, trying to inch away, but he held her fast to the edge of the bed, holding down her knees, putting himself in such a position that he could view the most secret parts of her.

"Tremaine! What are you—don't I—" She sucked in a breath as his hot mouth descended upon her trembling flesh. She lost all coherent thought. Her upper torso fell back against the bed and she thrashed and moaned, but he held her fast, inflicting sweet torture upon sweet torture until she reached peak after shattering peak.

Spent and gasping, she could scarcely believe the intimacies of his lovemaking. Finally, he joined her on the bed and drove himself into her once more.

"Lexie, my love," he muttered, collapsing against her moments later. "You are going to be the death of me."

She smiled with pure feminine pleasure. "I hope I *shall!*"

Chapter Twenty-one

She was a slave and a captive and she knew it. Lexie lay against Tremaine's hard chest and thought about the last night and day. She'd barely gotten out of bed. Normally, her actions would have made her blush and wonder and tear herself apart with self-recrimination, though she was past worrying now. But Tremaine was in for a big surprise. He might think he'd found a way to keep her a willing mistress, but Lexie had plans of her own.

She was going to leave under cover of night as soon as he fell asleep. She was heading for Denver. No matter how much she loved Tremaine, she knew from hours of physical lovemaking that he didn't feel the same. Even though she sensed he was giving her all he had to give, it just wasn't enough.

He stirred and turned to her, nuzzling into her neck. Lexie's gaze traveled over his magnificent shoulder to the pair of breeches, tossed carelessly over the chair. He'd gotten a message today, one that had bothered him, but when Lexie had asked who knew he was in Katieville, his mouth had clamped shut in implacable silence.

Her curiosity was now driving her wild.

She tried to escape from his embrace but he clutched her more tightly, opening lazy blue eyes. "Where are you going, Sundown?" he asked in a voice that could only be described as sated with pleasure.

Lexie's heart ached at the deception she'd planned. Truth be told, it would take little persuasion to remain his mistress. But not once had he mentioned love, or marriage, in all the hours of feverish lovemaking. Theirs would be a soulless union, destined to failure. Lexie knew that her love for Tremaine would not be enough. Unlike Ella, she needed to love and be loved in return.

"I'm hungry," she lied. "I thought we could go downstairs and eat dinner."

Tremaine drew in a deep breath, closing his eyes for a minute, his sensual lips curved in satisfaction. A pain stabbed in her chest at the sight of his long black lashes and tanned, chiseled face. "All right," he said a moment later, throwing back the covers.

He was climbing into his clothes. A lump swelled in Lexie's throat. "Would you mind—just bringing something back?"

He regarded her in concern. "Something wrong?"

"No, I just—don't want to get out of bed." At the boyish look of delight that crossed his face, she blushed to the roots of her hair.

"I'll be right back," he assured her, and let himself out of the room.

Lexie flopped back against the pillows. The message had gone with him. Glancing out the window, she mentally counted how many hours of daylight were left. She'd learned, from spending so much time in this room, that there was a last lonely eastbound train that swept into the station around midnight. She intended to be on that train.

By the time Tremaine returned with a pewter tray in hand and a maid bearing another one, night had fallen in earnest. Bright stars pinpricked the velvet sky outside the hotel window. A crisp fragrant breeze swirled the frothy curtains.

The maid left and Tremaine set Lexie's tray on her lap. "They think you're sick," Tremaine said, grinning. "Everyone offered their condolences." He reached into his pocket.

"I even have a sympathy card signed by all the staff of the Katieville Hotel."

"Thanks," Lexie said, feeling like a fraud. Apparently, the staff hadn't seen her sneak out to the railway ticket office this afternoon and purchase a one-way fare to Denver. Lexie looked down at the savory beef stew and dumplings and felt her appetite leave in a painful rush. Absurdly, she wanted to cry.

"Lex, what is it?" Tremaine asked, concerned.

She carefully placed the tray on the table next to the bed. "I don't want food after all. I just want you."

Her solemnity baffled him. He perched on the bed beside her, looking down at her, a half-smile hovering on his lips. "You have to eat sometime."

"Tomorrow," she murmured and pulled his mouth down to hers.

The paper crackled beneath her fingers and she had to carefully fold it into the pocket of her skirt. Longingly, she eyed the mother-of-pearl-handled pistol, its barrel just visible beneath Tremaine's pillow. He'd emptied the cartridge and squirreled away the bullets, but Lexie had hoped she could use the pistol as a threat if nothing else.

But it was too big a risk to take.

She tiptoed carefully to the door. Her hand on the knob, she glanced back at Tremaine's sprawled masculine form. She could see the smooth muscles of his bare back as he lay facedown, one arm cradled beneath the pillow. Fighting down the urge to kiss him goodbye, she closed the door softly behind her and ran lightly down the stairs and through the lobby of the hotel to the cool summer night.

The train depot was straight ahead, a mere thirty yards from the hotel. Lexie shivered and glanced through the hotel's front window to the clock behind the reception desk: 11:34.

Hurry, hurry, hurry. She rubbed her elbows briskly and walked over to the bench that served as the railway depot. It seemed like forever before the train wheezed to a puffing stop. The noise of its arrival made Lexie want to clap her hands over her ears and glance anxiously to Tremaine's hotel window. She did neither, but when the brakeman stepped down she slipped her arm through the handle of her reticule, felt the paper in her pocket, gathered her skirts, and leapt aboard the train.

Only when the train chugged and churned from the depot and the yellow lights of the hotel were a golden blur did she lean back in her seat and expel the breath she'd been holding. It was dark and there was no opportunity to read Tremaine's strange message.

When the conductor came by in his brass-buttoned blue coat and cap to punch her ticket, Lexie asked, "How long is it to Denver?"

"About eight hours, ma'am. We've a few stops between here and there." He handed her back the stub.

Lexie closed her eyes. Another train wouldn't pull into Katieville until 6:30 A.M. If by some chance Tremaine hadn't missed her yet, he would have to wait until nearly noon.

It gave her ample time to find Harrison and garner his support. Only with her brother on her side could she withstand her own treacherous desire to be with Tremaine.

The swaying of the train came to a sudden screeching halt and the whistle screamed high and piercing. Lexie jumped and opened sleepy eyes. Were they stopping at another small mountain town? Outside her window rows of buildings flashed by, some modest clapboard affairs with false fronts, others built of sturdy stone and brick. She realized they were finally in Denver!

As Lexie waited for the bumping rail cars to slow to a stop, she remembered the telegraph message. Pulling it from her pocket, she read the puzzling missive:

All is quiet. Stop. Sheriff visits twice daily. Stop. Garretts are keeping watch.

The message was simply signed: Cullen. Lexie read it through twice more, an anxious feeling growing in the pit of her stomach. Garretts are keeping watch? *Jace* Garrett? What was he watching and why? All is quiet . . . Sheriff visits twice daily . . .

Lexie had no further time to figure out the baffling message. She let the brakeman carry her reticule and help her down to the platform.

Carriages for hire were lined up on one side of the railway

tracks. Lexie, feeling suddenly lost and friendless in this big city, showed the first driver the envelope with Harrison's address written on it. He quoted her a fare she thought exorbitant, which she paid without a word of protest. She only wanted to be safe.

The carriage lurched into a stream of traffic that rapidly thickened as they wound their way through the city to a cluster of professional buildings, which housed Dr. Breverman's small school.

Dropped on the doorstep of a rather tired-looking brownstone building bearing a sign with Dr. Breverman's name listed on a swinging plaque near the gate, Lexie swallowed her misgivings and marched up the steps, rapping the brass knocker loudly. The sound seemed to echo within an empty chamber, but very quickly a young girl in a starched black dress opened the door.

"I'm here to see Dr. Breverman. Actually, I've come to see Harrison Danner. Does he live here?" Lexie glanced up the narrow stairway that turned left at a landing and slanted upward to the second floor.

"Yes, ma'am. He's livin' upstairs, he is. In one of the doctor's rooms for let. But he's in surgery now, I'd suspect."

"I'm his sister," Lexie said to the maid's questioning glance. "Is there somewhere I can wait for him?"

The maid inclined her head and showed Lexie to the horse doctor's waiting room. There was only one other person sitting on the straight-backed velvet-cushioned chairs, an elderly man who worriedly rubbed his hands together.

A few minutes later a brisk man with a pointed gray beard walked through the door of the inner office. "Colic spasms," was his blunt answer for the waiting man. "Nothing your other horses will catch."

"Thank you. Thank you!" He shook Dr. Breverman's hand, and Lexie knew without being told that this was the man she admired and yearned to study with. When the elderly man had shuffled to his feet and out the door, the doctor turned inquiringly to Lexie.

She crossed the room and held out her hand. "My name's Lexington Danner. My brother Harrison is a student of yours, Dr. Breverman."

The doctor's bristly eyebrows lifted. "So you're the sister hankering to be a horse doctor."

"He's told you about me?"

"Oh, yes." The doctor smiled. "Your brother's inside. If you can stomach an autopsy, my dear, please come in."

Lexie followed him into the surgical room. Harrison and another young man were cleaning up the area, and the corpse of a small horse lay on planks stretched across four sawhorses. A strong smell of ammonia burned Lexie's nostrils.

"Lexie!" Harrison exclaimed upon seeing her. He pumped water into the sink, washed his arms, then came to squeeze her in a bearhug.

"Since you wouldn't come back to Rock Springs, I thought I'd visit you here," she said lightly, forestalling the questions hovering in his eyes.

"And Pa and Mother agreed?"

Lexie's reluctance to answer prompted Dr. Breverman to kindly suggest, "Harrison, why don't you take your sister upstairs and get her settled? Jim and I will finish up."

Shooting the doctor a grateful look, Harrison guided Lexie from the surgical room and up the stairs to his room on the second floor. "Pa and Mother don't know you're here, do they?"

"Not yet. But Tremaine knows."

"You told him?" Harrison was surprised.

"He followed me and caught up with me in a little town called Katieville."

Lexie was unaware of the shadow of regret and unhappiness that clouded her emerald eyes, but Harrison, always astute to her feelings, said, "And did he try to force you to go home?"

"No, that's the strange part. I don't really know what he wanted—" She broke off, remembering his hoarse rasp, *I want you.* She cleared her throat, blushing, avoiding Harrison's eyes. To break the tension, she pulled out the crushed wire and handed it to him. "Does that make any sense to you?"

"'All's quiet. Sheriff visits twice daily. Garretts are keeping watch'?" His green eyes filled with puzzlement. "Where did you get this?"

"Tremaine got it. It came to the hotel in Katieville. I had to steal it from him to find out what it said."

"He didn't try to stop you from coming to Denver?"

Lexie wrinkled her nose. "No, I didn't tell him I was leaving. Although I suspect he'll be here soon. Harrison, you've got to promise to help me. Tremaine might want me to leave with him, and I can't. I want to stay here with you."

"And Dr. Breverman," he added wisely.

"And Dr. Breverman."

"If Tremaine didn't try to talk you into going home when you were in Katieville, why would he want to now?"

"Oh, it's too complicated to go into!" Lexie turned away from him, flustered. She walked to the window and peered out to the teeming street below. A handsome carriage was parked in front of the brownstone and the sudden resounding slam of the brass knocker against the front door made her jump in her skin. Tremaine! But he couldn't be here already, could he?

"Lexie." Harrison's hands dropped lightly onto her shoulders. "What's going on with you and Tremaine?"

"Tremaine—I—nothing!"

"Are you in love with him?"

"No!"

"He's in love with you."

Lexie had been about to launch into a harshly worded lecture about Harrison's letting his imagination get the best of him, but the words died in her throat. Tears starred her lashes because he was so wrong.

"I've seen the way he looks at you," Harrison reminded her. "You think I don't know what's going through his head? If I didn't think he loved you, I'd knock his teeth down his throat."

"That's not love you've seen," Lexie choked out bitterly.

"Lexie, it may be a surprise to you, but Tremaine's not exactly hurting for women, if you get my meaning. If he was after a mistress, he'd take one. That's not what he wants from you."

"Well, what does he want, then? My God, Harrison, he's put me through hell these past months! One minute I feel like he adores me, the next he doesn't want any part of me!"

"That's Pa's fault," he stated positively. "He didn't want any of us letting it be known you weren't his daughter. He sent me a letter to that effect last Christmas."

Last Christmas. The fog of misery that had clouded Lexie's judgment lifted a little. Pa had asked her to keep her relationship with Tremaine a secret. She'd thought that had been Tremaine's idea, but he'd said it had been Pa's. "That wouldn't stop Tremaine. He wouldn't listen to Pa unless he had his own reasons. Especially not after we'd—"

"After you'd . . . ?" Harrison prompted gently when she cut herself off. He glanced down at her bowed head and sighed. "So the flesh is weak, eh?"

"Oh, Harrison." She thought of how she'd spent the last few days and made a pitiful sound. "Very weak."

"When Tremaine gets here I suggest you and he have a long serious talk. Pa will realize how unreasonable his edict was as soon as he understands how you and Tremaine feel about each other."

Lexie shook her head. He was simplifying things too much. "There's a lot more to it than that. He's never even said he loved me."

"There's a lot more to loving than three little words."

"Three little words he knows I need to hear!" Lexie retorted. Bitterly, she closed her ears to Harrison's well-meant advice. No, what Tremaine felt for her was not love. If he'd loved her, he would have said as much when she'd revealed her own feelings.

There was a knock on Harrison's door. Lexie and Harrison exchanged looks and she anxiously grabbed his arm, certain that Tremaine had caught up with her. Her heart beat unevenly. Harrison gave her a reassuring wink and opened the door.

A familiar gentleman stood on the landing, smiling blandly. "Mr. Danner. Miss Danner," he greeted them.

It was the man from the hospital, the same one Lexie had seen at Celeste's party. She sidled closer to her brother. "I don't know your name," she answered coolly. "But we've met before—at Willamette Infirmary."

"Ah," he said. "You remembered. Let me introduce myself. My name's Victor Flynne."

Neither Lexie nor Harrison accepted his outstretched hand and, after several uneasy moments, he dropped his arm. Harrison glanced from the gentleman in the fine clothes to the suddenly icy woman beside him. He couldn't decide what surprised him most: his unexpected visitor, or the frigidly polite stranger who looked so much like his wild, untamed sister.

"What do you want?" Lexie demanded haughtily.

"Well, now, I'm on a quest for a very important gentleman named Ramsey Gainsborough. He's been looking for his daughter so I suggested we check with her brother in Denver. And here you are."

Lexie blinked in confusion. "Ramsey Gainsborough? I don't know what you're talking about. You've made a mistake. My father's Joseph Danner."

Harrison growled, "Get out of here. We don't know anything about anyone named Gainsborough."

"Ramsey Gainsborough was left for dead in his Kentucky plantation home, a victim of a blow from an iron poker—courtesy of his wife, Mrs. Eliza Smythe Gainsborough. But I assure you he is very much alive," Flynne went on smoothly as he stepped past a white-faced Lexington Danner and settled himself on Harrison's shabby couch, adjusting the crease of his slacks. "He's staying in Rock Springs at this very moment with his *wife's* family, and he's very anxious to meet his daughter . . ."

Tremaine stared out the open window of the carriage at the sun-dappled Denver landscape through bitterly derisive eyes. What a fool he'd been to believe Lexie's whispers of love. Women were all the same, he thought scathingly. Even Lexie. A man could never trust them to be honest. Like Eliza, Lexie was careful to hide her true feelings, showing only clever, tantalizing glimpses, like a magician twirling a cape. Now you see it, now you don't . . .

And he'd almost told her he loved her.

"Can't you go any faster?" he demanded of the driver, pounding his fist against the back of the carriage.

The man didn't acknowledge Tremaine's request but the horse's hoofbeats quickened.

Tremaine was too angered by Lexie's deception to recall the many things about her he admired. His nerves were raw and sensitive. Seeing her lying soft and sweet and innocent in a tangle of bedcovers, knowing she wanted him, knowing she loved him, had melted some of the ice surrounding his heart. He'd begun to doubt his own cynicism. There was such a thing as love, because it was tearing at his insides like a wild animal.

And then he'd woken to find her gone, without so much as a fare-thee-well. She'd slipped away while he was still dreaming of her. Tremaine snorted in disgust. His wounds were too raw and open for him to think rationally. All he wanted to do was wrap his hands around her lovely, white throat and strangle her.

And make sure she didn't return to Rock Springs.

The carriage stopped and Tremaine climbed out, paid the driver, and walked to the front door with barely a glance at his surroundings. He was bent on retribution.

There seemed no point in knocking when he wasn't going to wait on the stoop anyway. He walked right into the house, saw the door with the gilded frosted glass that listed Breverman's name and hours, and strode inside.

There was no one in the waiting room. The door to surgery was similarly closed and Tremaine yanked it open. He found a gray-haired man with a pointed beard, his black bag in hand, just getting ready to leave.

"Can I help you?" the man asked, scowling at Tremaine's abrupt entry.

"Where's Harrison Danner?"

"Who's asking?"

"My name's Tremaine Danner. Harrison's my brother."

Tremaine couldn't have predicted the man's reaction even if he'd tried. Breverman's nostrils flared. He looked furious. "Your brother and sister were visited by a man named Flynne. Apparently, there are family problems. They've already gone to the train station."

"Flynne! Good God. They're not going to Rock Springs?"

"I'm afraid so," said Breverman, calming down a bit. "I don't mind telling you Harrison's left me in a bit of a lurch. I've got sick animals to tend to, Mr. Danner. Too many for one man. None of my other students are as naturally qualified as your brother to help divide the load, and I . . . Say! Where are you going?"

But Tremaine was already a memory. Before Breverman could get over his surprise, the eldest Danner brother was on the street, hailing another carriage.

Chapter Twenty-two

The night was dark save for a fuzzy quarter moon. Clouds had rolled in ominously all afternoon and were slowly blanketing the moon's feeble light. Jason Garrett stood at the juncture of his land and the Danners', damning himself for being so citizen-minded. But because of the mysterious worries of the Rock Springs sheriff and that old fool Cullen, he'd offered to be on the lookout. There was trouble at the Danners. He didn't want that trouble to spread to his place.

The rattle of an approaching carriage caught his attention. He prudently stepped behind the shelter of one of the nearby towering firs.

The carriage swept by in a thunder of sweating flanks, pounding hooves, and swirling dust. Jace hadn't been able to see more than a glimpse of its passengers, but warning prickled the hairs on the back of his neck.

He was in a quandary of indecision when he heard a new horse, approaching from behind him. Moments later Kelsey appeared astride her bay mare. Jace glowered. His sister was a worse hoyden than Lexington was.

"What's wrong?" Kelsey asked, sliding from her mount.

"I'm not sure, but something's going on at the Danners'. That Gainsborough fellow's got new company."

"What are you going to do?"

Jace swore beneath his breath, disinterested in lifting a finger to help his neighbors. He would like nothing better than for misfortune to smite Tremaine Danner. But he had a reputation to maintain in Rock Springs, and if he let Cullen and the sheriff down, he would be hard-pressed to give an account of himself. "Guess I'd better warn the sheriff," he muttered, walking in the direction of the clearing where his own mount was tethered.

"I'll ride to the Cullens'," Kelsey said in sudden decision.

"Not astride, you won't. Go back to the house and slip a sidesaddle on. You're a Garrett, remember."

The clear look from Kelsey's brilliant eyes made Jace uncomfortable. Damn the wretch, was she laughing at him? But then she was gone in a flash of steel-shod hooves and flowing magenta-red hair.

With a sigh, Jace climbed on his horse and turned its head toward Rock Springs.

The carriage rounded the last curve and Lexie, who had traveled home in a numbed state hovering somewhere between reality and a kind of twilit netherworld, drew in a sharp breath at the sight of her mother standing on the widow's walk. Eliza's folly, Pa fondly called it. *Oh, Mother,* Lexie thought painfully.

Why hadn't they told her the truth? When she thought of the dreadful secret her mother had been forced to hide, she felt sick inside. Sick and compassionate. Now she understood Eliza's attitude. She'd been born to privilege, yet she thought she'd murdered her husband and left him for dead. Though Victor Flynne hadn't said so, Lexie knew her mother would never have struck down her father unless she had a good reason.

But her father was alive.

A queasiness filled her stomach as the carriage pulled beneath the portico. Harrison touched Lexie's hand and the driver of the carriage helped her out. They'd left Victor Flynne in Portland. Flynne had done his job and was no longer interested in seeing them home. "I'll wait for my payment here," he'd told them, then seen about hiring them a carriage for the long trip. The man was a dirty snake but Lexie and Harrison had been too upset to care.

The front door flew open and Eliza came outside, her blond hair unwound and lying in long waves against her shoulders. Lexie had only seen her mother's hair loose when she was getting ready for bed; her dishabille now said more about Eliza's state of mind than any words could.

"Lexington!" she cried in surprise and horror. She drew Lexie into the trembling comfort of her arms.

"Gainsborough's man, Victor Flynne, came to Denver," Harrison said as his mother reached past Lexie to grab his hand. "He told us Gainsborough was here."

"So you know." Eliza sounded tired and grief-stricken. Her voice was nearly inaudible when she added, "I wish I'd killed him."

Lexie was shaken by this side of her mother. Another time she might have been delighted at Eliza's show of strength and pride. Tonight she just felt scared.

They went inside the house. The door to the den was closed, but it suddenly swung inward and three strange men walked into the foyer. Lexie's gaze fell on the elderly gentleman with the ivory-handled cane. Ramsey Gainsborough. *My father,* she thought dully.

"Lexington?" he asked with extreme politeness that set Lexie's nerves to screaming. His face was a grotesque caricature. "How pleasant to finally meet you."

The cruel look he sent Eliza's way brought Lexie out of her near trance. She had a sudden mental image of how the days since Gainsborough's arrival had been spent: Gainsborough seizing every opportunity to inflict tiny wounds on his wife. His wife. Still his wife . . .

He clasped Lexie's cold hand within his. She felt nothing for this man. Nothing but anger. Lifting her proud chin, Lexie demanded, "What do you want?"

Gainsborough's brows arched. He'd never fancied having a daughter and when he'd heard about Lexie, he'd seen her only as a tool to achieve his own ends. Her defiance was unexpected. But now he saw a bit of himself in her—and more than a little of Eliza—and he saw his means for punishment and retribution.

"Well, now, child. Ah'm your father."

"I'm not a child."

"Ah can see that," he answered, amused. "You're a young lady. One ah've never had the pleasure to know. Ah think it's fair that ah get my turn."

"What do you mean?" Eliza asked sharply.

He turned to her, his smile unpleasant. "Now that ah've met my daughter, ah want my chance to get to know her. Ah want her to come back to Kentucky with me."

Lexie withdrew her hand as if his touch were poisonous. She felt Harrison stiffen beside her and was vaguely aware of Pa, Jesse, and Samuel, entering from the kitchen. But all she saw was this calculating man with the cruel eyes. "You may have sired me," she said boldly. "But you are not my father!"

"Your mother left me for dead. Ah intend to have satisfaction," Gainsborough said flatly. "The members of this household have been trying to reason with me these last few days, but ah will have justice." In his peripheral vision he saw the way Eliza's fingers dug into her blond son's arm and Gainsborough smiled to himself. "Ah could be persuaded to take you as an exchange for her freedom, however."

"Don't do it, Lexie," Pa said, his voice taut.

She glanced at him, saw the white bandage that covered his arm. "Pa?" she asked faintly, worriedly. Her gaze flew to Jesse, one side of whose face was a green and yellow bruise.

"He has no scruples," Eliza whispered, but her whisper was a harsh, resounding rasp. "Don't trust him. Don't leave with him. He only wants you in order to hurt me."

The two men behind Gainsborough shifted their weight, poised on the balls of their feet, watching the entire Danner family. It was a scene that had been enacted many times since their arrival. The Danners were inured to the threat. They each in turn begged Lexie not to listen to the ruthless man who was her father.

But Lexie was no coward. "I'll go with you," she answered amidst a roar of rebellion from her brothers, father, and mother. The gunmen drew their weapons.

"For God's sake, Lex, wait until the sheriff gets here," Harrison implored. "Gainsborough can't make you leave!"

"But he can prosecute our mother." Lexie's voice was devoid of emotion, her green eyes narrowed on Gainsborough, her mouth a terrible thin line. Drawing her shoulders back, she glowered at the hired thugs. "I'll go with you to Kentucky, Mr. Gainsborough, if you promise to leave my family alone. I'll even pretend to be your daughter. And I guarantee to make your life a living hell."

The house was dark and silent as a tomb when Tremaine arrived. It was late. Well past midnight. A hot, whipping wind rattled the trees and moved the clouds rapidly across the sky.

He slid from the saddle, looped Napoleon's reins over a fencepost, and walked stealthily across the dry field grass to the side of the house.

He heard a soft sound in the bushes and drew Lexie's pistol just as a shadow leaped forward, a rifle barring his path. "Who goes there?" the sheriff's voice rasped in a whisper.

Relief and alarm flooded over him in equal measure. Here was help, but the fact that the sheriff was at the farmhouse at all made his hair stand on end.

"It's Tremaine. What's going on? Is Lexie here?"

"Yeah, she's here," Jace Garrett's voice sounded in disgust from the stand of fir near the corner of the house. "And this has been a fool's errand if I've ever seen one."

"What are you doing here?" Tremaine demanded, his impotent fury finding a perfect target.

"Keeping an eye on your woman," Garrett sneered. "But it looks like a cozy little family reunion to me."

The sheriff brought Tremaine up-to-date on the atmosphere inside the house. "When Jace saw a strange carriage go by, he thought he'd better let me know. But it turned out to be your sister and brother. Cullen asked Jace to help keep an eye on the place," he added as an afterthought.

"Lexie's not Dr. Danner's sister," Jace said in a suggestive tone that made Tremaine want to lunge for his throat. He had to control himself with an effort and remain civil. But he'd be damned if he'd be beholden to Jace Garrett for anything. If Jace were here, then it was because it suited his own purposes.

"Cullen's around the other side of the house, but nothing's happening," the sheriff went on. "Now that you're here, I suppose we can leave."

Tremaine nodded. The sheriff stole around the side of the house to inform Cullen and Jace walked up to Tremaine. In the darkness the two men eyed each other with dislike.

"If you plan to make Lexie your wife, in the future don't ask for my help," Jace said.

"I didn't ask for it now."

Jace shrugged. "You'll never make a lady out of her," he threw over his shoulder like an epithet as he strode into the inky blackness and disappeared.

Jace, Tremaine realized in dawning surprise, had come as close to offering his blessing as he ever would.

For a moment Tremaine was undecided on what to do. Though the other men seemed to feel he'd overstated the danger, Tremaine had been there when Gainsborough's gunman had shot his father. The threat still existed. It was real. And none of his family would be safe until Gainsborough was dealt with once and for all.

The flare of a match glowed from the windows of Pa's den. Someone was awake! Tremaine melted backward, into the shadows. He couldn't see the features of the person inside, but he watched the direction of that tiny, wildly flickering flame.

Inside the room, the golden tip of fire reflected against a glass panel. Glass . . . Whoever it was had stopped in front of the guncase.

Gainsborough! Tremaine's blood froze. With the silence of a stalker, he slipped inside the house through the back door.

Lexie lay on her back, staring at the ceiling, listening to a fir bough scratch delicately against her windowpane. They'd all pleaded with her to reconsider, even to the point of growing furiously angry with her.

"I won't let you go with him!" Pa had roared, but Lexie hadn't turned a hair.

Even Eliza's hollow-eyed plea to wait for the Good Lord to interfere hadn't persuaded Lexie. The Good Lord might take His own sweet time.

Besides, what did she have to stay in Rock Springs for? Her dream had been to become a horse doctor. No one here had ever supported her. Not even Tremaine.

She ground her teeth together and blocked out Tremaine's image, remembering again her mother's telling words. "Didn't Tremaine find you?" Eliza had asked anxiously as soon as they were out of earshot from Ramsey Gainsborough.

"Yes, he found me. Why? Did you send him after me?"

"We didn't want you to come home! We thought he'd keep you away until Ramsey got tired of waiting for you."

Lexie hadn't told her mother how nearly successful Tremaine had been. His method for "keeping her away" had the power to hurt her worse than any imagined miseries Ramsey Gainsborough might have in store. Yet she wouldn't give up a moment of it. She might need those memories to savor in the near future.

Heart aching, she slipped from beneath the downy comforter and crossed the cool oak floor barefoot, stopping in front of her dresser. In the oval mirror her reflection was ghostly: long untamed hair, a white cotton shirt, bare ivory limbs. What she wouldn't give for a midnight ride to soothe her tormented soul, but when she thought of Tantrum the pain in her chest threatened to suffocate her.

A sound beyond her door pulled her out of her private hell. Someone was walking stealthily down the hallway. Could it be Gainsborough? He and his men stayed in the empty rooms downstairs, but she could believe he patrolled the house at night.

Lexie grabbed her silk wrapper, then flung it aside and pulled one of her cotton dresses over her head, fumbling with the buttons. She crossed the room soundlessly, wishing she still had the pistol she'd been forced to leave in Tremaine's care, and quietly opened the door.

The murmur of voices sounded from the upper stairway, a hushed murmur. Lexie crept along the wall, recognizing the low, chilling drawl of Ramsey Gainsborough.

She reached the top of the stairs and saw through the french doors that Gainsborough was on the widow's walk—with her mother! Eliza's blond head was bent, as if in deep sorrow. Carefully Lexie crossed the cool floor to within earshot of their hushed conversation.

". . . if you want me to beg, I'll beg," Eliza was saying in a dull, flat voice. "You can prosecute me and let me rot in jail. That's what you want, isn't it?"

"Ah must admit, the idea holds an attraction for me."

"You don't know Lexie." Eliza's head came up proudly, a faint smile curving her lips. "She's stubborn and smart. She won't do as you bid and she'll thwart you any way she can."

"She'll come to learn my ways," Gainsborough answered confidently.

Eliza actually laughed. "She's your daughter, Ramsey. She'll do as she pleases."

Somewhere below her, Lexie thought she heard the dull sound of a softly shutting door. One of Gainsborough's men? She shuddered.

Ramsey Gainsborough had the awesome nerve and bad sense to actually reach out and caress Eliza's smooth chin. "Ah could make you come with me, too, wife," he said silkily.

Eliza's gaze was stony. "Only by force."

He chuckled softly, drawing closer. Horrified, Lexie watched him lower his head for a kiss. Her stomach churned. She ran forward, prepared to stop him, when Eliza suddenly jerked back and slapped him full across the face.

"Bitch!" he spat, slapping her with all the force of one brawny hand. Lexie screamed. Eliza stumbled against the rail, gasping. Lexie charged for Gainsborough. He turned, eyes wild, nostrils flared, and backhanded Lexie with one lethal blow.

Lexie went sprawling. Her head reeled. She tasted blood. "Mother!" she screamed, and then screamed again when she saw him grab Eliza by the hair and hit her again.

The man reaching for the Winchester rifle in the guncase was a dark shadow outlined by the thin light of the candle, but Tremaine recognized him instantly. "Pa," he hissed softly. "What are you doing?"

Joseph Danner whirled around, his face unreadable in the blackness. "Tremaine?"

Crossing the room, Tremaine peered into his father's face. "You can't shoot Gainsborough in cold blood."

"He's kidnaping my daughter."

Tremaine's blood froze. "He's taken Lexie away?"

"She's upstairs asleep but he intends to take her back to Kentucky with him."

Relief crashed over him. "The hell he will," Tremaine growled. "I'll kill him first myself!"

"Stand in line."

Joseph's grim resolve made Tremaine smile. "Lexie won't go. She's—"

The sound of a thud and a short, pain-filled scream shattered the stillness. Of one mind, Tremaine and Joseph ran from the den to the foyer. A crash sounded.

"They're on the walk!" Pa yelled and tore through the front door.

Tremaine dug into his pocket for the pistol. Unlike his father, he mounted the stairs three at a time, cresting the last one at the same moment Jesse's door flew open. Tremaine ran for the open french doors, Jesse at his heels. Lexie was just staggering to her feet. Gainsborough was furiously beating Eliza with his fist.

"Let her go!" Tremaine roared, taking careful aim.

Before he could pull the trigger, a streak of silver-blond fury slammed full-body into the small of Gainsborough's back. "You bastard!" Lexie screamed, hitting and crying.

"Christ! Lexie!" Jesse yelled.

"Lexie!" Tremaine cried simultaneously.

The shock of Lexie's weight sent Gainsborough barreling into Eliza. For a heart-stopping moment Eliza's fragile body was crushed against the railing.

"Lexie. Ma—" Tremaine choked out, stepping forward.

The ominous cracking of rotten wood rent the air at the same moment Pa's Winchester exploded. Wood splintered into shrapnel. Eliza's terrorized scream wailed like the wind. The rail disappeared behind her and she teetered precariously on the edge.

"Mother!" Lexie sobbed, reaching for her as Gainsborough pitched forward into Eliza, their bodies whirling in the sultry blackness.

In a slow-motion trance Tremaine Danner witnessed a replay of his own mother's death, as Eliza plunged to the ground two floors below.

Chapter Twenty-three

Lexie's ears rang. She didn't know it was from her own screams. She ran to the rail. Strong arms encircled her and she fought like a madwoman, kicking and growling and trying to inflict as much damage as possible on her attacker.

"Mother . . . Mother . . ." she cried in anguish, scratching the arms that held her.

"Lex," Tremaine uttered brokenly. "Stop."

"Let me go!" she sobbed, kicking backward.

"I'm going down," Jesse said from somewhere in the blackness. Lexie couldn't see. Tears blinded her. Fear choked her.

"God damn you! Let me go!" she screamed.

"I've got to go down," Tremaine said in her ear. "Come with me." She nodded jerkily. When he finally released her, her legs felt detached. "Can you walk?" he demanded tersely.

"Yes." She pushed him away, but trembled so violently that Tremaine grabbed her hand, pulling her gently behind him. At the bottom of the stairs she found her legs again and ran into the windswept night.

Her first sight was Gainsborough, a bloody, crumpled mass from the combined effects of Pa's bullet and his fall. He was still alive and groaning. Lexie tore her numb gaze from him and searched for her mother. Eliza was a small huddled form. Pa was bent over her, examining her. She was still as death.

"Pa," Tremaine said gently, placing his hands on his father's shoulders.

A tearing sob rasped from his father's chest. "I broke her fall but I couldn't save her. Just like your mother. Just like your mother."

"Let me examine her."

"She's dead," Joseph said, staggering blindly to his feet. "She's dead. She's dead." He bent to pick up his Winchester.

A red haze of misery descended on Lexie. *Mother, I love you,* she thought in anguish. *I wish I could have told you.*

Pa stumbled toward Gainsborough's writhing form. He raised the rifle to his shoulder, his finger trembling on the trigger.

"No!" Lexie screamed.

Everything happened at once. Men ran from the house. Guns roared. Someone yanked Lexie's arm nearly from the socket. She saw the silvery flash of a knife. Vaguely, she recognized Harrison bearing down on her. And Jesse, gun in hand, a dark blur.

The Winchester blasted again and glass shattered. Lexie struggled. The grip on her arms was bone-crushing. Tears coursed silently down her cheeks.

She felt the cold barrel of a gun press against her temple. A voice snarled near her ear, "Get back or I'll kill her!"

It was the gunman called Pete. All motion ceased except for Gainsborough, still writhing on the ground. A last whistling rasp of air passed through his windpipe as he mercifully died.

"If you want a hostage, take me," Tremaine said quietly.

Pete had her head pulled back by the hair. Lexie couldn't move. The other gunman was kicking the gun Jesse had dropped out of reach. His face was slashed open from Harrison's knife. Harrison, Pa, and Jesse stood still and wary. Tremaine advanced slowly toward Lexie, his hands raised.

"Gainsborough's dead," he said quietly.

"Then so are you, Doctor," Pete snarled in rage. He lifted his gun and shot, the blast a yellow stream of fire. Tremaine fell backward.

Lexie twisted and bit into Pete's hand. He howled and hit her with the butt of his gun and she fell by her mother. Dimly, she saw the even rise and fall of Eliza's chest. She wasn't dead! Her mother wasn't dead! Pa, in his anguish, hadn't even checked.

Grunts and groans and the sickening crunch of bone connecting with bone sounded around her. *Tremaine,* she thought with sharp pain. *Tremaine!*

Harrison was nearest her. The glint of his knife flashed in the moonlight but it was held tightly in the hamlike fist of the other gunman. The man slashed viciously downward and Harrison sucked in a breath of pain.

Lexie didn't remember moving, but she leaped on Harrison's attacker, ripping at his hair. Blood spurted from Harrison's shoulder. The man clawed at Lexie. Then Jesse slammed his pistol across the side of the man's head.

A rifle blast nearly split Lexie's eardrums. Samuel, standing small and fierce in the doorway, was taking aim at the now fleeing Pete. Calmly, he shot again, but Pete disappeared behind a leafy frond of fern and melted into the blackness.

Harrison groaned and slipped into unconsciousness. Lexie placed her hands on the wound near his shoulder, holding with all her might, fighting sobs, until Pa relieved her. Her hands were sticky with blood.

Tremaine lay still. Blood smeared his temple. The bullet had struck him in the head.

"Pa." Lexie's voice shook.

Her father was pulling back the blood-soaked wad of Harrison's shirt. Nausea scalded the back of Lexie's throat. Her brother's arm was nearly severed from his shoulder.

"Go to the Garretts, Samuel," Pa said. "Get help."

Jesse was gathering Eliza into his arms. "Mother's alive!" he cried, chokingly.

"Take her upstairs," Pa said, his face transformed by joy and disbelief.

Lexie's own heart was heavy with dread. Tremaine lay quiet as death. She knelt beside him and touched his cheek. There was so little she could do for him. "Don't you dare die on me," she whispered fiercely. "Don't you dare die on me."

She laid her head on his chest and cried, great rolling sobs that couldn't be stopped. She cried for all the wasted time. For all the pointless misery. It couldn't come to this. It couldn't. "I love you. I love you so much," she murmured brokenly. "Don't leave me. Please, please don't leave me."

To her amazement he suddenly inhaled deeply and his eyes opened. He stared blankly around, as if he didn't know where he was. "Lex . . . ?"

"Tremaine!" She was beside herself with joy.

"God," he moaned, drawing air through his teeth. Lifting a hand, he tenderly touched the side of his head and winced. The bullet had grazed his temple rather than entering his skull.

Lexie's tears ran unchecked. "How dare you walk in front of a gun?" she demanded furiously, nearly hysterical with relief and rapture.

"It wasn't—one of my—brightest ideas," he panted, struggling to sit up. Seeing the chaos surrounding them, he muttered grimly, "Help me to my feet, Sundown. Pa needs us."

"I need a surgical nurse," Tremaine told her in the kitchen half an hour later as she handed him his bag. "Can you handle it?"

Lexie nodded. She was worried sick about all of them: her mother, Harrison, Tremaine. But Harrison was bleeding to death in front of her eyes. He needed help now.

Lexie glanced anxiously at Tremaine. He'd bandaged his own head, assuring her testily that he was fine. Harrison lay on the table, pallid as death. Jesse, who had helped carry Harrison inside, stood near the doorway, his shirt covered with Harrison's blood. Pa was upstairs with Eliza. Knowing his own skills were rusty, he'd reluctantly allowed Tremaine to perform surgery on Harrison. Even though Tremaine was injured, there was no time to wait for another surgeon. Harrison would bleed to death before he arrived.

"Hand me the carbolic, then thread me a needle," Tremaine muttered tersely. "Pray to God he doesn't wake up before we're finished."

Lexie's hands felt fat and numb. This was Harrison. Her brother. Her best friend. *Please, God, save him.*

Tremaine worked with incredible efficiency and singlemindedness. Beads of sweat appeared on his forehead and his face grew white. Lexie swallowed her fear. Tremaine stitched the torn muscles and vessels together, periodically using a scalpel to cut away tissue he couldn't save.

Lexie worked by rote, obeying his commands, mentally detaching herself from her task. She couldn't think that this was Harrison, otherwise she would fall apart completely. She couldn't think about Tremaine's injury. She couldn't think about anything.

It seemed an eternity before Tremaine was stitching Harrison's skin together. Jesse was sent for fresh bandages. Tremaine's eyes were dark pits in his pale face.

Hoofbeats pounded outside. The front door burst open. Samuel and Dr. Marshfield appeared as one.

"Check my mother," Tremaine said without looking up. "Make sure she's all right."

Marshfield didn't argue. He went upstairs just as Jesse returned with the sheets. Tremaine took the sheets, ripped them, and wound Harrison from neck to waist, pinning his right arm to his side. "Help me move him to the couch," he told Jesse in a tired voice, then ordered, "Stay with him. I've got to check on Eliza."

"No. You've got to rest!" Lexie cried.

"In a minute."

Lexie went with him. They entered their parents' bedroom together. Eliza lay on the bed, quiet and peaceful. Pa sat beside the bed, anxiously holding his wife's limp hand.

"She'll be fine," Marshfield was saying. "Just needs rest."

Tremaine didn't listen. He checked Eliza's pulse himself and looked in her sightless eyes.

"No broken bones," Pa said gruffly.

"You saved her life, you know," Tremaine remarked, his fingers exploring the swelling at the base of Eliza's skull.

"Tremaine," Dr. Marshfield said quietly. "Let me look at that head injury."

"I'm fine."

"You're about to fall on your face. As a doctor, you ought to know that—"

The look Tremaine sent him would have turned a lesser man to stone. As it was, Marshfield clamped his lips into a tight line and shook his head.

Pa drew a breath and asked fearfully, "What about Harrison?"

"I think he'll live, but he may lose his arm. Time will tell. But we Danners are tough," he added, his mouth twisting.

Marshfield went downstairs to check on Harrison, and Lexie walked Tremaine back to his room. "You've got to lie down," she ordered gently.

This time he didn't argue. He collapsed on the bed and fell instantly into a sleep that frightened her. "Tremaine?" she whispered.

His quiet breathing encouraged her but she couldn't shake the fear in her breast. "I love you, you know. I love you so much." Her voice broke. "I'm sorry for everything. For all the terrible, stupid things I've done. All I ever wanted was you. Just you. If I could do anything to change things I would. I love you. My God, how I love you."

She laid her head on his chest, tears squeezing from her eyes. Her heart lay heavy inside her breast. What if he didn't awaken? What if he'd used his last reserves of energy saving Harrison?

"Damn you, Tremaine," she sobbed quietly, wrapping her arms around him, burying her tearstained face in his neck.

He sighed heavily. Lexie's heart jerked at the feel of his hand tangling in her hair. "How can I sleep with you swearing at me all the time?" he muttered wearily. "Didn't I tell you I was fine? Now leave me alone, Sundown."

Lexie's tears changed to joy. Tremaine wasn't going to die! "Blackhearted bastard," she whispered cheerfully and laughed aloud at his disgusted groan.

Tremaine's words proved even more true than Lexie could have hoped. The Danners were tough. Tremaine managed to recover so quickly that Lexie was almost embarrassed by her fears of losing him. Harrison's arm began to improve. Though Tremaine warned him it would never be completely useful—there had been too much nerve damage—he would probably be able to lift it and his hand would even have some movement. Harrison's comment was, "Thank God I'm left-handed. Breverman would kill me if I couldn't finish my studies."

Eliza's recovery was slower but when her blue eyes opened Lexie was at her side. "Mother," she said in a wobbly voice, scarcely believing her mother was actually going to survive. "I love you."

Eliza hadn't been able to answer but the warmth in her eyes spoke clearly. Two fat tears traveled down her cheeks, and Lexie clasped her hand and sobbed uncontrollably for long minutes.

When she'd finally pulled herself together and Eliza had fallen asleep, Lexie went blindly back to her own room. She was drained, emotionally and physically. The last week had been a nightmare and only now did she feel she would ever truly awaken.

"Lex."

It was Tremaine's voice, from the doorway. Lexie saw his beloved reflection in her oval mirror. She smiled at him tenderly. Since that night when she'd thought she might lose him, they hadn't had any time together alone. Her lips curved lovingly. She actually turned toward him, wanting him.

"I have to leave for a few days," Tremaine said. "Pa can take care of Eliza and Harrison while I'm gone."

"Leave?" She was stunned. "You can't leave! You've barely recovered! Where are you going? How can you leave?" she demanded in a shaking voice. "What could possibly be more important than making certain your family survives?"

Tremaine was maddeningly uncommunicative. "Pa can handle any crisis. I'll be back before you know it."

If Lexie thought she could argue with him, she was soon disabused of that notion. Within the hour Tremaine, astride Fortune, was on his way in the direction of Rock Springs.

Lexie was furious, but no one else seemed to find his departure particularly newsworthy. "Tremaine's all right now. And he's got a life in Portland," Harrison reminded her.

Jesse added, "There's not much more he can do here."

Even Samuel remarked, "Pa knows as much about medicine as Tremaine does."

Surprisingly, Lexie found the most sympathy from her mother. "Don't worry so, Lexington," she whispered. "He'll be back."

She sounded so positive that Lexie asked, "Do you know something I don't?"

"Tremaine is settling scores," was her rather disturbing answer.

Five days later Tremaine did return. Lexie was instructing Annie on how she wanted the table set when the sound of pounding hoofbeats announced someone's arrival. The hoofbeats went right on past the house toward the stables and Lexie knew it was Tremaine.

"Set another place," Lexie said, gathering her skirts and hurrying outside. She couldn't decide whether to throw herself into his arms or kill him. How could he just up and leave when there was still so much to resolve between them?

The air was sultry and thick; the smell of wild roses and dusty field grass combining in a curiously sensual mix. Lexie, who had taken special care with her appearance tonight for lack of anything better to do, cursed the thick petticoats and folds of her skirt as she went to meet Tremaine.

The lantern was already lit in the stables when she opened the creaking Dutch door. Tremaine was just closing the gate on one of the box stalls. He turned to greet her but before a word was out of his mouth, Tantrum's head thrust forward and he snapped at Tremaine's shoulder.

"Tantrum!" Lexie cried in delight and the gelding tossed his head and whinnied.

"Beast," Tremaine muttered, smiling. He eyed the gelding distrustfully. "He never will learn any manners."

Lexie rubbed Tantrum's velvety nose. She was nearly speechless with gratitude and, when she turned to Tremaine, he swept in a breath at the love and joy on her face. "Thank you," she said softly. "I don't know how you found him, but thank you."

Tremaine's smile was full of unspoken mirth. "Silas Monteith was happy to turn him over to me."

Lexie gazed at him quizzically. "Why? He was delighted with Tantrum when I sold him to him."

"Monteith thinks I have information that could—er—cast aspersions on his already suspect reputation."

"What does that mean?"

Tremaine grinned like a pirate. "It means I blackmailed him."

"What? How?"

"Never mind. Monteith's in for a big surprise, however. Between my testimony and a few others', I think he may be in jail soon."

Lexie blinked in disbelief. "For what?"

"Murder."

Lexie's head whirled. She realized belatedly that she'd been unfair to Tremaine. Mother was right. He had had his reasons to leave. "So that's what you were doing in Portland."

"Among other things." Tremaine thought about his vain search for Victor Flynne, but the wily investigator had moved on. Probably for the best, considering what he thought of the bastard.

Slowly, his expression changed and his hands encircled Lexie's arms, pulling her toward him. For a moment his gaze dropped to the milky mounds of her breasts peeking above the daringly square neckline of her gown. "Were you expecting company tonight? You look—ravishing."

Lexie peered at him from beneath her lashes. "Tremaine, I . . ." She trailed off at the whisper-soft kiss he brushed against her lips.

"You know," he murmured. "I wanted to kill you when you left me in Katieville. I figured you for another untrustworthy woman."

"Something changed your mind?"

"You." He regarded her in deadly earnest. "The way you helped me with Eliza and Harrison. The way you would have gone with Gainsborough to save your mother."

His words of praise lifted her heart in a way she wouldn't have thought possible. She couldn't help smiling. "How long would you have kept me in Katieville?"

He growled lasciviously. "As long as it took."

His kisses were growing longer, each more soul-stirring than the last. "Took for what?"

"Took to get you out of my blood and Gainsborough out of Rock Springs. Looks like I failed at both."

This was such a bold confession that Lexie struggled against his restraining arms. "What do you mean?" she demanded breathlessly. "You're not saying that—that you *care* about me, are you?"

"You know I care about you. Let me show you . . ."

"How do you feel about me, Tremaine?" She held his arms back, searching his face. "Please. I need to know."

In all the experience Tremaine had had with women, he'd never faced such supreme honesty and openness. He sighed, fought back years of self-deception, and said, "You are everything to me, Lexie. I can't seem to stand being away from you. You're the most aggravating, bullheaded, bewitching woman I've ever had the misfortune to know, yet I can't live without you. Whenever I've thought of taking a wife, I've endowed her with all your qualities." He smiled crookedly, a bit embarrassed. "If that's love, then I love you. I've always loved you."

Her utter silence was ego-shattering. When long moments had passed and she still hadn't answered, Tremaine grew impatient. "Well?" he demanded. "I bare my soul and you say nothing?"

"I was just wondering." Lexie smiled at him, her green eyes alight with mischief. "Was there a marriage proposal in there somewhere?"

"Wretch," he muttered, dragging her soft body against the hardness of his. "Yes, there was a marriage proposal in there. What's your answer?"

"Yes," she said sublimely, lifting her smiling lips to his.

Tremaine laughed and took what she offered so beguilingly. After several long moments, he murmured, "Let's go back to the house and announce our news." He slipped his arm around her waist and led her to the door.

"By the way, your friend, Celeste, is getting married, too, I understand. To Peter Caldwell."

Lexie snorted. "She's no friend of mine."

"Did I ever tell you how she tried to force me to marry her? No? Well, it wasn't much of a story anyway."

Tremaine doubled over with laughter at the hard fist that slammed into his stomach.

Epilogue

Denver, Colorado
Summer, 1884

Tremaine held up the squawling red-faced infant, scrutinizing it as if for flaws. "Looks like his mother," he pronounced.

Lexie, from her seat by the window, laughed. Jamie was a week old and Tremaine was still bemused by his noisy son. "I should have known he'd be a boy. You Danners are notorious for siring sons."

"You're a Danner, too. Again," he reminded her dryly. "And soon to become a horse doctor."

Lexie sighed in perfect contentment. Dr. Breverman had been the soul of understanding; first, about letting a woman apprentice, second, for not allowing her pregnancy to interfere. And Tremaine had been wonderful about working at a Denver hospital so she could finish her training even though the clinic in Rock Springs was waiting for him. "Only a few more months and we can go home," she said aloud. "Do you really think Harrison's serious about wanting me to work with him? The Rock Springs farmers aren't going to take kindly to having a woman horse doctor. Pa's right about that."

"Harrison has a right arm and hand that work, thanks in

346

part to you. Yes, he's serious. The farmers will come around."

"And Billy Greaves? Are you really going to bring him to Rock Springs to work with you?"

"He's already there, my love. Staying with Pa and Eliza." Tremaine brought Jamie to his mother, and Lexie cuddled the child to her breast. Jamie nuzzled her breasts and when Lexie offered one to him, he sucked greedily.

She smiled enticingly at Tremaine. "Like father, like son," she murmured.

Tremaine kissed her lips and grinned. "You know, Sundown, as much as you try to hide it, you are a lady."

She smothered a sound of mirth. "A lady horse doctor?"

"Exactly." He grew serious. "I love you, Lexington Danner."

Her eyes misted with the ready tears of a new mother. "And I love you, Tremaine Danner. I always will."

He looked at her tenderly. "You always shall," he corrected her.

And they both laughed.